Taking Lives

Taking Lives

Michael Pye

Alfred A. Knopf • New York • 1999

This Is a Borzoi Book Published by Alfred A. Knopf, Inc.

www.randomhouse.com

Library of Congress Cataloging-in-Publication Data
Pye, Michael, 1946–
Taking lives / Michael Pye. — 1st ed.
p.   cm.
ISBN 0-375-40260-8
I. Title.
PR6066.Y4T35 1999
823'.914—dc21   98-28256   CIP

Manufactured in the United States of America
First Edition

This book is entirely a work of fiction.
The criminal who inspired it is still at large.

Taking Lives

One

Two boys ride the bus through Florida. One of them won't be alive much longer.

This is summer, 1987. Hot skies going basalt, boiled air. A road straight and bone-colored through grass and marsh.

Neither of the boys belongs here, you can tell. They stare out of the windows, but they don't want to be caught doing it.

The highway leads only on. They see towns that repeat one another like puzzle pictures: spot the eight differences in oceans of crabgrass and civic pink oleanders.

The first boy is Martin Arkenhout. Seventeen. Doesn't talk to people much; he doesn't have the habit. Besides, he's foreign—Dutch, blond, tall, white, lanky—and he can't stop himself feeling scared and superior all at once. He sees the crackers on the bus, and he thinks they're potato eaters out of some beach-party van Gogh. There are Hispanics, too, with the dark skin that looks rich to him, but he won't reach out. He's a careful boy.

He works out kilometers and miles to judge the speed. He slouches back to the bathroom and pisses into the lurching tank of liquid, then weaves back to his seat. He gets to wondering, eyes glazed, whether he truly wants to be here: a kid, going to be just a foreign kid at some American high school for a year, expected somehow to grow up.

Each stop, he gets off the bus and buys more Pepsi. By eleven in the morning, he has a fair caffeine buzz, his eyes very open on the world but with not much to see.

"I don't know why I did this," someone says.

Arkenhout looks up.

"I thought this was a really cool idea," the second boy says. "See America."

"Where are you going?"

"College. The way hard way."

"Oh," Arkenhout says. "So am I."

"You're not American?"

"I'm Dutch."

"Cool." The word sounds like absolution for being foreign. After a while, the boy says, "You have those marijuana cafes, don't you?"

Arkenhout says, "And Rembrandt."

"Yeah, yeah. Sorry."

This second boy is tall, blond, and white, like a snapshot of Arkenhout that's been retouched: hair seriously cut, more worked out, less tired and more brown.

"Seth Goodman," the second boy says.

Arkenhout thinks the name sounds like a fiction; he remembers nineteenth-century novels in English class.

"Christ!" Goodman said. "The bus—"

The doors are already shut. A parting signal of blue-black exhaust. The boys run and hammer on the doors and after a false start and a moment, the driver opens up.

"You didn't hear me shouting?" he says.

They both apologize, remembering the same lessons: nice boys.

They sit apart for the next hour and a half. At the next stop they buy chili dogs and coffee.

"I'm going to New York University," Goodman says.

"I'm in America for a year abroad. Before university." But Goodman doesn't seem to mind the canyon gap in status. They're both on the road, after all.

"Where are you from?" Arkenhout asks, politely.

"Jackson, Michigan. In the Midwest. Famous for its giant waterfall with colored lights."

"This is my first time in America."

"Really. You play baseball in Holland?"

In the next few hours, Goodman starts explaining. He starts in slogans: how he takes the bus for environmental reasons, how he wants to see America. He pulls up a bit of personal information: he will major in journalism. So far, he's an entry in a yearbook, concise and shiny. But after many more miles, he tries really hard to think of Arkenhout as this guy in the locker room he's known forever: so he mentions Tracy, the girlfriend in the hometown, who's a gymnast and dark, and how they get it on in the bleachers at the giant waterfall with colored lights.

He deserves a whole lifestory in return, so he thinks, but he'd be appalled if it turned out to be too foreign.

Arkenhout just says he's going to some Tampa suburb to be a schoolkid, which he's obviously done already. He doesn't have anything easy to say about home or parents. He particularly doesn't say out loud that he will learn America like a lesson because he is good at languages—not just neat sounds from a clever mouth, but the ability to listen to how people don't say a thing straight and then repeat it.

Goodman says he'd like to stop off before Tampa, pick up a bus the next morning. Arkenhout reckons he'll do the same. Just this once, it's not what everyone expects him to do; that's the whole attraction.

The bus draws into a station dressed up with bits of white column and brick siding. The boys pull their bags out of the belly of the bus. They talk a bit about that green flash in the sky you get in Florida, so they've both heard.

≡

Technicolor evening. Cracker eyes. Small motel, old pink, two double beds, TV with the colors shifted like a very old 3-D movie. Bathroom with crumbling mosaic and a barrier like a police line: this side sanitized for your protection, the rest at your own risk. Palm trees in a very little motion, a shine more than a move.

Goodman talks about New York. "You meet people who matter," he says, which must be his father's phrase. He'll work out where the career paths run, get invited, although he's not sure to what.

Arkenhout starts to think he's carrying his own name—Martin, Arkenhout—like a too-big case your mother packs, which he'll sooner or later have to lug home to Holland.

He remembers to call his new American family in Tampa to say he's missed the bus, been delayed.

He pays serious attention now. Goodman doesn't bite his nails. Arkenhout does; better stop. Americans have such glamorous, managed teeth, but Arkenhout's are good, too. Goodman doesn't say much about his hometown because he's leaving it. While he's in the shower, Arkenhout thumbs through his diary, finds an orderly list of emergency numbers: home, relations, doctor. The credit card that paid for the motel room is in his father's name. So that's how Americans do it, Arkenhout thinks.

Goodman comes out of the shower in white socks. He lies down on the bed, brown and naked, and he smiles. Arkenhout notices the sharp side of his belly muscles.

Since they've only just met, since they have nothing in common except not knowing each other's stories, it is natural to ask about parents, brothers, sisters. Goodman's are all in one house in a clean, small, distant town, not unlike Arkenhout's small town, except the Dutch are by the dunes and the sea. "My father's a doctor," Arkenhout says, as though that meant much more than a profession. Goodman has a brother and a sister, but he says they're "way heartland."

Arkenhout is curious about everything. He learns the motel first. Outdoor flamingos, paint bruised. An old apple of a woman, brown and soft, running the office; she has a gun just showing in a desk drawer. Rooms like boxes. No questions asked, or even contemplated, once the credit card runs through the machine.

Once, in the night, he thinks Goodman is watching him. He pretends to be asleep.

The next morning is smotheringly hot.

Arkenhout can barely hold his list of questions, and Goodman now wants to tell: or at least to brag a bit, to instruct the foreigner.

They eat grits for breakfast with eggs. Arkenhout manages. Goodman starts laughing. "I never ate this"—and he catches the waitress's judgmental eye—"stuff before," he says.

The bus seats stick to bare thighs. Goodman explains New York like a tabloid and a guidebook. Arkenhout listens, but he also watches the light show of sun and tangled branches through the windows.

Goodman is suddenly impatient. "This sucks," he says. "We should rent a car."

"I don't have my license," Arkenhout says. "Not with me."

"I'll drive," Goodman says. "They won't rent to a teenage alien."

"O.K.," Arkenhout says. To himself he says, "I Was a Teenage Alien." He likes the sound of it.

He's told his sponsors in Tampa which bus he'll catch, but getting a car sounds like much the same arrangement, only with a welcome bit of elastic in it. "Cool," he says, experimentally.

At the next main stop, the boys quit the bus and Seth Goodman, boy advocate, tries to talk Hertz into giving him a car. This doesn't work for two kids roaring indefinitely through Florida. But the clerk, who's absurdly muscular for a paper pusher, skin hardly containing the biceps, says there's a place down the road, and he smiles as the two blonds amble off.

The place down the road is the local sunset home for cars. The rate is high, the car a faded Taurus, but the credit card solves everything.

They swing out of town on the highway. The flat, banal business of hard travel has turned into an adventure—radio on, fast breeze, open road, a sense of chances. They sing out. The weather is loud like old rock 'n' roll up ahead.

But the road doesn't turn into a story. It just runs under them like clockwork.

They start looking for laughs. A brown plaster gator, on big haunches for stability, rears out of the grass. A sign promises a wonder of the world: five dollars each.

The office is papered in cobra skin, a sign says. There's a live cobra out back who sways to the sound of comb and tissue paper, and raccoons in cages, with clever hands.

"I saw this jungle before," Seth says, checking out the skimpy bushes. "Saw it on *Star Trek*."

Arkenhout nods. He's seen that show.

Under the boardwalk, in the muddy pools, a couple of corrugated things shift. One hinges open on great teeth, yawning. The place smells of inattention, not like home, not for either boy.

"They'll chew you up so your mama won't know you," a man in overalls says helpfully. "You want to feed them?"

Goodman tries out some hog call he once heard from a TV weatherman. Nothing answers. He picks up a bucket of chopped chickens, all shiny flesh, black blood, sawed bone, and rattles it. He tips the bucket into the mud. A snap and a flurry and the flesh is all gone.

"Your mama won't know you," the man in overalls says. He never gets tired of saying it.

The boys need the next thing. But the car won't start.

"I don't see how the battery could have gone flat," Arkenhout says.

Goodman says, "We'll sue them." He's heard his father say that.

They push the car off the hot tarmac forecourt and onto the road. It splutters, the engine turns, and the car dies again. Goodman lets out the handbrake, opens the front doors, and the boys try to run with the weight of the car on their shoulders. This time, it comes to querulous life.

"It's a long way to a service station," Goodman says.

"Maybe they'd help us at the gator farm." But the hut is locked, and nobody answers.

Goodman drives like an aunt. He never makes the main road. The car dies just out of sight of the highway and out of sight of the men who mind the gators, in a slight bowl of land between trees.

Goodman sits there, drumming his fingers on the wheel. Suddenly he doesn't look a prince; he looks a boy. Arkenhout feels older at once.

The heat rests on the skin and sounds filter through the windows: things moving, snakes and gators, in the ditches and the swamp. There shouldn't be blind hollows in flat Florida, and Goodman is fretting to be out of this one just as soon as he can.

"Shit," he says. "The car's on my father's card. We can't just leave it. And we can't phone and we're out here—"

"I'll walk to the highway."

"Nobody'll stop for you. They'll think you're hitchhiking."

Arkenhout says, "They'd stop in Holland. I think, anyway."

They hear cars buzz past unseen on the highway. They hear the little, tentative crisscross movements in the bush, and one splash.

Goodman is out of the car and he's almost running, never mind the sun. He's going fast to get away from the situation, so he can turn all the nature around him, browsing at the edges of his eyes, into a harmless frieze, a movie tracking shot.

Arkenhout says, "I'll come with you." He can't do anything else.

But Goodman is running away, that's obvious.

≡

Arkenhout stands in the shade of a tree at the roadside. He watches Goodman wave, make like a hitchhiker, put up his hand as though he were trying to stop a bus or a cab. Nothing works. He's a suspect boy, sodden, carrying nothing, in the middle of nowhere. He doesn't even seem to have a car. It's best if Arkenhout stands out of the way, so the drivers don't know there are two of them.

Some guys stare ahead and gun the engine coincidentally. Some look disapproving, as though they wished for the courage to stop and deliver a proper sermon. Two stubbled men in a pickup swerve toward Goodman where he dances on the road, and swerve back at the very last minute. He feels a hot metal wind.

Arkenhout watches. He savors the heat, the extreme, the sense of being lost: which means anything is possible. He slips out of sight a minute to piss.

He hears nothing on the road. Then:

"Hey," Goodman is shouting, "Hey!"

Arkenhout buttons his fly. From the gully he hears a soft slamming sound, a car diverted for a moment from its smooth progress, then the car carrying on, but faster. Goodman isn't shouting anymore.

Arkenhout liked being able to hear Goodman. The quiet makes him anxious. He strides back out of the gully.

He looks down the road. A scorch mark leads to Goodman, a pointer of black rubber. Goodman lies, one eye shut and black, one eye staring open. His mouth is bloody, frothing a bit. His legs are cracked and bruised, bone and sinew poking through bare skin. It seems as though someone was furiously angry that he dared to stand on this road at this time, angry at the very existence of people like him.

The road is silent. The little rickety movements in the bush are held down by the sheer weight of the sun.

Arkenhout feels in his own pockets and tugs out money, passport, postcards for his parents. He's fine. He's fine, he tells himself. He's grown-up, so the spasms in his stomach, the taste of eggs and old cola in his throat, can't be happening.

He doesn't want to look more closely, but he thinks that Seth's eye, the open one, moves a little. Maybe it's some mechanical reaction in a dead body, like current through a lab frog. Maybe he's alive.

Arkenhout tries to remember things learned in the Scouts: bandages, moving the injured, CPR. You don't move a body that's cut and broken like Seth. But the body is out there on the blacktop, and soon there will be traffic. Arkenhout feels obliged. He darts out and he tugs Goodman back to the scrappy crabgrass at the roadside. He acts like Goodman is a stranger, and checks his pockets: money, credit, ID. Arkenhout has a Timex, fake gold; Goodman has a Swiss Army watch.

He feels himself in a still, cold state where thinking seems to be peculiarly clear. He knows this can't be right. He's here with a boy he doesn't know. He's a foreigner, and people don't like foreigners around here, not even Seth Goodman. He's seen the movies, and the TV. He's panicking.

Cops do not understand what's improvised in life. A cop will think that riding the bus, hiring the car, lead inexorably to this broken body on a roadside.

A foreigner and an all-American boy, and the all-American is dead. Or dying.

He listens. There is no sound of an engine in either direction. He puts his head down to Seth's heart, which is struggling away.

Then there are Dr. and Mrs. Arkenhout to consider. They'd hate the idea of something so sensational happening to their son. They might even bring him home, and he couldn't stand going back to all those empty manners.

He picks up a heavy, faceted stone and hits Seth's head, two times, and then throws the rock into the ditch. This is mercy, because there's no way to call help, let alone make it come. He holds the head in his hands for a moment, checking it impersonally. The teeth are loose, he sees. The face is so spoiled it could belong to almost any boy the same build, age, color.

A truck goes by, a high chrome train on twenty-four wheels. For a moment, Arkenhout thinks the truck will stop, but it barrels on. He wonders how long it takes to stop a monster like that.

He holds Goodman's hand. The nails are unbitten. He bites them.

≡

Three miles, four miles down the highway, which once seemed so straight and now bends and shimmers, he's dry and almost out of breath. Nobody's moving, nobody passing. He has the whole damn world to himself.

The sky rumbles and blackens behind him.

He has two sets of papers in the jacket that trails in his left hand. He has Martin Arkenhout, who's a kid and a visitor. He has Seth Goodman, who's already at college and can do what he wants. He has blond hair, the proper height. Easy. The watch on his left wrist is now a Swiss Army watch.

He could be Seth Goodman better than Seth Goodman ever could. He can make Seth Goodman anyone he can imagine.

There is a diner, finally: a yellowish smear of brick between pines. He says there's been an accident, asks for a phone.

A waitress gives him coffee when he wants water and points him to the phone. He can see the waitress wants to be sympathetic, wants to mother the boy and believe him; it's natural. But she's experienced, so she also wants proof of his story.

"College boy," she says.

"Yes," he says, "Ma'am."

She beams, so close he smells the metal of old coffee on her breath.

But the smile is for the other diners. To Arkenhout, she says, softly, "Where's your freaking car then? Where is it?"

"We broke down," he says. "By the alligator farm. And then we tried to get someone to stop on the highway."

It's all true, but still she snorts.

"He was Dutch," Arkenhout says. "He thought they'd stop for us."

"Foreign. What were you doing with a foreign boy?"

"Just traveling."

She skims about the diner for a bit, ferrying salad to a pasty couple by the window, more coffee to a pencil-thin black queen, a plate of meat and French fries to the middle-aged couple in plaids.

"It sounds terrible, sugar," she says.

He has never gambled before, but if he had, he'd recognize his bright concentration on a single chance.

He watches rain come down in clots, rain with the force of hammers picking at the road and scouring the roadside. Just for a moment, hail makes the air rattle.

He can't eat, although the waitress says he should eat.

He knows when the sun comes back from all the brilliance that lies about on the ground.

≡

He has the phone in his hands at the police station. He's not at all sure that this can work.

"You sound different," this woman's voice says down the phone. She's Mrs. Goodman, mother.

"I did what I could," he says. Say as little as possible. Mimic Seth's particular flat language with your clever mouth.

"It must be shock, dear," she says. Then it's as though she remembers the boy doesn't tolerate endearments anymore. "Seth, I mean," she says. "They'll find the body when the storm stops, all that rain. I know you did all you could."

Arkenhout is dizzy, falling down all the implications of what she says: that he is going to be found.

"Come home. We'll take care of you," the woman says. "Until you're yourself again."

He hears the father snapping and hawking in the background. He thinks he should say something, but the silence, he guesses, only helps his credibility.

"The cops," he begins tentatively.

"Police. Police, Seth."

"The police said bodies do get moved. There are alligators around here. I left him on the roadside because I couldn't just leave him on the road . . ."

"It doesn't bear thinking about," says Mrs. Goodman, and she means it. "You can come home now. You know that. If you want to."

He's guessing: that she longs for him to rush home at once and forever, that the real Seth would pose as a man and refuse. They're not used to separation, he can tell; so they're trying very hard to do it properly.

He knows that much, but he doesn't even know what Seth calls his mother: Mum, Ma, Mother, by her Christian name, by some nickname, and whether she'll notice if he never calls her anything at all. Then he remembers that she expects him to sound, very slightly, not himself.

"I'd rather carry on to New York," Arkenhout says. "I want to get started."

Mrs. Goodman breathes hard. There is a pause, a bit of talk, and Mr. Goodman says down the line, "We'll get you a ticket, Seth. It'll be waiting at the airport. You're all right, are you? You have seen a doctor, haven't you?"

"I'm all right." So they don't parade feeling, either; like his own family, they think they can park emotion like a car until it's needed. "I'll call you from New York."

He puts down the phone. He's very aware, on his skin, that three cops are watching him.

An older sergeant, black, takes him into an interview room.

"Son," he says. "You should know we still didn't find your friend."

Arkenhout thinks they're questioning his story. He sets his face blank.

"There's tire marks, nothing else. The rain and the hail just mashed down the verges and there wasn't a body to see."

Arkenhout says nothing.

"I know this is hard. You want," and here the cop fishes up a word from talk shows, "closure. I promise you. We find him, I'll call you. I'll be in touch right away."

=

He stretches on the dorm bed, chilled down by the air conditioner. He's early for the semester; his roommate will not arrive for another week. Everybody seems to know there was an accident, so he has a brief buzz of glamour. Everyone is also very kind. Counseling is offered.

But he's thinking: It can't work. They'll find the body. You can't ruin a body enough to escape all those medical records, dental charts; what if Seth Goodman was fingerprinted once, or had his appendix or his wisdom teeth out? He should have inventoried Seth's body while it was alive.

Then: If they find the body and send it back to Holland, what if his parents decide it's not him? The possibilities run about his skin like sweat.

It's only when the call comes from Florida—boy found, badly cut up and smashed, major injuries compatible with car accident and the rest from being tugged about and mauled by gators, everything rotted down by weeks in warm, sluggish water; some contusions that might be from the head going downstream against a sluice; the body photographed, cataloged, identified as Martin Arkenhout because that was the name it ought to have, then burned in a plywood coffin because the remains were too foul to be shared with the grieving parents, and the ashes sent back to Holland—that Arkenhout stops seeing the kind black Florida cop on guard over his bed.

He punches the air, once. He's rid himself of a skin. He can take up a new life, know people he shouldn't know, invent himself.

At this moment, Fifth Avenue shining with the dust in the air on a brute summer's day, he owns the city.

=

And for a time, he is blessed: fearless because he doesn't know quite what he ought to fear.

He does Seth Goodman, student, just right. He cracks books at midnight with a pencil light on his desk, and gets to the great vaulted emptiness of the library at opening time and wades through his courses purposefully. His roommate likes the peace. He signs up for physical anthropology, all that measuring and reading of bones.

But he also hangs out just a measured amount—sprawled on sunny benches in the sun in Washington Square, out in a posse for a couple of beers, coinciding at the gym so he can spot his roommate. There's nothing missing.

The Goodmans call. But he's never in his room when they call. "He's out a lot," his roommate says. "At the library." The Goodmans want to know if he's well, if he's working. "No problems," his roommate says, expecting Goodman would do the same for him.

"We didn't want to bother him," Goodman's mother says. She doesn't mean it.

Arkenhout calls back. Mrs. Goodman says they'd love to come to see him in New York, but Seth knows what his father feels about the city. Arkenhout gives a sage, brief "Uh huh."

Since he doesn't know anyone, he decides this means he can know anyone at all. He cruises SoHo on the nights the art season opens, the galleries open out like souks and people spill out of them on a tide of thin white wine. He gets talked to, invited: he is seventeen, a personable volunteer. He remembers enough names from trips to the Stedelijk Museum in Amsterdam—Haring, Nauman, Koons, that kind of name—to sound a bit informed. He doesn't worry people by mentioning his favorite: Malevich. He's smart enough to know these people don't like true disturbers of the peace.

Out of this drifting come offers. He's useful, so the galleries have him around like furniture. He's helped shift glass snails, jokes on paper, brass pornography. That leads to parties; he samples a whole social round. He's inscribed in this group and that group, but people single him out because he has a party trick. He's blank like someone his age, a surrogate son, a potential lover, someone to mold, but he gives great attention. He doesn't mind egos spilling out their stories. He's hungry for the information they let slip in between their words.

In class, he's the one who doesn't ask the dumb questions, who knows not all the world is green-grass suburbia; he was taught that at school. He clatters ineffectually at the gym, but he's helpful. He goes his own private round among the galleries, now down on West Broadway helping shift boxes, now hanging out in some remote Chelsea space to make it look peopled. His roommate finds a girlfriend for the afternoons when Goodman is reliably never there.

Then there's Thanksgiving.

Arkenhout is Dutch. He knows about St. Nicholas, about Christmas, maybe New Year. He doesn't know about Thanksgiving, this late-November roadblock to his life; so he's startled when the Goodmans leave a message that they'll send him the ticket to come home for Thanksgiving and how long can he stay?

His roommate says, "It's lame. You got to let the parents know they don't rule you."

Arkenhout sees Christmas loom behind Thanksgiving on the calendar and a full month of vacation behind that. He needs alibis.

"You going home?" he asks his roommate.

"No way."

He has six weeks before Thanksgiving, maybe four before he has to call and say precisely when he's coming; or so he thinks.

His luck is cracking.

But then he's down one brilliant day on West Broadway, just hanging out in the big white back office of a gallery, and David Silver walks through: a name off museum banners. Silver has an impassive face, like he's Saran-Wrapped his feelings. The two see each other very briefly, but very clearly.

Silver starts talking too loudly. He needs a new assistant, so he says—part-time, afternoons, then Christmas, maybe summer.

Arkenhout says, "Mr. Silver."

The two stand like two screens opposite each other; all anyone will see is what they project.

"You want the job?" Silver says.

The artist's house is a mansion, behind shade trees on a quiet street, with a courtyard and a bare glass studio that mysteriously is without heat or glare. Among the spindles and towers of apartment blocks that surround it, it seems arrogant.

Silver is working on huge blind canvases in which, like a puzzle, there's a figure hidden: the critics find some kind of leper from an altarpiece, a specter of death or disease. Arkenhout thinks it's the artist himself, hiding in his work. A bit later, in a sensational piece in _Artforum_, a Canadian critic will say the hidden figure is Seth Goodman, and pick apart what that means for the story of David Silver. Silver, as usual, will refuse to explain or even talk.

There are three other assistants. Very quickly, Arkenhout figures out his importance: he's not responsive like the great artist's other arrangements—Jeff, Raoul, Henry—so he makes the whole household more opaque. But he's wrong and cheap about that.

"He's queer, isn't he?" the roommate says.

"I don't know."

The roommate looks skeptical.

Arkenhout reckons something different, based on the books and the profiles he has studied: that Silver sees a bit of himself in Arkenhout, the self that came out of Arizona at the same age because there was nowhere to go but New York, the self that is discreet as a mirror.

"I've been invited to work for David Silver," Arkenhout tells the Goodmans.

"Oh," his father says. "That's good. If you still have time to study. Your mother took me to that big show of his in Washington, once."

Arkenhout is relieved they know the name. He says, "It means I won't be able to come home for Thanksgiving."

"Your mother," says his father, "will be very disappointed."

He's grateful that Silver has just enough celebrity to excuse anything Arkenhout does, that the name is big and gilded in the Goodmans' minds. The Goodmans send him, UPS overnight, a pumpkin pie which arrives cracked. There's also a letter from his father: love, prefaced by oblique talk about the great city, and how a boy shouldn't grow too far away from his parents. Arkenhout knows it is a begging letter.

In mid-December he's up at Silver's house, copying some articles that Silver claims he won't ever read, when Raoul passes him the phone.

"Your father's coming," his roommate says.

"Coming?"

"He's on the New Jersey Turnpike now."

"But—"

"He's coming to some meeting in New Jersey, and he's coming to take you to dinner or something. He's an hour away, two hours if the tunnels are really bad."

Arkenhout puts down the phone. He catches Silver's eye. He doesn't have the right to bother Silver, but he hasn't any choice.

"My roommate says my father's here."

Silver says, "You want to see him?"

"I suppose so."

"I could talk to him. Say you're out of town on an errand for me. Taking something to the National Gallery in Washington, maybe."

"But he'll want—"

Silver remembers evading a father; he sees his own story in Arkenhout. "There's work here, house-sitting for the vacation. You could pay for spring break that way. I didn't think you'd want to come to the Caribbean—"

Arkenhout stays in the studio that night, on a futon on the floor, in a garden of high painted canvases.

Mr. Goodman sits on Arkenhout's bed, in Arkenhout's room, trying to sense the presence of his son. He shouldn't have surprised him. He shouldn't have come to New York at all. The place is a kind of afterlife, an altered state.

He takes down a book from the shelf. His eyes water. He counts the pens in the coffee cup, twice. He won't invade the boy's privacy by turning on the laptop. He sees clothes in a clean laundromat stack on a shelf and he takes the top T-shirt. He holds it up before him. He smells the good domestic smell of soap and artificial freshness.

The roommate stands in the doorway. "Sir," he says. "Sir, I'm afraid it's a bit difficult for you to stay here." His girlfriend is hanging back, between giggles and annoyance. "Sir?"

Mr. Goodman looks as though he would bury his face in the T-shirt. But he gets up slowly and says "Thank you" with mechanical manners and goes heavily down the hallway.

The Goodmans' Christmas card plays "Joy to the World" when it is opened, as Arkenhout does in David Silver's empty house.

≡

Seth Goodman is a success: a social creature, in a world Martin Arkenhout never expected to know, which doesn't seem narrow and self-righteous and beery like the Amsterdam artists he used to read about in the magazines. Seth Goodman wants to live on, if he can.

The Goodmans write letters now. They don't call much. There doesn't seem any point. The letters are sometimes brief, and sometimes they say much too much about life back home in Jackson, Michigan, as though they were trying to pull Seth back with detail. At first, they're angry Seth does not tell them more. Then they seem to get scared they'll push him away; they write about "growing pains."

Just once, they talk about cutting off the allowance unless Seth comes home.

Arkenhout on a subway train out to Park Slope. A black woman in a pose of sad tiredness, sitting sideways, face rolled up. A dapper Sunday suit and a pink Sunday dress on children traveling with shiny prayer books, and a very small, thin, blank Chinese man with a bag of windmills.

He gets it, suddenly: an F train epiphany. The other passengers think he's waking up from drugs or sleep; they pull back from him.

He can't be just Seth Goodman. That's a trap, too. These people out in Michigan want to see a Seth Goodman, and they'll start to get literal soon, and ask what happened to their real son.

He's supposed to visit people who live above a Chinese takeout on Seventh Avenue, in a second-floor cave of chocolate wood. Instead, he goes to the Botanic Gardens and sits on the lawn among the early lilacs, running the circuit of his situation over and over again.

Seth Goodman mustn't be missed, or else there will be questions. He can never go back to Martin Arkenhout. But he can't be Seth Goodman anymore, so he must become somebody else. In the papers, he's read how easy it is to steal someone's name and credit; but that doesn't seem quite safe. A living person may notice what is done in his name. So he needs papers, but he needs more than papers: he needs a life to inhabit.

He watches the families parade past: the Japanese in knots, the wide shoulders of West Indians, the occasional old ladies in twos or threes, a few Hasidic Jews so dazzled by their children they hardly see the flowers. They'd be missed, he thinks, even if they had lives worth taking.

≡

This doesn't seem terrible at the time because he's busy finessing the situation. Not being Arkenhout, not being Goodman, he's all concentration. He can read the little gaps and shifts in people with senses they don't know he is using: taste, say, or smell, like a cat, or a prickle like fever on his skin.

"You work for David Silver?"

He is in some photographer's apartment past Tompkins Square, at a party for someone's unemployed black art administrator boyfriend: there are many large women, who treat the gay men like cabaret and the straight men like treasure. Arkenhout now brings a powerful seriousness to these events. He feels the sheer efficiency of his own body, as though he were always running a short race.

"I said, you work for David Silver?"

The man asking is dome-headed, with a stick body, jointed awkwardly, which is sad because he is also young and insistent.

"Sometimes," Arkenhout says.

The man is impressed. He'd like to ask what Silver is really like, but he wants to seem sophisticated enough to know Silver someday; so he says, "I'd like to own a David Silver."

"They're for sale."

"You have to deal. There's a short list. I sent a check last time and—"

Arkenhout calculates. A Silver drawing is a half million, a painting one and a half; it's a reality you can't miss in Silver's house, that gives the corporate hush to the marble hallways.

He wonders about being rich.

Besides, this dome-headed man, free of physical grace, still can't be more than—what?—early twenties. It's time Arkenhout fast-forwarded his life, strode out of student days into real life. He's not preparing for some douce career. He might want to tour the world, and Seth Goodman doesn't even have a passport.

"Someone said you lived in his house."

"Over Christmas. He was away."

"With all the pieces—"

This guy must know people, or he wouldn't be here, but he's no social magnet; he foists himself on talking groups, then shuffles out of them. He's not cute, sharp, or with someone. From his anthropology of art, Arkenhout deduces: the man is here because he's money.

"The Museum of Modern Art show," he's saying. "I thought that kind of missed the point."

Very soon, it's going to seem significant that Arkenhout does not try to get away. He'll get dinner out of it.

They eat at a Vietnamese place in SoHo, which would be like an Edward Hopper cafe except for the paper lanterns, and the green lights in the fish tanks in the window. The man's name, Arkenhout now knows, is John Gaul.

He has an accent Arkenhout doesn't know, odd long vowels. He talks about wanting to be a collector as though it were a career, but how dealers won't somehow take him seriously. He wants the fine pieces, the great pieces, but he's marked down for works on paper, minor drawings, paintings by people who don't get covers in *Art-forum*. He's an unconvincing buyer, as he's an unconvincing man.

He invites Arkenhout back for a drink, and it's early, so Arkenhout goes. The doorman says it's good to see Mr. Gaul again, and will he be staying long?

Arkenhout half expects a pounce, but Gaul just frets around his apartment finding bottles of wine. And Arkenhout stares: at glass walls, puffed-up sofas, room after room, a corner cabinet of ladylike porcelain, a pair of old oils of bright, open autumn that might suggest taste but more likely are spares from a family house. The man isn't poor. What's more, he bitches at dust in corners, at the state of the heat, as though he hardly used this weirdly overgilded empire of an apartment.

"I'm going to the Bahamas," he says, as though it is another worry in a burdened life.

Arkenhout never, ever acts impressed. He knows better. He makes Gaul keep raising the stakes.

"My uncle left me a house there. Big and pink, my parents say. I never saw it."

"Really?" Arkenhout has worked to get his "really" just as vacant as anyone's in New York.

"It's real estate. You have to check out real estate. You never know."

"You know people there?" Arkenhout says.

"You don't get it, do you?" Gaul says. "You don't have to know people. You pick them up as you go along." He's starting to sound angry.

Arkenhout says nothing. He hates to fill up useful silences.

"I hate to be bored," Gaul says. The phone rings and he goes to answer it.

A bored man, always in motion, about to go somewhere he never went before; Arkenhout sees the promise in this. Gaul's jacket is slung across the shiny, stripy couch. He can hear Gaul's voice in the next room but one.

He doesn't touch the jacket. He stands looking out of the windows across to the islands in the East River. He thinks about touching the jacket, checking the cards, the signature Gaul uses. In the restaurant it looked like a half-circle for the *G* with the rest trailing away like a fine hair. Credit cards get you almost anything, ATM cards get you money around the world.

There is a credit card slip on the side table, tucked into a book. Arkenhout doesn't think; he acts on instinct, stuffing it into his pocket. He has a bit of Gaul now. There may even be information.

Gaul isn't talking anymore. He is standing at the door.

He knows something has happened. He sees satisfaction on Arkenhout's face, that's all. But Arkenhout isn't furtive, isn't hiding anything. Besides, he's not some hustler. He's David Silver's assistant, a kid with entree. John Gaul really wants to say nothing at all.

"The doorman will get you a cab," he says coldly.

≡

The next afternoon, Arkenhout hangs out at the house of David Silver, shifting canvases out of the cool hall into the sharp summer light of the studio. Jeff and Raoul don't help. Since Silver will soon be back from some German junket, they're playing away the last hours that feel free.

They have their passports out; a cartoon of Bugs Bunny with his mouth full, not of carrot; and the laser copier in Silver's clinical white office. They have glue, fine blades, a small machine for laminating. They've brought Bugs down to a postage stamp, a perfect color miniature, and they've produced page after page of the inside page of his passport, the one with birthdate, state of birth, all on a tasteful watermark.

"You could slip the plastic off the page," Raoul is saying. "The photograph bumps up a bit, so that's not a problem. And you use the thing a few times, it looks wrecked anyway. Then you just put the plastic, the page, and the cover back together."

"Just," Jeff says. "That's all we have to do."

"It's technique. Like they teach you at art school."

Arkenhout watches carefully.

"You could spoil someone's trip that way," he says.

Raoul and Jeff are still discussing where Bugs Bunny was born: Burbank, or Brooklyn.

"There's this guy who keeps chasing me," Arkenhout says. "We could fuck up his passport—"

Raoul and Jeff look up, interested. They like things to be discreet about.

"Get the passport when you see him," Jeff says. "You can do it."

Raoul has the laminating machine, the neatly cut rectangle of plastic, Bugs Bunny's in-flagrante picture, the faked-up version of his particulars. He brings them all together and, a few minutes later, shows Arkenhout the result.

"The type looks wrong," he says, "where it says place of birth."

Raoul says, "Then don't change the details. Switch the picture, just the picture, don't let him know, and the next time he tries to leave the country, he's Bugs Bunny and he's under arrest."

That afternoon, Arkenhout walks through the meat market down to the Hudson River. He sees old warehouses hollowed out with neglect, windows long gone, nettles growing in deep basements. Nobody cares about them. Nobody checks them.

≡

John Gaul is shifting about his apartment. For a few minutes after lunch, he even agonizes. He doesn't want to lose this chance of a connection to David Silver. He is suspicious, and he hates to leave suspicions unresolved. All these are clear reasons to call Arkenhout. But he doesn't trust Arkenhout. His life gets invaded so rarely that he reckons he can at least choose the invaders.

Still, he calls.

Arkenhout calls back at seven, and he's willing to go to dinner. He goes to a hardware store on Sixth Avenue. He needs a box cutter, he says, but they won't sell him one because there is a school around the corner. This does not seem logical to a sensible Dutch boy. He has the dorm room to himself. He takes paper from the printer and practices his own signature, his signature as Seth Goodman. He wants to see how much variation people take for granted.

He gets to the designated bar under a violet backpack, which irritates Gaul; it makes the boy look like a student, not a man who knows David Silver. Both men have a beer.

Gaul says he's sure the house in the Bahamas will be a zero. He'll be back in a week. Arkenhout says he might like it, might stay there. Gaul says, "I could, I suppose. I could always stay anywhere." Arkenhout ignores the self-pity in the voice; he notes down absence of planning, limitless possibilities.

"I just want to know about it," Gaul says. Daringly, he adds, "Silver has a place in the Caribbean, doesn't he? I read about it once."

"I never went to the Caribbean place," Arkenhout says. "I was just the house sitter."

Gaul thinks it's too early for dinner, but he wants to be on the move. Arkenhout follows. Gaul takes more beers, then gin, then a glass of red wine. Arkenhout doesn't. Evidently Gaul has given up on impressing Arkenhout and is juicing himself for some more direct attack.

They take a cab into SoHo and get tucked into the corner of a gray restaurant that claims to be Provençal. Gaul is so precise he's like a tin toy at table; Arkenhout simply eats. At the end of the meal, Gaul has coffee and more coffee. Then, when he stands, he is punctiliously drunk, a man who has just remembered the program for standing, walking, turning.

Arkenhout hails a cab.

"I don't want a cab," Gaul says.

Arkenhout pushes him in the small of the back and he tips into the cab seat. Gaul sits there, not quite sure enough to complain.

Arkenhout thinks he can kill, probably. The boundaries weakened when he took a rock to Seth Goodman's head. Besides, it will be Seth Goodman's crime, and he will not be Seth Goodman anymore.

The cab driver squeals between lanes as though he wants to jolt Gaul sober.

The problem, Arkenhout is thinking, while Gaul is thinking someone is being kind to him, is the body. It would be too much luck if the cops muddled up the bodies as they did in Florida, and besides, Gaul is that much older than Seth, with more time to have broken teeth or bones in ways that get recorded. So the body has to be lost for a long while.

The doorman doesn't rise from his desk when Gaul sweeps in, so Gaul wants his name, his apologies. The man can smell the drink, so he understands.

The doorman hardly notices Arkenhout.

In the apartment, Gaul throws off his jacket and sits down suddenly on his striped, shiny sofa, and lists a little to the left.

Arkenhout doesn't even have to sympathize with the man. There is no man to attract sympathy, just a few random functioning elements with no core of purpose or life.

Gaul is snoring now, still startlingly rigid, with the dark East River behind his fatuous head.

All Arkenhout needs now is information. He opens his backpack and puts on rubber gloves.

He takes Gaul's jacket into the hall, in case Gaul should suddenly surface, and checks the credit cards, the ATM cards. The signatures are simple enough and, besides, everyone varies their signature subtly. Hardly anyone checks with the eye of a graphologist.

Fine. He can access the money, but is the supply constant? Gaul seems to think he can travel anywhere; that's good. He seems to travel on whim. But perhaps that's just the appearance he wants to give. With all that movement, he can't simply wait for his credit card bills at a fixed address; there must be someone who settles them for him.

There is a rolltop desk in a side room, closed but not locked. Arkenhout opens it, hears the mechanism jar, then listens hard to Gaul, who is snoring and gasping down the hall. He pulls papers out, letters with long trails of names on the envelopes, a passport; next to the passport is an air ticket, Delta, round-trip to Nassau going out in two days and the return open. So Gaul is going, and doesn't know when he'll be back.

There's a lawyer's letter attached to the ticket with a rubber band. Gaul is to "introduce" himself to the agent, some woman on Bay Street. If he has to "introduce" himself, then he's not known. The lawyers have arranged credit in Nassau, they say. He might want to stay for a few months.

John Gaul wouldn't. He wouldn't have the patience to stay out of people's way. But Martin Arkenhout might.

He's a boy in a foreign country still. He's not sure he has read everything right. But he has the ticket, the money, the cards, the possibilities; and he needs a new life. Why should it matter how long this life can last?

He closes the desk carefully, but he keeps the ticket and the lawyer's letter.

He walks back to the room where Gaul is sleeping. Now it comes down to this: how to kill someone, how to make the body disappear.

It isn't time yet.

He makes himself coffee, and sits in the hallway. There is a stack of heavy art books, catalogs, and monographs, but that doesn't seem distracting enough; instead, he looks around for magazines. He has to settle for a thumbed paperback of some English whodunit that's been read over and again.

One o'clock. He goes to the desk to see if there's a letter opener. He finds one that is surprisingly sharp. There are paper towels and large black garbage bags under the sink; he helps himself and stuffs them into his backpack.

One-thirty. Gaul has toppled to his right, torso and thigh and calf a zigzag of black.

Arkenhout remembers the doorman saying it was good to have Gaul back and how long was he staying? After the date on that Nassau ticket, nobody here expects to see John Gaul. Nobody will particularly care, except to avoid the possibility that he might complain.

Two o'clock. Arkenhout takes off the rubber gloves, pulls Gaul up, slaps a cold washcloth across his face, waits for his eyes to creep open, then focus, then see.

"I've got to get the car," he says.

Gaul doesn't want to think because it would upset the delicate balance in his head. He looks around for his jacket, pulls out the keys.

"Come on," Arkenhout says.

"Where are we going?" Gaul says.

"We're going to see David Silver. It's a"—he can't quite bring out the word without giggling, so he tries again—"a surprise."

Gaul works at being sober, works furiously.

"I should change," he says.

"It doesn't matter." But Gaul insists on cleaning his teeth.

"There isn't much time," Arkenhout says, shepherding him through the door. There are two other apartments on this floor, owned by old-money relics, so Gaul says, who won't go wandering this early, and would never dare hear sudden movements through their fog of sleeping pills.

When the elevator comes, the operator is trying to stop yawning.

"I'll get the car," Arkenhout says. "Wait for me out front."

Gaul needs every ounce of his concentration to prepare for the moment this kid is offering him like a Christmas parcel: to meet a man impossible to meet. He nods to the elevator man.

The elevator doors snap shut at the garage level. Arkenhout pulls out the keys. He looks around the acreage of shine, white bruisers, sleek town cars, even a Jaguar that belongs to some old-guard traditionalist.

So what the hell does Gaul drive?

He ought to know, he ought to have found out. It was such a simple thing to ask. But they'd always been in cabs, and besides, he had other things to consider that made up a future and not just the next hour.

Only you can't get to the future except through the next hour, he tells himself, thinking he sounds like his father at his most sententious.

He checks the keys. There are two sets, with no color code to distinguish them, no license number cut in the metal.

"Sir?"

He expects security, some official kind of challenge. He spins round. But he sees only a man in a mechanic's overall, the night garageman.

Arkenhout says, "John Gaul's car," with all the authority he can summon. When the car arrives, he doesn't know if he should give the mechanic money.

He collects Gaul at the front of the building. The man is perfumed like a bar, breath the caricature fresh of peppermint, with skin like egg white over paper: not in good shape.

"We're meeting in the meat market," Arkenhout says.

For a moment, Gaul doesn't understand. He thinks of social meat markets, sexual ones.

"The one," Arkenhout says, "where they sell meat."

He takes Tenth Avenue downtown, a wide channel of dark and moving red taillights, and cuts across toward the river. There are people around, of course; he expected that. There's more light than he remembered, the meat trade starting up, the night trade drifting off in high heels and Lurex.

He parks a block away from any lights. He waits a moment. There may be someone stirring behind a Dumpster, a door shutter about to rise up rattling and reveal a store set with carcasses. He wants to be sure.

The street won't do. He puts the car into reverse, and pulls around the corner to the side of one of the hollowed-out buildings. Headlights sweep the end of the street.

Gaul wants to ask what's happening, but he always knew this meeting could never be ordinary.

Arkenhout pulls the backpack from between the seats.

He sometimes read thrillers as a child. He collected ways to kill: odd expertise about when blood flies, where to cut and when, how poisons work, information that clearly belonged to the adult world and leaked through Agatha Christie to a nation of ten-year-olds. None of it helps now.

He is terribly aware of Gaul breathing. He hits him once with force on the windpipe. Gaul's head breaks forward.

Arkenhout takes a thick black garbage bag out of his backpack, puts it over Gaul's head, and pulls it down. He molds the head in the bag until he can find the artery at the neck. He takes the sharp letter opener, and he drives the metal deep into the meat of Gaul's neck. He pushes Gaul forward, pinches the hole the letter opener has made.

He's thinking: Gaul wouldn't take his car to the Bahamas. The car will just rest in the garage until Gaul comes back, as secure and unquestioned as any leaseholder.

Besides, Gaul's blood in Gaul's car is easy to explain.

But the blood is flooding. He tries to dam it with paper towel from his backpack. He shifts the body across so it leans on the door. He backs away from the blood.

It isn't raining tonight, the convenient Florida rain that washed away the questions he should have answered.

Good, he tells himself. Now he'll have to solve his problems. Now he'll have to learn a way.

But he has a horror of the body in the leathery intimacy of the car. It is unpredictable. He starts to wonder if the whole eight pints of blood will spurt out through that simple puncture in the neck, if Gaul couldn't simply stifle under the black plastic that forms a cast of his high forehead and his thin nose.

Gaul's legs kick out.

Arkenhout gets out of the car, opens the passenger door. He expects the body to fall onto the sidewalk. He half expects eyes to open in that plastic face and Gaul to kick his way along the dark street. There is a smell of lard and blood from behind the closed steel doors.

He drags the legs out of the car and cocoons them in black plastic. He tugs Gaul bodily out of the car by the waist, constantly reaching up to make sure the body is as much covered as possible. At least this is a street where blood is ordinary.

He props the body on a wall beneath a wide industrial window that has no glass.

He can't go back now, so he finds the strength to tug Gaul up to the windowsill and let him fall on the other side, down to an open basement with struts and weeds and iron spans all lying around. As it happens, nobody sees him, or likes to ask questions, or believes what they're seeing.

He moves the car by the river on West Street and walks back to the building. If anyone sees, John Gaul is out about some sexual business he doesn't want known.

Inside the empty building, there's moonlight and the light of streetlamps making bars across the floors, camouflaging the bags. Arkenhout climbs down the inside wall, stone by stone. Once he gets down on the rough floor, he's a kid with a backpack.

He has a box cutter in the backpack. He puts on rubber gloves, then holds a garbage bag in front of him as he slashes across John Gaul's face. The blood oozes. He cuts the cheeks away, and the eyes. For a moment, he wonders if one eye was open, like Seth Goodman's eye on the roadway.

He lets the head fall again. He picks up a rusted pipe and hammers teeth out of place. The flesh softens sound. He pushes the body under an iron beam and he covers it deeply with old wood and metal.

He can hear the rats running. In a story, he'd call them to help him.

He puts paper towel, black and soaked now, into the garbage bags and he leaves the garbage bags in a Dumpster. It would be foolish to throw them in the river, to do anything that might make people inspect them; better to take this chance. The bags will go anonymously to the landfill, the body will be lost, and it could be years before anyone knows that a life was taken at all.

≡

John Gaul is going to the Bahamas. His passport, credit cards, and letters of introduction go with him. There is nothing untoward in his New York apartment—although the maid wonders why he used all those garbage bags—and his car is parked in the proper spot. Nobody asks questions.

Raoul and Jeff think it's a brilliant joke to put Arkenhout's picture into Gaul's passport: a social time bomb, waiting for the first sharp-eyed immigration officer.

Arkenhout reads the passport while Raoul and Jeff play with the pictures and make it his passport. He reads about tetanus and mumps shots, no Cambodian goods, all the plant and animal pests and diseases that could come with foreign meat, how mutilating a passport makes it INVALID. An American passport, to European eyes, is a three-volume novel.

David Silver insists on using all the time he's paid for, as though he knows Arkenhout won't stay. Arkenhout picks up toner for a laser printer, two dozen lilies, peach sorbet, a newly mended chair.

When he's finished, he says, "I'm afraid I can't come here again."

The artist has a closed, turtle's face, and it doesn't change. He says nothing.

Arkenhout wants to start an explanation in the silence, but he stops himself.

Silver says, "Make sure you've been paid."

≡

In Nassau he gets the point of all this. He grows up. He isn't some creature of circumstance, living someone else's ambitions. He isn't just his crimes, either. He can sample everything.

He gives the agent the lawyer's letter, and he gets the keys. The house has been empty for years, the agent says, and they hardly knew his—John Gaul's—uncle, but everything has been cleaned and painted and primped. She is glad to see someone living there.

It's not, she says, the grandest part of Nassau. It's a private drive of eight houses or so, all on their half-acres, all the colors of coconut ice and sherbets. When he asks about the house's history she gets edgy; later he discovers that the house was once overrun during a drunk dinner party by robbers who kept the guests hostage for nine hours.

One day the house blossoms with termites, grubs boiling out of mattresses. Arkenhout stands outside and laughs with wonder; then he leaves the maids to cope, and walks down to the beach.

There is a zone in the water where the light and the sea become a flashy kind of luster. Above, the sky is clear blue. Below, the sea is clear green over white sand, with tiny silver daggers of fish. Arkenhout comes up through the shine and goes down again where the soldierfish parade, breaks into the brilliance of the sun and back into the brilliance of the water. He's found joy.

He boozes, goes fishing. Saturdays, he drives past the police cadets' barracks while they're burning the week's evidence, and a parade hangs on the fence, inhaling. He takes up with the dowager class who make the introductions; very seriously, one tells him of his brand-new post office box that "the number says so much about you." He sort of breaks some hearts, an upper-class resort boy who stays while the girls go home.

The house is pink, with two frangipani trees, pink wax flowers with the smell of his mother's bath, and the red glare of poinciana blossom and the vanilla mauve of poor man's orchid. Even the storms come to delight him with their jet-black skies and their ferocious cuts of lightning.

He sails with new friends on seas that keep the promise of those small, square postcard pictures in the family encyclopedia. He comes to think of Miami as a kind of tropical Sears Roebuck you approach by plane; but he never goes there. He's superstitious about testing his passport in America.

Mornings he sometimes sits down with the fishermen selling from underwater trays at Potters' Cay, tells tourists who trust a white skin what they should pay for their lobster and grouper. Sundays he goes down for the fried food and music on the beach at church cookouts, with large black ladies in frocks with proper white collars; and in the evenings, he has dinner. He almost becomes the protégé of a property man who thinks he could learn things.

And he watches. He watches friends who leave cocaine blowing on mantelpieces. He watches the old ladies, and their tame tabby-cat priests, all carefully not talking about what they must know: the drug business all around them, a famous murder and its consequences, this marriage whose only problem is homosexual incest, another open arrangement where the husband is shamed if he doesn't have a Friday-night lover, and sleeps on friends' couches so his wife shall not know. He assembles a pathology of people who aren't where they belong.

They don't ask questions, he notices. If you stay, they make up the story they want; the past doesn't count if it happened off the islands.

John Gaul's accounts and credit cards make him more than respectable—the people who have to stay out the summer in the islands are not at all rich—and his sailing and fishing are enough common ground with a few white Bahamians. Black Bahamians think of him as plain white, which shocks his Dutch heart at first. He soon learns to avoid the banking classes, not much more than English telex clerks, stiff as the pink starched napkins at their dinner tables; and the black Bahamian lawyers, who stroll in black wool suits in August as a badge of pride, and who have the kind of power he doesn't understand. Someday, he may have to pay one, and that is relationship enough.

He goes traveling, on a whim. He takes the direct flights only, to London, to Kingston once, to Frankfurt. He buys books always. He graces places, his carefulness mistaken for manners because he seems so sociable.

He's in Tunis, visiting. He wants to see Roman ruins, the low wreckage of old Carthage, things from schoolbooks; he's drawing on the images that remain out of schooldays so he can preserve some kind of continuity between his various lives. He has to remember he must not remember what Martin Arkenhout or Seth Goodman knew.

He goes to Gide's village, not that he knows about Gide except as an entry in a kind of mental dictionary: French, queer, old. The village is white blocks stacked tightly together. There is a bar for tea, a great shaded room. On the wall hangs a single picture, like an icon: a young man stripped to the waist, muscles used more than built, but definitely posing. The photograph has been taken from a slight distance, not the forced closeness of pornography, and the man seems indifferent to the camera, except that the camera was the only possible reason he would strip and stand with his ribs of muscle flexed.

Arkenhout wonders: if this is the son of the house some generations back—the picture had a period air, fifties maybe—whether it was taken by a friend, an admiring uncle, someone who collected the man on the beach; why it had been given to the bar, and why it hangs as the one icon on tall white walls. It doesn't seem to be about sex; at least it was some kind of desire that depends on never touching. The man's body seems like function taken to a polished degree. Arkenhout wonders if it is some kind of bait.

He never forgets the photograph. It is an ideal: how to be a man, to be strong, calm, and quiet in the face of the very desire that makes you worth recording, to concern yourself with strength that matters, and to be beautiful without caring. He forgets the details of the picture, even though it sends him off to a Nassau gym in a panic of self-consciousness, but it always stays in his mind as a square on a wide white wall, larger than a snapshot, smaller than an eight by ten: instructions, somehow.

≡

He takes out of Nassau two memories. There's Junkanoo night, walking the dark streets with fires rolling in oil drums, the sound of cowbells and drums starting tentatively at first, then brazenly, then furiously. There was also a night of hurricane in a shuttered house, when the storm boards ripped off windows and he stared into a dark garden where the trees strained and broke against a faint gray light. He had parked the car, for safety, in the middle of the lawn. Its lights, uncannily, went on.

He doesn't remember the next killing at all.

He picks new lives. He's in Paris for a while, being an expatriate American, links up with a small old lion of a movie director who's forever being honored, but not paid. He becomes a kind of secretary. He's there when some fiftyish French movie star, once famously and now desperately blond, tells the director she doesn't swim in the Mediterranean anymore; *"On ne se baigne pas dans une mer juive."* He watches the director transcend that moment, for the director is a Jew; but Arkenhout has too much moral certainty to forgive him. When the money runs out entirely, and the director is hocking his old Citroën, the pump-up kind, to pay to lose his stomach cancer, Arkenhout moves on.

He watches even lives he will never steal, collects them just for the information: two Guatemalans in Rome who fake eighteenth-century Sacred Hearts for the Florentine market; a poet who thrives on being rejected by women he fancies, and likes Arkenhout to steal them; a sect of devout fraudsters playing golf in Marbella; the floating life of a bodyguard, padded out with the authority of whoever he's guarding; the life of parallel persons, the ones at airports who are not rushing with families, carrying half an office in a bag, fretting over bookings, who can travel whenever they want and wherever they want, if only they can bring themselves to want one specific time and place. It isn't money that makes this possible, although they need money, of course. It's a lack of mooring to the ordinary, crushing rhythms of practical life.

He's in Brazil awhile, up in Fortaleza, where it's fun to be rich but the mosquitoes still bite you, and then out in the grassland interior, sweating out days that smell of the leather of working horses. He thinks of trying Australia, but the visa seems too complicated. For a while, he roisters about, no fixed abode, but he finds he does like a community where people want to know him, but not much about

him. He gets tired of beers and bars sometimes. He has a year on the
fringes of the movie business, being part of entourages.

On the one hand, it works so well. He catches glimpses of other
people stuck in jobs, places, marriages, credit ratings, and he glories
in the fact that he alone knows how to reinvent himself at will, to get
on with the next bright life.

On the other hand, he has a career like any other young professional, with its demands and crises: like the need to move on. He has
to work at being casual and shiftless.

Then he makes a mistake.

It is 1996. He's in Switzerland, on the great lake near Lucerne, with
a lease on a small farmhouse on a slope of green velvet fields. He likes
playing at being settled in a place where tourist strangers are always
passing through. Guard down, he feels himself on holiday: in the
quiet, in the morning mist and sun over the lake that make eerie king-
doms of air, in the sound of cowbells and the regular passing of the
lake steamers down below. He contemplates mountains. He lacks
occupation, and doesn't care.

His name, for the moment, is Paul Raven. He has an American
passport again, collected from Raven's office in Los Angeles, where
the man was scattering money about the town to break into movies. It
made good sense for Raven to disappear to Switzerland for a while.
Nobody would ask questions. It was Arkenhout's idea he should disappear somewhere that nobody knew him.

He sometimes walks all day on the high paths, along the mountain
ridges, until he's not sure he can hold enough breath and summon
enough will to make the last kilometer home. He swims in the lake
waters, where they're jade and not the black of shadow. He wakes
early in the morning.

He hears hammering on the door.

Now, seven in the morning is a possible time to go calling in rural
Switzerland. The neighbors have already tended cattle and pigs, have
taken the first glass of coffee with sugar and their own pear schnapps.

Arkenhout goes down the wood stairs and opens the door.

There are three men in uniform.

"Fremdenpolizei," the largest one says.

In ten years of wandering, he had always slipped past uniforms, not on the watch list at Customs, not anyone's idea of an illegal migrant, solvent and sensible enough to raise no questions.

"Foreigner police," the man repeats. "Herr Raven?"

For a moment, Arkenhout does not know whether to nod or argue.

"You are in breach of your visa for Switzerland," the cop says.

"I suppose—"

"Your visa expired yesterday."

Arkenhout takes in the great black water of the lake, the last paper of snow on the mountains, the smell of coffee on the man's breath.

"So—" the cop says.

Arkenhout tries to remember what the problem is: whether he gave the wrong number somewhere, whether he's miscalculated his welcome, whether he seemed to seek employment just because one dumb night he was half-offered a job animating tours for the over-sixties, by a man who knew perfectly well he could not give the job away. But remembering doesn't help.

He's allowed to collect his personal papers, and a single suitcase. The police take the keys to the house.

He's on a train to Basel, discreetly handcuffed to one of the cops. An old lady, in first class, picks apart the hems of napkins. She never looks at the police.

At Basel station, which is half French and half Swiss, he's left to buy a ticket. He chooses Cologne. He knows there's money in Cologne.

He is escorted to the train, settled in his proper seat and carriage. The handcuffs are removed only when he's seated. The Fremdenpolizei cover the end of the platform just to make sure he leaves.

And the train slips out into Germany.

He has never made a mistake before, not like this, not a mistake so catastrophic that he's been noticed. He depends on not being noticed. He doesn't even have the usual protections, the possibility of charging to the American consul and demanding protection, because authority must never take a particular interest in his name or movements. He shares this taste for privacy with all the major tax evaders he's met: invisible when they move or settle or spend.

He has almost a day before the train reaches Cologne. He doesn't have cash in his pocket. He has Paul Raven's credit cards, of course, but the problem must be something he doesn't know about Raven.

Still, he walks to the restaurant car and eats sliced veal and dumplings, in honor of his old Swiss hosts, and pays with the credit card.

He's nobody now, nobody in particular, on a moving train, staring out first at forest, then factories, then at the Rhine. He can't trust his name. He isn't ready to take a new one. He counts castles that are stuck in mid-river or on horror-movie crags. If he can't trust Raven's name, he'll need to make money, fast. He stares at the white sun behind the clouds. It might be easier in Amsterdam, he thinks, weak for once; the fact that he speaks Dutch would entitle him to a community. He knows the rules of the place.

The train runs on from Cologne into Amsterdam. Nobody will know him; Amsterdam was a foreign country to him growing up. He can surely find a job.

≡

The office, a room over a red-light brothel, gleams like hellfire when he starts the evening calls. Six schoolroom desks, six phones. Six men wheedling.

"... wanted you to know before anyone else ..."

"... unique opportunity. I tell you, we're not sharing this with just anyone ..."

He sits with a list of dentists, one of pensioners, all suckers just longing to be told they alone were going to do something so clever, so profitable, it would dazzle the world. Naturally, he always says he has to be discreet, and so do they.

"... this gold mine," he says, "unworked for thirty years. Astounding assays. Of course, anyone could have mined there, but the only people who thought ..."

"... casino in Las Vegas. Yes, a casino in Las Vegas. And you're in on the ground floor. They want to be very careful about their sources of financing ..."

"... the world's waiting for this device. Antitheft. Anticorrosion. Antigravity. Antimatter ..." And he says all this matter-of-factly, trying not to make it into a song, trying to keep it flat as though he were barely suppressing his own excitement.

If they ask—an accountant in North London, a company director in Kent, sometimes expatriate bankers in Brussels or Paris—he tells them, "We wouldn't ordinarily share this unique investment opportunity but you are a client so valued we want your goodwill more than anything.

"I'll need your check by Tuesday," he says.

Occasionally, they'd be difficult. "Where," a Scots voice asks, "are these shares traded?"

"Spokane," Arkenhout says with absolute authority, or "Denver. There's a huge market in penny shares."

"You want more than a penny," the Scots voice says, weak with sarcasm. Three minutes later, he buys; the ones who think they know the right questions are always the easiest.

Arkenhout finds he likes this game, likes the regularity and the sense of occupation. It's a holiday from the way life averages out, which to him is mansions and palm trees and lakesides.

It can't last, of course. He's made a life out of staying alert to the moment when trouble starts to start, when people look as though someone has been asking questions, when a credit card takes a minute longer to pass scrutiny. So he's alert in Amsterdam, too, even though he's cocooned in all this ordinary life.

He senses being watched. He doesn't take it personally, because he's on home ground. There are a few strange phone calls to the office that, strangest of all, come from the Netherlands.

There is a smell of police on the air.

In this occupation, you don't hang around for the cops. Arkenhout and the others shut up the office one night and never go back.

They do, however, find the manager in an agreeable apartment down by the American Hotel. He is at first unwilling to concede that he owes them money, let alone favors. He becomes prissy and sure like a schoolmaster. There is a discussion, some of it physical. The manager is full of praise now for such good salespeople, promises to pay all the commissions due and perhaps to hire the team again. Then he passes out.

Surprisingly, he keeps most of his words.

In the new office, between a piercing parlor and a greengrocer, there's even a brass plaque, although not for the company name the salesmen use. There are scripts, and a line of product: a brand-new Denver share issue every three days or so, a rush of money, followed by stock prices sent out sea mail so as not to alarm the punters. This time Arkenhout, who was so effective getting the due commissions, has a privilege: he can buy on credit to sell again on the first day of issue to the rush of punters who really believe in secret information, runic keys to gold, gadgets with magic. He makes money.

There is a price, of course. He is summoned to a concrete bunker of a hotel close by Schiphol Airport. A billboard outside says the hotel is nine feet under sea level, because there is nothing else to say.

He sits in a room with a view of grass and more grass.

After an hour, a very short man called Moe appears. He does not let Arkenhout say more than "Good morning." He explains that he is saving capitalism by finding money for people the banks turn down. He tells Arkenhout that the rules about stocks and shares are unconstitutional. He says, including Arkenhout, that we are all good Americans here.

In case Arkenhout's attention should wander, Moe has a few stories to tell: how he started in the vending machine business on Long Island before friends—and he says "friends," not "buddies" or "associates"—invited him to take over their stock business in Denver. He preaches a bit more. Then he offers Arkenhout the job of running the Amsterdam operation.

There is no question of refusing, of course.

"Cookies?" Moe says, producing a box from the deep pockets of his jacket.

"I'm very honored," Arkenhout says.

"We'll tell your boss tomorrow," Moe says. "He's coming to see me tomorrow."

The implications sink in while Arkenhout is driving back to Amsterdam. Here he is, stuck in honey, which will drown you as fast as shit. At least as a salesman, he gets to leg it when trouble arrives; if he were Moe he could preach about being a stockbroker to the risky classes; but he's middle management, and middle management goes straight to jail.

"... we're calling out of office hours," he breathes down the phone, "to keep this call absolutely confidential." We're also hoping you had a bit too much to drink at lunchtime, he thinks, that your pulse is up and your skin flushed and you're ready to see Jesus in a slice of bread. "This opportunity won't happen again," he says, which is true—unless the sucker lists circulate and the man is cold-called again, or unless he buys, in which case he becomes a supersucker and they won't waste the really good salesmen on him anymore.

He leaves the office as usual and goes back to his apartment in North Amsterdam for the last time.

He thinks, on the ferry, how proud his parents would be that he has a career, an office, a promotion: a proper citizen. This, he thinks, is ironic, if irony is a bad enough, spiky enough word for the situation.

Tomorrow, the old Amsterdam manager will be his enemy. But the old Amsterdam manager is not in the custody of the police; he is free-ranging, with spiteful friends. Moe, too, is around the place, and he is not accustomed to being refused or even disappointed. Arkenhout can't please both men, but he senses a whole criminal city behind each.

So the next morning, when the banks open, he draws out his money and closes the accounts. He takes a train to Utrecht and puts himself in a small hotel.

≡

This particular night, he doesn't want to be alone. He has cash. He calls an escort service, asks for a very Dutch girl, pays her for the night. She doesn't like the idea of a whole night, maybe she has children she must care for; so he throws in another hundred guilders over the agency fee. In the middle of sex, he knows he's fucking to put away his fear.

Being scared is something new. When situations are bad, he calculates his way out; he anticipates, he researches and checks, he operates in communities where people do come and go quite abruptly and nobody asks questions. But now he's in a nation of settled, documented people, and he has no time at all.

He should have started looking for a new name months ago. He shouldn't have slipped for a moment into this easy, structured life.

The girl has soft, wandering breasts with huge nipples. He puts his head between them. She lies there, eyes closed fiercely, keeping herself asleep by sheer will.

He's awake early. He's angry with himself, which he knows is not useful. He has to find a life to take and he has days, not months, and he is starting from scratch. His heart scampers, his eyes seem to dive into situations and read them out; he is wound and ready.

Grietje leaves early, a bit disgruntled at all the intimacy on top of the sex.

He's left blank. He scarfs breakfast, stokes up on coffee. He thinks about starting in the bars, even though it is barely ten in the morning; he needs an easy victim. This time, the money doesn't matter. He just needs a new name.

It is the strangest time he has ever known. He works the streets like a kind of whorehound, looking at everyone male, twentyish, thirtyish with the same starved eye: as substitutes for himself. He might be cruising for sex, except there's no sense of play and he wants information first, not afterward with a cigarette or a coffee.

In two days, he finds nobody. Nobody at all. He doesn't even have a candidate. He starts going farther afield, although he knows he's in the absurd position of seeking the perfect random encounter.

He goes to the border towns that stand by raised river courses, eats pizza, drinks beer, hangs out. He looks for the unconnected one, the outsider. He draws out people's stories by the simple trick of staying quiet. Sentences hang in the air. People feel they owe him another detail, and another. Usually, all he hears is the beer bubbling in the voice box.

Christopher Hart is different. He doesn't have the usual saga of injustices done him, politicians despised, marriages survived. He doesn't, at first, launch into any simple, one-side-of-the-paper explanation of himself. He just drinks like a hero.

Arkenhout tries being a talker, for once. He starts off in Dutch and Hart says nobody ever talked Dutch to him. He says *"dank u wel,"* and that's all he knows.

Arkenhout says he's just back from Germany and looking for work. He doesn't lay the burden on Hart; he just shares the story, two men looking at the bottles behind the bar from parallel lives.

Hart says he teaches at a university. Arkenhout almost backs away. Professors belong to place and institution. They can't travel without a grant form in triplicate, or think without a subsidy, or write a book without putting their institution under their name on the title page. They go about in specialties where they've watched the same faces and reputations for decades. He could never take on a professor's life.

But Hart is the outsider in this place, the vulnerable one. He's the best Arkenhout can find.

"You're at the local university?" he asks.

"Sort of," Hart said. "I'm on sabbatical. To write a book. So I can't very well complain if I don't have a social life. I suppose."

"You're here long?"

"Another half year. If I don't just run away. You can get awfully tired of all the straight roads and the flat fields."

"You could run away?"

"I suppose so." Hart took schnapps and pitched it into his beer. "What kind of work do you do?"

≡

The next day Hart is not in the bar, and Arkenhout is irritated. The professor is letting him down, inhabiting the life he needs and living it without style or glory: a plain man in a bright world.

Besides, there isn't time for all this. Arkenhout needs a change, and quickly, and then he needs to get away with reliable papers and reliable credit. This next life doesn't have to be perfect, just feasible for a while.

He rings the local university, a modest place whose low buildings hunker among trees, and asks for Professor Christopher Hart, visiting scholar. He's put through to the Department of Fine Art; that's new information for him. "But Dr. Hart hardly ever comes in," a rather blowsy voice tells him. "You'd be better off calling him at home."

He takes the number. He'd have preferred an address, so he could go watch for the signs that Hart leaves on a landscape: what people will miss if he's gone.

The number helps. He calls, and there's no answer. He remembers Hart saying he couldn't complain about his lack of a social life; so he lacks a social life. There is no answering machine to take messages from distant friends or lovers; perhaps this year people don't call.

Arkenhout tries the local real estate agent. He needs a house, he says, for maybe six months. The agent, he says, helped his friend Christopher Hart.

And he did, as luck has it. "There isn't much around here," the agent says. "Dr. Hart got the last house on the market. For rent, that is."

"It'll be back on the market, though? In six months?"

"In six months. You want to see the details?"

The agent pulls out a loose ring binder of colored sheets. He shows a house in the countryside, painted green, high gables, a garden of shadows, all low shrubs, and a driveway that seems to be the most important feature. Arkenhout takes the address.

The next morning, he's there at nine-thirty. The cleaning woman has just arrived, so there is no housekeeper, which is good.

There could be a girlfriend, a boyfriend of course, but the man was in a bar on his own, talking but not cruising except for simple company and someone to hear his voice. Of course, that could mean he's just lost a girlfriend or boyfriend; but he would have spilled all that out after a few beers. At the very least, he'd have hinted at the duplicity of other people. People do.

Still, Arkenhout checks. He walks up to the door and asks the cleaning woman for some Christa or other. The cleaning woman says the professor lives there quite alone. Sleeps alone, too, from the looks of it, she says, not wanting to waste even an empty bit of gossip. Then she gets moralistic, five feet of muscle in a housedress, sermonizing on the doorstep. A bachelor rattling about in a big house like that, she says; it doesn't seem right.

Arkenhout wonders how sound will carry on this flat, wet land.

He's already decided the rent for this great, remade farmhouse is an excellent sign; Hart, although he's young, must have money. He drives a VW Golf, new. He dresses sharp.

But there is always the possibility of a parallel life. So Arkenhout waits a few more days, goes for long walks in the country, goes fishing one day, then hires a car and waits for Hart to use his VW to go to his other life, whatever it is, if he has another life. All this time, Arkenhout is the bit of shadow under the tree across the road.

Arkenhout checks Hart on the Web, checks his taste for anything troublesome with a few key merchants of worldwide sucker lists: no kiddie porn, no need for mail-order sheets, not wicked, not domestic. He is nothing in particular, available to be stolen.

Arkenhout finds himself asking all the questions, except the right ones.

=

Hart comes out of the back door covering his head as if it is raining. But it is only mist. He gets into the car, creeps down the drive, creeps into the road. Arkenhout can't follow like that, can't keep him in sight without tailgating, because of the mist. Besides, he can't drive that slowly. It isn't in him.

Hart seems such a cautious bastard, afraid of trees and the green and the mist and the cars on the road. He parks at the station and takes the Amsterdam train. Nobody knows him. Fine.

At Amsterdam Central, Hart walks off like he is hiking mountains. He bustles down streets full of early-morning hookers suss-suss-sussuring from the red windows, and students piling their bicycles alongside the bookshops or the cafes. The man needs a life, Arkenhout thinks, which strikes him as funny in the circumstances.

Hart goes to the side of the Rijksmuseum, through those little formal gardens with their bits of sculpture, and through a door marked PRENTENKABINET. He is still researching, evidently.

Around lunchtime, Hart leaves to eat in a cafe across Museumplein. He orders croquettes, of all the low things. He eats fast, he drinks one beer, and he goes back to work.

Arkenhout decides to take a chance and come back only at closing time—watching like a father who tactfully watches his son come home on his own. The day has tired Hart. The brisk lope has turned to slack shoulders and a dutiful stride. There's nothing ahead of him except the evening.

The station, the train, the VW, the house. The daily woman has gone. One light comes on in what must be the kitchen, another in what must be the living room: probably some huge, open, cold living room. Another in the gable of the house, which must be his bedroom, reached by sharp, narrow stairs. Arkenhout wonders why an English-man would feel at home with what the Dutch like.

He feels his skin go cold.

≡

Hart lets him in; why wouldn't he? If he's surprised, he puts it down to different manners, another country, and he's glad of company. He brings beer into the tall, open living room, by a hearth whose huge stones seem cold and shiny damp. He waits for Arkenhout to come to the point.

There's just one more thing that Arkenhout feels the need to know: if Hart went away, where would he go? He needs Hart's life for only a brief time, so he wants no complications.

"I shouldn't have come home," Arkenhout says. He can sense Hart draw back. The man doesn't like confidences; his alertness is pure defense, not curiosity.

"Five years in Germany," Arkenhout says. "Frankfurt. In a bank. Better than nothing, I guess."

Hart says, "I'm off next week, actually." He only means he's not available for this kind of chat, but Arkenhout can't believe his luck has finally turned. "To Portugal. I thought I'd get as far away as possible."

"The Algarve?"

"God, no. Somewhere in the center by the mountains. Where nobody goes."

For the first time, Arkenhout checks out Hart as something more than a useful set of data. He's a fine case of presentation, who does just enough at the gym to stave off scholar's stoop in his narrow shoulders, who has one Dolce & Gabbana jacket to hang on a gawky frame, who animates his eyes and face even when he's not interested, like a man who someday wants to be on TV.

He's training to be a star of some kind, Arkenhout thinks.

But what kills him is the fact that he's already written the letters—they lie unposted on his desk—that tell his university in England and his hosts in Holland that he's going to Portugal for a while.

≡

By the time Hart is dead, the Brahms CD has reached the *Academic Festival* Overture: *Gaudeamus igitur juvenes dum sumus.* A little effort, and Arkenhout is starting out again.

Hart is alive for the first two movements of the Second Symphony, though. The garotte goes around his neck at the start of the *Allegretto grazioso*, keeps turning like you turn a can opener until the breath is out of his body and his neck is cut through.

Arkenhout lays him on the patio on the usual bed of garbage bags. It is dark and there are fences. He waits for an hour so the blood will ooze instead of spurt, and he trims Hart's identity with a good sharp knife to a rerun of the *Allegro con spirito*. You always cut the balls, because if they do find the body, that suggests some sexual motive. Sex makes it anonymous.

It is careful work. Arkenhout washes away the blood with ammonia. He operates so the body can be wrapped and weighted and sunk into water in several places. If you don't cut, the body keeps its natural buoyancy and comes up black and accusing.

He dematerializes this Christopher Hart so well that by the time he drives away in the VW that night he is Christopher Hart—alive, well, creditworthy, just on the move.

Gaudeamus igitur. He gets himself a beer.

Later, the cops will say Arkenhout is a master of disguise. But he never tries to change his face, his body, his way of walking or dressing. He simply takes papers, money, and a whole life, to live as himself under someone else's name.

He checks the details like nervous travelers check their cash and tickets. Paul Raven has disappeared, which is what you would expect him to do in his circumstances; and if he was dubious enough to be slung out of Switzerland, who's now going to be surprised that he has gone to earth? Christopher Hart is going to Portugal, where he always meant to go. No questions at all arise.

He wants to find the same escort girl from Utrecht, and show her a good time this time: no neediness, no all-night warmth, just action. But he's not stupid. It's his good time so any girl will do.

Later, he packs Hart's clothes: not many, mostly khaki. Better not to leave them in the house. He remembers to leave money for the cleaning lady, so she won't talk. The keys he will take with him, as Hart would, since the lease has six months to run. He likes that phrase: six months to run.

≡

Mrs. Arkenhout always goes shopping in Amsterdam.

She's the mother, decorous, docked like a neat little boat outside Marks & Spencer with a bag of black socks, knickers, and sweet wine, wondering if she has time for a piece of pie and a coffee before the train.

Then, amid the mutter and clatter of Kalverstraat, she sees the dead walking: Martin, her son. He is tall, blond, and just as he should be.

She hugs a few clichés to her. Martin, she thinks, to the life. These young people all look alike. Nowadays. A face in the crowd. A mother knows. Then she sees how the tug and pull of the street is taking Martin away, just like ten years before, and this time she won't stand for it. She knocks her way through the crowd. She ricochets off the nicest people, not even meaning to say "Sorry."

He stops in front of an open store, by a machine that makes business cards while you wait. He'll need cards, being a proper professional man. She can see him feeding his name to the machine, who he is and where he lives and how to reach him, the name of his company and his position, what has became of him since the telegram—"the" telegram, always—announced his death.

But the man feeding the machine turns out to be another blond.

She panics. You can't meet the dead and then lose them, not in a shopping street, not in a mall. It isn't right.

She thinks of shouting Martin's name. But even in passion, she's proper. She only stares around, and people watch her stare. She feels herself change in their eyes from a doctor's wife with a position and a garden into a ghost of herself, an unremarkable, dotty, and disrespected lady in an oddly nice skirt.

She sees him again in the line for a tram to Central Station. She can't waste time, because the tram might come and pull away and she'd lose him. The train doesn't matter anymore. She thinks she can explain why dinner is late.

The tram pulls up. It is painted over with huge eyes, like an articulated billboard, advertising sunglasses, but she doesn't have time to see that. Martin gets on, so she gets on. Her heart bothers her.

He is at the snout of the tram, she is at the back. She pushes and frets forward, her shopping bags following awkwardly and clashing with people's shins and buttocks.

She is just behind him.

She thinks about how long she must cook the pork for dinner. She tries to remember when the next train goes. She sees a boy with earrings and she is glad Martin doesn't wear earrings.

And now, if he doesn't suddenly turn and acknowledge her, she is going to have to speak.

She knows about thank-you letters, and the size of invitations and when to offer sherry and when genever gin. But there is nothing in her books for this.

"Excuse me," she says. But she doesn't touch him.

The tram sways on a bend, pitches her against him. Her shopping bags fall and leach neat socks across the floor.

"Do I know you?" Martin says.

It is Martin, she's sure—his eyes, his manner, shoulders too broad for the bookworm face, the fingers like tapers blunted at the end. She knows that he knows her, and still he is saying in that offensive tone and in English, "Can I help you?"

She is meant to say "I made a mistake. I'm sorry." But she hasn't made a mistake, and she isn't sorry, and she will stay here until the end of the line and she will make him remember.

"Martin, I'm your mother," she says.

Martin pulls away.

She knows he knows her. Mother and son isn't a matter of a face uncertainly etched into memory; it's body memory, very old.

She says, "Martin? I am your mother."

He is leaning on the door button when the tram next stops, but he doesn't run. He allows two girls to get down before him, leggy, juicy girls. He turns back then, and he says, "My name is Hart, Christopher Hart."

He says it in English, although she spoke in Dutch; which is odd, because the English hardly ever understand Dutch.

The tram door snaps shut. She stoops to salvage the socks, absently rolls some into balls out of habit, all the time apologizing to the air.

≡

The nearest police station is on Warmoesstraat, not a respectable street. Mrs. Arkenhout arms herself with her position as a doctor's wife, and sweeps past the pushers, the chip eaters, the bleary dummy people who stand quite still on corners like a bored audience at their own lives; and past the sex-shop windows, people and their pets, splayed ladies, industrial equipment; and the coffeehouses crowded with the kind of people she doesn't know, but maybe Martin has become.

She explains the problem to one of those designated kind policemen they have in Amsterdam. Afterward, she realizes how it must have looked: a red-faced woman talking so exactly and carrying wine, explaining how she had seen her dead son walking on the street and asking for something to be done about it. Naturally, the policeman offers her something hot and sweet.

Then he makes a show of checking a computer file, and tries not to look surprised when he finds an old story on the screen: Martin Arkenhout, Dutch exchange student, found dead in Florida.

"I want to see the inspector who asked us questions," Mrs. Arkenhout says. "The one who investigated Martin's death."

"You understand that Martin is dead, don't you?" the nice cop says.

"Please," she says. She knows what she knows, which is photographs, a neat, clean, manila file of them presented to her ten years ago: details, all horrible, in silt. A forearm with a fake-gold Timex, with roots of flesh where the shoulder had been. A fragment of chest with an indented nipple; she didn't know about Martin's nipples, not a boy's nipples. Some perfect teeth, scattered in sets. All these and more, the policeman said, had been pulled from a great river of grass.

"Martin is alive," she says. "I saw him."

"I'll make a report," the cop says.

She hasn't wasted her time, she thinks. For the wife of a doctor, someone will do something. Surely?

≡

Leave Martin Arkenhout for a moment. He's catching his breath at the back of some cafe, taking an interest in a beer. He'll be telling himself that his mother didn't know him, that the meeting never happened, that officials will calm her down and send her home and think she's sad. But she'll make sure the authorities do something, he knows. She'll want to find him out of love but, being the decorous woman she is, she'll pretend she's just offended by the untidiness, the impropriety of seeing the dead on public trams.

The whole chain of his life depends on disconnections, so he knows his situation is bad. He just doesn't know how much worse I am going to make it.

≡

I am not a policeman.

I am not a fanciful man.

I've simply tried to tell you all this in one of his languages: what he'd done, who he had been, before he broke into my life.

He fooled me, but then he had many languages. He knew art English and plain English, and bar English and dinner party English in expatriate mouths with that odd precision you get from too many euphemisms. He knew how to dress up his mind in a language, not just get the vowels and endings right.

He chose who to be. He chose what happened next, and where. He animated each minute because he never dared let anyone else do it. He must have been a fearfully busy man. I find it more relaxing to have this single personality of mine, formed like yours by the usual circumstance and history.

Now I want my own words for what happened next.

I know some of this because I lived it, some because people told me, some because in the end there were police reports. I have put this together like a history from documents and interviews and memories.

Everything here is true. I don't want anyone making the mistakes that I made.

Two

My name is John Michael Snell Costa. That explains almost everything.

Costa is a Portuguese name. Snell is English, my mother's name, but it is there only by Portuguese custom. The first two—John Michael—are what a Portuguese father calls a boy born in London when he wants him to pass for English.

I do pass very well, on the whole: perhaps too dark, shorter than the absolutely average, the name a bit odd. I suppose I'm sometimes too obviously serious—about women, about the art I file away in Solander boxes. I'm reserved even when I drink too much; I don't have a boisterous, slap-happy, separate drunk self. My accent started with the BBC and got a bit demotic later as fashion changed.

But don't think I belong. I would hate to belong.

I'm out on monochrome streets, on my way to work, passing people all in a blind, resentful rush who long for the day to color up. I'm rushing, too, that's the cleverness of it all. I'm in step on the escalator, always in the right line. I know how to box myself into the right moves.

I look around and see the self-conscious stylists who've bought and paid for their identity—biker, jock, queer, Armani, banker—and I'm right there with them. Because I fell in love with paintings, hopelessly, I play a keeper at the Museum. I have the clothes, mostly flannel. I have the degrees.

I like the job, I should say. On the streets, everyone is running in this pale, stressed present tense, no history, future indefinite, scrambling to invent themselves every minute just to stay whole. We keepers get to mediate between a past that's stored and documented, that is registered as important, and some possible future in which people will look at it again.

I'm also a romantic, without much opportunity. What I do is keep drawings, tend and study them: reddish lines, brown wash on paper that stains and crumbles. I protect these things.

But I'd guard wonders, given half a chance. I'd be a knight in armor, by a grail in a tower, kneeling on watch for centuries.

≡

The taxi dropped me at the north entrance.

There was a gentle riot all along the Museum railings, crowds blowsy in open summer clothes. At ten, exactly, the guards consulting their watches with great drama, the gates folded open. The mob promenaded ruthlessly up to the famous portico. The daily invasion of the public, physical museum had begun.

But I walked past them, and through the green door of a decorous Georgian house to the side. Keepers know that the Museum itself—its powers, purposes, and history—is in these offices and it looks out on the plant that supports it the way Victorian mill owners looked at their mills: which is to say, unseeingly.

I walked the warren of students' rooms, past labs that cut up bodies of stones and fussed with odd worms in exotic woods, down corridors painted in pale, official colors with a sense of respectable dust even in mopped corners. I loved this walk. I was deep inside the Museum, opening up the soft privacy of this solipsists' place that was kept separate from the big, open circus of the public galleries and the wider world only by doors marked (I noticed this on my very first day) EMERGENCY EXIT.

I cut through a basement like locked cells, each stacked with objects, a world tour in bric-a-brac. I passed the Hindu sculpture where a scream of cats came to be fed, offices where small, broken things were filed in drawers until a monograph could be built on them. All the higgledy-piggledy confusion of the Museum's private parts, its lack of maps and its trick, dogleg corridors, were an occasion of triumph: I won through.

I was on my own territory, under the dome. The sense of achievement died quickly.

Carter was waiting in my brown and stuffy office: a small, neat, anxious man, like a mouse in a cleaning coat, with a vigorous toupee on a tired face. He had four folios balanced on his knees.

"Good morning," he said. "Good weekend? Yes? I thought you should see these. I'm not responsible."

He waited for me to clear a corner of my desk, and put the books down. They were perhaps twelve inches by twenty-four, bound in slick white parchment that had stained with time, their edges shaggy like a pile of thick papers.

I said, "What's the problem?" knowing that Carter always thinks there is a problem.

"See for yourself."

I went to touch the books, but Carter coughed. "Gloves, sir," he said.

I said, "You can't do anything without latex nowadays." It's a ritual joke that slightly stirs Carter's dust, which is the point. I pulled on thin white surgical gloves.

"Fifteen pages," Carter said. "There are pages missing. Someone has taken fifteen pages."

Each book was labeled "Liber Principis," the Book of the Prince. I knew of them, of course, although they were kept in the cage of a reserve collection: albums of paintings, seventeenth century, made by artists attached to Prince Maurice of Nassau when he was governor of Dutch Brazil. They were lovely things, full of exact living animals, trees, snakes, and people, but they were much more: the first attempt to record precisely what was in the New World instead of populating it with conventional monsters. It was as though, on each page, you could see wonders directly through the eyes of the past.

"I'd never have known," Carter said, "but for the routine checks. We've been having dehumidifier trouble in the cage. Staff have handled them, conservation had them three years ago. Besides that, there's only one person. Professor Christopher Hart."

"Oh, God," I said. "We have a suspect." I could see that Carter was hot for mousy vengeance, but he said nothing.

"You're absolutely sure that no other member of the public saw these?"

"Hart had to get special permission, you remember. In the circumstances."

Carter blamed me for the permission, I could tell, blamed me for the fact that the books did not stay safe in their wire cage. I saw the ghosts of liveliness penned up in those cages. He saw his few surrogate possessions, to be protected like his pension and his mortgage.

I had my hands, palms down, on the scratched white parchment of the covers.

"I'll handle it," I said.

≡

Christopher Hart at that moment was these things on a table: three credit cards, a bank card, a Eurocheque card, four library passes, one photo pass that opened doors to his university department, a gym card, two frequent flyer cards, one out of date, one colored gold, a passport, an American visa in the new style with a photograph, a driver's license, a separate identity card, a red season ticket to Arsenal Football Club, a computer warranty card.

They were all Martin Arkenhout needed, usually.

They're what authority requires to let us walk onto a plane, look at books, touch our own money; they don't just prove who we are, the cards are our identity itself. Power wants us numbered and not named, carded and not just remembering our name, address, telephone number, purpose, social security number, PIN, and so forth. Power has good reasons. As long as we have papers, we cohere; we don't shift like character or personality or desire. We're available to be managed.

In the end, he boasted to me about all this: how all he had to do now was to fill in the details—what Hart wants, eats, loves, hates, believes. He was already sure he could make a better life for Hart than Hart ever could have.

He doesn't know about Hart, you see. I do, which is knowledge that can kill me.

≡

"You understand the problem," the deputy director said. He was a fleshy man, the ruins of a rugby player, out of whose bulk came short, sharp puffs of startlingly aesthetic opinion.

"I think so," I said. "These books are not supposed to be in the Museum in the first place."

"I'm not sure the Museum would say that. I'm sure the Museum would say it cannot by law part with objects in its collections, however they arrived; that makes almost everything easier. But in this case, the Museum would particularly like not to say anything at all."

"Family secrets," I said.

"Exactly."

"For the record," I said, "I suppose we ought to review the history of the Liber Principis?"

"Do we really need to?"

"For the record," I said. I wanted as much distance as possible from any future awkwardness. I wanted the deputy director to handle the Museum's honor, while I attended to the art. "The paintings were made by Albert Eckhout for Prince Maurice of Nassau. Maurice ran short of funds and decided to sell them—which he did, to two German princelings. Maybe each one thought he was getting the whole collection. At any rate, each bound up his own albums of the paintings, and each called the albums the Books of the Prince. The albums all stayed in Germany."

"Yes, yes," the deputy director said.

"Sometime early this century, the Prussian National Library acquired both sets. War broke out. The holdings of the Prussian National Library were sent out for safekeeping in case Berlin was razed. The Libri Principis, along with some Mozart autographs and so forth, disappeared. It's a matter of public record that one set turned up in Cracow, and decades later the Polish government admitted that they had it and let in the scholars."

"A mistake," the deputy director said. "Books would live forever if nobody saw or moved them. We could keep the whole universe of knowledge in perfect safety." He coughed, a little embarrassed at parodying his deepest instincts.

"Of course," I said, "it was easy to see how some books left in Saxony might make their way to Cracow. It is a little more difficult to explain how the other set arrived in London."

"Enterprise. Spoils of war. Most museums owe everything to enterprise and spoils of one war or another."

"Until now," I said, "there has been no public acknowledgment that we hold the Eckhout paintings. I suppose unkind people would ask how we acquired them in the first place. They might talk of theft."

"Or transfer. The Museum taking responsibility when the Prussians failed to look after things."

The books had a presence in the room: the embarrassment of something wounded on the sideboard. I lifted a volume and spread its pages with indecently bare fingers: they had a delicate smell of paper dust and perhaps some kind of old, scented pomade, as in the library of some grand house.

"Unfortunately," the deputy director said, "we live in an age where everyone is supposed to be open, and everyone apologizes for history. We don't send the Elgin Marbles back. But we don't hide them, either. So the director, in his wisdom, thought one younger scholar should be allowed to look at the Eckhouts. A confidential matter."

I considered the pages. Each had a net of captions, but only the odd-numbered pages had pictures, sometimes more than one: the album was a plan for something more ambitious than itself.

"We can hardly bring the police in," the deputy director said. "And it's hard to avoid the inference that whoever stole these pages knew that very well indeed. It is an embarrassment to lose things. It is worse to lose something you should never have had."

"Only one person outside the Museum handled the books. Christopher Hart."

"You're perfectly sure there could be no question of some insider at work?"

I shrugged. "I'm not a detective," I said.

"This is very unfortunate. The Museum values its relations with younger scholars. The Museum depends on them. But it was Hart, definitely, and only Hart?"

Evidently some of the pictures had never been set in place, because the paper was evenly discolored. I turned the pages like a policeman at first, noting the few places where the gaps were shockingly bright inside a weathered frame, where a painting had long protected the paper on which it was mounted. Then my eye caught on a page that had been cut close to the spine. The insult to the album brought the object alive for me, took it out of the inert category of evidence. I felt anger for the integrity of a perfect thing that had been spoiled.

I was not supposed to feel this. It was politically incorrect. It was historically dubious, too, since the albums were an arbitrary assembly of what survived, what patrons liked, what nobody had managed to steal or ruin over long years, including whoever found the books in Germany and then thoughtfully dropped them off at the imperial storehouse of the Museum.

But I found myself falling into the bright, exact pictures.

"Perhaps you could talk to Hart," the deputy director said.

"He's in Holland, on sabbatical, so his department says. He hasn't been seen for a while. He told everyone he might go to Portugal, but there's no forwarding address."

"God," the deputy director said.

A tiny nameless insect, jagged crimson and black, crawled up the page. A snake, gold underneath, black above, like a player come up to the footlights in a melodrama. Three snakes on a page: diamond-backed, splashed with red, saddled in black, all writhing to break the frame.

The deputy director said, "The bugger wouldn't publish, would he?"

Goats, I saw, warm and a little nervous against mottled grounds, ears and horns turned in. Llamas with the faces of cartoon politicians. An anteater had proved so astonishing that it was a mass of uninvesti-gated brown hair ending in a snout. There were gorgeous cats, a mon-key whose features—tired eyes, worn teeth, low ears—looked human and scared. I have never understood how people can pull back from the seduction and presence of paint, its physical depth and crust, and look only at slides, use abstract nouns, throw concepts and theory around instead of looking with passion. Paint is food to me.

"I don't have to emphasize discretion, I hope," the deputy director said. "Except for the record," he added, mocking me. I should have put the books down. I should have concentrated on this exchange, however empty and pompous it was. Instead, I was looking into a round, kind face at the front of the album, someone with a thatch of hair, shining cheeks, a faint suggestion of stubble above wide lips, eyes just out of focus as though the artist could not quite meet them, or perhaps the man was drunk.

The album was not a set of pretty things, a carnival of oddities: it was a new world seen with wonder. Instead of conventional assemblies of root, flower, insect, and memento mori, the kind of overstuffed images the Dutch also made in that century, this was precise and astonished, and deeply personal. It was like a grandfather's stories of discovery.

A woman, bare-breasted, holding a root up like a torch, a vermilion sash about supple brown legs. Then a soldier, bare with a bow and arrow and a ring of crimson around his head, absurdly like medieval millinery. A chief, mitered and robed like a bishop. A mother, a tiny baby clinging to her neck.

"The Germans tried to get the albums back from Cracow, I think. That could be trouble," I said. "We're not very plausible heirs to the Prussians."

"The law does not permit the Museum to alienate anything in its collections. Anything. So of course we insist on keeping them."

Reluctantly, I left the woman with the sash. I felt I had been in her company a moment, that I could turn back and ask her things: how the cold of a vault felt after the forest.

"It's possible," I said, "that whoever stole the pages simply wanted to sell them. He wouldn't find it hard. They're rare, portable, exquisite, and anyone could appreciate them. There'll be some sausage king of Saxony who has them in his private safe. Or some banker." I withdrew my hands reluctantly, as though the books had been touching me back. "You could hang them in your drawing room quite safely, too—nobody ever published them, and almost nobody has seen them for the past fifty years."

"Perhaps." The deputy director tumbled his fingers against the desk. "I did wonder something else. I wondered if the pages were meant to be sources for an argument, Hart's argument," he said. He was outlining a crime he wanted to commit, I could see that. "Perhaps he wants to control them, so he controls the story he's telling." The offense changed: from a theft, something banal and greedy, to an affront to everything the Museum was supposed to represent.

"Perhaps he wants to destroy them, so nobody can argue with him," I said.

The idea stood in the room for a moment, as shocking as a leper.

"This is a community of scholars," the deputy director said. "I suppose we must acquire the habit of suspecting one another. Body searches as you enter, body searches as you leave. Metal detectors and X-rays. Warrants for everyone's libraries. But I would have thought from Hart's reputation, from the papers I've read, that I knew him.

"We really must talk to Professor Hart."

I knew the "we" included only me.

=

Christopher Hart, so Arkenhout told me, bought his rail ticket from Amsterdam to Cologne with his credit card. No problem. He had his passport with him, but nobody needed to see it at the German border.

He caught the tram to the end of a suburban line in Cologne, and walked up three flights of stairs to an apartment where an Indian with bloodshot eyes took his papers away. There was no receipt, nothing written.

He nursed a beer for four long hours.

When he went back, his face matched his name. The Indian—and his two cousins—mended identities like shoes, and with the same professional indifference. He paid in cash. The Indians accepted most currencies.

On the way back to Amsterdam, the dull, gray border station at Emmerich acquired something like glamour: a place of ordeal. He could see gray-uniformed policemen on the long, empty platforms. He wanted to show his passport to one of them, to be examined and searched and proved to be Christopher Hart, professor. Nobody came.

Then he asked himself: Did I really give a name to my mother? Did I really say out loud that now I am "Christopher Hart"?

≡

I left early, through a fire door into the public museum. Crowds roared at me, on their way to shop for cultures, gods in the nude, all those unbiddable spirits of river and earthquake and birth that we hold behind strong, official glass. Occasionally, someone would be stopped by the huge brown eyes of—say—a Coptic portrait, would stand against the crowd for a moment; and then would scuttle on to the next obligatory sight.

I watched the guards watching all this. They were older men who certainly drank beer and ate pies, who had been dutiful in the army and would not answer back, who paraded through the galleries at night and shut them down. They tolerated cameras and sensors and the mumbo-jumbo of security, but only because they knew in the end it came down to their nightly ceremony of big iron keys.

I thought they belonged to the same world as my father: people who ate Marmite, knew the name of Max Jaffa, knew what they meant by "tradition."

My father was on my mind, anyway. He had left messages on the answering machine, all starting uncertainly as though he felt self-conscious talking to himself this way with only a vague hope that someone would sometime find the message. I called him, but he was out. He liked to spend the late afternoon in the Portuguese cafes along Ladbroke Grove, talking without the nagging burden of perpetual translation. He'd be drinking little coffees, and eating cakes with eggs and almonds. I don't know what he discussed.

Anna wasn't home yet.

My father's story is an old one. He came to Britain as a laborer, became a waiter, polished himself up until he was running a hotel restaurant. All this time, he made sure I would never be him. He turned me into a dark, nostalgic Englishman, attached to cricket and kings and chestnut trees like nobody English could ever be again.

But my father, I came to realize, did not like the process. With his friends, he still spoke Portuguese. When I came home from school, even my "Hello," my "Good afternoon," the word "Dad," were betrayals of true, Portuguese language. Fish fingers, gobstoppers, stuck him in the heart. But he couldn't say anything about betrayal. He had already slipped across enemy lines and into the bed of the English-woman who became my mother.

She died of a cancer so quick it was like a special effect, as though she'd briefly relaxed and all her defenses crashed at once. I was ten. I know now what my father did. He made me safe at all costs. The highest of those costs, to him, was Englishness. Other families went back to Portugal when the girls were thirteen, just when Englishness might get between their legs; but I was his son, his only child, and I could stay on to become an alien myself.

I went to university, which nobody in my family ever did before. My father was proud, soft and nervous. I got my higher degree, because I was to be proofed against digging or serving for a living.

I can't imagine how my father explained all this to friends who ached for home.

My father was back at half past six. He said he wanted to go to Essex on Saturday, to take a boat out fishing for dabs. I knew there was no way to refuse him.

Anna still wasn't home. I felt her absence, a coldness where she should be occupying a chair or standing at a window. She was pre-occupied, of course. Her life went by the rhythms of the college where she taught—breaks, exams, committee crises—and to the frequent, brutal pain in her head that beat her down. But she was more preoccupied than usual. I thought she was wholly involved in something, someone else, and she could not even pretend that things were normal. It was more comfortable than admitting to the distance between us.

Anna came home, but I still felt her absence.

≡

I have the police file here, copies, anyway: neat reports, no paragraphs, sometimes a note in the margin. The file says that, around this time, Inspector Van Deursen and Sergeant Visser went out from Amsterdam to interview the Arkenhouts. One or other of them has scrawled at the bottom of the first page: "Nice people." And then: "artificial fire in hearth. gave off no heat at all."

They asked if Martin Arkenhout had tried to contact his parents.

His mother said, "No, actually." I think she must have said it with shame.

"You haven't moved in the past ten years?"

"No."

"And this man on the tram—he gave you some other name?"

"He said he was Hart. Christopher Hart. He said it in English, but, you see, I'd spoken to him in Dutch."

"You're quite sure you could not be mistaken?"

"Yes."

"You know there are penalties for wasting police time?"

At the end one of the policemen had made a light penciled note: "Very practical. Very distraught but couldn't show it. Drugs?" His colleague had annotated the note: "Prescription drugs. Husband a doctor." He had underlined the word *prescription* fiercely.

≡

My father took the oars while I pushed the rowing boat out onto the flat estuary water. I couldn't have stopped him. He was seventy-six, wiry still, proud that he could wear the same suits as at fifty. His hair was a white, immaculate helmet set on a Brylcreem boy grown old. The tendons of his arms looked thin, though, and they were wattled with spare flesh.

He fell asleep once on the drive down from London. He was bright, almost young, when he was animated; but I looked sideways at him, his mouth gaping, and I saw the skull exposed beneath the skin.

But at this moment he was heroic, his eyes bright with a kind of exasperation.

"Hurry up," he said.

I didn't know if we were about to miss the fish, the tide, or perhaps some imaginary train going home. He couldn't wait any longer; he had lost the resigned patience of middle age.

I jumped into the boat, and he pulled away. Occasionally, the oar feathered the water, but usually his muscles remembered as acutely as his mind. After a dozen strokes, he said, "You can row later."

I said, "Oh. Thank you."

He rowed into the channel. The mud bottom slipped away under us. The skies were enormous and pale, and there was a mean little wind and a burning sun all at once. I could see the marshlands around us: vetch in bloom, salt channels cut in the mud and rushes.

He was going out to sea. The strokes were already an effort, but he concentrated hard. He didn't speak, so as not to show that his breath might be short, and he didn't smile.

I said, "Isn't it a bit late in the day for dabs?"

He said nothing. I looked back at the flat shore, the fence of reeds. A gray heron sat in an attitude at the edge of the water.

He put down the oars quite abruptly. I wondered if he had run out of energy, or if his heart was troubling him, but he looked strong and bright.

"Get the lines," he said.

We hooked and baited the lines, then cast them over the side. The little rowing boat was caught in their grid, and we stayed put on black water, waiting.

I knew better than to talk. I sometimes used to talk on walks in Surrey when I was a kid—Green Line bus, a few hours in the forest—and it was my fault the cuckoo or redstart or fieldfare or siskin flew away and never came back the whole day.

"We came out too late," my father said, accusingly.

"I was afraid of that," I said. "Aren't we too far out, anyway?"

We had both set our backs to the monument on the estuary: the towers and blocks of a nuclear power station. We were determined to see only water and marsh.

"I have this account. Poupança Emigrante," my father said.

"I don't understand."

"A bank account in Portugal. For emigrants."

"But you're English."

"I've sold the house," my father said.

I didn't, for a moment, know where to look. The marsh was a black line in the bright light. The sky was washed pale. There was no particular cloud in which to find faces or a map, as I used to do as a child with my father. There were no other boats out on this kind of eccentric expedition.

"I said, I sold the house."

"I heard you," I said.

"I'm leaving next month."

"You're leaving?"

"I've been building this house in Portugal. I want your advice on it."

The boat turned a little, uneasy on the change of the tide. The lines looked likely to snag, and I started sorting them, pulling one in, straightening another, like someone tidying a room.

After a while, I said, "I don't understand."

"I'm going home. To Portugal."

"You always said England was your home."

"I said a lot of things," my father said. "We're not going to catch anything out here at midday."

"I don't understand."

"You and Anna must come and see me, when I'm settled. Meanwhile, I'm putting the rest of the money in a Portuguese bank. Sixteen percent interest. Can't get that here." He always was concerned with money, not skilled at it but interested. He once asked if he could make money buying and selling the kind of paintings I know about.

"You're sure—"

He stood up in the boat. If he'd slipped, moved suddenly, moved in anger, he'd have tipped the boat to one side and the dark river water would have soaked into our clothes and tangled us in long, green weeds. I wanted him to be calm.

He stretched himself, arms high behind his neck, and let his knees sag for a moment to stretch out his hamstrings.

"Surprised you, didn't I?" He was grinning.

I took the oars this time, and I took us back into shore so fast the water sounded against the bows. He'd said nothing about this, nothing about a house in Portugal, or wanting to go back, or about selling the house in Stockwell where he had lived so long with my mother, and with me, in the smell of bay leaves, coffee, and pine disinfectant. It was shocking how little he had ever said.

The boat beached under us. "Steady," my father said. "Steady." He looked into the pale sky and said, "There's rain coming."

≡

Anna came into the room after me and lay down on the bed. I could tell she was making a point by not touching.

"He never said anything," I said. "He must have been thinking about this for months, years maybe. It takes time to sell a house. It takes time to build one, for Christ's sake." He wasn't settled, after all; he was thinking of, maybe longing for Portugal, planning a house there with particular rooms and doors and gables. "He never said anything. He never even wanted to travel. Remember when I wanted to take him to—"

Her stillness interrupted me. It was louder than words.

"You bother me," I said.

And she did: caught my eye, caught my breath at the most unexpected moments, broke into my planning and reading and left me smiling. I always had to wonder how long she could hold on. She hadn't asked any questions, which was a bad sign. She'd been once to the bathroom, for medicine for her head.

"Maybe I should go with him," I said.

"You're the one who wanted him to be so independent. You're proud of him, really."

So it was going to be a lucky morning, calm as milk. At least she could engage with what I said.

It was not always like this. I had got into the messy habit of loving her totally and always being wary, both in parallel, alert for the moment when the pain in her head came back and temper broke up talk and words flew out sharply and the pain was present in the room like some wrecked ex-rival who now felt entitled to demand kind and polite attention.

I lay down beside her. I felt at home there, but I knew I couldn't touch her because touch was one feeling too many for her.

She'd go for a walk. I'd go for a walk. We'd manage, somehow.

≡

That same day, according to Mrs. Arkenhout's diary, which she gave to the police, Hart went home.

I can't imagine he decided where he was going. He'd have taken trains, got off too soon, waited for the next train all along the line—in hamlets, in art deco stations all gray and yellow and tiled, and on bleakly open halts. He liked coffee. I can guess he drank coffee, then another coffee.

He reached the town where he grew up. It's a half-hour's walk from the station to the Arkenhouts' house, so he must have arrived at about four in the afternoon: the time when the domestic world would be drawing Mrs. Arkenhout again, time to get dinner ready, to finish the ironing, to water the garden, to be at all costs ready.

He didn't need to find the way. He'd be halfway there before he even looked around. The houses were like a set of bright toys from a model railway, as clean, matched, colored, and artificial, and this fanatic neatness stood on land that was just as artificial, stolen from the sea. It was all so engineered and unlikely: a clean frame for growing up.

I know he remembered getting on his bicycle and riding over green polder land and still being always in sight between the flat, rectangular fields, behind the tall trunks of poplars. I know this because he told me, but he said it all happened in England. He rode down to the dunes and the sea, stripped off so nobody would know him by his clothes. He would walk about a soft, hilly sandscape, thinking he was alone for a moment, and a head, two known heads would appear over the next dune and trap him again in himself. Already, he didn't just want to be alone. He wanted to be someone else.

When he could see the house, anyone in the house could see him. The garden still had that awkward quality: a garden that was required by the unwritten civic rulebook, but not loved.

Out here, there couldn't be any question about it. He was Martin Arkenhout again, the child demanded by his parents' marriage, proof there was nothing defective about them. He was Martin when he played here, schemed here, did homework, tried to get off with girls. The place remembered him and took him back—as if he could ever get away.

He must have been shocked by all this: the ease with which he slipped back past all the identities he had stolen, into the one he had so effortfully escaped.

He was a few hundred meters from the house and there were only three more buildings before the road gave up at a gate. For the moment, he might still be visiting the Boerrigters, or the Fields, if they never did manage to go home to the Malvern Hills, their dream of heights. Once he'd passed all their houses, he could only be Martin Arkenhout going home.

I suppose he was just trying on the possibility of going back. After all, he didn't have the history for it anymore.

To fill in Martin Arkenhout he'd have to write himself a kind of novel to fill in the past ten years. Martin slouches through college. Martin drops out and gets back on the tracks, Martin in plaid pants, smoking dope, dreams of fulfillment and applies, when the dope wears off, to a bank, a firm of accountants, a cultural foundation. College stops, so Martin stops reading. Martin gets on a job like a railway train that's carrying him somewhere someone else has decided. Martin lives with a girl in an apartment in Utrecht because they can't afford Amsterdam; hey, Mum, look at me, I'm a commuter. Martin's girl has an abortion. Martin leaves his girl. Martin fucks up. Martin takes Prozac. Martin would not have been good as Martin.

He'd burned this house down in his head, buried it in sand.

He stopped in the lane. He couldn't afford to be seen, to start more people asking questions, but he could hardly be more conspicuous: a stick figure against flat land.

He saw his mother at a window. She couldn't truly see his face, of course. She'd see a tall stick of a man out walking, an outline against a sky pale with heat; like a picture, she could make up the meaning later.

≡

Mrs. Arkenhout let the newly washed curtains twitch into place; I can see her doing it.

There was a man out there walking along the road. He was coming this way, but he'd stopped short. You had to keep an eye out nowadays, neighbors looking after neighbors. But perhaps he was going to see the Boerrigters. Perhaps he was just going for a walk now the sun was less ferocious.

Then again, perhaps it really was Martin. She told herself not to think this; it wasn't useful or proper. She suspected herself now of conjuring him back because it seemed even more impossible that he'd gone, so abruptly, so meanly: a statistic from some Southern state she'd always imagined as hot, dangerous, not very clean.

The man didn't turn at the Boerrigters'. He had nowhere left to go except their house. If he came, he might kiss her or he might kill her. He might tell her things she didn't want to know.

She must call the police; that was the proper, citizenly thing to do. But they already thought her peculiar, even mad: a woman who sees visions.

Out on the road, the man kicked a stone for a moment, stood aside for a passing car that must have been lost, and then stretched hugely.

Mrs. Arkenhout pulled the lace curtains shut. She watched him in the mirror above the fire until he walked briskly away. She put all this in her diary.

≡

My father wanted coffee while the movers worked, but he truly wanted the coffee he could make for himself. This pale, milky stuff in a café cup had been an insult at first; now it was the perfect reason for leaving England. He drank it and didn't need to say a word.

We could watch the house through the plate-glass window of the cafe. Old oak chairs came out, then cheap sofas. There was a big, obvious brass bed and even a hatstand. The men strained under the heavy stuff of a life. I didn't like to ask what he was taking with him because that would tell me what objects—a table where I used to write, my mother's boxes from her dressing table, mugs we each used—were being abandoned.

"You've got everything you need in Portugal? Already?"

He said, "I bought Portuguese things."

"I don't see why you want to leave all your life in London. I don't get it."

"I'm going because I can go."

"You could always have gone back. But you didn't."

He said, "I can go back now."

He left the sense of a story on the air, something he was not going to tell, but he didn't make sense. I'd always imagined him as some kind of hero, a man who got away from the endless rule of the dictator Salazar; and it hardly mattered if he was really chasing work instead of liberty, since he had the courage to go.

But he could have gone back when Portugal turned into a democracy in the 1970s. Instead, he waited tables and he stayed in London.

He said, "Don't ask questions."

"Fine," I said.

He stood up suddenly, went for change, and pulled his trouser pocket inside out with a rain of little coins. He scrambled to pick them up, then set a pile on the table to pay for the coffees; he didn't need to ask the price after so many years.

I said, "Is there anything I can do?"

He glared at me, and he stiffened his back and walked to the house. I'd have known he was scared if he had been anyone but my father.

He went inside to check they'd taken everything, he said. I stood by the road and watched the last pallets and pieces of felt packed in the back of the van until one of the movers snapped out some sarcasm, and I walked back to the Underground station.

I had grown so safe I was boxed. I didn't even know how little I knew. I had become ordinarily English, busied myself with career and marriage, and I never saw any need to help pull my father into his adopted country. I had always assumed my father was naturalized and settled like me.

I went to my mother's grave, a marble rectangle topped with marble chips, under a tangle of old trees. I didn't know quite what to do. I knelt and brushed the seeds and leaves away, cleared some bird droppings from the marble letters. I felt I should be able to explain things.

I said out loud, "He's gone." The words were stifled by the soft, cold air.

≡

It was decided by a consensus, not by any colleagues with names and faces, in one of those discreet Museum committees for which I did not quite qualify, that I should go to Holland and find Christopher Hart. He would not refuse to see me if I arrived suddenly in town; he might not be quite clear what I wanted, but it would be wise not to give him any notice, just in case.

I packed methodically, Anna keeping out of the way: trousers folded over sweaters so they held their creases; jackets inside out, the sleeve seams exposed and rough; shoes in their sleeves.

Anna said, "You must have something to eat."

I couldn't think about anything except going, and Anna knew it. "Or some coffee?" she said. Each of us hated to have the other distracted.

She said, "I wish I could come with you. We could go to Leiden together. I love the gardens in Leiden."

She didn't mean it. She was letting me go as she always did, entirely concerned with me but not holding me.

"I'll only be a couple of days," I said. "I left the hotel numbers for you, and the flight numbers."

I tugged the zip around the garment bag. I held her for a moment, her warmth and my warmth making a kind, closed zone, like lovers.

"I don't think Fred is very well," she said, meaning the cat, a checkerboard veteran who had been feisty in his time. "I'll take him to the vet."

We both knew this was something we always did together.

"You'll need a taxi," Anna said. "I'll book a taxi."

"I could drink some coffee," I said.

Anna led me by the hand into the kitchen. She'd put out cereal and yogurt, of course; she would feed me if she could. She had already made coffee. It had not been a good night; I could tell by the marks under her eyes. I was overwhelmed by her kindness for the moment, and the sheer peculiarity of her: fine, sharp-faced, the memorable legs that were perfect and too short all at once, like a sample.

"The taxi's coming," she said. She didn't like good-byes.

≡

The next day, according to the police file, Sergeant Visser decided to find Christopher Hart. He pulled the hotel registration forms and the computer records. He found one Christopher Hart, British passport, registered at a cheap hotel on Rozengracht. Since Hart had checked in the night before, his passport was still with the hotel clerk, who handed it to the police for copying.

So they had a picture of Christopher Hart they could show to the Arkenhouts.

When the sergeant went back to the hotel, scenting a crime but still unable to name it, Hart had already left. It seems he'd returned from morning coffee, morning paper, morning walk, climbed the stairs, and found the clerk waiting for him. I can see the man now: his shoulders tense with righteousness.

"The police came. Wanted to see your passport."

Arkenhout said, "They didn't say why?"

"They never say anything. If there's any trouble, maybe you'd better find another hotel. In fact, I think you'd better find another hotel."

He said, "Yes."

He didn't know what else to say. He'd never been the one the police come after; his name was always on the body left behind. He just knew he couldn't be found, not yet.

I suppose he packed his bag, collected his passport, settled the bill, that the clerk stared at Hart's credit card as though there had to be some conspiracy coded in the hologram and was distinctly put out when authorization came chattering down the line.

"You want a cab?" the clerk said. "To the airport?"

"No."

"I thought you'd want to get away."

He said, "Why should I?"

The clerk remembered everything he said for the police, down to "Have a nice day."

He was out on the streets, no fixed abode, no fixed name, known as Martin Arkenhout and as Christopher Hart, which was at least one name too many. The police file says nothing about the next twenty-four hours.

But imagine: this man lived by forms, address, occupation, nationality, write in the squares, sign below, all anybody notices. He once talked to me about Tinkerbelle, the machines that capture every transatlantic phone call, more in an hour than anyone could transcribe and read in a working lifetime; he said the point was that nothing went unobserved. Your every move is conditional. And all these years, he had used that fact, tricked with forms and cards and passes and papers, and the bureaucratic reflex they produced; he was shocked to discover the bureaucrats could use the papers too.

He had never truly had to bluff before, because there had been nobody to challenge him; he took a new name and he immediately moved on. But now he had to be perfectly Christopher Hart, whoever that was: professor, scholar, writer, and whatever else. He owed the dead man a kind of debt, and all because of one stupid answer to one sudden question on a tram.

Also, he had to act a character. He couldn't just continue himself under another name.

He couldn't get his head around this notion. He said—he said it about another time, but I'm sure he meant this time—he saw the city like filing boxes, people shut away by firm and occupation, going deliberately from one place to another by arrangement. Even the loungers in the sun were tourists, day-trippers, time wasters deliberately aware of their designated gap in the organized day; they knew their place.

He had become the anomaly, expecting to be singled out. He couldn't stand at a tram stop with conviction; no destination. There was no particular reason for him to be in any street at any time. Passersby, the ones with even the slightest purpose, had the advantage: a net of obligations and appointments and habits and other people's expectations to hold them in place. But he'd done his peculiar work, stolen a life; and now he was too fraught to live it.

He couldn't think straight, so he tried going out of his mind: spacecake, a couple of beers, some sinister peppermint schnapps.

But he could still see only through his own eyes. He looked at the high gables of the houses, the shifting trees, the low light breaking up in the canal water, a big moon hanging in the blue and neon sky, and he went out of time. He wasn't held to any particular name, or personality, to being a person, not even to being in that present moment. He wasn't a serial killer, orderly and regular; he was a willful consumer of lives.

Restaurants closed down, dim lights at the back, naked tables, stacked chairs. A few people were belched out by the pubs on a breath of smoke and beer. I imagine him panicking. It wasn't chemical panic;

it came from the heart. The disconnection with the city became the city shutting him out. It was a still summer night, but it seemed very cold.

He told me he stared in a bookshop window, trying to connect with titles, subjects: not just to know what they were, but to bring back what he knew about them and thought about them, to reconstruct himself around that skeleton. It didn't work.

There was a packed bar across the road, sociable to the point where people rubbed against one another as if they weren't quite sure they could stand.

$$\equiv$$

Maybe we grazed each other during those days. I was in a bar one night and I remember a face at the window, which struck me as odd: it was a grown man, thirtyish, stoned, big gray eyes, playing the part of a child waiting for Daddy, staring with wonder at a grown-up world. But the wrong drugs could turn anyone that way.

I didn't seek out Hart at first, not while there were museum people, collegial types, to see. I knew I was no policeman, not even a moralist; I was in Amsterdam just to help clear up an embarrassment. I could never track and shadow and bluster. I never understood the English criminal and cop in whodunits, both so decent the killer leaves the room to kill himself when he's found out, to avoid any social awkwardness; and I don't have Bay City luck, where the private dick is hired by the woman who did it, sees the guns go off from the heart of a martini, and coincides with crime so often he breathes complicity and suspicion along with the gin. I felt very separate from Hart's crime, across a sea of call slips and study rooms.

I did what I do best, which is talk to colleagues.

"So what do you want?" Van Ostaade said. He was a short, slight man, with a face on the point of vanishing entirely into fine-etched lines, a curator at the Rijksmuseum.

"Want?"

"Of course you want something. If you were just here for sex and drugs and rock and roll, you wouldn't be calling the museum." I thought it interesting that his museum, too, was "the" museum.

"Could you tell me," I said, "the five most likely fences in Amsterdam for mid-seventeenth-century paintings."

"Attributed or not?"

"Attributed."

"Good names?"

"Known names."

"How many?"

"Enough."

"You're having a rough time, aren't you? I heard about the Persian book covers. And the Japanese chest. And the Medici casket and those Louis XIV bottles. You ought to be more careful."

"Security," I said, "is being upgraded. So they say. Meantime, these pictures are my department, which is why I'm here."

"You think they might be on offer in Amsterdam?"

"It's a big market. Our thief, if he is a thief, is here. You do have some nice, plump, shiny dealers with very interesting back rooms."

"I hope you haven't been doing business with them," Van Ostaade said. "I could tell you stories about people at your Museum—"

"Before my time," I said.

"Oh yes," Van Ostaade said. "Yes, of course. What are these paintings—landscapes and burghers?"

"Flowers. Birds. Insects. Animals. People."

"That about covers it," Van Ostaade said. He finished his beer noisily.

But my answer had to be careful; he knew that.

He was grinning anyway, features a bit slack and wet with the beer. The volume in the bar turned up suddenly. "You're talking about the paintings everybody thinks they understand, so everybody wants them," he said. "Anybody could sell them. There's nobody you could rule out."

I said, "I need the dealer. A likely dealer."

"Are you buying stuff back? I'm not sure the police would like that."

"No," I said. "Not buying. Maybe anticipating a deal. Negotiating, if I have to."

Van Ostaade was kind enough not to skewer me with a few shrewd guesses. He did say he would ask around to see if anything spectacular was on offer in town. He'd be truly discreet. He'd be happy to check their own print rooms, too, in case the same gentleman had come visiting: would I tell him again just what kind of pictures were involved, and who was suspected?

I didn't, of course.

We drank for a while, and the woman at the next table plumped down off her chair and scrambled back, her face loose and grinning, then fell down again and was propped by her little squirrel hands on the table. Everybody agreed she was a great little drinker, always had been.

≡

The police file has Hart's credit card statements, so we know he didn't find anywhere to sleep; there is no hotel record. His eyes must have been open on needles.

At four in the morning he was out in the huge, shiny spaces of Schiphol Airport buying a ticket to Oporto. Nothing much moves in an airport at that time. There were Surinamese women pushing wide mops, and banks of unmanned check-in desks like stalls at some fair that would open soon. Or perhaps the fair has been abandoned forever: just steel and plastic, no prospect of escape or business or fantasy, nothing moving ever again. But it was clean.

He checked in for a 9:50 flight at 4:35. I guess the check-in clerk said something: maybe just "You're early. Rough night?" The clerk was so obviously right he expected no answer.

Hart showed his passport, his boarding card to get into the main concourse.

He never usually had a sense of anxiety when he tried out a new identity. He was one in a crowd, no reason he should be checked and cross-checked. But it was odd to be in the airport so early for a flight, and he was the only one crossing the immigration line.

Hart's passport was the old-fashioned British kind, a black, covered volume. The immigration man could have given him his full attention, but he only waved him through.

The police were interested in Christopher Hart. Immigration were not.

The shops were mostly shuttered, nowhere to duck out of sight.

He was among the overnight losers whose planes never came, who snored and kicked and curled up miserably where they could: trainee refugees just waiting to go back to the middle class.

At 5:15, he took a bed in the day hotel. They have pure, cool boxes of rooms. I don't imagine he slept well. He sat on the edge of the bed, trying to think things out, brain racked and thoughts kicking his eyes from the inside.

Then he remembered: Hart's VW. How would he explain Hart leaving his new car in Holland when he would need it in Portugal? He had to go back and get it and he had to do everything meticulously. He seemed to be acquiring a talent for doing things wrong.

=

The next morning, I went to look for Hart. It sounds absurd, but I had the polite assumption that everyone would tell me the truth, the arrogance to think Hart would fold the moment I found him.

I had never met the man, remember, never seen him; he was a reputation to me, someone I'd read in the journals, who was constantly needing more from the Museum. I preferred to stand back when he made his demands, let him apply in writing, answer him in writing. I'm not good at being importuned, or bullied.

I took the double-decker train and a taxi to the university, where Hart was last seen: a shy institution just outside an inland town, low glass boxes covered in shrubbery and quick-growing trees. I found the department, and the department secretary, a practical woman, and I put on charm like a suit.

She said people were always asking for Hart, but he was never there. He'd been there, of course, taught for a semester, but they hardly saw him now. People were "always" asking for him? Well, people did ask for him. More often than usual. Usually people didn't ring up for academics at the department, because they knew they would never find them there.

She thought Hart was living just out of town. He'd found a farmhouse to rent. Something in her tone suggested he had been too ambitious, that he should have settled for rooms or a small apartment, camouflaged himself like the block in which she sat. "Of course," she said, "he did talk about going to Portugal. For the summer, I suppose. Somewhere remote, near Coimbra. I don't know if it was just talk. He never notified us he was going, so probably he hasn't gone."

I wasn't any kind of hunter yet. I was still exasperated, as you are when someone breaks an appointment without warning, arrives late for a meeting or, worse yet, exactly on time for dinner. I put myself on an old solid bicycle, a two-wheeled tank with gears, and I spun out along the roads in the direction of Hart's house.

I could have phoned him, of course. Perhaps the fact that I didn't phone him meant I was already hoping to surprise and shock him: the well-tempered bureaucrat eager, without admitting it, for the chance to be the kind of avenger who rents out by the hour in paperbacks.

But he was not at home. Home didn't even look like a home. The garden had not been touched in weeks; it had rained and the growth was fierce in all directions. There was no car visible, although on the drive at the side of the house there was a dry patch where a car could have stood quite recently.

I walked up to the windows and looked in on a high cream living room with a piece of dubious art on the fieldstone mantelpiece: southern surrealism with round alabaster breasts from every angle and in every plane. The house was clean enough, but dead.

I imagined I could make a true story out of the room. I only had to look long enough.

≡

The police file notes that Hart was a no-show for the Oporto flight. A handwritten note—I should by now be able to distinguish between the inspector and the sergeant—says simply: "He drove?"

But it can't have been that easy, not on the long, long roads south. He had too much time, without distraction, to think about how quiet and convincing he had to be for a while, until the police lost interest in his mother's odd visions; and how he could start all over again. He said once he liked the look of the fjord country in New Zealand: crisp, bright, and far away, black water, cut mountains, white snow.

Meanwhile, there must be nothing of interest about the predictable, respectable Christopher Hart.

He may have thought, too, about what kind of life he would take next. Of course, he never told me this.

≡

The cat lay in the wrong corner, paws bent under, waiting. I put down the garment bag, walked into the living room, and he rose politely to greet me. At once, he sagged down. I picked him up and carried him into the kitchen.

Anna had everything ready: needles, plastic-capped, and a solution of electrolytes hanging from the wall in a fat plastic bag.

I laid the cat down on a towel on the kitchen table.

You watch a kitten, a young cat in its first few years; you watch it hunt and play. But when a cat is this age, you're far more conscious of all the times he has watched you: your witness, proof of what happened while you were together.

Anna showed me how to check the flow of liquid, how to snap the plastic cover from the needle, how to find a fold of loose skin and slip in the needle. Only she didn't quite do it right. The cat leaked, fur drenched black, a little trace of blood. We got it right the second time, and waited while the fluid slowly dripped into the sick animal.

"His stomach's blown up," Anna said. "And he's very thin. He cries at night."

It was as though we were both fighting for our shared history, as tired and vulnerable as the black-and-white cat that was dying more slowly thanks to us. We were so fiercely concentrated, we felt grief as though it was just an interruption to what we could do.

Two days later, the cat started to shift about, unable to find comfort. He was all spine and stomach now, a great cancerous ball suspended from a sagging back. His fur spiked up from lack of interest in grooming.

"Fine," Anna said, before I could say anything.

The vet offered to catheterize the cat "so it would be quicker."

Neither of us wanted the animal to suffer more. Neither of us wanted the power to decide on his end. We were in such confusion, we didn't stop the vet and the nurse taking the cat away, and bringing him back, after a while, with a plastic tube sticking from a bandaged paw.

Anna bent down to mark him, her cheek against his cheek.

The vet fed the plastic tube.

The cat collapsed like a balloon without wind, suddenly but also radically so that the familiar, animated creature was cold bone and fur.

Anna went down to the ground, too, and I had to push bits of furniture under her as she fell. I couldn't see for a moment. We were entirely separated by a common sorrow.

The vet left us with the body as you might leave parents with a dead child; but of course, we never had children. Some women are allergic to the sperm of some men, but by the time science knew all that, we'd been through five miscarriages—all the hope, then the rush of clotted blood, then the sheer confusion of hormones and emotions. You flush futures down the toilet because there's nothing else to do. We didn't go to any more doctors after that.

I helped Anna up from the floor. I did it only as a friend.

≡

The deputy director agreed I must go to Portugal. I didn't suggest it, but somehow he agreed, and then insisted. I did say that my father had newly moved there—the deputy director thought of some ruin in the Sintra hills, with jasmine, lemons, roses, and Moorish features— and I would like to take a few days to see him. The deputy director agreed again.

Anna didn't. "They can't make you run about the continent looking for people," she said. "That's the job of the police."

"I can't talk to the police," I said, patiently. "It isn't like that. It's what the English call 'delicate.' "

"What do you mean, what 'the English' say? You're English."

I didn't say anything.

"You can't just detach yourself."

"I know."

"So when are you coming back?"

"I can't tell."

"Surely they can tell you—"

"Nobody tells me. I have a job to do. It's that simple."

I put down the phone. I had things to do: a memorandum to revise about what we might buy from some truck tycoon's collection just passing through Sotheby's, a few sharp calls to maintenance about a suspect piece of glass in the roof above our prized Solander boxes of Raphaels and Leonardos, a personnel matter—a promotion of one grade—that would probably take longer than any of the above. And there was the constant nagging issue of visibility: the Museum's and therefore mine. Our department had so far failed to produce a thick, shiny gift book, and scholarly monographs were no longer enough. The Museum press needed product.

Anna would call back. I'd call back. She might be able to leave things hanging this way, to be continued, but I never could. I can never stop trying to reason.

She called back within a half-hour.

"Listen," she said. "Some doctor called from Portugal. His English wasn't good. But I think there's news about your father. It wasn't a good line."

≡

I hacked at some odd lamb on the plane to Lisbon, drank a small plastic bottle of red Bairrada wine. I have to tell you: all sense of rush and purpose simply stopped. I just felt cold. The white cloudscapes mocked me: a baroque, sentimental sky that ought to have fat, pink cherubs lollipopping about.

For this news about my father was disconcertingly vague, filtered through the doctor's English and Anna's understanding of it. I didn't know the doctor's threshold of panic, but I did know my father would never see a doctor without some alarming reason; anything else was "wasting the doctor's time." So the news could require great feeling from me—grief, compassion, horror—or nothing more than exasperation at a false alarm. If it was a false alarm, my father would blame me for coming. I couldn't be ready, either way.

I couldn't lose him.

I'd always been able to judge myself against my father, tell who I was by not being my father, and now the measure and the history might be going out of my life.

Everything started all over again, strapped in a bus seat at 35,000 feet, in the vague place and time above clouds.

≡

I stopped for coffee on the motorway north, somewhere the espresso was parceled out from a chrome-and-white samovar and the sandwiches were date-stamped. Foreignness began to register, first on the ears—the high, rushing pitch of a man's sentence, the way a thought rose at the end to peck at the air. Then there were the municipal buses, shipping cargoes of ancient widows from town to town; a folklore group in black hats and red scarves; a man holding his mobile phone nervously in his hands, always aware of it, aware of it not ringing; everyone else, phone to ear; and the drivers tailgating as though travel were a social business, in tiny white cars with no speed to speak of, but every electronic and assisted and automatic thing there is. Portugal, as my father liked to say, is overrun by the Portuguese.

There was the gray shine of olive trees, vines thrusting and clambering, roses boiling out of lawns; and villages called Inferno and Chaos and Valley of Darkness, choices you could make off the modern moral path of the motorway.

I chose the turning to Fátima, and stopped after a few miles in what was now my father's town. It looked like the other places I'd passed: the shop with the gas bottles lined up outside, the church which was a box freshly whitened, houses thrown up against one another with a fountain, some ice-cream signs, some trees, some old onlookers standing awkwardly still. There was a black circle of ash at a crossroads, remains of an old bonfire; that was odd.

For a moment I thought this little town was as I remembered it, but then I realized I remembered nothing at all. I had seen pictures, read letters, heard my father assemble our hometown like a model kit for Christmas—always under stars on a clear night—but I had never stood there before.

I called into the shop, which had one side selling coffee and drinks. I introduced myself: the son of José Costa.

The man behind the bar said, "I'll send Miguel to fetch him."

"I'll walk there," I said.

"He'd rather come here," the barman said, with authority. "You don't know the way. He does."

I know what I expected: warmth, perhaps, men smiling, women kissing me, being put at a table with a glass of aguardente, being accepted back as another missing piece of the village. It didn't happen. I was baffled like a grandchild out visiting whose grandparents go on playing cards.

One old man, with a face so smooth it could have been pumiced, asked if I was *"o historiador,"* the historian. So that was what father said I was: a scholar, or maybe a teller of old, audited tales. He said there was a feast in three nights' time and that I must come. I would be staying with my father, naturally.

I wondered about the "naturally." It was odd to be known but not to be wanted.

Miguel came back on his bicycle, a very quiet ten-year-old, and said Senhor Costa was coming. I went to the door of the bar and looked both ways, but all along the tight street of houses I could see nobody coming.

A bus passed, filling the whole street. Nobody breathed for a moment.

"Uma bica," I said. I did remember the word for a good, small coffee.

I thought people passed and commented on the fact that I was waiting in a bar for my father instead of going to his house. But of course they would comment on any stranger.

A half-hour passed. I had nothing to read, and nothing to think.

Another ten minutes. Miguel was whistling briskly. A tractor went by with a trailer behind it, and an old skull of a man, legs splayed, working the tractor with a grimly concentrated look. I thought of Grandpa on a slow-mo Harley. I thought of death on a slow rig.

Another five. By now, the end-of-day drinkers had come into the bar for a *copo*—a glass of wine—or a beer. They gave me space, and they huddled companionably. I began to be infuriated with my father, to wonder why nobody would simply show me his house, why he was taking so long. He didn't want to seem sick, I knew. He never did.

I asked Miguel if he could tell my father one more time that I was waiting. Or perhaps he could show me how to find the house.

"I'll go," Miguel said.

He came back very quickly this time, and he would not speak to me. Instead, he stood reporting to the barman. I picked out words in clusters: "now, now, now" and "white, white."

I went over to Miguel and I said, "Tell me. Tell me this time."

"Your father," the barman said. "You'd better go. He's not well."

"He's alone?"

"I should think so."

This time, the barman gave me directions: two kilometers along the Fátima road, down a track to Casal Novo, a house with a huge stone chimney and a garden. I couldn't miss the garden, because it was full of things.

Miguel said he would come and guide me.

"There," he said.

I wish I could have missed it: a beige bunker on a flat base, like a huge box in the maize fields. A staircase jutted up to the first floor; it had its own pineapple finials. The huge chimney split the house with large, dull stones lined in white mortar. The roof ended in eyebrow tiles and a pair of terra-cotta doves, swooping as boastfully as eagles. As for the garden, it was certainly full of things: a fountain of more madly piled pineapples, assorted lions all from the same mold with dark sleep lines, a *mannequin pis* off to the side, like a rough page from a plasterworks catalog, with a few bright roses for decoration.

I stared. I remembered plain white walls in Stockwell.

"He's here," Miguel said, and jumped out of the car.

My father must have heard the car, because he came to the front door and opened it.

I shouted, "Dad."

I could see he was holding himself upright, arms tight against the door frame. He was being a good soldier. But he couldn't smile.

"Dad, I'm coming up."

He seemed to watch me running up the steps, but with no expression in his eyes. Then he couldn't hold himself anymore. He fell softly. His bones went in every direction under his skin. His face was a greenish white I'd only ever read about before.

I took him up in my arms. I don't think I ever did that before, but I knew he would be very light under his dark suit. I held him and asked Miguel where the nearest phone was.

An old woman in black, working among the maize, saw me on the steps and she began a high, almost animal cry, an endless shriek.

I asked him all the questions you're supposed to ask after a heart attack: about pains in the arm, pains in the chest. He shook his head.

I carried him to the car. There was nothing much to him. I strapped him into the backseat. Miguel said it was twelve kilometers to the hospital. My father said, "Eleven."

The old woman cried on, a signal to the whole valley.

At the little hospital in the next town, my father was laid out on a gurney and taken away. I tried to follow, but a male nurse stopped me.

"I have to look after him," I said.

"He's dead. Didn't you know?"

A policeman came up to me. He wasn't in uniform, but he wore his authority fitted tight.

I remember how I strained for a moment to be entirely practical. If my father was dead, there was a funeral to arrange, and I didn't know how to do it here. There must be a hospital office that could help me handle such things. Then I would need death certificates, dozens of them, probably. There would be people to notify. But who would I notify? I had already told my mother that my father had gone away. I could tell Anna, at least, if only I could find a phone.

I folded on the ground, the power to stand gone, then the power to speak. I had time, in the middle of airless, drowned breathing, to think how ashamed my father might have been to see me like this.

Miguel was still there. He put his hand on my head as though I were a dog, a gesture of odd comfort.

I thought of how my father made me separate from this country he never let me know, how we lost each other years before he told me the house in Stockwell was sold.

I was an orphan of long standing. So I told myself: I should know what to do.

Three

I spent a half-hour with the priest, who extolled the virtues of heaven like a salesman of swamp lots, and then an effortful hour with four aunts I had never known before—who were worn out with rigorous wailing, and now wanted to welcome me, make sure I was one of the kind that comes back to Portugal and fits again, but found I wasn't, that I was even unsure of the language. I could see it shocked them when I said my father's name, making José sound like Spanish, with a breathy *H* at the front instead of a solid *J*. Still, they launched into arias of births, heart murmurs, burnt houses, new marriages, and I could barely pick out enough nouns to understand the subject. The names were all strange.

At nine, the undertaker came; at least, I thought he was the undertaker. He was a sly man, paws up to his face. He led me through the village to the garage of a furniture store on the outskirts.

My father lay in a coffin on a trestle. "Usually," the undertaker was saying, "he would be in his own house, but there was nobody in the house and we thought, in the circumstances, it would be better—"

He levered up the tinfoil he'd put over the face. The face was a shock, the jaw bound in place with a cloth around the skull, and netting over that. Now that there was no more will to hold the face together, I'd never seen my father seem so at ease.

The undertaker gave me a blanket.

I knelt by the coffin, between cold concrete walls, with the faint smells of oil and onions and something like formaldehyde. But the body was not embalmed. It had been cracked into shape, tied there, and the nets were to keep off the flies.

I tried to say "good-bye," tried to say the word out loud. I couldn't; this still body was such a plain reminder that my father was not there to hear me. For a moment, I had a sense of how loudly emptiness can roar at you: like everything you hear with fingers in your ears.

I stood up, found the undertaker waiting just to the side of the door.

"You don't want to stay?" he said. It was obviously an issue, a duty he was not prepared to explain.

I said, "No." I tried to give him back the blanket.

"Usually," he said, "there would be others to join you. I have some wine if you want to wait."

I knew then I had no choice. I covered my shoulders with the blanket, and I sat waiting by the open garage door, with my father trussed and netted on a trestle just beyond. A few people passed busily.

I wondered why nobody wanted to remember my father in the place where he always thought he belonged.

I watched the flies turning in the white light of the streetlamp, bright like fireflies. After a while, the undertaker put his portable TV on the windowsill across the alleyway, flickers of blue light in the dusk, so I could watch some dance show while I waited.

≡

There are a number of hotel forms in the police file. Hart tried Lisbon first, but evidently he did not fit; perhaps nobody noticed him. He spent two days in the hills around Sintra; plenty of exiles there, growing sour in pretty gardens, but he didn't settle. He went south to the Algarve, and I can understand why he found no comfortable, sociable place along the concrete facade of the beach.

To judge from the gap between the hotel forms, he quit the coast and drove north in a day. He came to medieval streets in the center of the country, a university town on a hill, and put himself in some shiny old-new hotel with imitation pools in a dummy atrium and an old manor house at the front. Coimbra, he obviously decided, would be a credible destination for a runaway academic.

If he tried to find an apartment, and I suppose he did, he'd have been out of luck. Apartments to rent hardly exist, except for the long term. He had an alibi for six months, but nowhere to put it.

I called his university again, of course. They still had no forwarding address in Portugal. They thought Professor Hart must be traveling, a word that seemed like sin in the mouth of the secretary. I called Holland, too. They were waiting to hear from him. You could tell they would happily wait a long time.

Anna sent me all her love, like a parcel.

≡

For the funeral, they brought out a long Renault hearse, broad bearers in a line in the seats behind the driver, coffin clear through the glass sides, with a blue-and-gilt blanket to hide the safety belts that held it in place.

Nobody had come to the wake. Everyone came to the funeral. The church's banner went first, then the men in gowns of white and blue over their working clothes, then the crucifix, the priest, and the hearse—slowly down the main street, serious but not quite silent. Behind all this, a string of infuriated modern cars were held up on their business, waiting for the road to clear. There seemed to be triumph in the eyes of the old, bony aunts as they walked their memento mori into the faces of the city types behind.

The coffin came off the hearse, and I took my place to help carry it: a sudden, wrenching weight.

A single electric candelabra burned in the chancel of the church. I remembered what a church should be: dark and Victorian, gilded, with bright glass and the smell of incense and wax. But here the reredos went up in rough steps of gold and sky blue, there was a Madonna strung with pearls, three severed heads under her feet, and a saint flying red ribbons as long as himself, with a trident: odd, unofficial gods.

The priest rumbled his words through a microphone. The congregation took up the words, answering before the priest could finish; they couldn't wait. There was no theater or teaching, just a dialog they knew as intimately as any talk in the fields or the bar.

Because I was thinking of doing things properly and not making mistakes, it was not until I turned around and took up the burden of my father's coffin again that I was entirely overwhelmed. A whole community, this village, villages beyond, had come down here at five on a working day for a mannerly farewell to my father, and to save his soul, if they could.

We walked the church steps, down a tight lane toward the skull and crossed bones over the cemetery gate.

I felt the coffin handle slipping in my hand. I wouldn't be less strong than the other bearers, the one who broke this sense of community. I held on. I wondered how a man who had become so slight and bony could weigh so much.

The sky was full of wet light and soft, gray cloud, and along the way I noticed things that took my mind briefly from the rip in my shoulder. Here, hollyhocks massed like spires on the edge of a maize field; here, a practical concrete clinic among houses held up by tree trunks and plaster; here, hay already scythed down and full of prickly flies and grains; and, if I held my head up for a moment, the light playing along the top of the mountains beyond.

There was a moment for the bearers to rest, and then the lane turned uphill. Rain seemed imminent. Then we were through the graveyard wall, into a square of sand and neat marble tablets, memorial photographs, family plots, tiny metal lanterns on each to make the streets of the dead seem decently suburban.

There was one shiny white marble house at the end: an emigrant's last resting place, windows slightly curtained, and the family name above the door.

I hadn't thought to ask, and nobody had thought to tell me; I'd expected an ordinary, dug grave like my mother's, ropes to lower the coffin, the finality of earth falling on the coffin lid. But the name on the bright pink house, with shelves for many dead, was Costa.

My mother lies in a hollow of gray marble and green grass in a South London churchyard. So, for the moment, José Costa would lie alone, second shelf of four, having made an investment in his son dying in the right place, his son's sons if ever there were any.

The priest spoke again. The coffin lid was raised so people could finally say good-bye, but I did not go forward. Flowers from gardens lay around, gladioli in scalding reds, fountains of montbretia.

The doors of the vault closed as delicately as those in a house of glass, and were fixed shut with a padlock. I wondered who had a key, if I should ask for one.

The crowd spread out about the business of tending their own family memories. Nobody rushed away, but everyone else had things do to, fields to tend, houses to clean, time to waste before dinner.

I knew I was expected in this small marble house. I was expected to want to be boxed and filed alongside my father, in his very particular notion of a resting place. It was a neat bit of postmortem pressure: to be a good son and lie here, to think until I died whether I should.

I rather wished my father had chosen the permanence of rotting underground rather than this state of waiting for doors to open on something better.

I wondered why my father had to start from scratch in his own town, why there was no family vault for him to join. I wondered at the polite duty of the funeral, the lack of strong tears.

I had picked up flowers from the ground, violent pink and black-red roses bound together with grass. Now they hung in my hands and I didn't know where to put them. I realized the caretakers were looking down this suburban street of the dead, politely impatient.

I needed something to dry my eyes, to blow my nose, the kind of thing a father has. I remembered: playing penguins, draped in Dad's huge tweed jacket; waiting for Dad to free a bee that was trapped in my hair; talking big on a night walk before some exam, and seeing a shooting star. For all the impossibility of my father's change of worlds and country, for all the ways my father made me grow away, it was not bearable for my father to be gone.

This show of feeling was improper for an Englishman, even more shocking for a Portuguese. It was impractical, too, burning my eyes. I tried to go casually to the other side of the marble tomb, where I would be less obvious, until I could get back my breath.

I saw, across the marble, already a little etched into the delicate surface of the stone, scrawls and lines of spray-gun black, broad tarry strokes on the fine pink marble. They made a date or a number: 1953.

You can't feel shock on top of shock. It fails to register. I went back to my car, started the engine, and edged through the quiet streets. It was as though the whole town had done enough feeling for the day, and closed itself down.

I was shivering when I came to the main road. I ought to complain and protest, but I wondered why nobody had warned me. Perhaps nobody had noticed. It was as though the pink tomb, with its bubble-gum veining, was a boast; and the curt black lines were an order to shut up.

Perhaps nobody minded.

≡

I had to see a lawyer, settle an estate of whose size and ramifications I had absolutely no idea. I wondered why my father had chosen a lawyer in some small town called Vila Nova de Formentina, forty miles away: Maria de Sousa de Conceição Mattoso.

I unlocked the door to my father's house.

I expected to be overwhelmed. I always had an acute sense of smell. My father didn't smoke in London, or keep a dog, so that house had a minimal smell: crowns of bay leaves rusting in the kitchen, and the erstaz pine of the rasping stuff my mother used to clean. I didn't smell either of those in this secret house. There was cedar oil for polish, though, and dust in the old air.

I expected photographs, a kind of potted life, but there were none. There were no souvenirs; those had mostly belonged to my mother, and been too much trouble to ship. There was one picture on the wall, but I had never seen it before: a bank of tiles that showed a brown caravel on a blue-and-white sea.

I wondered if I could second-guess my father, find the coffee beans and the grinder in predictable places, the cups, the sugar, and the drinking water (my father never trusted London water for serious coffee). Somehow I still didn't doubt that there must be some continuity from London to this house, from father to son.

There was no coffee, no drinking water. I pulled open cupboards one by one, tugged at drawers, put on the light in the larder and looked around on the wooden shelves. I was furious: the bastard dying and not leaving even a fucking cup of coffee.

Maria Mattoso said, "Mr. Costa?"

She had come through the hall silently, but not in order to take me by surprise. Maria was all business. You could take her for some thin city girl.

I thought I should apologize. Instead, I offered tea.

Maria said, "A glass of water, please."

She sipped a very little and put the glass neatly down. There was no extravagance in her, I thought at the time. I noticed a silk of hairs on her arms, dark against dark. I also wondered why I was noticing this so much.

She was a lawyer, after all. She was there to talk about money in savings accounts of one kind and another, earning rates of interest that seemed wild; and the house, of course, and some land with grapes, and the contents of the house. Everything went to John Michael Snell Costa with the provision that I give a tenth of the estate to some orphanage two towns away.

"Do you want to keep the house? Or to sell it?"

I said, "How would I bloody know?" and then, "I'm sorry."

"You have time," Maria said.

I thought how clean, how distant she seemed: a sharp, bony spectator. I wondered if my father had fancied her. He'd been a spectator, too, in London; they'd have had that in common.

"There are no complications, are there?"

"If you keep the land that goes with the house, we might have to file with the Ministry of Agriculture since you're a foreigner."

"But my father was a foreigner."

"Born here. There shouldn't be a problem. It's just some olive trees, a few hectares, and some grapes."

"Of course."

She said, "I expect you know the land."

"I've never been here before."

"Oh," Maria said. She was a little shocked; she was used to families being together and knowing all one another's business.

I had a sense of being overheard. I didn't want to be in the house anymore. But Maria was conducting a meeting, and her manners held us in place.

"He was a remarkable man," she said, politely.

"I suppose so."

In a few minutes, carefully but not obviously, she placed me as married, no children—well, no living children. I worked in a museum, had been at Oxford; *senhor doutor*, for sure.

"Will you go home now?"

"No," I said. I surprised myself.

"If you want to sell the house, we can start that without you. If you don't mind who buys it—"

"I've got nothing to be sentimental about." I was talking very loudly, so he could hear me.

"If you don't, lock it up and go away. Come back when it's kinder weather."

I really hadn't noticed until then, but it was a relief to blame heat for my sense of tiredness and the way my emotions sank and welled. I was ridiculously aware of sweat staining the one good dark suit I had with me, and how improper this was in front of Maria.

"Someone spray-painted the tomb," I said. "I ought to report it. I ought to have it cleaned."

She looked blank.

"Marked. They've written on it, at the back."

She said, "Why would they write on a tomb?"

"1953. I suppose it's the date of something."

"People have such long memories around here," she said. She stretched with grace. "Your father always said I was a wonderful lawyer because I didn't have memories. Just files. That's why he came to me in the first place."

The grace confused me. One minute she was buttoned up in her lawyer's role, precise as a stamped document, and the next she stretched as though she had no self-consciousness at all.

She'd done such intimate things—written down and packed away my father's life, seen him alone when he couldn't use social training to mask what he felt. She must know things I never knew. I told myself that was the only reason I felt such a quick sense of closeness.

=

The dinner for the *festa* was in someone's garage, just like the wake should have been, at a long wood table, with the aunts busying about with goat stew, roast suckling pig, little fritters of salt cod and potato, red local wine with a soft, dirty undertow, roast peppers, cut oranges, potatoes boiled and fried and roasted. The fan at one end took out the faint back taste of diesel and turpentine. Lean back, and the wall was sharp with chisels and blades, loud with a many-colored root ball of electric wiring.

I sat near the head of the table, still in my one jacket in the heat, while everyone else was down to shirts.

I drank. The wine went down light and almost sweet, too young to have lost the taste of grapes. The men came up to me, leaned across to me, grinned their bare grins at me, and told me a few things about my father. Much more than telling, they were asking—about his life abroad, his wife, his times.

I wondered which of them had marked his grave, and whether that was all they meant to do. But my wondering drowned in the wine.

The men told me their things: how the heat had affected the grapes, given the sudden wrong rain in June; about the emigrant who'd come back to find his palace under interdict, took a shotgun, and blew the head off the woman who did planning for the local council; about who was sick, who was well, which families went off hotfoot to Brazil and should have waited a year longer for the sake of seeing the new train, the new road, the new water pumps; about how Erminio's pines burned just in time for him to plant eucalyptus with the new subsidy, and he'd got the insurance, too; about how his lawyer, that Maria, was looking good these days.

They tugged me under the wine, into a small place with its huge assumptions, and the more I drank, the more I thought I understood and the more I laughed. Once, I lost track altogether and began laughing without a reason, and a moment later everyone joined me.

So I mentioned my father: just those words, *"o meu pai."*

"He didn't come here much."

"But my father—"

There was a little well of silence in the party, but it soon filled with talk and noise.

The tables never emptied. After fish and goat and pig there was cake with bilious roses and pale icing, and all this was strewn about the trestles with paper plates, glasses from the bar, big white bottles of red wine, jumbles of beers, and a small archaeological find of pig bones. There was a bit of singing, shouted down at first. I thought, head now insecure, there would have to be dancing. I was close to crying wine, but I've always been a controlled drunk; except for the few times I tried to kill someone.

I'd dance, this wholly separate "I" that belonged only in this village on this night, with—Graça, perhaps, or Manuela, or Adelina, maybe a widow straight and keen in her sixties or a young woman with sweet, rounded breasts and belly and cheeks or an aunt as stringy as boiled goat. I'd dance like a Londoner, like a Portuguese, like a scholar, like a husband—whatever I was, I could dance it.

The wine was my alibi for not entirely knowing where I was.

There was also Anna in London, which seemed an impossibly distant place. I couldn't even tell how we had come apart. I knew her warmth, her refusal of regrets, the way she used to turn in bed in her sleep as though she ached for touch, and yet the way she could play the brisk, rhetorical teacher on demand. I used to love those contradictions, feel tangled with them.

We almost lost each other once before. She was to be a musician, at nineteen, going to Siena for months at the Chigana Academy: to perfect the viola, to learn to conduct. She went with such huge ambition. I saw her vanish through the gates of the academy into a shaded courtyard, and I went back to Britain, unsure of where we stood. She called me months later from a hospital in London; she'd turned a leg on slippery steps, and bone and tendon had pulled apart. She asked if she could be pregnant, because the doctors had asked. I didn't think so, and I was right.

Then, apart from a few parties, we went off to different universities and different lives. We met again, by the kind of luck that suggests someone was trying, in the study rooms of the Museum. She was now an art history student; she was not quite good enough for performing, she said, and she always acted on judgment, practical and ruthless. I was in my first six months acclimatizing to the manners and dust of the place. We lucked into passion, in all the hidden corners of the Museum, in the unchecked stacks, in the storerooms; the place was a great, gray continuum in which we were the only brilliant colors.

Anna will be having dinner with someone I don't like, an old friend, while I am away; so I thought.

I felt hot, too, and clammy all at once. I took off my jacket, walked outside, and remembered too late I was close to the mountains, in the foothills of the Serra Estrela: the kingdom of rocks between the Portuguese forest and the Spanish desert.

The wet shirt stuck to me, and showed off the skin. I shivered and I started to dance, cold and wet and moving just so the blood would keep turning in my head. I skipped to one side, to the other. I beckoned to Maria to join me, but she didn't like to dance; or she was simply fastidious and not at all sure of me. I beckoned to the aunts.

I remembered my father cold in the ground—except the body was above ground, and couldn't be cold in the heat, and was marked out with that arbitrary number: 1953. I was sad as a bear.

One of the older men, emperor's face on a laborer's body, must have felt pity for me: a party without goers. He sat on the metal bench outside the garage and talked up to me.

"You mustn't mind what they say about your father," he said.

"But they don't say anything."

"It has nothing to do with you. Nothing. You weren't even born."

"In 1953?"

"They shouldn't have touched the grave."

"I want to know—"

He stood, the body that seemed so strong oddly uncertain on its joints. "No, no," he said. "You don't have to know things. We're glad to know you."

The other men, a moment later, erupted out of the garage onto the road and joined me; and they brought the women with them.

An old man had bagpipes, red cloth with yellow trimming, and he'd started to blow and pump. There was a big drum not keeping time. There was a confusion of moves and beats, and in between them the undertaker and his wife, both round and solid like bars of fat, dancing a quick, light, startling dance.

Someone broke away with much whispering and went off to fetch something that couldn't quite be mentioned; or so it seemed. I was in a circle now, throwing myself around, glad that the blood and muscles were moving again, that the wine was working out of me. Maria was moving around with a man, and they weren't smiling.

Shutters opened, windows opened on the sounds.

And then from down the street there was the sound of shots, mortars, rocket fire; and nobody seemed to care. I had police nerves, city expectations; I thought there were guns heading to the party and I froze for a moment in the middle of the dancers. Then I looked up to the sky and realized someone had found the mortars for the next village *festa* and was setting them off in a patch of cabbages behind the road, one by three by one, so the raw music went to the beat of a drunk drummer and a sky with the tracer tracks and blasts of war.

I was beating back death and shame with noise.

The bagpiper started marching in place. The drummer came up behind him. The mortars announced a procession, so they'd have a procession: but not, this time, the procession of the dead. They turned off the main street, older people following, younger people starting to think about tomorrow, and they pitched up a hill through a tunnel of mimosas and pines.

I tried to dance, to march, to get my balance back. Maria came up behind me and said quietly, "It's a long walk."

I said, with soft, drunk sincerity, "Are you coming?"

Maria shrugged.

But nothing was going to stop the procession, even though now it was just the piper playing, and the drummer wavering from side to side on the track. The procession was about the habit of walking, the power to walk. The muscles kept going when the breath was short, and the breath allowed for farts and rallies from the bagpipes.

I went with them.

The track twisted around. There were olive trees, it seemed from the silhouettes. On a corner, two women were lighting the candles in a little shrine, faces lit gold from underneath. There were fireflies, brilliant intervals rubbed lightly on the darkness.

At the top of the rise, the road fell back to the next village. I expected the sound of dogs, nervy hunting dogs yelping together, and maybe shutters closing, lights going off; but nothing moved.

The music died. In the silence, I started to shiver.

≡

Christopher Hart left a message on the answering machine of Maria de Sousa de Conceição Mattoso. He left eight other messages that day with other lawyers picked out of the Yellow Pages, all saying that he needed advice on renting a house in the area, any area.

Maria was the one who answered.

She climbed to her couple of rooms up some narrow green stairs, next door to an engineer and a shoe repairer. She heard Hart's voice: young but otherwise difficult to place, probably English.

She kept the shutters closed while she called him back. So she first spoke to him in an office from some film noir, pools of light, shadows of blinds cutting up the wall.

This Mr. Hart was in a hotel thirty miles away, and wanted to do the usual business: rents and leases. It had been usual for only twenty years or so, since the first foreigners came here, slipped south from the port-wine valleys or north from Lisbon and the misty pretensions of Sintra—a lost Dutch poet, an English diplomat, a truck driver with a passion for racing pigeons. They were so few and so unexpected that nobody opposed them; they were simply new neighbors.

Twenty years ago, of course, you could assume a lawyer here was a man with a belly who condescended to the world. But Maria de Sousa de Conceição Mattoso never had a belly.

She liked to think of the foreigners as her friends. She cared for them. Most of them came to her sooner or later, unless they were so sly they wouldn't trust a local foreign lawyer on local foreign business, seeing Abroad as some kind of Masonic conspiracy; and they brought their world to her—in bits and stories, like presents. In turn, when they needed it, she explained things.

These things might surprise you: She never kept office hours. She had no secretary, no receptionist, not even her degree on the wall. She went where she was asked, and when she was not asked, she spent time as she wanted. She did all this on ground that never slipped under her, ground she knew best: the town where she grew up.

I want you to know Maria.

She met Hart in the bar under the office. She liked the bar because she could drink coffee and watch the town square; but you mustn't make the wrong picture out of those words. The square is really a gap with a garden, a concrete fountain, and a line of pollarded lindens, in among the fire station, the town hall, some shops, the insurance office, a bank, the agricultural adviser's office, and a car park. It's clean and shaded, but not picturesque at all.

Hart drove something shiny and he parked it where the firemen park. She didn't know the marque of the car, but it was so clean the firemen didn't like to complain.

He was tall, absurdly tall in the low bar; he had limbs high above eye level, a purposeful smile that everyone saw from below at an un-kind angle. He was blond, well made, but somehow like one of those security people you see around heads of state on television: no per-sonality, just purpose.

"You're not at all what I expected from a provincial lawyer," he said, which may have seemed charming at his height.

She offered him coffee; he wanted water.

"This is a lovely part of the world," Mr. Hart said.

She said, "You know it well?"

"I came here by chance," he said. "But I'd like to stay. I was think-ing about three months."

He sounded like a conversation class, people in rows who each ask how the others are, and each tell the others blankly that they're quite fine. She was glad when he talked about needing two bedrooms, good roads, good water pressure, something "private but not remote"; busi-ness fitted his language best. She thought he was arrogant, too, not wasting anything personal on her.

She asked if he was alone, and he looked as though he knew why she asked, which he didn't. She asked what he did for a living, and he said he was a professor who wrote books; it seemed inquisitorial to insist on knowing his subject, his tastes, where he taught, where he came from. He seemed very young to be a professor.

He had only one answer, anyway: to promise he'd pay all the rent in advance. "I have a lot to do," he said.

=

I lay in the bedroom at my aunt's house, with a dim bulb in an amber shade and a wardrobe painted with blue, red, and yellow flowers and garlands and a Virgin Mary tucked almost out of sight by the door. I couldn't sleep for the wine.

I just had to find the bastard.

I told myself all this was about my duty to the Museum. I've been around the Museum twenty years, so my interests and doings are part of the records and fabric of the place. I almost believed my own story, except that I knew perfectly well this was all about buying more time in Portugal.

I could at least call universities. I never knew there were so many in Portugal: new, private, scientific, scattered all over Lisbon and half the country.

I bought phone cards at the bar and called bureaucrats to a background of game shows, once a barful of midday wasters all roaring at what the Portuguese consider the ultimate joke: flamenco.

These calls were diligent, not hopeful. Nobody recognized Hart's name. Of course, if he had come to Portugal to write, to be on his own, he would not necessarily need a university; but I thought he might visit some library. If he did, nobody knew about it. I thought he might need to go somewhere he and his place in a hierarchy were recognized.

I called the Museu de Arte Antiga, the Gulbenkian Foundation, the National Library—anywhere a man might go to check a reference dutifully, or to be addressed without irony as Professor Hart. I worried for a moment that curators might think I was warning them against Hart in some way by making such a strange call; simply to get through to any responsible voice I had to say I was from the Museum.

But then I thought: The man's guilty. I had the certainties of a cop.

I could do nothing else on the phone. I couldn't talk to the police, for obvious reasons. I couldn't simply access some register of tourists that would tell me where the man had stayed or was staying. The Dutch police file had all these facts, but at the time, I couldn't know that; and besides, the file was in another country and on the other side of walls.

I did deduce one thing, though. There were big cities with universities, and I didn't think Hart would go there: not Oporto, not Lisbon. He was not trying to draw attention to himself. He had not even left a forwarding address. Besides, his British university couldn't suggest anywhere he had connections, since New Historicist views of the Dutch Golden Age are not big business in Portugal; he had no contact to visit.

That left the obvious: Coimbra, a town rather than a city, properly picturesque, a proper medieval university with a guidebook, towers, a rosewood library, mosaic steps, and statues. Hart would have heard of Coimbra.

It was fifty miles north of me. I put myself on the motorway again.

=

Maria remembers the next morning, too, how her house smelled of coffee and new bread—*broa*, the thick, moist corn bread. She opened a window, and the breeze was cool, blowing from the sea in the west. There was cloud and mist instead of dust.

Her mother was in the kitchen, with a rumpled man in his fifties. She'd been running, perhaps, or moving boxes in the store; she had strength like a peasant woman, even if she spent it on books and inventories.

"Amandio was saying we might go to the beach," her mother said. "For the day." Her enormous dark eyes had made her a beauty once; now they invigilated customers.

"It'll be a lovely day," Amandio said. "Get some air. Maybe get your mother in the water." He smiled like an all-day drunk.

"I'll make more coffee," her mother said, and she left Amandio and Maria sitting across the narrow plastic tabletop.

"You'll be glad to get me out of the house," Amandio said. Then he said, "Won't you?" insisting on an answer. But she didn't answer. She buttered a piece of warm bread, and she said to her mother, "I'd like to have people to supper. Next week."

Her mother looked at Amandio first; Maria noticed. But she didn't look long. "Of course," she said. "I love to cook for your friends."

Amandio and Maria could not stay in the same house much longer.

Her mother was a widow, and widows are entitled to a life. Maria meant that. But Amandio was a part-time salesman, and he'd been ingratiating so long that he was all oil; his features—nose, eyes, and mouth—seemed to perch on the edge of oiled hair, oiled skin. He sold bathroom fittings, kitchen taps, that kind of thing, and he'd once waited until her mother's shop was closing to make a formal, knees-bent declaration of how he felt for her. It was like a bad local movie;

he should have posed and sung *fado*. Instead, she laughed so much she took him to bed, and he'd persisted ever since. Maria often wondered if she was his only widow, because he didn't seem to mind her laughing at all.

"We're going to the sea, then," Amandio said.

"I'll leave supper," her mother said. She always seemed defensive about Amandio, as though she knew he wasn't a serious proposition. "Carlos Alberto has the shop." She gulped a bit of coffee. "It was Carlos Alberto's day in the shop, anyway."

Maria went to the office. An older couple called in, worrying about wills. Someone called about a neighbor who'd left steel beams across a right-of-way. There was an *escritura* in its long, slow progress, and she wrote a letter, tapped it out on an old Olympia typewriter, explaining there was no need to worry, that the house was already theirs, and the proof would come in the slow rhythm of paper.

Then she found Hart his house. This wasn't so easy. There are houses all around where people don't live, but some of them belong to emigrants off working in France or Germany, and they mean to come back. Meanwhile, these houses are their refuge and their new dreams; they don't rent them out. There are old houses, too, wrecks with slipping roofs and walls bellying, but nobody could live there; the foreigners see "possibilities," and then take years to change the gold river stone into something square, white, small, and decent, to put in bidets on the ground floor where the pigs, chickens, and wine barrels used to be. Then they want to be here in summer. In summer, if a house is habitable, it's not available: someone is dreaming there.

But there was a French writer, a gray, square man, who'd just gone home abruptly because of some oversight—forgetting to pay tax on his American income for thirty years, something like that. He'd lived in a rented place in Formentina, which is a famous mountain village, in a long, low house painted white, peaceful except on days of pilgrimage to the chapel of Our Lady of the Snows. But there was no need to mention that; Hart was much too young, foreign, and modern to know anything about pilgrims. He probably thought the roadside walkers, feet bound up and staffs in their hands, were only ramblers.

Besides, it was a lucky day when Maria took Hart up to Formentina.

The high *serra* was clear and the smell of pine had been softened with dew overnight, and the village was full of new flowers—daisies and big, blue, shaggy agapanthus.

"There aren't any streets," Hart said.

"Not as such. It's too steep. Just paths."

"Where do I park the car?"

She told him he'd have to leave it by the main road, but he knew that already.

"Why don't people live here anymore? Portuguese, I mean?"

"People live here," she said. "But a lot of them left in the fifties. They went to Brazil, mostly."

"What happened?"

"They couldn't make a living out of charcoal anymore. It was too rough in the winters, and too far out of town." No point in telling him her own theory: that people around there live for *"saudade,"* the rush of nostalgia and longing, and you first have to leave a place to feel *saudade.*

"Is there piped water?"

She wanted him to see Formentina as she saw it. She always loved walking there as a child: dozy bees in plumes of white heather, slate roofs colored like starling feathers, white houses, yellow borders around their windows, then the dark, dry stone houses that fit into the fold of the mountain, some of them deserted, some of them spoiled. She slipped between them on steps that sometimes opened on unused lots, sometimes on sheds. One street had a fierce, clean stream. She showed the place like postcards: moments when everything is sharply lit and bright.

But when she stood still and looked for herself, the cute, bright image came to odd life. Goats came out of a cellar. A woman entered her garden with dung in a basket on her head. A man tugged an endless rubber pipe around for irrigation. A man wove willow twigs like gold strings. Two young men fussed over an ancient SEAT car that was parked at the edge of the road.

Already, she was afraid this would not be enough to hold Hart, that she didn't know how to keep his attention.

She felt like a civic booster, mentioning the daily bus that swept down to the town where she lived. She cataloged her town: a library, four pharmacies, three banks, a gymnasium for power lifting and another that metamorphosed into a billiard hall, a market twice a week, a hypermarket that had opened with feathery widgeon stuffed in the freezer and now sold frozen pizza, a cordon of new pink apartment buildings, and cinema on Fridays.

She meant that Formentina had none of these things, so he'd need to come down to Vila Nova.

He loped ahead, overshot the house, and turned back, looking almost angry. She thought how vigorous he seemed, too much motor for his spinning, ineffectual manner.

But once he'd walked into the house, as she had expected, the deal was done. The rooms seemed to hang on the hill. You sat by the windows and the woods rushed away from you, down to the vague white and tile of the town of Vila Nova. You couldn't believe that you could sit, drink, sleep here, with neighbors, but also with the mountain and forest circling you. At least, that is how she saw the place, after small-town streets.

"Storage space," Hart said. "I need storage space. I suppose I could find a carpenter?"

"How long are you taking the place?"

"Three months. Maybe longer."

"Tell me what you want to do, and I'll ask."

He was fidgeting around drawers and tables and cupboards and wardrobes, as though he had a whole life coming by steamer that would need careful laying out. But he couldn't have been more than thirty. You shouldn't need to carry your whole life at his age.

"I'll take it," he said.

She could have told him things. She knew about the old routes over the mountains to Spain, the mule trains that once stuttered up them and the places they took refuge, where the Lisbon court cut snow to keep in caves against the hot weather. She had an exact sense of what a garden should look like in summer: poles of bright green beans, tree cabbage on its high, gnarled stems, sweet, shiny onions lying on the ground. But she realized she hadn't the least idea what Hart saw here, why he wanted to be here, what all this meant to him.

≡

I know what Christopher Hart did next. Maria told me, because she was the one who saw him.

She drove out of town on the old road south, past the tile factory that's undercutting a whole hill to get clay, past dry fields of corn, through pine forest where the bracken was already rustling brown like paper. She was looking for a breeze, but the sky had gone dusty, just waiting to split apart in a storm.

There was a blue haze in the pines. It could have been heat, or smoke. She stopped the car on a wide turn in the road and looked down into the valley. She'd seen these fields so often she didn't look properly at them: a rough grid of beans, maize, potatoes, coriander and garlic and onions, scraps of earth slotted one into another.

She saw something shifting in the woods. If she'd been a hunter, she'd have cocked the gun. But this animal moved around with a shameless noise, flickering and rising. It was a big animal, broad enough to bother the trees: fire walking.

A bush burst out in neon orange, then the red and orange licked their way to the edge of the road and the tall, dry grass stems went off like sparklers. The brambles ran like fuses into a hedge. The air shook so you could hear it, like a ship when the engines start turning.

She was three turns of the road above the fire. She could see it was only starting. She ought to tell the nearest village, to call for the volunteer firemen.

But she'd never been this close to fire before. It was a spectacle, a firework show, lights seen through the trees of a park. It was so usual, it couldn't hurt her. Besides, the sound of flames held her still. The sound surrounded her even if it was only on one side; it seemed to prophesy where the fire would jump next.

A very tall man, blond, was walking into the fire. Nobody's tall around there; it's Celtic territory. Nobody's blond, except the tourists. So even from that distance, she knew the man was Christopher Hart. He was trying to beat back the flames with his jacket, as though he never meant the fire to catch on this scale.

She drove away quickly. She called the *bombeiros voluntarios*, the firemen, of course. They assembled, but the rain hammered down and the flames weren't hot or strong enough to persist.

There was almost no more rain that summer.

≡

I tried library registers while the librarians were not looking. I asked concierges in great concrete faculty towers if they knew a Professor Hart.

I called my aunts to tell them I would be staying a few days in Coimbra. I called the Museum to ask my secretary to check, yet again, whether Hart had left a new forwarding address in Portugal. If he had gone purposefully to ground, then to me that seemed like a confession of crime.

The aunts said Maria had called. I called her back and got the answering machine. I left the number of my small hotel.

She rang at six. I dashed along the slippy polish of the halls, past a convention of dusted aspidistras, and took the call at reception.

"I didn't know you were in Coimbra," she said. "That makes things easy. Come to lunch tomorrow, in Vila Nova de Formentina. I've got some papers for you to sign. You must meet some people."

I didn't yet know her habit of assuming everybody should know everybody if they were foreign.

We went to lunch at a place with chairs of lace ironwork with unforgiving seats and small round tables. We ate a dish of salt cod, roasted, with oil and parsley and onion and chickpeas. Three people joined us.

There was an emigrant newly returned from Holland, a man in his late twenties, a computer maven; a painter who lived alone in a hill village; and an academic, a gangling man with hair white-yellow, in his late twenties. He came late and he did not have time to eat, he said.

"Christopher Hart," he said.

≡

In the room in my hotel there was a single small mirror. I presented myself: John Costa, museum functionary.

Hart was hardly going to run from the Museum. It would be an admission of guilt. He'd rather act as though he thought I was some kind of intellectual social worker, come to check on his intellectual pregnancy, hand out more kinds of welfare, make sure he was condemned to being properly all right.

I presented myself to the mirror: avenging angel.

More like Keystone Kop, I thought. I can be threatening, but it takes passion. I can't loom at a door and fill it up with muscle and make a man shrink away. I certainly can't force a cold thief to give up the goods just because I say so.

So I presented myself to the mirror in a darker guise: John Costa, dealer.

You have to understand about dealers and keepers. Dealers are a special kind of gentry. They have special buffed pink skin that shines. They have double-breasted suits and their yellow ties are knotted in great blossoms of silk. Their shoes are perfect, polished brogues. They are the ones who get taxis when all humanity is trudging in the sleet, the ones who never turn corners but only cut them.

They constantly call the Museum.

I'm an honest man, but they still take me to lunch, somewhere far from the Museum, in silkiest Kensington, and propose that I could just forget an inconvenient fact or accept that a certain provenance is not entirely impossible or help separate art from (say) Italy in one of the traditional ways. They do this quite subtly, in the sense that you could not prosecute their talk, not even after the second bottle of wine, but they do it directly. They want the Museum's authority when their own seems in doubt.

John Costa, dealer: with a proposal that Hart might consider, a suggestion that there are works he knows about that the Museum can't acknowledge, works that might fetch a wonderful price.

The skin's wrong: too dark, not Anglo-Saxon pig-pink. I had no truly expensive suit in my wardrobe; I had nothing black for my own father's funeral. But I can look creditworthy in a crisp white shirt, suggest by understatement the presence of unlimited money just out of reach. I could bluff, surely.

≡

I would have hired Maria Mattoso to negotiate the next meeting with Hart, like some lease or contact; but there was no need. She wanted a season ticket for whatever game the foreigners were about to play.

I wanted the meeting, so naturally I drove the long miles to Vila Nova de Formentina. All Hart had to do was drift down from Formentina to Vila Nova.

Since we had no particular agenda, just a kind of social duty, we met on the terrace of the bar just above the market.

I arrived first, perfectly shaved, shaved as a penance. Hart turned up in pressed jeans and a flannel shirt, the neat young academic as lumberjack.

I told Hart that I'd called just because I was in the region. I talked about my father's funeral, and he offered careful sympathy. Then I asked what had brought him down to Portugal, underlining the question just a little.

He joked: about a whole year of blonds and common sense and herring, and not being able to stand it anymore.

Maria sat straining to hear what we were really saying.

"I always thought we should meet," I said.

Hart looked quizzical. Of course, he'd wonder why we never had; he must know my name.

"I admire your iconographic work," I said. "It's something to have things to say about flower pictures. We should be grateful." He didn't respond to flattery. "You are," I said, "our distinguished colleague." I rather missed the huge Portuguese words—the banks call even their most dubious customers *"excelentissimo"* in letters—that are not even meant to be convincing.

Hart said, "I don't know your work, I'm afraid. Your area."

"I once wrote a thesis about Duccio and the issue of whether he painted in his own hand."

"Duccio," Hart said.

"It was a perfect academic piece," I said. "Three laps around the subject, with footnotes."

I was sure I should not have said that. Soon the effect of the perfect shave would be dissipated; my learning would expose me, a minor academic bureaucrat out bluffing.

"But you," I said, "have the gift of finding things that nobody else finds. In the most unlikely places."

"Really?" he said. I should have noticed it was the proper, affectless New York "really," an invitation to try again, if you must.

"The Museum is not entirely happy, of course," I said. "But the Liber Principis really should be published. The collection is astonishing."

I didn't know, but he was exercising his schoolboy Latin: the book, nominative, of the prince, genitive. He was no wiser.

"And, of course, very valuable. Anyone would want a part of it. The Museum's claim always seemed to me rather tenuous, in any case."

I thought he got the point. "Your interest," he said. "It's business or duty. Or pleasure?"

"All of them. It's always good to know things first. And there's always money in it."

I read Maria wrong. I thought she was unimpressed by the talk, that she was watching everyone else. An old woman in black, struggling to hold red dahlias for the market. A girl who couldn't not smile. A man in a black cardboard suit, one arm ending like a pig's trotter. Five bank clerks in shirtsleeves on the verge of making a joke. Cops weighted on the spot by their stupendously polished boots.

"So you deal, do you?" Hart asked. It was all the sense he could make of someone talking about books and money in the same breath.

Maria leaned forward. She had me placed among the bureaucrats, the decorous professionals, and she would not easily change her mind.

"I do business," I said. "Material people wouldn't find anywhere else, material they want to keep for themselves. They don't mind a gap in provenance as long as the story is convincing on the whole."

Maria said, "What's provenance?"

"History," I said. "Who owned a painting and when, and where it's been."

"You mean they don't mind buying stolen goods?" Maria said.

I smiled. It was meant to be a knowing, sophisticated but non-committal smile. I was lucky it didn't fade under the glare of all that interpretation.

"We must have dinner," I said to Hart. "We have a lot to discuss about the Liber Principis."

I could see Maria was about to ask questions again. But Hart got in first.

"How long will you be here?" he asked, as though he was sure it would not be long enough for a meeting.

"For a while," I said. "I have family business to settle. I'll be around."

The whole conversation, Maria thought, was like listening to the radio and having the battery die on you slowly.

When we left, Maria says, she had more coffee and more water. She was puzzled. Foreigners usually arrive when they've run out of life elsewhere: tired, retired, maybe angry, looking for a change so complete they often forget mere material details like having an income. They don't come, like Hart, like John Costa, trailing their old lives with them and living them still, strongly enough to start a fight.

Something truly foreign had arrived.

≡

It was too hot for business, but Maria went to her office anyway, shut off the phone, and sat. She would have gone home, but it was lunch hour, and Amandio would be there.

He now came to sleep at the house. Her mother was kind in the evenings, distracted in the mornings, stocking and managing and watching Amandio like the shop itself. One night, she tried to make *broa*, even though the cooking cousin was around. She fixed flour and water, fed sugar to the yeast, pummeled the dough, and let it rise until it got up out of its bowl and started over the table in a soft, deliberate flood. She squeezed it, pummeled it, but it had a fearful resiliency. She slapped it onto a metal sheet, still growing, still moving, and burned it thoroughly.

Amandio tasted. He smiled vigorously. Maria didn't.

"It doesn't bother you, me being here?" he said.

"Of course not."

"I wouldn't want to bother you," he said. He was eating the *broa* steadily, doing his duty by Maria's mother. Maria wasn't. Her mother looked on.

"I know you've been used to having Mother to yourself—"

Maria said, "I have to go to the office."

She felt displaced for the first time. It wasn't just a matter of losing the steady comfort of home. Home was life. The local rule says people stay in their family, at the family house, until they're married. True, she should have married years ago, but despite her different kind of life home still bound and defined her: this house, this town, this valley.

Anywhere else, like the few weeks she once spent in Paris, she'd have to rely on illusions and sketches: other people's maps, guides, histories, geographies, memories, anxieties, what you read in the paper, what they tell you on TV news, a road-sign world, all warnings and indications, which she'd never be able to grasp as entirely as this small place. Here was the place she knew best, knew in her bones and on her skin, season in, season out.

She found Amandio snoring in a chair one night, flesh like the raw yeast rising in the *broa* and a slick of oil on top.

The next day, she bought a new dress, two new dresses. One was quite short. She thought about changing her hair color. These were not things that usually concerned her, but it was good to make such tiny decisions. It was practice.

One afternoon, she looked at an apartment in the nearest big town: three rooms, fourth floor, a block painted the color of smoked salmon. The walls didn't seem enough to separate people's lives, and the blocks were jammed together in a new part of town; there was scaffolding and raw brick in every direction.

She liked that. She didn't smoke in the apartment, although she wanted to, because she needed the place to be full of new air.

≡

I crowed to the deputy director, explaining punctiliously how I had done the impossible: found Hart.

"And?" the deputy director said. "And now what?"

≡

Christopher Hart lay in blue water in a borrowed pool, staring at a blue sky: suspended like a vacationland billboard or the covenanted pleasures of a cheap cigarette.

Maria watched. She had found him the pool, after all.

They were on a hillside, looking out to trees and scree and fields, but

Hart said he saw only perfect blue. He told Maria he wanted the English words for this particular blue: robin's egg, perhaps. Gentian. Cerulean. He thought about drowning in this blue. He wanted to live forever in this water until the faint, mean chlorine bleached him white.

That would have been easier, I suppose.

He can't have liked people who knew his stolen self, who had business with Christopher Hart. In the places he used to choose to be, people take you at face value, then they take your face value and pick that apart, then they magnify rumors and tease one another with possibilities. Everybody makes up themselves and then everybody else.

Anytime he touched the poolside, levered himself out of the water, he would have to be Hart the professor again: a character already written. He had to cope with whatever it was that this John Costa reckoned Hart had done, or might yet do. But he wanted to be any Christopher Hart he could imagine—subject to credit and bank balances, of course.

In the water, still cool under a hot sun, he turned and swam a couple of lengths, water smoothing muscles down. Out on the dry tiles he expected a world he already knew, more or less: wild daughters, people who teach, probably a cokehead falling out of a dress, unintellectual people with days so empty they start to hunger for a new book, people who take up art, the gardeners, people who drink, and, of course, the designated fuckers: the ones who produce the gossip for the rest. There would be divisions by nationality, each group allowed its interest in the old country—because it was ruined, polluted, blackfaced, or steely, because none of them meant to go back. There would be class divisions for those who liked them.

He levered himself out of the pool, shook himself like a dog. Maria says it seemed the pool was suddenly claustrophobic, that downtime was alarming him. He nodded to her, and ran off to change. He didn't say good-bye to his hosts.

He drove away up the hill. She heard brakes going on sharply, wheels dragging against stone in a sudden turn. He'd come to a dead end.

He came down the hill at a furious pace, speeding and braking, until he could rush out onto the bends of the main road below. There, he drove like a man racing, a man with no destination or purpose except getting distance under his wheels.

≡

"I'm glad you got on with Christopher Hart," Maria said disingenuously.

"We've talked a bit since," I said. "We keep running into each other, somehow."

"You'll have things in common," Maria said, meaning: coming from somewhere else, being part of cities and a world of words she didn't know.

"About my father's house," I said. "I think it's time I moved on."

Maria said, "You want to shut it down, or sell it?"

If I said "sell," there would be an orderly, unemotional process of breaking up my father's life and passing it on to someone else. It would not be my responsibility. I couldn't stop it anymore.

I said, "Shut it down, I suppose." Then I added, because I needed someone to listen, "I can't sell it yet. I feel strange selling something when I don't quite know what it meant to him."

Maria said, "Lock it up. Go away and think."

"But I'll be here a little longer."

"You have business?"

"In a way." I had a man to intimidate or persuade into confession, a man who so far seemed remarkably uninterested in my various hints and offers; if he had stuff for sale, he was not selling to me. I could hardly tell Maria this.

But I did say I wanted a house. I asked if there might be anything in the village where Hart was living. Maria said that might be possible, because people had holiday houses in Formentina.

She found me a house by the week, for at least a month.

I called Anna to explain.

"Come back," she said, using her close voice, none of the crispness and diction of her usual talk. "You've been away long enough."

"I know," I said. "It's just that this Hart business—and my father's estate isn't settled."

"You have lawyers for that."

"It's more complicated than that. Personal stuff. That business with the grave."

"I can't talk long. I have to get to college."

"I love you," I said. I am a creature of habits—work, love, dinnertimes—and sometimes habit saves you from decisions. "I miss you, I'll come back as soon as I can."

"Just don't get lost there," Anna said.

"I asked the Museum for a month more."

"I feel like bloody Penelope. Except I'm not knitting. I'm writing lectures."

"I'm coming back."

"You're only saying that because you thought of staying."

I wondered if she was teasing me. I didn't think so. Neither of us liked this sensation of a past cracking under us like ice.

≡

Maria came by just to see if Hart was all right, if the house was all right, on her way to fetch water, because she happened to be passing. But she didn't feel the need to list the excuses.

Hart couldn't close the door on her, or send her away. He knew the rules for small places too well. He told me so.

She showed him the spring, a mile and several folds of mountain away: a park big enough for seven trees, a pipe in a mass of official tiles where water always ran. But there were people there, two families packed up in a taxi and a pickup truck, and they were pulling leaves together to make a fire to cook a picnic. She pointed out the mountains to Hart, the purple of heather, the scent of pine, and she changed the subject to lunch.

On the way back, she had run out of things to say. But the attention she was paying had become electric.

≡

I parked the car in Formentina. I took out weekday luggage, the kind that goes out on a Monday, back on a Friday: neat, black, on wheels, a statement that a man travels with a job to do. I carried it to the door of the small house just above the road. I unlocked the door.

I put on all the lights in the house even though there was no need for them. I was signaling: I'm here, in the house between you and the road.

Of course, a dealer wouldn't need to do such a thing. His persistence would be so sweetly oiled that it seemed inevitable, and resistance simply bad manners. I didn't have that trick.

I went up to see Hart late that afternoon.

He didn't bother with any preliminaries. "Maria says you told her you work at the Museum," he said.

He could have known that already, known my name and the little hieroglyphic block of my signature from times he'd asked the Museum for favors.

"I should explain," I said.

I had wanted him to think I was some corrupt dealer operating on the black. I just couldn't bear the notion of doing it well, of convincing anybody: Maria, for example.

"But you talk as though you deal in art," he said. He paraded his sense of puzzlement.

"I think I rather gave that impression," I said.

"You said as much."

"Dealing isn't the point," I said. "I am assistant keeper of drawings at the Museum. I'm concerned with the Liber Principis. The Museum is."

"You want to buy this book? For the Museum? Or one of those clients who doesn't care about provenance?"

"I'm not going away," I said. "I'm here on family business."

"The Museum must be very understanding."

"Yes," I said. "For the moment, yes, it is."

I was sure I left a threat on the air. He'd know he had only a short time to hand back what he had stolen. He'd know I was serious because he'd think there was a profit in this for me. I could leave him to worry now.

After all, we were neighbors, so he couldn't move without either dodging or acknowledging me. I could monitor his morning walk, a late coffee at the bar, a trip to buy in the Vila Nova market. He had to worry, too, if all this was deliberate, or if it was just a malign coincidence born of the fact that it's tough to find a house to rent, by the week, for a month in the summer.

Our stalemate had an address at last: a village halved by a road, and halved again by a stream, full of color and stone. I was happy to be settled for a while.

I made coffee, as he did, longing for something to read, someone to talk to, looking out on the valley as he did, watching weather boil up black and furious out of the west. I really thought that I had only to wait.

≡

I was right. I just had the equation totally wrong.

I know now, from the police file, that the Dutch had already asked the Portuguese Guarda Nacional to make discreet inquiries about any-one saying he was a Christopher Hart. It wouldn't be simple—Hart was a European citizen, so he could move in and out of Portugal with-out a record—but they had the hotel registrations, and those were quite enough.

In a day or so, Martin Arkenhout would be quite sure of what he now suspected: that he had stolen the wrong life. He'd know, too, he had to cling to being Christopher Hart, or face the unraveling of a whole career.

I saw this happen. I just didn't realize it at the time.

≡

He came down the slate steps carefully. Cloud overgrew the houses like old vines, broke up the geometry of their dark, solid shapes, whited out some of the woods and left the rest gray and shadowy.

He thought I couldn't yet be awake, that the light in my house must be from last night. And if I was awake, I wouldn't be dressed before dawn and ready to run out. And if I was, he could lose me.

He started the car. The cloud held the sound close to the road, but made it seem monstrously loud. I would be awake now, for sure, scrambling out of my morning system and routine.

From here, there were only two ways to go: up and down. Up, the road snaked into bare mountain, then fell away into a valley, a lake, a dam. Down, the road went to a familiar town, with a dozen choices of town after that.

Hart headed down. Looking back on the road, all he could see was a white wall of cloud. The village had vanished. He must have vanished, too.

He told me he thought about running for Guarda and the frontier and crossing into Spain. Or he could get to an airport, get a ticket out, to anywhere people took less interest in Christopher Hart. He had a whole day ahead of him: a whole empty, resounding day.

Sometimes a great Volvo truck came up out of the white and went past with a speeding whine, sometimes there were car lights ahead; but that didn't matter. Inside the cloud and the white, the tunnels of trees, he was alone enough. The day was opening ahead of him, sun burning off mist and cloud and drying the damp road.

He was moving again, in control again: invincible.

≡

I heard the engine start. I made more toast. Hart's anger, I thought, had to be useful: a man who feels trapped may give himself away, or even surrender.

I went up to his house, of course. Neighbors might notice, but on a weekday there are not many; and besides, foreigners were known to know one another, to be in and out of one another's lives. The door was locked. I could see a plain, oppressive order, everything personal—even used cups, spare sweaters—tucked away out of sight. Hart hardly dented the house, let alone marked it for his own.

Nor did I. My own house was cold and dead, like all rented places. You wouldn't want to know what last happened there.

I missed Anna. I waited to leave a message on the answering machine because I like to do that: I can say exactly what I mean to say.

Then I called the Museum. The deputy director was oddly expansive. He urged me to take my time. The more time I took, of course, the more certain I must be of resolving the problem of the Liber Principis; that was clear. But that did not seem like a serious issue. I thought Hart was nervous already, and his nerves were all I had to work on.

I thought how I would explain what I was doing in the Museum's elegant and euphemistic official prose: what phrase I would use for intimidation. "Interim discussions," perhaps. "Soundings."

The day opened around me, cooler than most, with a bright sky clotted with huge white clouds. Now Hart was gone, I had only one pressing duty, and that was personal: to complain, again, about my father's grave.

The Guarda Nacional Republicana had a brick barracks in a maze of low, wired walls, and an incongruous fig tree sprawling over its military neatness. Inside, there was an odd air of hospital, but a hospital where people sweat.

I asked for someone whose English was better than my Portuguese, the self-deprecation trick. I gave my name and sat on a bench. A breeze tugged at the photocopies of faces on the "Wanted" board.

"You are John Costa?" a man said.

He had to be senior, old even, in his starched white shirt. He wore his paunch like decorations under a long, thin face that didn't match the body. He had the manner of an officer trying not to pull rank, just this once.

I stood up. The man didn't seem to have the usual blankness of a policeman, the wall on which you're supposed to project all your guilty thoughts. He almost seemed kind. I expected him to say something doctorly: "What seems to be the matter, then?"

Three cops in boots and uniform saluted him crisply, and the kindness dissolved.

"I am Captain Mello," he said, in English. "At your service."

I said I was sorry to disturb him. "But someone has vandalized my father's grave," I said. "I wanted to see what was happening."

"These things almost never happen here," Mello said. "I'm sorry."

I thought we might apologize the day away.

"They've spray-painted on the back wall," I said. "The usual scrawl, and a date: 1953."

Mello shook his head.

He said, "It's a very un-Christian act. Unforgiving."

His concern seemed gentle, unlike a policeman, and intense. He said my name again. "John Costa. Such a pity."

I said, "Should I make a report—"

"No, no. That won't be necessary."

"But you don't even know where the grave is."

"We have the report. We're doing everything we can."

I thought this must be the standard bromide for a distressed son, but he was watching me as though he expected to find something out.

"I didn't understand the figures," I said. "1953."

He said, "Vandals. They don't understand what they write half the time."

"But you have an idea, don't you?"

I was brushed off and out of the barracks in minutes, an exercise of authority I hardly noticed until I was in the car park.

≡

And then I was alone in my father's country, perfectly ignorant, with everything to discover.

It was one of those rare days when you snatch back a little of a child's most ordinary privileges—to wonder, to chase after wonders, to put together a landscape, a history, a place as you want out of stories, dreams, misunderstandings, and what you see. There are no experts, revisionists, conference papers, no catalogues raisonnés and guidebooks and politics to cut in between you and sensation. Everything is sharp, and not yet spoiled with words.

I thought Mello could have told me my father's story. Then I put the thought aside, and I gloried in the high colors and the brilliant light.

I made an expedition. I followed the Mondego River down past castles, green rice paddy, down to the sea. Then I went north a little, where the coast is rocks and alcoves, but it wasn't a day for that kind of craggy wildness. The sea just persisted at the foot of cliffs.

South, then. There was a fishing village with rooms to let that opened onto a vast crescent of a bay, white sand filled in with more white sand, cabanas in striped canvas rows along a city of board-walks. The place smelled of coconut oil and iodine. There was a circus tent closed up and waiting for the evening, and a few fishing boats with high, bright prows and sterns pulled up by the sea of car-park tarmac.

Everyone edged out on the hard, hot sand. Beyond that, the sea stopped them: gray, busy with kelp, alarming small children with its cold and its spitting and sucking.

A father was taking his son to the edge of the water, showing him the whole ocean. The boy stared, and wouldn't move.

We don't have children, Anna and I. We never had the clean mercy of a scientific explanation, not until it was too late; we thought it was a pain we had to share and tend. We came to confuse it with love, I think now.

I couldn't see the ocean anymore, just the concrete blocks, pink and white like a matchbox town, that ringed the wide sands and the sea.

≡

I saw Hart, glimpsed him really, in a serious working port, with freighters riding rusty and high. He must have taken a wrong turn. He glared at me, and accelerated out of town over the long, high river bridge which is an estuary wide.

I followed, of course. He had to think I was on his trail, always. He had to be unnerved.

Below the road were salt pans, all as regular as Dutch fields, squared off and neat; but instead of a uniform green, they were sometimes full of dark water, sometimes almost white with salt, with a red tinge and a black vein in the white. There were buildings scattered, too: huts, stores, refuges.

For a man who's angry, this landscape is a melodrama. Someone running away could scrabble down to the salt water, fade from one dike to another, hole up in a brick hut with nothing to drink or eat for miles. Death by condiments. He would drown, sucked down by the salt. He would be blinded by the whiteness of the salt and stumble into machines or deep water or the path of a car.

After the bridge, Hart turned off down cobbled roads, then a main road, then a kind of wrecked avenue with sea pines and yucca and the occasional sandwich shop, the sort of road that always leads to some superannuated seaside town.

I saw just a man running. I didn't imagine how he was reinventing me in his mind.

At the end of the avenue, he lucked into surfer heaven: a long, narrow beach that ran away forever, slammed by waves, sea curling back as translucent as glass but with fine white lines of spray. The buildings stopped. Gulls massed. There were only occasional stark black figures in wet-suits. Once he was on the beach itself, he could see only sand and the ocean, and people playing in the ocean, and a black dog on its hind legs trying to wrestle back the waves.

He spat on the sand three times to pardon himself.

The farther he walked down that beach, into a distance of spray and light, the more he fancied staying there. He threw himself into that sea, worked his way out until he could feel the muscle of the water under him, and rode it back to shore. And when he was scattered back on the sand, there was still nothing beyond the glinting screen of the ocean, and the long procession of white sands. No distractions. No problems.

I wanted to be his problem.

He had no choices, either; I know that now. On that mile of spare sand, he was still the boy from an orderly childhood, rectangles of green dirt, straight-sided canals, greenhouses flickering at night like ghost industries. He had only the Arkenhouts for parents, and if ever he stopped moving on, he would fall back into the scrubbed regularity of their world and it would scour and sweep and shine him to death.

I watched him on the beach. I found the right road by luck, away from all those families on the big beach, and the girls in brash shorts working the truckers on the main road; but then, there aren't many destinations on this coast. I saw his car parked among surfers' vans; and then there was only one direction he could walk, on the edge of the sea.

I liked his agitation. But he didn't see me as a guard on his life, or a Nemesis; and he wasn't ready to crack. He saw me as the kind with a job, an office, a wife to tug me back to London. I'd leave him, soon. Besides, he had all the venom of an adolescent's fine feeling: he was better than anyone settled. Settling was compromise. He didn't compromise.

He waded out again into the water. I saw him flail at the waves, not swimming but fighting the ocean; and then he was washed back to the sands very suddenly on the fierce run of a riptide. He sat down on the sands.

He saw me waving from a distance. He knew nobody else, so he knew it must be me, even though I was far too distant and indistinct to be identified.

He stared out to sea. Civil servants came and dropped hints to him about stolen property, and then would not leave him alone. Christopher Hart might as well have had lovers.

And there was such a choice, a whole tribe he could have culled: solo barflies, solitary walkers, the disengaged, people abroad for reasons they'd forgotten; men out trying to think up a new life; the ones too absentminded to keep friends, or too vicious, the dumb but creditworthy, the wanderers who might someday stop long enough to decide what they were pursuing—a people of lost boys who catch too many planes. But he hadn't stolen one of these shiftless, rootless lives. He'd stolen Hart, and Hart was of interest to others.

He could always steal another life. He would get it right this time. There must be some expatriate whose sudden exit would surprise nobody.

He wondered again about me.

John Costa had a wife in London, a life, a job, certainly a mortgage: obligations and maybe loves.

But that meant John Costa was sure to have a passport and credit and all the vital things. John Costa was a museum keeper who dropped hints about stolen property, who might have reason to disappear. The longer I stayed, he reasoned, the less likely I would simply go back to the office. I was up to something.

Apparently, he did think I might have dreams and fancies. But he thought they were just cinema, finished without consequences when the lights went up. He didn't know much about movies, either.

It was the first time he thought about killing me. He promised me later he dismissed the thought almost at once.

≡

By the time he caught up to me, suggested lunch, asked advice on which among the unfamiliar fish he should eat, bought me a glass of white port like some tourist with a sweet tooth, he was almost adhesive.

"I ought to be flattered," he said. "You following me. I thought I was just an anonymous professor."

"I just happened this way. I'm hardly invading your privacy—"

He said, "You're here, though. You wouldn't be here if I wasn't."

I shrugged and poured vinho verde.

"If you weren't here," he said, as though he was thinking matters out, "nobody would know me."

"Maybe not."

I didn't want to have some sophomore talk about identity, or be eyewitness to some premature midlife crisis.

"But if you're here—" he said.

"You know I can't leave until we have things sorted out. The Liber Principis."

"Really?" he said.

"You know that."

"I can count on that?" he said. I thought he was being ironic.

We took the fast road home, a two-car convoy under a turning sky that was no longer blue and bright, but sepia, smudged with black. There was a smell of baked air. Where light ought to flicker through the trees there was only smoke, until the road pulled us on, out of the woods and onto the flat, wet rice paddy. Then the smoke stood behind us like a wall.

≡

Hart stopped abruptly at a roadside castle: battlements, underpinnings, a church built inside the walls.

I overshot for a moment, then quit the road fast, alarming the posse of small cars running behind me.

The castle was stuck with a crown of bright blond stone, newly fixed, and everything below had been hollowed into the hill: caves, sooty cooking places, old holes for latrines, stones rounded by a hundred years of romantics who wanted a seat with a view, enclosed by

an outer wall that had mostly become a high grass dyke. I wandered.
A goat stared at me. I trailed around the entire outer wall and climbed
to the stone enclosure at the top of the hill.

I didn't look for Hart. I assumed he would want to find me.

I crossed into the inner keep, down onto a floor of set stone rubble.
I could see nobody, hear nothing moving except the cars streaming
past on the road below. The stillness bothered me.

I ran the steel steps and gantries up to the battlements. The view
was red earth and the dusty greens of summer trees, and villages like
clusters of white boxes. But I wasn't looking properly. I was listening,
and looking out of the corner of my eye for Hart.

The man had nowhere to hide. He had no reason to hide. There
weren't even pools of shadow to hide him under a high, overhead
sun. His absence hung in the air.

I stood against the cross-shaped arrow slit in a corner of the battle-
ment, looking down and around the circle of the keep. I thought I
heard a door close. But a ruin has no doors that close with that tight,
quick sound.

The afternoon heat came down like hammers on my mind. I told
myself that was the problem.

I walked the battlements, checking where I could see down into
the keep or on to the hill around the castle. I came down quickly to
the main tower, and the way out.

Hart's car was still there.

I couldn't imagine what he might be doing. I assumed he'd turned
off to see the castle as a distraction, that he was playing the tourist for
a moment.

I went back to the undercrofts of the ruin, the hollows and caves of
the place. I went gratefully out of the sun. Papers blew about. A fine,
small breeze worked the olive leaves on the hill.

I found a hollow behind the main cooking cave, and walked into it:
just curious, I told myself, about the place. A dog flustered out, nervous and yelping. I turned back toward the sun.

Hart was standing in the entrance of the cave. He had a knife in his
right hand, something solid in the left.

I said, "I thought I'd lost you."

I couldn't see the expression on his face.

He took the knife and began turning an orange in his hand so he could pare away the peel in a neat spiral.

"We'll have to sort this out," I said.

"I don't understand."

"I'm only interested in the Liber Principis. If we can just sort out—"

"I guess it interests everyone." He didn't know what he was saying, so he was perfectly deadpan.

I said, "We'd better go."

He dropped the orange peel to the ground, where it glinted like oil in the sun.

"We can talk later," I said.

As I went past him, I thought I felt something like a shiver across my hand.

Hart said, "I'm sorry."

He smiled. I never saw a smile like that before.

In the car, I watched a fine line of blood open on the back of my hand. I wiped it away. I thought at first it must have been some accident I'd failed to notice, but my hand smelled of orange.

$$\equiv$$

On the way back he drove kindly, so we moved in the lockstep of a convoy: safe, protected.

But he hated the idea of "protection." He told me later he much preferred the idea of being pursued; it was less alarming than the awful, regulating persistence of goodwill.

He took a wrong turn. But it might not have been a wrong turn, so I followed. He ran several bends ahead of me, then felt obliged to slow for a while.

Two kids were hitchhiking at the roadside: stringy, blond, undressed, too young and foreign-looking and gigglingly innocent to be truckers' tarts. He stopped.

The two blonds scrambled up to the car and smiled energetically, as though they didn't know enough to calculate their appeal. He laughed back.

The kids wanted the next town but one. They packed in beside

Hart. I could almost smell the oil and the baked blond skin on the girl and the boy; I was interested, too.

Hart showed off driving, of course.

But then he stopped the car suddenly and pitched both kids out onto the roadside. They looked startled at the failure of skin and charm. They stood while he drove off, and the girl gave him the finger.

≡

Then he was the one, again, who suggested a drink. He came bounding down the steps before I could wash my face and change my shirt. A little above my house he slowed for a moment, settled his collar, arched his back, and then walked on as though he was distracted by all kinds of professorial thoughts. I watched the change.

He said, "Maria left me a note. The police have been asking where I am."

"Did she say why?" I knew the Museum would have made no official complaint; we are discreet about sin in general, and the sin of theft implies the sin of inattention to security.

"Someone trying to find me, I suppose." He shrugged. "It's a good job I've got you to vouch for me," he said brightly. "You're official. You matter."

"And you have the reputation," I said. "We just have titles in the Museum. We just wear the titles for a while, nothing personal."

He said, "But your being here, it makes things easier."

Later he said, "The mountains close in on you after a while. You'll see."

"I like the mountains."

He was restless like a boy in his chair. He stood up, went to the window, paced a little, said his apologies, and went out to walk down the crease of the valley.

He broke a stick from a dead bush and thrashed at brambles and tall grasses. A dust of yellow powder hung in the air. But on the way back, he remembered to turn to my house and he waved and grinned like a good holiday neighbor.

Four

Maria was reading a book about fire that summer. Someone must have left it in one of the houses for rent: a book full of diagrams and graphs, pictures of spiked plants from burned places. Some days, it filled whole afternoons.

The wind was coming hot from Spain each day, and in the afternoons Vila Nova was closed. Open a shutter, and the whole house would sink under the heavy rush of the heat; you could bruise yourself on it. Even the smell of the town was cooked: pine and eucalyptus in the lumberyards, market trash, a thin fume of glue from the carpet factory, hot roses in dry gardens.

The foreigners were all pinned down by the heat, as you'd expect— too hot even to fret or feud and call a lawyer. So Maria could read about grass trees and orchids that flower only after fire, how animals don't panic in fire, that they double back through the firewall to the safety of ground that has already burned. She read about hawks that fly into the smoke plumes to catch the escaping grasshoppers, and beetles that dance into fire itself, scramble down branches where the sap is still boiling and the wood is red hot. Even English beetles do this.

Fire was on everybody's mind that summer. Only Hart and I were too foreign to be worried.

Maria was curious enough to go back to the site of the fire where she saw Hart dancing. She told herself she wanted to check the book, to see if ants came out to steal the hard poppylike seedheads of the eucalypt, if bushes broke into flower on scorched stems, and small, round mice came stirring up the ash. Maybe there'd be a grass tree or an orchid; she could dream.

The brambles were just spiked tangles of black string. There was a small new clearing, some uphill scars on old trees. She was glad the fire had been beaten back. Mountain people live the same way with snow and its sudden, deadly shifts, floodplain people with rivers; they're nervous, and they like a little triumph.

She walked into the wood, reading the fire: how it moved, where it started. It had spread out from a single point, as a fan does, and it had stayed small enough for the point to be obvious.

It was Thursday, hunters' day. Guns popped in the quiet, popped again and again. After lunch and wine, there's a lot more ammunition used, a lot less blood spilled; anything moving is a target when you can't quite see through the trees. Men start shooting eagles and wondering why the dogs can't find them. They fill a cat with shot in the hope it might still turn out to be a rabbit.

She was in a clearing under the black knots of a burned mimosa. All the fire's tracks led back here.

She felt uneasy. Hart was far away, but she'd seen him here, and his presence or absence had started to matter to her. She was ready to make a story out of anything she found.

Under the mimosa were burned sheets of paper. That's not unexpected; people dump rubbish out here because it's easier than finding a legal way to leave it, cars sometimes, tires and metal angles often, drums and plastic and cans and the five-liter wine bottles, papers that nobody misses much.

This leaf of paper was thicker than usual, though, thick as a photograph. Its surface was badly blistered. She picked it up and turned it over.

She couldn't read it, of course. But she was sure for a moment she was looking into eyes.

=

My house was under siege: buses lining the road, blocking the tight corners, letting off a muddle of old people in good clothes who all tried to stand in the shade. I watched from my window like a village spinster.

The old herd seemed to remember a purpose suddenly, and they moved off up the hill. I thought the path would break them, but they went steadily forward and upward, hauling their bodies ahead: hundreds of steps, irregular and sharp-edged so you had to come at them with your mind alert and work your calf muscles to go up.

It was too hot to dress, too hot to move. I stood at the window in shorts, trying to make sense of the old people moving with such grace and purpose. They were going to a cross that bore a Christ with the wounds painted in.

They had found their own speeds now, women in black linen, men in clean shirts. The path zigzagged on the slope, so they seemed to fill my whole field of vision, to take a quiet landscape and fill it up with effort. Some women went on their knees. Some went on bare, bloody feet. A few stalled like flies caught on paper, and some looked back to call to the others, but mostly they went forward in a serious, concentrated quiet.

My father was never part of this, I think. But I can't be entirely sure. He came from here, and he knew about these things; they could be buried deeper than a son can ever find.

I thought I heard someone at the door. I went to open it, and there were five peaches piled on the doorstep.

≡

Hart watched the pilgrims from his steps. He was thinking he'd chosen a place that was all too particular and special.

He told me:

Before, he'd always chosen places that were nice, neat generalizations, the kind people choose when they run away to spend their money, with mansions, often pink, and gardens with palm trees and pools, people endlessly tan, just enough booze and drugs to ease you through days in the shade and the water. There might be boats like floating houses, too, and servants attuned to whims of iron. These, usually, were his places of choice. People didn't talk about salvation, much less crawl on their knees about it. It would have been bad manners.

He'd chosen average people, too, with credit. Christopher was turning out different, not all what he had seemed: which was a fixed quantity, anonymous, professorial, predictable, who had half a sabbatical year left that anyone could steal. This other Hart interested people: museums, even police.

Well, he was interesting enough now. His life had been stolen. He was fairy-tale stuff: alive and dead at the same time.

He tasted the sweat on his forearms. He went to the shower and let the brown water stain him. The past few days, the world had dried up so much that water now came unfiltered, because filters could impede the slow flow.

He didn't want anymore to see the bent, dark figures who were coming back down the scorched hillside, as though they'd found something at the top.

≡

Maria de Sousa de Conceição Mattoso stood in the doorway. She didn't announce herself; she was just there, a silhouette against strong sun.

"I was passing," she said.

Hart brought her in.

"Everything O.K.?" she said. *"Tudo bem?"*

"I guess," Hart said.

"I thought I'd call by. I was on my way to—"

"Yeah." His mind was too busy to let any real reaction through.

"You can get down to the dam this way," she said. "There's a beautiful lake." She seemed bird-boned and slightly at an angle to the room. "It's very beautiful there," she said.

He said he was sure.

She sat on a wooden chair. He expected her to cross her bare legs, skirt riding up to where the chair cut her narrow thighs. But she sat as though she were in a classroom.

He said, "Would you like some tea?"

They both laughed. He thought how English he was being. She didn't think at all.

He didn't have time for this. She had all the time in the world. He had to make up a performance, and she was just curious, waiting for anything he might say that would tell her more about him.

"I'll make some tea," he said.

She sat quietly in her chair, eyes bright. She watched him take water from the tap for the kettle.

"There's the spring above here," she said. "It's better, I think. You get water up where nobody lives. No pollution." Then she thought she might be too insistent and she said, "Not even the snakes."

He stopped what he was doing.

"The snakes. People say they get in the water and poison it. With their skin, I suppose."

"You believe that?"

Maria said, "I don't believe anything very seriously."

He set the kettle on the stove.

"I mean," Maria said, "sometimes it's good to believe in snakes in the water and usually it isn't. It's like ghosts."

"You believe in ghosts?" But he wasn't really looking for an answer, Maria could tell. He was looking to fill up the space in the room with talk.

"Do you?" he said.

He sat down again, this time back in his chair with legs splayed. She liked the fact that he was strong but still a little awkward, like a young stork.

She smiled. "People have time to believe all sorts of things around here," she said. "We don't have anything else to do except make up stories."

It was an invitation, of course. He knew that. He just wasn't sure, this minute, how to respond—as Arkenhout, as Hart, as himself. His breath was a little deeper now, his pulse a little up.

She stood up and went to the window. On the way, she had to brush past him, her brown arm against his.

"You ought to keep the shutters closed," she said. "You need to keep the hot air out in summer. Once it's in, you never get the house cool again."

He said, "I guess."

He watched her bend to pull the shutters into place and bolt them, her small bottom angled up. She moved as a flirt might move, but entirely without self-consciousness. She neither smiled nor stopped herself smiling.

The room was very dark.

"You could put the light on," she said.

He didn't move.

"I'm afraid I'll bump into the furniture," she said.

"You won't."

"It's after the sunlight," she said. "I can't see anything."

He didn't move from his chair. She picked her way across the room as though she was trying to avoid him.

He didn't know the rules. She didn't know there were any rules.

"People like having you here," she said. "They like having a *senhor doutor* down the road, a man with degrees." She must be sitting down now, making polite, even deferential conversation.

"You don't find it dull here?" she said.

He wondered what harm it could do to tell a single story: pick out a Bahamas night and dress it up with moon and night flowers and drums, tell her about some tourist moment in Vienna, maybe. It would be just a postcard, nothing personal.

He started to think the whole rousing moment was over. It wasn't.

He felt her fingers start in the hollows of his neck and trace across the muscles of the shoulder, then down his arm.

"I can read you," she said.

She covered him with her body, lightly, holding back at just less than arm's length; then she let her arms fold and she lay pressed against him. He could make out her eyes in the dark, a shine of faint gray. All the rest was touch.

She was fragile bones sticking him, a child or a runner. She was a wing more than a hand. She was hands asking questions. Then he felt the full warmth of her, and her wonderful persistence, as though she were going under his skin to find him. He found himself arching and moaning and turning as though he were doing a whore's tricks under her weight. She pulled his head back by the hair.

He stood up and took her into the bedroom, wrapped around him. She fitted his strength exactly. She kept her lips together on his neck, the breath playing and prickling there.

She pulled off her dress briskly. His clothes seemed cumbersome by comparison. She lay carefully on the bed, expectant but patient in the half-light, hardly moving. He thought maybe she'd run out of play, that all she wanted was the waiting and the darkness and the possibilities. He'd have understood that. He felt the same way about killing.

But he was wrong. He went to bury his face in her, and taste the salt in her sex, but she pulled him alongside her. He couldn't tell if she wanted him, or the peace she might find when she'd left him and gone away again, but she wanted to fuck immediately and furiously.

He fell on her, caught her on the mattress with his whole weight. She came back up against him with much more strength than he'd guessed. She found him and took him in. There was a second of child-like surprise: that they were joined at all. Then there was nothing but bellies smacking and sucking against each other, the roar of their breath in their throats, the mutual heat.

Afterward, he watched her breathe, her small, round stomach shifting above coarse black hair and her sex.

"You always lived here?" he said.

"Always."

"You never wanted to go, I don't know, to Fortaleza, or San Salvador? Or Rio?"

She opened her eyes and smiled.

"Fortaleza," he began, "is—"

He knew enough to panic at what was happening to him.

=

She still had to go to the spring for water, a hundred cold liters in plastic bottles pitching about in the back of her car. The only way back was through Formentina again.

I happened to be sitting on the steps of my house. So she stopped, of course. We said a few empty things, and she drove on, but she was still printed on my retina, like the sun when you stare too long.

Her own thoughts, though, were all domestic. She tried to imagine what it would be like when getting water for the house, going to the hypermarket; all these jobs were no longer services or duties or favors done for others, just her own necessities. Life on her own would lack a lot of moral gilding.

She had rehearsed what to say at home, what the others would say and carefully avoid saying, but in the end it slipped out while talking over coffee: that she was going to leave the house.

Her mother said, "You don't have to."

"It's time I did."

"You mustn't go on my account," Amandio said.

"It's not because of anyone. I just think I ought to have my own house."

"You'll have to run it," my mother said. "And you'll be alone."

"I suppose I will."

"It's not good for people to be alone," she said, as though she'd only just found the antidote and was not sure it could last. "You need your family. You'll have to have someone to do the cleaning and cooking."

Amandio said, "You ought to go out more." He'd managed a variation on his smile: something avuncular but not disinterested.

"I do," Maria said. "I always do."

And that was that: a life turned upside down in a minute. It wasn't just a change of address. People live in their families here, in the net of who was born to whom; that's their acquaintance, their gossip, their expectation of dancing, drinking, and eating. You don't often break the net, unless you marry or leave for the big city. Maria was not leaving.

Her mother took away the coffee cups and said, "Some of us have work to do." She bustled down to the shop, set herself in a back room behind tiles, pipes, brushes, screws, tools. Amandio went down to the shop, too, but he didn't stay; he had business somewhere else. Maria's mother surrounded herself with invoices, tax papers, receipts, with catalogs of pavement and lawn mowers, classified lists of bidets, specifications, with anything that made immediate sense to her. She glared, flirted, barracked with the customers who caught her eye.

She was furious. Maria was falling out of the ways that things are done, and that could not end well.

≡

The police called on me the next morning, the same Captain Mello who heard my complaint about my father's grave.

He was courtly, almost. He told me Formentina was lovely, that he was glad to breathe the air of the *serra*. He said he was sorry to trouble me—my Museum connections apparently put me among the *senhores doutores*, the ones who expect such apologies—but he wondered if I could just confirm the identity of Christopher Hart. Yes, the professor who had taken the house up the hill. I must know him, surely, from London.

I said, carefully, "I know his work. I wouldn't say I know him personally."

"Ah," said Mello. "But you asked for him when you came here. You found him. You did find him, didn't you?"

I said, "I don't understand. There's no doubt, you know. That's Christopher Hart. Seventeenth-century specialist, Dutch interests. A man trying to get noticed in the shadow of Simon Schama. He's work-ing on—" but I couldn't say precisely what, even in this odd atmo-sphere of casual conspiracy and plainclothes confession. "On genre painting."

"Yes," Mello said.

"Is there some kind of problem?"

"Not at all," Mello said. "A routine inquiry."

"The Museum has its own interest in Professor Hart," I said. "I don't suppose you could give me any idea—"

"I won't take up any more of your time," Mello said. But he didn't move for a moment; he studied me. "I knew your father," he said.

I didn't know what to say.

"I thought you came here for your father," Mello said. He sounded disappointed in me. "I think the grave has been cleaned," he said. "But you probably know that."

"I haven't been to the grave."

Again, he seemed disappointed.

"I was glad your father came back," he said.

"I had mixed feelings. You can imagine."

"He had to come back sometime. He couldn't stay away forever."

"That's what we're all supposed to think, is it? That we have to come back to the native soil?"

He shook his head.

He said, "I'm sorry, I shouldn't be taking up your time. You must have many things to do."

He walked to his car very straight-backed and thoughtful.

Within minutes, Hart came bounding down the steps, as though he'd counted to one hundred, two hundred, five hundred after seeing Mello drive away.

"You want to go for lunch?" he said.

I said, "The police were asking about you. Whether I knew you were Christopher Hart."

He didn't pause. "Really?" he said. "What did you tell them?"

"I told them who you are."

"Pity," he said. "I fancied being the man of a thousand faces. Someone like that. Not just some English professor."

"I'll call him back," I said.

He said, "Don't bother." He said it with surprising force.

≡

Hart was in another pool, swimming steadily up and down in perfect, chlorinated solipsism. The pool glinted, the universal shiny blue of pools, between roses and herbaceous stuff.

Around it stood the English, gins aloft, assumptions polished, murmuring that the police had asked the oddest questions about this Mr. Hart.

"Did they ask you, dear?" someone asked me.

"No," her husband said to me, firmly. "They wouldn't. They never do ask the friends."

There was a self-consciously well-kept man in his sixties, overworked muscles kept assembled by skin like carpet, whose younger wife was watching Hart's back as he slid away and back again, away and back again. They had West Midlands accents.

"Love it here," the man said to me. "Delightful. Really delightful. Delightful. You'll fit right in."

His wife was smiling at Hart's back.

"He's a professor of art history," I told his wife, helpfully.

"I'll have to ask him about Portuguese art," the wife said.

Her husband said, "What fucking art do these people have?"

Hart swam on, hearing nothing but the water and the occasional bubble of chat. He knew he was being watched, of course.

He pulled himself up from the water at the deep end.

"You swim very well," said the Midlands wife.

He wanted something more literal, more crude than that. He wanted her to take a proper risk. So he went back under the water, feeling clean and distanced, and waded out at the far end.

The wife looked suddenly red.

And Hart came back, dry and dressed: the odd man out. He had an audience of all the expatriates, not just one hot-faced wife. The police put an odd stardom on him.

≡

It was safe to be Christopher Hart for a while. Christopher Hart was identified by everyone's attention, by the *senhor doutor* from the Museum, who had no reason to lie. No officious, persistent cops in Holland need ask questions. They could feel pity for Mrs. Arkenhout, still strung out on her loss of ten years ago, still mourning in a mad way.

And if Hart was definitely Hart, that meant he had not lied to his mother at all. He took a perverse satisfaction in that.

But he had to use the time. This improvisation, like the last one, was more trouble than it was worth. The next move had to be secure and certain.

He didn't smell enough money, certainly not enough credit, around the pool. The expatriates had the price of a house sold in Britain less the cost of living for the months or years they had been in Portugal.

The Portuguese had an ominously settled look. They seemed to account for one another.

He was grateful for my presence, grinning at me in a soused way. I could be a museum keeper on the lam—who succumbed to temptation, perhaps, after finding whatever it was he was here to find, who was deeply distressed by the death of his father and ran off. So he could be me.

He wasn't inquiring anymore. He was checking.

He took me to the good restaurant by the castle and bought shrimp stewed in oil with bay leaves and garlic, and then roasted salt cod, and a bottle of serious wine: Caves São João Reserva, 1986, big and woody and red. It was his way of thanking me for saving his life, and surrendering mine. It was like being courted.

I don't know if it was the wine, in quantity, but I was stark awake at midnight, sitting up in bed. The silence seemed unusually deep: none of the machine noises of the wet woods, no cicadas and frogs like musical saws, no whirring nightjars. The world had narrowed down to this tight valley, and it was waiting.

Low in the woods, across the *serra*, there was the abrupt sound of branches tearing, a shout, a shriek, and then a fearful whining. Then there was a great sigh that seeped into the night like water into dry ground.

I closed the shutters then and crashed about the house, pulling down glasses, slapping them on tables, running taps, anything to break the silence that was waiting for me at the windows.

≡

The next morning there was a neat parcel on my doorstep: a leaf of cabbage as tough as canvas and tied up with stems. Inside was a piece of meat still filmed with blood.

My neighbor across the pathway, a man in his fifties with a grin suspended on two teeth, watched me open it. "Pork," he said. "Pork from the mountains."

I looked puzzled.

"They got a pig last night," the neighbor said. "There's been a pig around the maize fields and they went after it."

I said, "I didn't hear anything."

The neighbor nodded, approvingly. "It's good stewed," he said.

I introduced myself; so did Arturo.

"You bought the house?" Arturo asked.

"I'm just here for a few weeks."

"Oh. You want a *copo*?"

"It's a bit early—"

"I thought you were Portuguese."

"My father was. We lived in London a long time."

"And now you're coming home?"

I said, "You never know." I couldn't tell him I would certainly go back to London, back to my official self.

"You want a *copo*?"

We went into the shed alongside the house, a tiled cave that smelled of spilled wine and was masked in by the flourish and tendrils of vines. Arturo opened the tap of a barrel and poured.

"That's good," I said, even though it was raw, thin stuff. I drank slowly; my father once told me there's a half-wild grape that makes a methanol mixture that can stop the brain.

Arturo waited for me to finish, and poured another; there was only one glass. He settled on a concrete wall, still smiling.

"We didn't see you. We thought you might be sick."

"I was here," I said. "Just busy."

"We're always busy."

"I'm from London."

"I was in Bordeaux. Ten years. I drove taxis."

"Beautiful town."

"I love the city. Any city. The country's just work and dust. Work and dust."

"Yes."

"You're married?"

"I'm married. She's in London."

"She's coming here?"

"I'm going back."

"I came back from France," Arturo said. "People don't believe it, but I did."

"What took you to France in the first place?" But that was a dumb question.

"Hunger. We didn't have anything to eat," Arturo said. "So I left one morning and I went to France and when I'd got construction work and got somewhere to sleep I wrote to my wife and told her what I'd done. Then I sent money, of course. Then I drove taxis. I knew all the night people. Every whore in Bordeaux."

I felt the wine scouring my stomach. "That was in Salazar's time?"

"I sent money," Arturo said. "What else could I do?"

"You liked France?"

"I like towns," Arturo said. "Out here, you never go anywhere. You just stay."

"It's very beautiful here."

"Oh yes," Arturo said.

"I didn't know there was wild boar around here."

"Too many. You're not supposed to kill them. They're 'rare.' " He put the word in sardonic quotes. "Then they get in the maize fields and twenty minutes later you don't have food for the winter. So what are you supposed to do?"

"You stew the meat?"

"Zulmira was going to cook it for you, but maybe you don't like our cooking. She could get you onions, and bay leaves and some garlic. I'll leave them for you."

"Thank you."

Arturo said, "We thought you might have come to stay."

I said, "I thought about a garden."

"You want to make a garden? You can't plant in summer."

"Just something."

"Flowers?" Arturo said. "You like flowers?"

"There won't be time for beans or cabbage," I said.

≡

Hart would not avoid me now; he refused to run. Since the police came calling, I was his very useful colleague, to be cultivated.

He was good at silence, I remember. I told him more about Anna than I quite meant to, and without saying anything in particular. We mentioned the Museum. At least he provided a kind of occupation while I bought death certificates—impossible numbers, at exorbitant prices, from satisfied clerks—and adjusted all my father's goods and papers. I could have left the whole business to Maria but it had become part of settling my father down.

So we ate together: young chickens done on the barbecue with hot *piri-piri*, or *bacalhau à brás*—the soft, golden dish of egg and salt cod and tiny sticks of potato, the essence of fish and chips and eggs for breakfast all in one; salads of tuna and black-eyed peas, spiked with garlic. We worked our way through a culture of the seas, hot African pepper, a pig in every shed, a bean-eating nation with a taste for garlic and the sour edge of cilantro.

I'd have known my father better if I had thought of those meals as information, not just lunch. I know that now.

Hart became some kind of social director, the man who kept us amused. He proposed an expedition, at lunchtime in a cafe when Maria was there. He said we should all go to the monastery church at Lorvão. He'd read about it in the Michelin guide, maybe, and he imagined some spectacle of white and gilt.

Maria gave him an odd look, as though he must be making an inexcusable joke, but at the time I missed it. She did not come with us.

We drove zigzag roads, around bends of olive trees all tangled up with the brilliant blue of morning glory, past windmills on a bare hill. I had to stop him playing Abba at full blast on the car stereo.

The monastery was impossible to miss, the core of a small town with a fussing river: a white, palatial range with windows surrounded in stone the color of the crusts of new loaves.

The windows also had bars. I said something about that, but only jokingly.

The high metal gates lay open. I drove carefully ahead, past civic lawns and geometric beds of marigolds and red salvia.

"Ask someone," Hart said.

There was a man standing by a kind of kiosk, with a cigarette hanging unlit in his mouth.

"Please," I said. "Can you tell me where the church is?"

He looked at me as though he were looking in a mirror. And you don't answer yourself; people might think you are mad.

A second man came up behind the car, and stood still. A third arrived.

Hart said, "What is this?"

The stillness around the car was uncanny. Nobody spoke. Nobody made a social gesture: no smiles, no pointing, no pompous or angry shouts to tell us we were trespassing or in the wrong place. The men moved around us as arbitrarily as fish.

A door of the monastery opened and shut quickly. Two men bustled out wearing white coats. They seemed to be arguing.

I tried to get their attention by sounding the horn.

They turned briefly. "Closed," one of them shouted. "Closed." They waved us away.

Hart said, "They're doctors."

"I guess they are."

"Then they're fucking madmen, these men," Hart said. "I didn't know this was a madhouse."

"We just reverse out of here," I said. "There's nothing to be afraid of."

Hart said, "Maybe they're lepers. It's something contagious. I know."

I missed reverse the first time I tried.

Hart rolled up the window. He put the men on TV and watched them like a child watches danger on the screen: face slack, body rigid, open-eyed.

We crept backward from the monastery door. I was afraid the men would not part to let us through, but slowly they did. One of them, as we passed, remembered about smiling. He shifted his lips, opened his teeth; but his eyes stayed dead.

At the roadway, I said, "We should have asked about the church. You said we could get into the church."

Hart said, "I want to get the hell out of here."

I drove quickly up the hill.

Hart said, "Maria should have told us."

"I suppose she thought everyone knew."

"I saw my mother like that once," he said. "She smiled like a doll. She couldn't move all the time. I—"

Then he remembered that he was a man who must have no history.

"I could use a drink," he said.

≡

The drink must have occupied him, because his car was missing when I went for a walk that evening, even when I came back in failing light, with the sky gone the colors of a Cecil B. De Mille ending: peach, scarlet, pale blues and greens, all ladled indiscriminately across monumental clouds.

There was no light in Hart's house. It seemed so quiet I would be bound to hear the car coming back.

I tried the door.

The room was a holiday vacancy, with a laptop computer on the table.

I looked around. Some odd, old scruple stopped me rifling through papers, checking cupboards and drawers; at least, for the moment. I could say I was just waiting for Hart. I was sure I was entitled to check on him, to find out about him; but I found it hard to play the policeman.

The laptop was connected to an outlet, so there would be no loss of battery power to inform on me if I simply opened it.

I had no particular expectations. I just thought that somewhere in the work and letters, there might be some way to fashion a useful picture of Hart.

At least there wasn't any question about how he worked; the machine went straight into Nota Bene. I checked the names of files, then their dates, and then their lengths. I found "outline," a longish file, 73 kilobytes, that Hart had last touched a month or so ago.

I opened the file and read.

This was like meeting Hart at some cocktail party: a snapshot of Hart when he was trying to impress.

The outline was for a book about the time Prince Maurice spent in Dutch Brazil, a collar of land around Recife and Pernambuco. The prince went there, in the seventeenth century, to govern a tenuous colony that depended not so much on willing settlers as controlling the trading ports. He'd taken something with him. This new world was a place of monsters and legends, but he wanted to know what exactly was there, however strange, to give this unfamiliar stuff the same kind of names and classifications that the known world had. He threw away all the lovely myths in the hope of being modern.

He brought artists to record what grew and lived there. His doctor became his naturalist. He built palaces on an island (he never truly settled on mainland America at all) and from there he sent out painters and observers to find, fix, list, and explain everything. He sent Frans Post, painter, to make pictures that would bring new settlers: landscapes with downstage chorus lines of safe, exotic animals, set against blue mountains, with sugar mills and old cathedrals to imply a long, tame European past. He sent Albert Eckhout, painter, to record the turtles, the crested and disheveled hens, the beans, pallid mushrooms, great cats, and knobbled, glittering lemons: anything new.

So far, so unremarkable. Hart had a nice historical vignette. He'd obviously thought about the art on the dust jacket. The only thing missing was a point.

It came soon enough: a knockdown, drag-out routine. Hart, it seemed, was outraged by science raping the Americas, by the brutal intrusion of the modern, even if the worst sin of the modern seemed to be collecting watercolors. The modern stood accused of seeking hegemony over the bright fruits, the living, chattering things, the human beings classified in the albums. All of imperialism, of Eurocentricity, of patriarchy probably and certainly modern science and its ills, was implicit in these seemingly lovely pages. The proof was how aristocrats in the eighteenth century valued them: a confirmation that the albums were themselves corrupt.

It was exhausting stuff to read. The words were like millipedes in motion: articulated, shiny, and weird. There was fury everywhere, a determination to accuse the founders of, say, a botanical garden of complicity in everything Hart found wanting, including History for its failure to be like Hart. The pages spat ideas like little weapons.

I was relieved, for a moment. There was nothing to suggest Hart had a passion for revenge on his material.

But then came the flashy stuff: a discovery, a name maker, and, even worse, headlines—about this great imperial museum holding what it should never have had, about fifty years of concealment and bluff. Hart took it too far, of course; he ranted about the hegemony— always that big, blocky, violent word—of museums and historians themselves. He denounced, in no particular order, object fetishism, elitism, imperialism, the historical process (which seemed to be distinct from history or writing it), and the great sins of being modern, even the crime of linear thinking and reason's rape of the planet. But while he juggled shiny abstractions, he tried on a hero's role: a hero of the stacks, a treasure hunter adventuring busily against evil, with a degree.

I thought I heard a car on the road down below. I shut off the machine and went out up the steps, away from my own house, so I could seem to come back casually from an evening stroll in the woods.

I saw people biting at the fields with picks, carrying greens for the goats. It looked like stage stuff, set against this drop of slate and stone. But then again, so did Hart, a Jekyll and Hyde: at once the scholar Hart, with his footnotes and his moral certainties, and the criminal Hart who stole pictures and bluffed so well. I had to help him choose which role he liked best.

≡

I thought the light was playing tricks at first, although beyond the verandahs and shutters of my house there was little light to play. Something seemed to move inside.

I thought of an animal out exploring, a cat wanting a home. The third day I was in Formentina, there was a thud on the metal front door. I opened to a small, wagging pack of wild dogs, all smiling.

Animals don't unlock doors, obviously.

The house had a solid door at the front, and a bolt-hole at the back, up against the sharp side of the hill. I had never tried the bolt-hole before, never needed to. I pushed past brambles and grazed myself on stones to get there, stumbled on half an oil drum buried in yellowing grass.

The door opened too easily.

I didn't go through it at once. I knew there was a jumble of tools, cleaning chemicals, an old clotheshorse, and paint cans just inside an eccentric kind of hallway, and I didn't want to send the whole pile clattering onto the tiles.

The pile, I could see, had been tidied to one side.

I was the righteous homeowner, returning to confront some thief, but that was not how I felt in that hallway. I felt oddly exposed. The invasion was so orderly, so methodical.

The door to the kitchen stood ajar. I edged through it, trying not to make the hinges sing, and I kept low like a soldier, an odd instinct for a sedentary man.

One time in London, we found the house prized open and smashed, drawers tilted out, all our organized life scattered about at random, and shit in the center of the living room carpet. But nothing had been touched in this kitchen. The two onions, the bottles of red wine, the bananas with their flight of tiny midges, the cups and glasses, were all in place.

I heard my own breathing. I thought I would need to cough. I listened so fiercely, and I could make out nothing in the next rooms except the fact someone had been here, might still be here.

I couldn't dislodge a tool from the hallway pile, not without noise. I picked up a wine bottle.

I threw myself forward, knocked open the door to my living room.

The contents of my jacket were spread out on the table: credit cards, tickets, IDs, my passport, two checkbooks, a little leather pouch of cards.

I checked, but all of them were present, all the signs and proofs of John Costa's life and credit. That fact was more alarming than anything. I put the wine bottle down.

It might have been someone else, I told myself, and not Christopher Hart. I did not convince myself.

≡

He came to my house the next morning, asked if I wanted to come for a walk. The situation was in danger of becoming absurd: two men married by a crime, never quite losing sight of each other, but keeping quiet as though quiet made everything ordinary.

He showed me bottles of water in his knapsack, some chocolate. The walk was a challenge, not a casual thing.

We went up by Jesus on his white cross and kept walking up the goat track into the fringe of the woods. There was a little breeze. There was brown bracken, lavender in flower, heather and foxgloves and scrubby oak that grew like bushes; and through it the foresters had cut roads as wide as a bulldozer, clay-white and hot.

I suppose lovers go for walks that seem like this: inconsequential walks, for the sake of company. Hart paid me a kind of attention that was also a demand.

We didn't say much for the first mile. Then we both noticed that the roads had twisted about, that the folds of the mountain were more complicated than we had supposed. We weren't entirely lost, because we had up and down, the direction of the sun, and some sense of how the hill ran; but we couldn't point to home anymore.

"Easier to go up," he said. "We can see our way from there."

"In Switzerland they have signposts on the mountains. I miss them."

"We'll be fine," he said.

We walked a little faster now we had a purpose: to find our way. If we'd been boys, we'd have had everything to discover and talk about. As men, we just sometimes talked. At each fork in the path we slowed down because either fork would do and sometimes it was not clear which would lead consistently upward.

"If you want to make things good, you can," I said. "That's why I'm here and not the police."

Hart scuffed at white stones on the path.

"Think about it," I said. I walked on briskly.

I had no idea who was walking with me. I felt entirely safe, even here in the woods, where a man can slip, slip in the path of a hunter's gun, lie in the path of a fire and, presto, out of the woods comes a whole new John Costa, a tall and blond one, off where nobody knows him. Cartagena, maybe; Arkenhout had seen films made in Cartagena. He liked the thought of a colonial, tropical place.

I was well ahead now, walking soundlessly on the baking clay, making my point by being ahead and walking fast just like my father used to do. I turned and shouted for Hart to come on.

Hart wasn't there. He had cut off the track, to piss perhaps.

I stood there dutifully. The weight of the day came down on me: hot, sullen, with erratic, furious movement in the air somewhere distant. Far across the valley, where there was brown smoke in among the haze, lightning sliced the sky horizontally, straight as a knife. The woods seemed very dense suddenly, as regimented as planted fields.

Hart must be in the brush and the scrubby oak bushes and the heather. Perhaps he was watching me now.

I turned around, turned around again. I could sense a new, hot wind on the path: a shift in the weather, nothing more.

The lightning cracked the sky one more time.

I started running. I wanted to be out of the woods before the storm came. I wanted to be clear of whatever Hart was doing.

I missed my step on a tree root and I fell. My ankle turned under me, and the shock of the pain made me grunt like a hog.

Baked white tracks ran down and up through the trees, forking and twisting. I wasn't sure I knew my way home anymore.

I am sure I heard footsteps going away.

I couldn't stand for a moment. I thought the hot wind behind me might be fire, just out of sight, set somewhere behind a rack of stones or a thicket of new, bright eucalyptus. I didn't know how to run from the fire, or where to run.

Hart said, "You all right?"

He stood almost over me.

I said, "Give me a minute. I'm just winded, I think."

He was carrying a long strip of eucalyptus bark, the tough stuff shed from the trees like raw ribbons. He snapped it against itself.

Then he pulled a pack of cigarettes out of his pocket. I couldn't move for the moment, so I watched the match flare and die as though that was interesting, watched it fall still lit on the ground, just out of my reach. The ash fell after it, and finally the lit butt of the cigarette.

"Come on," he said. "We've got the day ahead of us."

He walked ahead now; he'd won that point.

I heard the birds clatter high up in the eucalyptus.

We were always going upward. I told myself that was common sense, that we would never easily find the track back down the hill, that we had to climb until the woods cleared and we were out on the bare *serra*.

But Hart's pace was racing fierce and mine had to match his.

I asked for water. He passed me a bottle, but he did not pause.

"You know you have some explaining to do," I said. "Why you didn't notice the Liber Principis was damaged—if you didn't damage it yourself."

"I have some explaining to do?" Hart said.

"We want the pieces back, unharmed. If we get them, probably the Museum will ask no further questions."

"You're a keeper," Hart said. "You're not a policeman. So why did they send you?"

"If this is an aberration, the Museum has no interest in pressing matters. We're only concerned with the paintings. To call in the police at this stage—"

"You mean you don't want people to know."

"I want the pieces," I said. "I'm not leaving Portugal without them."

The ground was too rough for easy, steady speed. Animals had slipped about in the wet spring, and left steps in the baked mud. There were stones, sometimes fallen tree trunks. In places, the pines massed so close they killed out any green thing living at their roots, and their fallen needles wrapped the ground ahead like rough brown paper.

"Nobody's leaving," Hart said.

I realize now what he had to think about. This crime of Hart's had acquired a name, at last, and some specifics. If he'd touched up a librarian, the Museum wouldn't care so much; nor if he embezzled, drugged, or indulged in interspecies dating. They wouldn't have sent anyone if all he'd stolen was an idea. But they cared enough to leave this John Costa here for days, even weeks, all because of something official, something with an index card and an accession number and an identity.

It was Hart's crime, just like killing Hart was Paul Raven's crime: it could not touch his moral holiday. But it could seriously disrupt his chances of a next life.

His arms pumped like an athlete walker, like a prizewinner. I was infuriated all at once by the thought of following him, but not sure enough of my ankle to try to overtake.

He was waiting for me to try, or to ask to stop. I wouldn't stop.

He didn't say anything now.

The dark in between the trees, which was a lack of life as well as light, began to break in strips and patches. Grass, mint, a little fennel reappeared, but only in clumps where the light caught. As we climbed, the clumps became little gardens and sometimes the gardens were like meadows.

We came out suddenly onto the high *serra*. The light was as hot as it was brilliant, a hammer on the skin. Lightning cut across the sky, and left the trees shivering in the electric wind.

In common sense, we should have turned back, not walked out onto bare moor with an electric storm massing above us. We should have looked around and got our bearings; so far our only direction had been upward. We should have stopped.

I wouldn't be the first to stop. He wouldn't be the first to stop. So we raced over the rough, dusty grass as though we had some destination in mind.

≡

When I called Anna next, I chose my time carefully, so I could hear her instead of the digitized voice on the answering machine.

"I don't understand," she said.

"It's a kind of stalemate," I said. "I just have to wait him out."

"Can I come? For a weekend?"

"I don't know how long I'll be here. It might all be finished this week and then—"

"I could come this weekend."

She couldn't, I was almost sure. She never could simply tear things up, not even an empty day in a diary; she guarded herself with timetables.

"If you want to," I said. I meant to be cruel.

"I'll surprise you," Anna said.

I'd stopped making a formal daily report to the deputy director. Hart was alive and well and behaving as you might expect, I told him, although he had no apparent routine for work. We were both shocked at this. At least I still had the sense to know that I should call, sometimes, in case I started to seem dispensable.

My trouble wasn't Hart, not yet. It was this place, this Formentina, this Portugal. It always came back to my father. He had returned to Portugal because he was settling again, so he'd chosen the practical low ground: with water pressure, power lines, daily buses, minimarket. I didn't need that. I could live high and picturesque, like any transient. The landscape to me was pleasure, a pleasure not unlike holiday: allowing the eyes to open wide without cutting a place down to the road you have to take, the address you have to find.

The trouble was, I was not in a hotel where people in uniforms replaced one another daily. I couldn't help starting to see the particular people in Formentina—to know their names, something of their stories.

I knew Arturo from his passion to explain things. He had fields of new apple saplings, planted as close as beans, and he said he had linden trees, his own plantation somewhere up among the pines; he also kept bees that blundered, drunk and fat, through the sweet bells of linden flowers. The condition of every day was work.

"I'm going to have an operation," he said, quite abruptly.

I said, "What's wrong?"

"They don't know."

I said, "It's a biopsy?"

"They'll know when they've done it."

"Is there anything I can do?"

"I was wondering," he said, "if you could take us to the hospital. On Friday."

"Of course," I said. "What time?"

"Eight in the morning. They could send an ambulance, but I don't feel like an ambulance. I feel like going down in an ordinary way, while I can."

His face was wrecked skin and utterly open eyes. He was very afraid.

≡

I thought of my father dying. I must have seen the moment, when he was propped in the door, when he was in my arms on the steps, but I missed it, too: the exact moment when the body was empty at last, the moment of difference. It was too powerful to be imagined.

But then, I could hardly imagine who my father was and what he felt when he was there.

It wasn't enough to say he loved the place, dreamed it; you can tend love, keep dreams, without ever going back. Usually, it's better that way. There'd been moments, away from Anna, when I got myself in and out of love in a day or so, in hotels in different countries, so as to have memories; but that was transitory, conference stuff, and I never wanted to go back.

Arturo came out of the shade and stood watching me, and I him.

He wanted to explain. He just didn't know what to explain. And I sat there, still unable to make up a life for him out of what I knew. He seemed almost content, but he sometimes sat down suddenly on stones as though movement had stopped being possible.

His wife, Zulmira, kept the key to the chapel, I knew that, and every night she went there to set a light burning; but how she ordered the world through saints and the Virgin, kept alive the hope of sudden miracles in a place that never seemed to change, I had no idea. I ought to understand it in my blood, for my father's sake. Perhaps it was the secret of how he, too, organized the world.

Arturo shouted up: "The grapes used to be a marvel at that house."

"Sure."

"Someone could plant grapes there again."

=

That day three policemen, no sign of Mello, parked on the road and ran up to Hart's house and opened it up like you open a tin can: without violence, but everyone can see what has happened.

"Papers," one of them said.

Hart said, "What do you need?"

He fished in the pockets of the Cerutti jacket, the one that was still a bit too smart for the valley, and he pulled out a passport.

The senior of the three cops took it, opened windows and put on a desk light, and peered at page after page. He seemed to care about the views of Her Britannic Majesty's Secretary of State, about the date and place of issue and the date of expiry, about the American visa with the barely readable photograph of Hart copied onto it. He ran his fingernail over the visa, checked the figures at the bottom against the birth date on page 4. Then he checked the emergencies section on page 94, which Hart, like everyone else, had left blank. Only then did he put the passport to one side.

"Do you have any ID?" he said.

Hart said, "You must be joking."

He knew that was wrong. He'd cleared Customs often enough in different countries to understand that you stand respectfully while they examine your papers because the papers don't interest them; they want your submission, or they want you to show nerves.

"I'm sorry," he said. "Yes, of course."

The university ID had a photograph. So did the back of his bank card. The Indians had done a wonderful job on both of them.

But he hadn't asked them to change the gym card. He'd meant to dispose of it, he should have left it in Hart's house, no reason for him to carry a card for a London gym all the way to Portugal. But Hart had carried it to Holland, of course.

The senior policeman was playing out cards now, dealing them into lines with a casino precision.

He'd see the gym card. It would be incongruous. It would be enough.

It was too late to take the card back. He'd volunteered it.

The computer repair card. The library card. The Greenpeace credit card, biodegradable.

"Where were you on the nights of June twenty-sixth and twenty-seventh?" the senior cop asked. He held the gym card in his hand. The photograph was just a Polaroid snap, colors fast settling toward beige and magenta; it was inconclusive, surely. The cop gave it the same grave attention he had given to every other scrap of Hart's official, carded being.

"I don't know," Hart said. "I could look in my diary—"

The cop threw the gym card down.

"Let me know," he said. "Or Captain Mello. At the police station. People in Holland want to know."

He shuffled the cards again and stood up, flanked by his juniors, with his perfectly inexpressive policeman's face.

"Just those dates," the cop said. "I need an answer by the end of the day."

When they had gone, Hart fell to the floor and started to do push-ups, for the sake of something he could control.

He was seriously alarmed, not by the check, which could have been any routine check on foreigners, but by the demand that he go down to the police station to fill in the last detail. They could have waited while he found his diary. He could have told them at once.

They couldn't possibly know what had happened on June 27, because it was nothing that left traces. He had to check the date himself. It was the night he went drinking in a warm, brown bar, sat about, and hunted; the night he met Hart for the first time.

≡

Maria let herself into the house. He was lying on the bed, fitfully asleep and still fully dressed.

She snapped on the light, abrupt as a policeman would be.

"*Olá,*" she said. "You sleeping?"

She looked at him with a directness he did not expect. It wasn't politely usual, or conventional. It had something in common with the directness of the older peasant women who had never learned any other way of seeing the world.

"I'm sleeping," he said. He lay still.

"Imagine if the cops came back," she said. "If we only had ten minutes—"

She turned off the light.

Five

I drove Arturo to the hospital in the morning, slowly, like some black car in a solemn procession.

The old man must have seen the mist in the trees most mornings of his life, seen it shift out of shape and drift through the headlights with the tar steaming below, but now he chose to stare at it; and Zulmira sat upright in the backseat. The two of them were sharp as scared animals.

Their daughter, Isabel, tried to take Zulmira's right hand. She couldn't break Zulmira's grip on herself.

The hospital had the manageable look of a picture in a prospectus: oleanders, parking spaces, towers of glass. But inside, it was frantic like a market, women in black, bags and bundles, a whole civilian population turned out to mourn its men in the wars: men cut up by machines, men whose hearts exploded or whose brains stopped because of the drink, men broken, men who wore out when they could least afford it. Every grating and corner was full of people waiting; the hard glass and tile of the walls had gone soft with cloth and eyes and hands.

Arturo wasn't quite expected, was about to be shunted aside to wait in line for an office that could tell him which line he should wait in next. There were processions of the sick between this office and the next.

I couldn't bear the sight of his resignation, his patience. I barged up to the admitting desk and used my proper bourgeois manner and the oddness of my accent to get attention. After a few minutes, a nurse came for Arturo and led him away, cardboard case in one hand, down a long, dark corridor that sometimes shone with the light from a far window.

Zulmira went after him at once. But a squadron of doctors bustled by, and she stopped out of deference. She sat down in the corridor and began to check the food she'd brought in another bag.

"He won't need that," Isabel said.

"They don't feed you in places like this."

"They won't let him have it."

"I brought the right thing, didn't I?" She appealed to me as if it was my business, a jamjar of bean stew in one hand.

"I don't know," I said. "He won't be able to eat much before the operation, and afterwards maybe he won't feel like it."

"He'll want this. To build him up."

Isabel said, "You don't have to stay. We'll stay."

Zulmira looked at me directly. Her right hand had relaxed a little, and in it was a crucifix: a metal Christ on a wooden cross. The crucifix had bitten her hand hard.

She went entirely blank for a moment, face like paper, eyes dead; and then she came back to us, still focused only on Arturo.

"He'll want the food," she said.

"You know he can't have it," Isabel said. "We'll bring him food when he's getting better."

"I made it for him," Zulmira said stubbornly, but she had no more energy. She'd watched over Arturo all night in this hospital before, watched him shaved and white, on his back on a gurney like something being moved in a barn, his face tired even though he was coming out of chemical sleep. She thought everyone has a measured portion of luck, and she wasn't sure if he would be there this time when he woke up.

Isabel said, "There's nothing we can do now."

"I can wait," Zulmira said fiercely. "I can."

I left them. I told myself I was only cluttering a place that was already confused, that I was somehow intruding. But so was everybody else in that corridor, bumping in and out of one another's lives, sometimes edging accidentally up on a death. I did think to check the ward number before I left, and the name of the admitting doctor.

I drove down into the town, bought an English-language newspaper, and ordered a coffee under the shades of a street cafe.

I kept clinging to ideas, even quotations, to save me from what I saw in Isabel and Arturo: their fear and their certainties, both. I remembered, as a kid, being corrupted for months by a line in Graham Greene—it must be in *The Human Factor*—where someone says something truly wicked: that pity is the only truly adult emotion. So I thought being adult meant detachment, the right to appropriate someone else's pain with your pity, to feel morally involved without feeling anything stronger. I know much better now.

≡

Someone passed me with those odd turtle gestures of neck and head that mean he wants you to know he thinks he's recognized you, but isn't sure he is entitled to talk. The someone passed again: Captain Mello.

I put down the paper. Mello stood there, smiling.

"Could I buy you a coffee?" he said.

I could say only "Yes."

He commanded a chair, summoned the waiter with small, authoritative gestures.

"They've done the best they can with the grave," he said. "The marble drinks paint, unfortunately."

"I'm very grateful. I just don't know why it was marked in the first place."

Mello said, "Some people have it in their hearts to forgive. Some don't."

"You knew my father," I said.

"Before he left, of course."

"He never spoke much about those years."

"They're gone," Mello said. "For better or worse."

I said, "For worse?"

"You look around you," Mello said, and he raked a quite ordinary shopping street of Benettons and Body Shops. "You know things aren't all better."

I saw a girl in a token skirt, with dazzlingly bare legs, two men playing drums and saxophone, windows full of pastel clothes, an old-fashioned barber, a bookshop full of academic titles, and a couple of other cafes spilling out into the street.

"We have a drug problem, of course. You can't park your car without some toxicodependent 'helping' you find a safe place, and staving in your windshield if you don't pay him. You can't walk all the streets anymore."

I saw tourists trying to make their green guides fit the sights.

"And prices," Mello said. "People say they were happier when you could get three sardines for ten escudos. Nowadays, money frightens them. They were happy in their place."

"My father wasn't."

"There were always exceptions. And people who worked abroad, of course, were exceptions."

"People worked abroad because they were hungry here."

"Is that what your father told you?" Mello sipped his coffee. "I didn't think so."

I wasn't sure I wanted this man's version of my father. But he at least knew some of the story, and there was nobody else who would admit as much.

"We knew you were here," Mello said. "I meant to visit you before."

I looked at my watch. "Forgive me," I said. "But I had arranged to see somebody in the hospital and I mustn't miss visiting hours."

Mello said, "It took courage for your father to come back."

"I don't know what you mean."

For an odd moment, the sun behind him, he could almost have been a priest: someone with the power to release and forgive, not a cop's power to seize and avenge.

"I'll let you go," he said.

Far down the street, past windows full of fake lace, and other windows full of ancient tin toys and dust, and a seed shop with a window full of grass seed in packets, I kept hearing Mello's words: "courage . . . to come back . . ."

Now the unspoken thought, the one that put gold around my father's name, was always that he had left a dictatorship to come to London. It seemed a heroic, not just an economic thing to do, a matter of principle to get away from all the police spies and the regulated life. I didn't want a policeman's view of that, not even if he implied there was enough of the old fascist hierarchy left to make my father a hero just for being back where he belonged.

Besides, I thought Mello was asking "Are you brave enough to come back?"

I went to the bank, made my usual polite apology about not speaking Portuguese well, then asked to cash a Eurocheque for 35,000 escudos.

In the next queue stood a bulky, formidable woman, felt-hatted, green-suited, obviously the chairwoman of something purposeful. She punched me quite suddenly in the ribs.

"You speak Portuguese perfectly well," she said.

I could think of nothing to say except "Thank you."

≡

The day turned cooler at last. A stranger's car was parked by the chapel, back open and scales visible inside on a bed of sacking.

The fields were deserted. Women crisscrossed in the village and the men clustered in the shade.

I sensed something on the air. The ox, usually silent, bellowed once.

Four square-built men came out in a scrum, women following with wide red plastic bowls, with plates, wine, eggs, and bread.

I supposed the foreigners were meant to stay away, whatever this was. Hart would be up in his clean white house engaged in his own business; no reason he should even come down. I found out later that I was a rather different matter. Arturo had wanted to include me, but the other men weren't sure how a man in such nice city shoes, city-shined, would react. And without Arturo, there was nobody who felt obliged or entitled to invite me.

I didn't go inside the house. The dogs ran about as though they had errands.

A woman I didn't know called across to me: "Senhor. Senhor João." She didn't think it quite proper that she should invite me, but she wanted to include me, since I'd done my duty by Zulmira and Arturo and Isabel, like a neighbor.

The scrum went into a barn at the roadside, stone walls with an iron roof that roasted the evening air. I followed. The women and some of the older men stepped around the pine cones and needles and heather and wood on the floor, keeping out of the way.

The pig was very young, very fat. The scrum threw themselves on the pig, one to clamp each thrashing leg and hold the animal down, a fifth to take a strong knife and cut the throat. It was very sudden, undignified but not brutal. Blood crazed the pig's white skin, like a pretty martyr on a tile.

The animal seized up still and rigid.

I'd never seen this before. I wondered if it was simply a routine for these men, something they knew exactly.

There was one who cut and slaughtered, while the others helped. He said he wasn't an expert; I asked. He said he knew a bit about doing this.

They laid the pig on the floor and took a blowtorch to the skin, over the sides and under the round buttocks, scraping the dirt from the trotters like a lady filing nails for the night, shaving the skin with trowels, cutting the ears and burning out the bristles. The fire was pale blue and I smelled gas, burnt bristle, the wet ocher shit the pig dumped in its last moment. Someone thought to stuff its ass with paper and a cork.

Then they took pine sticks and needles on a pitchfork and lit them, and perfumed smoke rolled up in the shed. They put the fire all over and around the pig, so it lay in a pool of flame and smoke and ash, the snout and mouth fallen apart in a loose smile. Each fork of burning pine was carefully tamped down. The white soot danced in the air.

They took heather and brushed the pig's skin.

"Makes it tastier," someone said in my ear. "The fire, I mean."

I nodded.

The animal was still entire, like a stuffed thing or a carved pig, its skin blistered with a little gold and a little black. The smell now was sweet and resinous, except for the burnt hair that caught in the nose.

The men laid the pig out on a scrubbed bench and carried it into the light. They took brushes and they worked the body clean. It had a cooked color now, not ordinary pink and white.

The slaughterer took a kitchen knife, washed it, whetted it. He cut into the cheeks of the pig's head, pulled the flesh away, and broke the mouth open. Blood rushed away: vermilion blood, shockingly dark, over long rows of small teeth and a loose tongue. The effigy of a pig was suddenly a real carcass again.

Someone pushed a glass of spirits in my hand. It burned my stomach and settled it. So I didn't turn away. I respected the practice, the method of these men, although one was rubbing the pig's buttocks and grinning. Everyone laughed, shifted, like a party that has just become a party with the first broken glass and the first drunk laugh.

The laughs disturbed me.

The slaughterer cut out the anus of the pig, a neat and new round hole, and tied up the intestine. He cut a circle in the middle of the belly. No blood ran.

Then the knife went through the pig's two back legs to make holes for a double hook. The men picked up the carcass and roped it to a beam in the shed, so it hung head down and just above the ground. The pig's face, now the tongue was gone, the gristle of the nose carved out along with the jaw, was a drunk grin of blood.

The laughing man ducked in with his own little knife. He ran a finger down the two rows of nipples on the young sow's belly. He sawed one off, rolled it between his lips, then chewed it and spat it out. He burst into kid's laughter.

Now I wanted to look away. Someone pushed another glass of spirits on me and I drank it.

The slaughterer began to cut between the pig's back legs, a careful, delicate line through the white of the fat, down and down. I went forward to see more clearly and more closely. He left his knife stuck in the flesh of a back thigh for a moment.

He took an axe to the breastbone. As the axe broke through, there was a fall and rush of blood that splattered into the red plastic bowls and colored them black. I stood back.

He opened the caul of the belly, and the intestines began to fall, plump, white, and shining. When they broke and stank, he tied them.

He put his hands into the cavity and worked the guts out with the sucking sounds of a vacuum breaking.

The shed was impossibly hot. My mind was roaring with the spirits. I couldn't tell what I thought anymore: if somehow I had a window into some past, if the prospect of blood excited me, if only the methodical ways of the butcher kept me from being entirely revolted, if I wanted to work the carcass myself, or if I wanted to forget I had ever watched a knife carefully go into a belly.

I wanted to say something urban: that if you eat meat, you'd better be prepared for how you get it. But I had nobody to bother with a cliché like that. I was alone with the magical transformation I had seen, that everyone else thought was ordinary and banal: from a live, screaming pig to an effigy, from a mess of organs to something now cleaned and trimmed that belonged in a freezer, or a butcher's shop. Life turned into a menu in a half-hour.

They pulled out the flat, shining liver, and the kidneys lying in their vast caul of fat. They took a saw and cut down the back of the pig to divide it.

I saw Christopher Hart watching from the doorway.

≡

A killer watched a killing. He was startled, he told me afterward. He'd got used to a green place, quiet, nice swimming pools, an available woman who liked stories, and here was a caricature of his own regular modus operandi. He was practical, too, when he killed. He loved change, not the killing that made it possible. He knew about the smells inside a body, the ones that were prickling in my nostrils. The blowtorch and the pine needles were a new idea.

He caught the sense of party: wine, fire, blood. He had never felt such a perfect stranger. The scales in the car said this was a simple economic transaction, but it was more than that: a victory over want, and even a little dangerous.

The carcass was cut almost in half. The butcher had one last job: to take his knife first, then an axe, and sever the clotted head from the neat sides of pork above it. He swung the axe and someone held the head.

There was a procession then: the limp sides of pig thrown over shoulders, the liver hanging from a slim white rope of organs, the head, the tub of intestines. The blood had gone already.

I was hot drunk, with an unreliable look. Hart watched me. In a minute or two, the women brought the blood back from the fire: clotted like the skin on paint, to be chewed with spikes of raw garlic and a dress of olive oil, along with salt cod and boiled eggs and *broa*.

I ate. I snatched at the blood and the cod. I suppose I never looked more vulnerable.

≡

"You don't want to drive," Hart was saying. So naturally I wanted to drive more than anything, wanted to drive to the sea and the mountains all at once, and fast.

Hart said, "You'd better get some coffee."

"Fuck coffee," I said.

He said, "Give me the car keys."

So I took the keys and settled in the driver's seat, ready to race away. It was so easy for him.

I started the car and slipped down the hill. By luck, I only grazed the low wall between road and valley. I pulled back and took the next bend too wide, trying to run away from the rocks. The trees stumbled about in my line of vision.

I knew this was wrong. The light had gone tricky and fussy, clouds over trees, not enough to define the sides of a road that lacked white lines. I was aware I needed to swing to left, to right, to run the bends accurately; I had driven this road often enough to know its character, if not its details.

I knew all at once I couldn't make it.

There were headlights up close on my tail, blinding me. I couldn't stop suddenly. I couldn't see a place to stop. I couldn't go on with the valley falling away to one side, straight down over ribs of rock and old tree roots. I could hardly hold the road but I was being pushed to go faster.

The lights were on top of me now, lights that made my head ache like blaring music. I thought I felt a slight impact, a nudge forward.

An ordinary macho would have wanted to overtake me, leave me behind. This driver stayed on my tail.

As drunks do, I had a sudden moment when I understood exactly what was happening. I saw a side road signposted up ahead, and I cut off up its steep ruts.

The engine stalled.

The car with the ominous lights went by.

I put on the handbrake and my head fell on the wheel. The sound of the horn woke me up.

I was still stupid, you understand. I let the car run backward to the road. I stopped there for a moment before, very slowly, another car crept around the bend with its lights full on.

The sun came out, low and brilliant.

Hart said, "Are you all right?"

"What the hell are you doing following me?"

"You're drunk. I didn't want you to kill yourself."

"You nearly killed me on the road. I couldn't see."

Hart didn't answer for a bit.

"I said, you nearly killed me."

He said, "I'll drive you back. Leave the car."

It's a wonder how reason hides reality. I truly believed, after that, that somehow he had saved my life.

=

That was when Anna arrived. She paid off the taxi, had a coffee, found out which house I was using; the barman spoke rough French. She'd asked if she could buy some of the bay leaves hanging in the bar, leaves gone brass-brown in the dry air, and he'd given her some. She used them to beat the air into a breeze.

We used to share moments like this. She baked in the shade, smiling when people went past, let her eyes fill up with all the various greens that ran up and down the mountain. There were so many cicadas rustling the air it seemed they made a wind of sound, a machine of some kind coughing like an old man in a bar corner.

I know Anna. The moment it was too late to cancel her ticket, she'd started to relax. She couldn't waste the money, after all. She missed me, I know, missed touch, the possibility of regulating her life by someone else's presence. It wasn't romance; it was how things were.

But she couldn't really see Formentina, and she knew it, and regretted it. Her colleagues said they dreamed of a life like this— green, not wasteful, not taken up with spending. Then they jumped in their Fords and went to spend plastic at a mall. They wanted healthy bodies, which they bought by the hour in a gym. They acquired peasant homes, but clean, sealed, lifeless peasant houses. They liked their world refurbished.

She, Anna, was just like them. She grinned at the fact.

She watched a woman washing at the public trough, a block of dark-green soap rubbed on white linen, the linen scrubbed and rinsed and rinsed again; and a man pulling a cart of greenery and brownery from the roadside, grasses and bracken and vetch. She wanted to talk to someone but she realized she was, in the most literal sense, none of their business: a woman in neat white cotton, a bit too smart, inexplicably fallen from the sky on their chapel steps and seeming to want nothing at all.

Sooner or later, even if it was only for an afternoon with too much wine, she knew I was going to think about living here.

But she felt comfortable in the shade, immobilized by comfort. She wasn't even watching the road when I drove up in some neat, shiny Opel, followed by a straw-doll man, lanky blond, in a VW Golf.

She saw me go back to confront the blond, and she says we seemed to be fighting, but the words didn't carry.

She got up, dusted down her skirt, held the bay leaves before her.

"I'm early," she said. "I could come a day early, so I thought I would."

I walked to her. It was the sun, I think, that kept my movements sensible and slow.

"Anna," I said.

She put her arms around me, and I put my arms around her a moment later. I tried not to breathe out whisky.

"I missed you. I thought I'd come early."

"I'm glad you did."

"I couldn't call. You said your phone didn't work up here."

I hadn't the slightest idea what to say or what to do about her, she could see that. She'd have to teach me all over again.

"I like the train," Anna said. "I got a very slow train. It stopped at every station and several farms. Then I got a taxi up here. Everybody seems to know Formentina."

"I suppose so."

"I was glad. I mean, it might have been some tiny village nobody knew about—"

Hart ran up the steps to his neat white house and slammed the door hard. I know now the only thing that kept me alive through that day was the arrival of Anna, "that woman in a long cotton skirt," as Hart said, "with her long English face."

≡

Anna stirred a bit on the bed. I was up, and we'd slept only a half-hour.

"I have to collect someone from the hospital," I said.

"Who? I don't understand."

"Someone from the village."

I got out before she could ask questions, left her on thin cotton sheets in a room that never stopped being warm, even with the shutters and windows closed tight.

I drove very cautiously, but once or twice I misjudged a bend.

The hospital corridors smelled of ether and pine and plain, denatured food. I found Zulmira and Isabel sitting like guards on either side of a door.

"He had the operation?" I asked.

"Yes," Isabel said. "They won't exactly tell us how it was."

"But he's O.K.?"

"We think so."

Zulmira said, "There'll be nobody to light the chapel."

"We're going home," Isabel said.

"But he'll wake up alone in there."

"There'll be nurses. There are two other men in there."

"He'll be alone. I always sleep here."

"You'll feel better if you go home and sleep."

"I suppose your husband wants you back."

"I expect he wants his supper, yes," Isabel said.

"He could drive us home."

"He has to go straight home from work."

"We shouldn't have to ask Senhor João. Jorge ought to drive us. I've stayed here before."

I knew my father's country well enough to know that conversations like this never happened in public. The one time I dropped wine-glasses on a stone floor and cursed and bellowed, I heard shutters closing on the houses all around me to spare me embarrassment. Either I now counted as a kind of local, or Zulmira was far too tired for shame.

"I'll try to find a doctor," I said.

I worked my way down the corridor. It was as tough as swimming in weeds. There were nurses, equipment, relations, a family party standing about in shock and not noticing other people trying to get by, two old men opening a five-liter white bottle of red wine and being told to put it away, a couple of doctors whose suits and coats seemed to stand away from their bodies like armor. I tackled them, got referred on, found a nurse who knew the records and told me it was a straightforward biopsy, the main danger the anesthetic, and he was well through that.

"It was a bit late, though," she said. "He can't go home until tomorrow."

"Should his family stay?"

"He's fine. He's not a young man, but he's a strong man. Take them home and bring them back tomorrow when he can recognize them, and they can take him home." She thought for a moment, and said, "If you could get his wife to see the doctor—" She smiled at me. "They think it's only the men who die. Country people."

I didn't understand.

I cajoled Zulmira to her feet. I talked a nurse into opening the door so Zulmira could see Arturo's chest rising and falling reliably in the middle bed.

In the car on the way home Zulmira said, "I'll make *broa*. They won't have *broa* there. It's all bread, white bread."

"You make *broa*," I said. "They killed a pig today."

"But Arturo wasn't there," Zulmira said.

At nine that evening, Zulmira put a loaf on my doorstep. Anna heard something move outside, went to the door, and saw her briskly walking away.

"Your neighbors must like you," she said.

You know what I was thinking? That I would be in time, that this time I could keep a man alive, that Arturo would be together with Zulmira again. No funerals, no burials, no graves. This time, I would do better.

≡

Maria asked Hart to come and look at her house the day she found it. She told herself she needed another pair of eyes.

It wasn't in the country, she couldn't quite manage that. Instead, it was on the outskirts of Vila Nova, on the edge of what they call the industrial zone, down the road from a lumberyard and a couple of warehouses for electrical appliances. The house itself was bright white, with a lawn and roses, and dark wood.

Hart said, "It's fine."

"I didn't know if it was sound or not."

"I don't know about those things."

She wanted someone to tell her that she'd judged right: that she could be comfortable here, that people would come to the house. All her life, she'd lived where it seemed natural to live—student houses, home mostly—and she had never made a choice she'd had to live with.

She showed him the kitchen. "Big," he said. And the other rooms, bare tile floors, dust and paint smells everywhere, odd bits of tarpaulin still lying around, a crack in a corner that snaked through the plaster from ceiling to floor and looked as though it would open onto a cliff of dirt. "I like it," Hart said.

"I still have to buy furniture," she said.

That wasn't the point; she knew it, he knew it. He paced about and opened windows as though he wanted to know what kind of view there was. It was the usual kind: the side of the mountain, flashes of wall, tree, roof until the point where you couldn't see higher without lying on the floor.

They waited for each other.

She showed him the kitchen: marble everywhere, a wide stove, dark wood cabinets. She tried the taps at the sink and he came up behind her, brushed against her, and stood back. She was waiting for the water to run hot, which was absurd since there was no gas bottle for the heater. The water ran. She turned off the taps.

"Hey," he said.

She was going to say something about the garden, but he was standing against her back.

She turned around. He was staring, it seemed, eyes soft and fixed.

She wasn't sure these were the right rules for domestic passion. Perhaps she should cook. She wanted to try out everything.

She stared at the wood and marble around her.

He kissed her left breast. She was aware of the smell of cleaning stuff: a kind of pine cracked in a chemical plant somewhere.

"It's fine," he said.

"I have to get home," she said. She realized she meant her mother's house.

≡

That weekend was the *festa* in Vila Nova de Formentina. Anna, of course, wanted to dance. We both thought a crowd would somehow fill the gap between us.

The church tower was lined in white lightbulbs, so it looked like a drawing in soft, bright pencil. Huge speakers saturated the walls with sound. Green bars of neon, ropes of light and bunting glittered in the little wind among the tired brown linden leaves.

I heard tunes I remembered from Italy, when Anna and I were first there: persistent, sentimental tunes like "Una Lagrima sul Viso . . ."

The kids lined up: boys in T-shirts like stiff white skins, girls in flounces of skirt. The band assembled: drums, synthesizer, guitars, and a saxophone star.

Maria Mattoso brought Hart down the mountain, and they danced together. Anna also wanted to dance, but first she wanted water from the bar. I pushed through the crowd to collect it.

A man in a uniform shirt and uniform trousers, with a gun, tapped me on the shoulder at the bar. He was in his sixties, perhaps, with a square, dark head and a neatly kept body.

"Captain Mello asked to see you," he said. I couldn't make out his own name; he muttered it. "I'm at your disposal."

"I don't understand."

"Captain Mello wanted me to explain about your father."

The music was loud, slippery stuff, old wailing tunes and a steady beat behind it; between Anna and me, the square began to roll and shift with dancing.

"But I'm here with my wife."

The man shrugged his enormous shoulders.

I climbed into his car. "I never knew about my father," I said. "He never talked about Portugal much. He talked about history, about the Templars and the Moors and all that. He just never talked about his own history."

"Difficult times," said the cop, who concentrated on driving.

"He left in 1953," I said. "During the dictatorship."

"The governor," the cop said. "He liked to be called *O Governante*."

"I always wondered what made my father leave." I picked at that sore without even meaning to.

"Listen," said the cop. "People left. That's how the economy worked. We built the roads in France and the houses in Switzerland and the sewers in Germany. We sent money home. That's how it was."

"I understand that."

"Then why do you want so many answers?"

"Someone defaced my father's grave. I wanted to know why."

"You sure you want to know?"

He had passed through Vila Nova to the outskirts, where tired buildings lined the road, white walls were streaked black with mold. He stopped the car outside one of them, a long block like a barracks with bars at the windows. There was no glass left in the windows, I could see.

"What is this?" I asked.

"Captain Mello asked me to show you something. He said it would be easier during the *festa*—nobody here. Then he wondered if you would come for a drink."

"I thought this was official business—"

"Listen," said the cop. "You wanted answers. Mello wants you to get them. Come on."

The door was padlocked shut until the cop opened it.

I was entering a dark, empty building with an armed cop whose name I did not know, but who said he was from Mello. I thought this very clearly as I stood at the start of a dim corridor. But some threshold had changed in me over the past weeks. This was not melodrama. It was the only way in which a mystery like my father could possibly be resolved.

The cop bustled down the corridor. There were broken doors into small rooms on either side.

"We're going down," he said. "It doesn't always smell good."

There was a wide, almost ornamental staircase in the middle of this functional heap of a building: azulejos of cherubim and Justice, of country scenes and dizzy-looking sheep and an ominous, radiant eye. The lights were so dim I caught only fragments of shining images on the tiles.

We started down the stairs.

Out of the basement came a smell of rotted meat, damp, something like lichen growing on the damp. It didn't smell empty, though.

The cop snapped on a light in a square, whitewashed room. The light was so much brighter than the rest that I thought for a moment the room was immaculate. Then I realized the floor was broken concrete, the walls cracked from each other at the corners, and there were the prints of rat paws on the walls, like handprints of a child.

"Mello said you should see this," the cop said. "I'm to tell you what I saw here."

"This was a police barracks?" I said. "Some sort of police place?"

"PVDE," the cop said. "*Política de Vigilância e de Defesa do Estado.* Then it was PIDE after the German war: *Policia Internacional e de Defesa do Estado.*"

"Defense of the State," I said.

"I don't know English," the cop said. "Well, I don't like this any more than you do, you know. I don't want to be back here."

He stood in the center of the room.

"Hooks," he said. "Up there. This pillar"—he pointed to a tree trunk—"was always here. You could tie a man up neatly. Arms behind, always. Rope around the knees. Then the arms could go up behind the neck.

"The electricity," he said, "was over there. Several outlets. They had their own generator."

"I see."

"They had other techniques, of course. They had what they called the 'camp of slow death' in the colonies. They could keep you in jail forever, just in case. But it all came down to the threat of this room. This kind of room. This is just the local version, the subsidiary room."

"For torture," I said.

"Of course."

"My father was here?"

But the cop was patrolling the walls now, as though he wanted to stay as far away as he could from the responsibility at the center of an otherwise blank room: the outlets, the pillar, the hooks.

"They used to like asking why the prisoner didn't defend himself," he said. "They thought that meant he wasn't any kind of a man, and they said so." His voice dropped. "This wasn't even the worst. They had hutches, too: dark, damp. You didn't get fed often. You stayed there, cramped up and shitting yourself, week in, week out."

I said, "I suppose—"

"You didn't want to know all this, did you? It's a bit of inglorious history. Well, you asked. You're being told."

"Was my father here?"

"Yes," said the cop. He spat.

"He was a prisoner?"

The cop said, "No."

I brought myself to say this with great difficulty, trying to get the words past a protective guard of memories of all my father's kindness and gentleness and propriety. I said, "He was a policeman?"

"No, no, no. You don't get it, do you?"

"You don't explain."

"Listen. It was better before the world war. The PVDE and the PIDE and all the rest of them, half the time they didn't know what they were doing. They'd forget to take people's pictures. They weren't good at taking fingerprints or keeping files straight. Amateur night. Then they had more contact with the experts—German experts from the Gestapo, mostly—and they got better. They learned to hurt people seriously. They started using sound torture instead of just whips and sticks and water."

The blankness of the room was suddenly appalling, like a void in what I understood of the world. Worse, I could not quite imagine what had happened there. We've softened the stuff of brutality into sadomasochistic chic, a jokey whipping on a music video; so we can't catch the desperation that salted the real pain. I can't, anyway.

"You've seen enough?" the cop said.

"Yes," I said. I wanted to be able to imagine and sympathize with those who had suffered there—those who must be right, because their righteousness was defined by bruises, scars, and even death, who fit the criteria for proper martyrs. I couldn't. I'd been too comfortable.

The lights went off and the darkness seemed to fill up the empty room. We were almost running by the end of the upstairs corridor. I could smell old dirt on my shoes.

"Mello's expecting you, now," the cop said.

≡

In the middle of the dancing, Anna stood about puzzled. I should have come back. I should have brought bottles of water. I should be out on the square now, turning with her in that same tight box step the older people performed with such startling energy.

The night was down completely. The light had a kind of glamour against black sky and the thin sickle of the moon. The square was parceled out between the generations, between widows and hopefuls, and people were flooding in from the side streets, laughing and shouting, everyone out in the night. Children danced between the taller bodies, in their own low world.

She saw all this, saw backs of half-familiar heads, thought she knew Arturo from the village but could never quite reach him through the crowd. She stood about the bar, where the men jostled amiably for beer and wine.

She came up against Hart's back as he stood talking to Maria.

"Where's John?" she asked. "Where is he?"

Hart said, "He's with you, isn't he?"

"I haven't seen him for a half-hour. He went to the bar and he never came back."

Maria said, "I expect he's talking." She says she had no high expectation of men's manners on party nights. But she agrees that Anna was alarmed.

"He's got away from both of us," Hart said. Anna looked furious at this assumed complicity, but she didn't argue.

Hart broke out across the square, being tall enough and broad enough to divide the crowd and see past them. Anna went back to the bar and tried to ask people, in a kind of proto-Romance she based on half-remembered Italian, if they'd seen me.

Maria says Anna couldn't find the words to describe me; so Maria tried to help.

≡

Mello's house lay at the end of a straight, narrow driveway that must once have been the road to a farmhouse, but now was hemmed in with boxes of apartments on both sides. It was a villa, with neat, low-growing flowers. Doors at the side of the house opened directly into a cluttered living room: papers, low lights, walls of colonial souvenirs.

"Good evening," Senhora Mello said. She was a rather distinguished woman, but she spoke in the manner of a tape, as though she had memorized just two words of English and everything about them: "Good eve, en, ing."

Mello sent her away. I meant to be shocked by the abruptness of his manners. Instead, I was glad to be getting on with things.

He led me into a study, and brought out a decanter. The room smelled deeply of cedar oil, almost enough to save me from the dirt and body smells of the barracks.

"I'm very sorry," he said.

"I don't understand."

"They have painted the date on your father's grave again. I don't know why people are so unwilling to forget—"

The wine was too sweet and the cold did not save it.

"It could be anybody," he said. "Children. Toxicodependents. Perhaps they use the graveyard to take drugs."

"But they keep painting the same date."

There was a brief silence.

"Your father's tomb is different," Mello said. "It is visible." He sipped his wine rather carefully, as though he found it slightly distasteful. "These days, people don't accept that kind of difference. They don't respect it."

Senhora Mello brought in a fresh cheese like dimpled milk, small black olives, a cut *broa*, salt and pepper. She went away immediately.

"You saw the driveway coming in," Mello said. "You saw all those blocks on either side. They don't respect the privacy of a quinta any longer. Everything has changed."

"This must have been very beautiful, very peaceful before the blocks were built."

Mello shrugged. "It was my father's house, too. In the middle of the town, a farm. Such a thing could not survive forever." He seemed a little resigned, a little angry: a man who'd clearly risen for many decades in a bureaucratic continuum, who was suspicious of the new permissions and possibilities. God help me, I thought this made him a reactionary, even a fascist, attached to the same brutal past he had gone to such trouble to show me.

I wanted to get to the point. I didn't dare.

"You don't think of moving out into the country?" I asked, politely.

"Nobody moved into the country in my day. You didn't buy land any more than you bought a new child. That's changed, too.

"The fresh cheese," he said, "is very good. It's not dangerous like they say nowadays. The goats are all vaccinated."

"And my father?" I said.

Mello put pepper and salt on the fresh cheese and took a fork to it. "Your father," he said, with the air of someone marking time before making a presentation.

"My father loved this place. He taught me Portuguese history." I'd begun to sound like a defender to a jury. "But," I said, "he never told me about himself."

"And you think—?"

"I don't know what to think. The house was a surprise, and the grave. As though he came back here and yet he wanted to separate himself from everyone."

Mello said, "The *emigrantes* often do. They go away, they make money, they want something that shows all that time and effort was worthwhile."

"He boasted too much," I said. I had said it out loud at last. "He didn't need that grave. He was telling people something."

Mello got up and brought an envelope from a crowded rolltop desk. He said, "I can just give you this."

I took the envelope. I didn't have a pocket for it, so it was stained with sweat by the time I got home.

=

Anna said, "Where the hell did you go?"

Hart said, "Where were you? You just disappeared."

I said, "I don't want to talk about it. Maybe I can get a taxi back to the house."

"All the taxi drivers are out dancing," Maria said.

"Then someone come with me. That way you can bring the car back later. I don't want to spoil the evening."

Anna said, "I'm coming with you."

Hart said, "Will you be all right?"

"I was only away an hour," I said. It was flattering, almost like being loved too much, to see how my absence unnerved them both.

When we closed the house door, you could cut the quiet in Formentina. Dogs stopped fretting. Cicadas and frogs were subdued, a chatter in the quiet of the night and not their usual bright song.

We heard plates smashing in a house in the village, then something metal—a pot, perhaps—rolling on tile. The sound of the accident filled up all the quiet. It made Anna whisper for a while.

"Why did Mello want you?"

"I haven't worked it out. He wanted me to read some papers."

I made myself a drink and opened the windows to get a breeze moving. The air was dusty and I thought I smelled smoke.

Anna didn't even suggest I read the papers to her. She went to the verandah and sat there in cool shade from the moonlight.

I would have liked a fight, something to stall the moment of discovering what Mello had to tell me. Instead, the best I could do was to fuss over finding a knife to open the envelope, not a perfect one I would blunt on paper, but a rough one. The edge I left was jagged.

I pulled out two sheets of flimsy paper, one headed with the name of the restaurant where my father had worked and signed by my father, one a carbon copy of Mello's reply.

I was sure I wouldn't know quite enough Portuguese to read an official letter. There'd be euphemism, euphuism, jargon, and code. So I went to get a dictionary even before I unfolded the papers fully.

My father in a blank white room with a hook, electric power, and a pillar. He was not a policeman. He was not being tortured. So what was he, and when and why was he there? He was a riddle in a box.

I couldn't stall anymore.

"Most Excellent Senhor Mello," my father began, with conventional respect, the kind banks give customers on the monthly statement. Then his full name was typed out on a separate line, centered and underlined.

"You may remember me from our days in Portugal, of which I hold such *saudade* . . ." my father wrote.

I knew this word *"saudade"*: the consuming sense of loss, the sweetness of nostalgia, and raw longing all bundled up in two syllables.

I left for London in 1953, as you know. I made my career and my life here, as best I could. Now I am an old man, and considering a return to my own country, to be myself again, to have a Portuguese house. Everything has changed, of course. I have changed. The country has changed. Everything is free and democratic now. I would be very grateful for your opinion on my plan to return—if there might be any difficulties of any kind, if it would be wise or even possible.

I held the letter up as though I could find some marks or secret ink, some special code in the way the words were organized on the page. But there was nothing exceptional. The letter meant what it seemed to mean: that my father had asked permission to come back.

He had signed the letter in his fullest, most formal way, with all the initials embroidered. There was a reference at the top as though the office typist had pecked it out, letter by letter, puzzling over the odd accents.

I opened the second letter.

Mello had written:

All Portuguese citizens are welcome to return to the country of their birth. Much time has passed since we last saw each other and the times have changed, as you say. If you have any problems at all when you return, you must contact me. I am a policeman, above all.

And Mello, when asked, had given his permission.

In a white room where a man is being tortured, who is the man who is not the torturer, not the policeman, and not the victim? My mind rambled about all that night. It seemed my father didn't run from officialdom, as I had imagined, but then he never said that he had. Perhaps he did some accidental or deliberate service to the state of the dictator. It was something people were likely to remember after so many years and my father, who had always seemed so assured and brave, needed to ask if he would be entirely safe if he returned. Or perhaps he was worried about the old-time attitudes that were still only a scrape beneath the surface of a democratic state.

Who is the man in the white room who is not the victim and not the torturer?

I remembered: how there had been no true mourners at his funeral, how the two marble houses, one for life, one for death, seemed such a deliberate defiance of everyone around, how I had been moderately welcome—because I was a grieving son, because I was a returning *emigrante*, because it was customary—but my father was not honored.

Anna went to bed. She didn't bother to comfort or question me. She knew we were past all that.

I stood at the windows. The air was cold now, but still smelled faintly of heat and ashes. Up the hill, I could make out the shapes of the houses, a few fruit trees in between them, and sometimes the shape of an agapanthus blossom against the shine from the slate. People slept; you couldn't risk nightmares and sleeplessness with a day's work ahead. I wondered if I would ever know such powerful tiredness.

It must be like that in all small places, separated for so long from any other places, where thirty years ago you carried a pregnant woman miles on a shutter before there was a road that an ambulance could tackle. There was only one place to live, so people forgot what they needed to forget in order to protect their lives.

When my father came back to Portugal, built his big, assertive house right by the road and his flashy marble tomb for a new dynasty, he thumbed his nose at memory and its rules. He was protected, guarded and official. He didn't have to care what neighbors knew; anything they did would disrupt their own lives more than his.

But memory, one night, broke out of its cage of manners and went to the graveyard and used a spray can to erase the shape and the boast of my father's tomb. It was one thing to tolerate the living man, and quite another to tolerate his claim to be one of them, only better.

The marks could not hurt the dead. They were an affront to the living: perhaps, it crossed my mind, to Mello himself, who had such a taste for order, and such concern at the toxicodependents and the girls in short skirts.

In bed later, the same questions went past again and again, like a paper parade on a zoetrope. Once I sat up cold, thinking that I was, as a matter of fact, a long way from home, mortgaged, with a marriage kept together by frantically doing other things. Once, I started walking around the house looking for comfort.

The village outside slept on relentlessly.

At four, I was wide awake. The perfume of coffee in the dark made me think about days of expeditions, rising early to get to fish in the canal, or to catch the train on holiday to some salty resort. At five, I had reread the letters a dozen times and found no explanation I wanted to hear.

At six there was pink behind the gray skin of the sky. Birds sang.

Hunting dogs, hungry and pepper-fed, howled at some imaginary sound. Detail, a dead tree here, a high tree there, appeared in the black blur of the woods. A man was coughing.

Anna came to the door and complained softly.

≡

I brought Anna coffee in bed and some peaches cut up in a bowl.

"What do you want to do today?"

"I don't know," she said.

We still had a joint talent for setting things aside.

"We could take a picnic up into the mountains."

"It's too hot."

"There's a breeze up there. I promise."

We wrangled amiably. Finally, I said, "It's hot everywhere."

"I'd like to see something, now I'm here."

"You mean art and churches?"

"Yes, I do. Art and churches." She threw the pillow at me. "That's how I make my living, art and churches."

"We could always go to Tomar," I said.

"Yes, please," she said. "I want to share this place with you. I really do."

I knew Tomar would engage Anna: a footnote in art history, a castle and a convent, Renaissance, Manueline, with a sidelong reference in a book by Umberto Eco, paintings by Gregorio Lopes, whose name she'd think she ought to know; somewhere she'd like and find interesting.

That was not why I wanted to go.

I remembered the nights my father turned Tomar into stories, rainy nights when I kicked about under the sheets while my father talked about treasure and secrets and holy knights and codes for the whole universe cut into stone.

Sometimes, all this was quite literal, a history lesson: how the Knights Templar, bound to God, built the castle at Tomar to battle the Infidel Moors—my father liked big phrases for the villains; he understood boys very well—how the Templars rode their horses to Mass and broke away to make the castle stones run with Muslim blood. We all took sides in those days.

My father sang the Templars' poverty, their dedication to God and to war, and then his voice would go soft because he wanted me to go to sleep. But I listened relentlessly. I made the Templars into a boy's club with huge broadswords, and mystery to set the hairs up on a boy's neck. I told Anna all this on a road that stretched ahead like black glass.

"You never talk about your father now," she said.

"I can't talk about everything," I said.

I remembered watching the Templars pass in my dreams, men as huge and grim as old stones, and their faces as worn. On nights when I had more courage, I burst with them out of their plain, strong castle on a tide of faith, which was strong enough to carry me even though I did not believe in their particular God or any other; and armed with something even more powerful, for which the closest word is "anger," an old worm in the mind. I was terrified to be with them, and terrified to find it was somehow inevitable I should be there. It was what it meant to be a man.

I couldn't tell Anna.

"I used to imagine the castle," I said. "It had halls and corridors. Lots of staircases going around and around."

"Like a swashbuckler," said Anna. "Like Errol Flynn."

"Castles always looked right in the movies," I said. "Great towers. And there had to be torches flickering away." I couldn't say that I thought of the torches as the memory of the place.

"You press a stone on a grave and a secret corridor opens?"

"No," I said. "No, the grave is the library. You have to read it for clues. Then you go after some great mystery. I never could imagine what the mystery could be, what lay in the next room. I was always on the other side of the door from it."

"It was metaphysical? Or was it gold?"

"There had to be a treasure-house," I said. "The Templars kept everyone's riches in wartime, like bankers."

"I know that," she said.

But she didn't know that the old stone knights stood on perpetual guard in my mind, immortals even after their individual faces had worn quite away. Sometimes I seemed to be among them when the stones breathed for a moment and the chain mail shifted. I used to be glad to feel my father's weight still on the side of the bed.

"Straight on," Anna said, holding the map.

We came over a hill between a barracks and a supermarket and we saw Tomar. The town was washed white, and the castle, from below, was a line of strong gold riverine stone, with a huddled tower and a range of battlements as wide as the sky.

It wasn't what I expected. It wasn't a story, only a fact on the sky-line, something that could be cased and labeled like museum stuff. The tall red geraniums were pretty on the white streets, I thought. The church was fine.

Anna said, "What is it? What's bothering you?"

We both picked up a tourist sheet about the Templars and read it over coffee. Facts were listed: how the Templars fought, how the order was dissolved around 1400 and the Order of Christ formed at Tomar on its ruins; and how the caravels of the Portuguese discoverers, on their way to find Prester John and India and America, carried the cross of the Order of Christ around the world. But this was not the history my father had laid out on nights when he and his son were both hungry for a missing wife, a missing mother; the man's stuff, the core of things, the strong, gray, purposeful, ominously patient knights.

"I'd like to walk to the castle," I said.

I was a tourist, but I was actually nervous. The castle at Tomar was the one great picture I shared with my father. If he was lying about this, he lied about everything.

≡

Walking seemed like a proper, pilgrim's way up the hill. The path led behind the town hall, up green tracks and along walls of soft gray stone tangled with ivy and bougainvillea.

We stopped on the way, under an olive tree.

"My father used to dress the story up," I said.

"Fathers do."

"I'd be warm in bed and he wanted me to be grateful, so he'd make me shiver."

Anna said, "I know some ghost stories too."

"He talked about this deep, deep well where the dead ride past in procession every night. There were vaults underneath, warrens and tunnels. There was the seven-branched candlestick of Solomon's Temple, the skull of someone called Beelzebub, the Shroud from the tomb of Christ, and the Holy Grail."

I started walking again over the disorderly stones.

"You don't understand," I said.

But she wouldn't let me block her out like that.

She said, "I only ever heard the crazy stories about the Templars. The ones that wash up in literary novels. All that stuff about an androgyne devil and kissing one another on the anus and the cat and the severed head. And the secrets of Solomon's Temple. And the Masons, of course."

"I got a book on the Charing Cross Road once," I said, "about the Templars. It was in French. Apparently the Templars had secret Masters from other galaxies, and they explained absolutely everything."

Anna said, "Wouldn't it be wonderful to simplify the world like that—to understand everything all at once with just one great mistake?"

We came to the outer gate.

I was cleaning the place in my mind, taking away the long buses, true common carriers, lined against the walls, and the chatterers at the gate trying to read the opening hours out loud, and the stand selling apricots and cold water. Anna knew not to break into this odd air of reverence.

I wonder what she made of my mood. I never knew.

We went through the gate into a sunken lane of stone. The lane turned and opened suddenly onto a terrace: orange trees and blowsy pink oleander and box hedges, benches in blue and yellow tile, a view of woods. Anna was delighted, I was shocked. I couldn't see blood and chivalry for this pretty park.

You sense madness in this, don't you? Or at least irrational and obsessive feeling. But this was my only way, I truly thought, to know my father's world and see the picture we shared. I needed to know this one thing.

Tourists bustled past us, camcorders cutting the place down to screen size and details. Anna pulled out the green Michelin for her own information.

Ahead I saw the true fortress: not the castle, but a round church buttressed down to the rock, its brute defensiveness only a little disguised by the new steps and terraces around it, a tower squared off for strength and with one huge, prophetic bell hanging above it.

It was the church that my father had told me about. I stood breathless.

The tourists fussed on. I thought I heard horses wheeling nervously, held in place by figures in gray armor, metal grazing the ground, hooves and weapons. I thought I smelled horses, too: sweat and dung.

But I didn't just think this. I did hear and I did smell. I was not surrounded by ghosts, but by story, a story heard by a boy when he's half afraid of sleep, when his father domesticates terror by telling him things he already knows by heart.

"The entrance must be through the church," Anna said, turning the Michelin pages.

Cloisters of blue tile and shining orange trees. A circle of a church enclosed in a gilded lantern. Below the church, a box of plain stone and light, bare and odd.

"Umberto Eco counted the steps," Anna said brightly. "For *Foucault's Pendulum*. He seemed to think the number mattered."

On the outer walls, stone flourished around windows, cut into sea stuff, coral and cables and astrolabes, then artichokes, then angels in armor, held up by an old bearded man and reaching up to a heaven of square crosses and battlements—built later, Anna told me from the guide, like the Renaissance cloisters and the aqueduct that stepped into the convent like a parade, and the buff and white hospital wings, all added to this core of my father's particular meaning.

"I think places like this are like Tarot cards," Anna said. "They were just playing cards to start with, then people forgot how to play and now they think the Tarot is mysterious. They'll tell fortunes by bus tickets next century."

Now I know the backsides of monuments very well, the bits that fail to fit; the Museum was full of them, a mad storehouse of things with the order and sense of the public galleries as a facade. I wanted to know what was private here.

"You want to see the rest?" I said to Anna.

She said, "Of course. It's extraordinary."

"I mean the rest that the public can't see," I said. "I have my Museum credentials. It's worth a try."

The women at the door made phone calls, and asked us to wait. We sat on the rails by the Charola, the great round and domed church, looking in on still gray light and the scaffolding that reached to the roof with broad stairs and wide decks and a sense of permanence.

The tourists paid and passed, a straggle speaking low out of awe at the oldness, the gold of the stone, the oddness of the place.

After twenty minutes or so, a man in his twenties rushed out of a stone doorway, said, "Mr. Costa, Mr. Costa" as though he was embarrassed not to have been there to greet the distinguished visitor, and introduced himself as "Manoel. Your guide."

I stood up and stretched.

"We can begin," Manoel said, "in the Charola."

≡

We crossed the ropes, stood inside the dome of the church. Manoel pointed out the single great pipe left from a stolen organ, the walls where once there had been paintings on wood, taken off for the glory and convenience of Lisbon clerks. He showed the spiky, gilded wood, the statues, the almost Byzantine line of the faint paintings on the wall. But my eye kept drifting upward to where the decks of the scaffolding hid the top of the dome.

Manoel noticed. "This way," he said.

We climbed on the kind of settled wood that sits inside church towers and holds bells. This structure, grand and solid, was supposed to be temporary, but it filled the view and redefined both light and space inside the dome. We reached a deck that ran all around the Charola, wall to wall, which was roofed in turn by yet another deck. We were climbing through attics of old air, light that was pale gold from the reflection of the timbers. The stairs cut into one another, branched off, sometimes divided into ceremonial pairs.

Finally, we came out inside the top of the dome. The scaffolding reduced it to a kind of circular, whitewashed corridor, suspended just under the sunlight of the top clerestory windows. There were tables set with brushes, pots, plaster knives.

"Nobody has seen this," Manoel said, knowing just what I would like to hear.

I expected the crack of beams under the weight of someone working, but all I heard was my breathing, Anna's breathing, a few ragged pigeons flapping at the windows, the slightest sound of the scaffold easing and settling in its frame of old stone. Manoel stood waiting.

Anna said, "But I don't know anything about all this."

We followed Manoel around the corner where the whitewash had been carved away from the wall.

I saw a devil on a pillar: only an attendant devil, but standing on a dog's hind feet with the nipples of a sow and the knowing face of a scavenger. We turned, Anna and I together. We saw Christ being beaten, the image so huge that we were caught up against open, staring eyes. We turned again, to a wall where a palace was faintly outlined and a knot of short, violent soldiers, and a virtuous face whose body had been ruined under the whitewash. It seemed strange the devil had done so well all these centuries.

"The Passion of Christ," Manoel said. "The pictures must continue around the dome."

"But who'd have seen them?" I said.

"They didn't have to be seen," Manoel said. "They were for the glory of God."

"They're extraordinary," Anna said. There was some greediness in her voice: a discovery, unknown frescoes, unpublished, more evidence perhaps of Italianate influence on Portuguese art, or, better yet, some independent sort of genius, a new Giotto, maybe two. She loved to be free of the classroom kind of questions, her students' passion for issues, not pictures, and facts that could be looked up in encyclopedias.

"This is from the time of the Order of Christ," Manoel said.

"Oh. Oh, of course," I said.

I imagined: some secret worshipper up so dizzyingly high with paints and ladders, putting these images onto new plaster. For I was used to frescoes that, being painted fast, held decorative masses stenciled on the wall, quick and sunlit effects, a bit of individuality added later. These had something quite different: an insistent, personal sense of pain.

I imagined the painter daring himself to work so high above the ground, to see the eyes of Christ in agony and the temporary triumph of a warthog devil with a thousand tits. All this would stay private for centuries because, after all the risk, his work was just vague lines and masses from the church below. So the painter worked—for what? For money, probably. For want of any other assignment. For God alone.

Anna said, "Are any of the restorers around?"

Manoel shrugged. "Sometimes there's money, sometimes there isn't," he said. "It has taken a very long time."

Anna was up against the wall, fingers tracing just above the thick whitewash.

I thought of my father's decent, practical Catholicism, nothing to extremes, nothing in particular. Then I saw the devil with the nipples, the scourge in the hands of a short, dark soldier, the graphic bigness of the dark eyes of Christ, their stare only magnified where the paint had cracked and chipped in settling.

The corridor of light between dome and platform turned claustrophobic.

"They have worked here many years," Manoel said.

But there was nobody working. The quiet was eerie. The only presence was this row of half-uncovered versions of the faith that animated the place. And I was an outsider to that faith, only confused and horrified by the devil, the whipping, the eyes.

"We should go down," Manoel said. "We have many other things to see."

I was ready, more than ready, but Anna said, "Could I look for just a minute more?" She smiled her English smile: radiance on a time switch, its purpose unconcealed.

I slipped on the first few steps going down. I was grateful to be out of the corridor of light, into the attics that followed one after another and down the last, wide staircase to the ground. I felt literally grounded: back where paintings can be classified and stored, explained and safely presented, where taxonomy takes over from impact as pity takes over from pain. I wasn't thinking clearly, you understand.

I was still on the staircase when I saw Hart beside the ticket desk.

He looked up, sharp and expectant like a dog. Anna was several minutes with the paintings, and Manoel went to help on the stairs with his elaborate chivalry, but when they reached the ropes, Hart was still there.

I'd come for something very private, something I could barely share with Anna, and there was this thief, this sociopath, this middling thing, a suspect professor. At that moment, the tables turned. I could have killed him.

≡

Hart knew that at once, noted it down. He hid the same feeling for a living—as you might say—and so he recognized it in others. Reciprocated, too. Then he went back to business: watching to see if the life of John Costa was worth stealing, if anyone would ask questions.

Manoel said, "If your friend would like to join us—"

Hart said, "That's very kind."

Anna smiled.

"We go next into the Templars' castle," Manoel said. "Please follow me."

"I don't want to spoil your visit," Hart said.

Anna said, "Of course not."

Manoel collected keys from the entrance desk, a heavy iron bunch, and unlocked a side door at the end of the last cloister. There was nothing on the other side except a narrow stone ledge that ran unguarded along the wall. The stone was shiny. We edged along, careful of broken blocks and the occasional jagged gap.

"This," Manoel was saying, "was the palace of Henry the Navigator. Are you all right, Senhora?"

The palace was ruins, marked out by archaeologists' tapes and flags. We picked and shuffled along the ledge.

Hart could have slipped and I might have been delighted to be rid of him. Whatever I was still supposed to do—guard or arrest him—it would be over.

Every time I hesitated a moment, looked out through the empty windows in the old palace wall to the woods, he'd catch up and brush against me, significantly.

Anna went forward very cautiously.

We came to a second locked door. Manoel rattled his chain of keys, selected one and got it wrong, then pushed a great bar of metal into the lock, and the door opened. We were in the tower of the castle itself.

Anna was disappointed, I could tell. This was just stones and defenses, a job lot of heritage. You had to read the books to find the battles and what they meant, and she preferred to find things by trusting her eyes. So she noticed that Hart watched me and I watched him. It was odd how alert we all were, with Manoel chattering.

Manoel, politely, pointed out the chapel: a room now suspended in a wall, the stairs long ago crumbled away. "The stores were there," he said, showing rows of practical cells. "And the wells," he said, pointing to a circular gap in the sweet grass that had colonized the castle.

Hart and I stood each side of the gap in the grass, and looked down. There was a pause of dark air, no walls to be seen, and then a pool of water. I thought the pool had shores rather than edges.

"One of the guides went down there once," Manoel said brightly.

We peered into the dark. All Hart would make out was a cave with black water, but just for a moment I saw the castle as it was in my father's stories: a place where heroes mount a strange, heroic defense of mysteries.

"What did he see?" I asked.

Manoel said, "He was on a rope, so he didn't walk around down there."

"Yes?"

"He said there seemed to be two doorways, either side of the pool. With stone across them."

Hart coughed.

"He said the stones looked almost like human figures. Like knights on guard."

I saw them breathe in my mind's eye.

Anna said, "We should get back."

Hart thought he'd found a fault line at last, between the odd sense of obsession in me and the practicality of Anna. He didn't have to be right. He only had to know that other people might have guessed the same thing, that it might not be surprising if John Costa went suddenly away on some quest of his own.

"Well," Manoel said, startled by all the sudden feeling in his audience, "there could be passageways."

Hart said, "It's almost lunchtime," and stuffed a banknote into Manoel's hand.

In the safe cloister beyond the ruins, Manoel was explaining to Anna this theory a friend of his had thought out, about water, air, fire, earth, spirit, and where their signs might lie, about the inner meanings of the coral and the artichokes. Anna listened very kindly.

Outside the Charola, in light that made us tie up our eyes, Anna took a picture: pines, tiles, architecture, and two men putting on the required smiles.

Afterward she turned to me, cold and angry for a second. "What are you doing here?" she said.

≡

Arturo sat on the steps of his house, cutting green beans.

"Women's work," he said.

"Everything all right?" I asked.

"More or less, *mais ou menos.* Everything all right with you?"

"My wife's here."

"She's Catholic?"

It was not a possible question for me, so I said nothing, and Arturo took my silence for a "yes." "Then she can get the key to the chapel from Zulmira if she wants it. Zulmira always has it."

"Thank you," I said. Then I realized I'd stepped back involuntarily while we were talking. "I'll tell her."

I did, and Anna said, "Don't men go to the chapel?"

"I think praying is women's work," I said.

"What's men's work, then?"

"Going away to France to make money so women don't starve," I said. "Being alone there and waiting."

"That old man did that?"

"He didn't even tell his wife. She got a postcard a week after he got to Bordeaux."

"And she was left alone."

"Alone with the children. You always think life can be made fair, don't you? Balanced somehow. Well, it can't always. He suffered, she suffered, the children suffered. But they ate."

"That makes it all right?"

I walked away.

"That makes it all right?" she said again.

I still didn't turn.

"What makes you think I don't know about pain. You think I just fake it, is that it?"

"No," I said. "No, of course I don't. But that's you and this is Arturo in a village called Formentina. There aren't always the same rules and the same manners for everyone everywhere."

"I know that," she said, following me. "Are you sorry I came?"

"I was going to take you out to dinner. A good dinner. Somewhere you'd like."

"So I go away with good memories?"

"It's a start."

She put her arms around my waist.

When we were driving up the mountain for a breeze, she said suddenly, "The Museum are being very understanding."

I said, "I suppose they are."

She noticed how I accelerated at once.

≡

Maria changed the rules for Hart. He never did local things, met settled people who saw inconsistencies; he was a traveler. He would never have asked Maria to the *festa*, but she asked him.

Even then, he only thought she might be lonely. He didn't reckon loneliness, except as a failure of planning that meant he should move on. He liked moving on. It saved him from a whole garden of tempting fallacies, like the notion that nothing is true until it is shared. And now he was set in someone else's identity, and alarmingly close to thinking the only way to save his self was to share the special souvenir edition of his past doings with someone else.

Also, he would have liked someone to fight with. He got nostalgic for raised voices and clear diction.

=

Anna, at the kitchen table, cut an onion. The knife slid off its wet shine, not like the soft, docile onions out of a supermarket at home. She set chickens on a tin dish, sparse and bony birds you could imagine on the run, unlike the plump, settled pillows she was used to buying. The tomatoes, too, were woody and green; they had a dusty redness close to their hearts.

She turned on the stove. The bottled gas seethed for a minute and settled to a low burn, and then went out. She propped the door open and tried again. This time, she burned her fingers on the metal of the door, but the stove stayed lit.

The phone rang, my cell phone. It was bothersome and persistent like all phones, but it was faint and she couldn't quite place where I had left it. Her hands were greasy from handling the chicken skin. She washed them, half hoping the phone would simply stop, but it didn't. She found it in the pocket of my jacket.

"My name's Mello. Perhaps your husband will call me."

"Yes. Of course. I remember. Your number—"

There was no pad and pencil, of course. There was a paperback with a heavy, laminated cover and she scratched the number into the shine with her fingernail.

She opened the door and stood out in the still air. Over where she thought the sea must lie, very distant, the sky had turned to a band of sepia. The afternoon heat even felt like a fire. She couldn't think why she had decided to cook on a day like this, in a place like this.

She went walking, slipping from one patch of shade to another, going slowly up the steps. The blackberries were almost ripe, she saw. There were bushes of spiky rosemary up against a drystone wall. She felt breathless in the dry heat. She knew she'd feel a hard ball of pain behind her eyes very soon.

She picked rosemary. The stems wouldn't break at first; they were too woody and resinous. She took tiny sprigs from around the curious dead-colored flowers, sprigs that could almost be fir or pine. She crushed them between her fingers and then she buried her face in her hands and the smell of sharp, medicinal oil, a concentrate of the rosemary she knew from cooler places.

A car droned down the curves of the mountain.

She realized suddenly that she had left the stove burning. She sprinted the steps and almost fell into the kitchen, tested the air with her hand as she walked in. She forced the rosemary sprigs into the cavities of the chickens, stuffed the tray into the hot oven and smelled her hands again: fat and medicine. The smell was in her mouth, too.

She pulled the shutters tight and sat in the dark living room. Some spare feathers on the birds were singeing in the oven, sharp as vinegar on the air, before the full, practical smell of skin and flesh cooking. The singeing smell was all right, she told herself. It was really all right.

I brought back water from the spring and carried the boxy five-liter jars into the kitchen. I called her name, but she didn't have anything to say. I put on the light in the living room.

"Oh," I said, "there you are. How are you?"

She went into the bathroom and ran water from the tap. But she couldn't drink the water, she remembered, and in case she had any doubts, it ran stained like coffee. She reached down for a bottle of the water from the spring, but it was empty. She took the prescription jar of painkillers and for a moment she thought she'd never be able to calm this sense that she was being reduced by pain to someone incompetent, without ordinary sensation, fumbling, even old.

I handed her a glass of clean water. She took the pills. I said, "Come and lie down. Please."

"You're supposed to ring someone called Mello," she said. "The number's on your book."

"On the book?"

"I scratched it."

She must have heard me on the phone, and wondered about my

distinct, official voice. "I'll see him this evening," I said. "I'll be glad to help."

≡

I knocked on the door exactly like a policeman: six loud knocks expecting instant attention.

"I think we ought to have a talk," I said.

He sat across the table, his hands folded like a steeple.

"You won't object if I have a look around," I said, without much of an interrogative rise at the end of the sentence.

"Hey," Hart said. He clearly thought he had the upper hand.

"I've been very patient," I said. "I've waited weeks. I thought you understood that I will not go away until we've recovered the Museum material."

Hart said, "What material was that?"

He had a reasonable grudge: being treated like some minor sneak thief, a professor carting off the odd Coptic portrait, Greek leg, bit of gold, when really he had stolen much more. He was something that slipped around in people's sexiest fears, if only they knew. And to be threatened in this amateur, bureaucrat's way, told what to do on pain of upsetting the way things are, when he was headline stuff and far more dangerous: that hurt.

This time, I did have an advantage. "The police wanted to know," I said, "if you knew a man called Martin Arkenhout?"

He paused only a couple of beats, but it was jarring, like a late woodwind in a bit of Bach. He got up and offered wine.

I couldn't know what I had said. I took the wine.

"Mello couldn't reach you on the phone," I said. "Then Anna sent me up. To see if you'd like to come down to dinner. She's cooking."

Hart was astonished. We were going to be so perfectly mannerly, so social, foreigners allied in a strange land, even though what brought us together was some crime. Sherry might be offered, might be taken. Probably we'd talk about Tomar since that was virtually all the three of us had in common.

"What exactly do you expect me to give you?" Hart asked. I thought he might be bargaining.

"There are at least fifteen images missing," I said. "I want them all in perfect condition. If any of them have been sold, I want to know where to find them—exactly where to find them, not just a dealer's name. If any of them have been damaged or destroyed, then there's no deal."

"And then?"

"Nothing after that. I go back to London, you do what you like. I'm not a policeman."

"What's Anna cooking?"

"She's roasting chicken. With herbs," I said.

"What time, then?"

I said, "Nine o'clock." From the door I added, "Let's have everything settled by then."

≡

I didn't go home. I hung in the shade, with a view of his windows. I learned that from Hart, the way he sometimes left silence open for other people to fill.

I didn't understand what I was seeing.

He was tearing open cases, one by one, emptying them in a muddle of shirts and shoes and plastic laundry bags on the floor.

He opened the black-bound notebooks Hart had bought in Amsterdam, tried to read the writing that fluttered like the line on some medical gauge. He examined books that had been butchered and digested, pages turned down, lines marked, notes spiraling around someone else's text like those snail's trails that freaks leave on library books; and he checked bundles of photographic prints of paintings and etchings, very new and shiny. He must have packed too few objects when he cleared Hart's house. He assumed the objects had been rented along with the house. He never guessed.

He now knew someone had made the connection properly: from Arkenhout to Hart. They would be checking along the chain for missing persons, sudden moves. There would be evidence soon; you could never clean all the blood, or be sure that all the cuts of a body would stay separate and nameless. The cleverness in what he did had been the lack of connections, and now that was all over.

I saw panic in his face.

Martin Arkenhout was back; that's how he explained it later. Arkenhout claimed Hart back so thoroughly he could hardly breathe. He settled a discontinuity of ten years as though it did not matter at all, opened up tracks he thought were hidden, and connections as subtle and chaotic as all those mathematical headlines about how the fall of a leaf in a distant galaxy can spoil your billiards shot at home. It was Arkenhout he had killed in Florida, Arkenhout who lumbered about in his memory, the thing that must at all costs be repressed and put away. Now the name was in the air again, and Arkenhout was like a cartoon ghost, a graveyard joke.

He could be laid to rest if my life was available for taking; but it couldn't be taken yet. Meantime, there was this dead life of Hart's to inhabit.

Martin had always been the winner, the man who knew how to reinvent himself perpetually, Faust with no need for some cramping contract with any passing devil. He did what other men just dream of doing, which is to change all the incidentals and take with him, life after life, only what's essential.

Until that moment, he had never doubted that there was something essential.

I lost him for a moment under the level of the windowsills.

He upended a small attaché case out of which fell neat, clear plastic envelopes of insurance documents, bank statements, letters, papers to show at a frontier. It seemed odd that Hart carried so much in a Europe without frontiers, as though in his mind he were adventuring off to some deep-woods Colombian silver mine or a dubious island or a country with a serious regime.

I couldn't tell what he was hunting. The papers shuffled over one another, skidded over the plastic envelopes; he made chaos around the room. But I had no notion, then, that he even needed to hunt for anything, or why I could see panic on his face.

He did tell me, later. Christopher Hart seemed alive and loose in that long, white Portuguese house: a dissembler, a twister, who was hiding things from this second Hart, his heir, himself.

Hart had one hefty blue Vulcanite suitcase on wheels, a kind of cabin trunk, called Globetrotter. He fumbled the irregular surface of its bottom, wondering if there could be something false. One of the white inside straps came away.

He started laughing.

He knew then he'd taken Hart's small but perfectly formed credit and left behind a physical fortune. He could surely have played Hart well enough to sell the pictures. He could have had money of his own, for once, which would not run out like other people's credit runs out when people start asking questions. The money could have bought him a life of his own.

He went to the verandah. The sun had begun to go down, and the mass of the pine woods was a little gold, a little pink: decorator calm. It was an ordinary show, seen from an ordinary kind of place. He was ordinary, too, caught now in a name and a history like everyone else.

He went back to the Globetrotter, with a knife. He levered up the bottom of the case, under the lining.

Nothing.

He couldn't be Hart, he decided. He couldn't satisfy this John Costa and produce the stolen paintings; so being Hart meant perpetual trouble.

If he was John Costa, though, then the link between him and Arkenhout and Hart was broken for good. He'd leave behind a body and a name that could carry all his crimes and adventures.

He told me he had never thought about a death this way before: as something satisfying, not just necessary.

≡

The next days were like dinner that night: a kind of dance, two people transfixed with each other, life and death, a third cutting in. Sometimes it was Hart who felt like the intruder, he says. Sometimes it was Anna. She says she could not calculate what kind of story was happening between Hart and me. We all had business that politeness forbade us mentioning, let alone finishing: a theft, a foundering marriage, the possibility of murder.

Hart's sleep broke up, so he told Maria later, on dreams—dreams that the summer had been brutal in Holland, too, and the water in the River Vecht was running low. He knew it was the Vecht from the bends, the chestnuts, the mansions, and the constant river traffic: small, brisk boats between the lawns.

His mother sat at a lock, drinking tea. The lock opened and a long boat edged in. The gates shut, and the water drained. But the water wouldn't stop draining until the floor of the lock was shining mud.

His mother was in the lock, trying to shift the boat with her shoulders. She couldn't move it. Her feet slipped. She was in the mud, her face up against something bare and white. She looked eye to eye into the hollows of a skull.

She said out loud, "Martin, are you all right, Martin?"

≡

This happened, but it was not Mrs. Arkenhout who made the discovery. It was a boy called Piet, eleven years old, son of an artists' union official and a teacher, who was helping on the lock and moved much faster than the old, official lockkeeper. He pulled out the skull, and said he wanted to keep it because it had wounds, and must be a famous warrior, probably Krull or Conan.

The police wouldn't listen to him. Instead, they started to run tests.

Six

Maria came to see Hart in the afternoon.

"The police have been asking about you. Again," she said.

"I don't know why."

"Checking on foreigners, maybe."

"They never check. Do they?"

She'd invented him already for the afternoon: fugitive in hideaway, risk of death. She put down a loaf on the kitchen table and stood there, slight and fragile in her summer skirt. "You ought to keep the shutters closed," she said. "People will know you're here."

He couldn't complain. His life, all his lives, depended on just this: being what people expected him to be.

She went about checking doors, closing shutters, drawing curtains in the dark. The light left was the shine on skin, the bar of bright wood under the front door, a few prickles of light where the slats in the wood ceiling stood proud of one another.

She came up to him in the doorway. She undid his shirt, began to tug it off, and then she threw herself against him as though she could force into this moment all the desperate, big-screen passion in all the cinema houses of the world, and she was smiling. Then she kissed him, forcefully.

He knew the cues, too. He had his hands high under her skirt, moving fast, no need for persuasion; she'd imagined them in a film noir, lost souls throwing themselves on this last fire. The choreography failed only at the usual moments, tucking out of pants, standing clear of jeans. Then bodies took over from the scenario, and there wasn't time or life to lose—him standing, her legs around him, her whole weight, it seemed, concentrated on bringing him as deeply as possible into her.

Their skin was slick and hot, their breath desperate. It was all as urgent, as proper for a condemned man's last night, as she could stage.

Then she collected her clothes.

"I just wanted you to know about the police," she said. "So they can't surprise you."

For a moment he wasn't sure if this, too, was part of the matinee story they had just played.

≡

My house acquired a routine in those days. It had been my cell, a refuge, a place without associations like a hotel room; but Anna's presence filled it with our shared life. The arrangement of chairs mattered now; it defined how we would talk in the evening. The bed was aired and crisply made.

And food was needed. The markets in Vila Nova were on Wednesday and Saturday. Anna had this vision of Provence laid out on tables from a glossy magazine: a dozen goat cheeses, maybe, and good leaves for salad.

We negotiated our way past the legless beggar, the cake seller, the flower persons, and the butcher shops into the market hall: narrow ways between narrow tables, women standing over bunches of greens, plastic sacks of eggs or white or scarlet or dark-brown beans, furred peaches, forests of high orange montbretia, resigned cilantro, and onions wet with juice. Beyond the women's territory were the cheese stalls, the boards of salt cod, the sausages strung on poles, the man who sold young chickens, the professional greengrocers with their sad green peppers and kiwifruit and nectarines from Spain.

The hall was practical enough: supplies of watercress or bacon, grainy apples or potatoes. But it was also medieval in its crowded insistence, in the way the women called you over, in the small heaps of what had flowered or fruited that morning all set out to be changed into cash. You could imagine you should be sliding on straw or mud, instead of civic concrete.

I said, "What do you need?"

"Ham. *Presunto.* Maybe some fish."

There were long, spiny fish, like armored eels, and cuts across some coarse, dark-fleshed creature. There was nothing entirely familiar. The sardines lay under the tables, some boxes lightly salted, some under blizzards of salt; those at least she knew. She bumped against the limits of her curiosity and her interest all at once: she wanted clean cod, filleted salmon.

I said, "We could always have chicken. We could eat somewhere."

"I want to cook fish."

So she bought *corvinho*, not entirely sure what it was, and a nubbly kind of snowpeas, and potatoes, and cheese, and peaches. She added parsley, lettuce, and some branches of dried lemon verbena to make tea. She took back specimens of the place.

I waited for her, up against the railings with the other gossiping knots of men who buried themselves in the talk and business of the place.

I saw Arturo, but not standing with the gossips. He was walking between the lines of tables, a bucket in either hand.

I knew men never come to sell in the women's zone.

People stepped to let him through because he should not be there and, besides, the market had been open two hours and the best was all gone.

He set the buckets on the table. He poured out pink, waxy potatoes that went running every which way off the narrow stone table.

The women nodded. Nobody spoke to him, though, or looked directly at him. The places on either side were empty.

I thought of him as a friend, an ally. But I didn't know how to acknowledge him, either; it was as odd for a man to be buying as selling at the tables.

Anna came out of the crowd, laden with thin blue plastic bags. I took some of them, and I walked her briskly out of the market hall.

At home she spread out the foods she had bought, as though she could read them like a map.

She laid little ambushes for me, too. "I wish I knew why you're so preoccupied," she said. And: "Did you find out anything about your father?" She said these things when I was sitting before a sunset, when I was cleaning boots, as though they might slip under my conscious guard.

Then, after a day when I said nothing in reply, she was suddenly angry: "I'm trying. Why won't you try?"

I stared at her.

"You're drifting," she said. "You don't engage with me. You don't call the Museum. It's as though London doesn't exist for you anymore."

I don't remember how I answered her. I hope I didn't say: "Don't be stupid." I expect I did.

We went to bed in the afternoon, separate sides of the bed because of the heat, so we both assumed. She broke the divide. She put out a hand and I thought she wanted me to hold it, but she wanted to touch me along the line of the spine as I lay there. Her fingers grazed my skin, made me anticipate.

"Turn over," she said.

I turned. I was hard, of course. She was smiling. But instead of falling together, instead of laughing or delighting in the moment, we were frozen with a kind of embarrassment. Desire was there all right, the usual responses; but it suddenly seemed inappropriate, almost embarrassing to take things any further, as though we'd only be passing the time.

She kissed my forehead once and lay down again, distant as though she'd still been in London, close as the length of my fingers. I got up and went to the shower and ran the brown water, hoping it would clear.

She made an elaborate fresh lemonade later, and we sat watching the valley down below: shine on the slate roofs, birds twitching between trees, the run of the stream.

I said, for want of anything else I could bring myself to say, "It's funny Arturo was in the market. I haven't seen Zulmira, either."

She nodded.

We both knew that afternoon was something more than a bad day in bed, naturally repaired in the next easy night. It wasn't desire that had failed us. It was connection.

≡

"You could go to see them," Anna said. "Maybe you'd better go to see them."

So I climbed the steps to Zulmira and Arturo's house, knocked on their metal gates, then tried the gates and walked through into the courtyard. It was an open space, with mounds for marigolds and lettuce, wood stacked under steading, rooms on two sides up concrete stairs, and animals: a pig parked in a corner, rabbits in mesh cages, a convoy of chickens picking at the world, and a kid springing at the end of a rope and halter. Geraniums went striving up one wall.

I called, "Zulmira? Arturo?"

Arturo came out of the shadow on the verandah. "Senhor João," he said.

"Everything all right? *Tudo bem?*"

Arturo said, unconvincingly, *"Tudo bem."*

"Really?"

He shook his head a little. "If you could drive me, me and Zulmira, into the town. I think we should go to the little hospital in Vila Nova."

"Zulmira's sick now?"

"I'll bring her down."

I said, "Can I help?"

But he had gone back into the shadow, and I was half-blind from the brilliance of the sun.

Anna, too, wanted to help. She wanted it even more than she wanted me occupied, although she was treating me now with the elaborate kindness you show to someone in mourning.

"There," she said. "There they are."

Arturo was coming down the steps, Zulmira at his side. I knew how Arturo's legs could sometimes fail him, but today he stared forward as though he was concentrating all his will on simply moving down. Zulmira seemed to hang on his neck. There were dark patches under her eyes, like old blood under the skin, and she stumbled, feet dragging on the stones.

I wanted to help. Anna wanted to help. We have the same instincts in such different forms: Anna is more sure that she can intervene in lives, while I was born to be a bureaucrat and find objections. But we are both kind, always.

Arturo didn't acknowledge me. He kept walking with Zulmira's arm around his neck. I was so used to her as a strong presence in the fields, chasing down a goat, cutting greens, picking at the ground with a hoe, that the slackness of her arm shocked me.

There must have been some sense of occasion, because Hart was watching from above. He caught my eye. He shrugged. The usual afternoon stillness seemed to weigh on us all.

Arturo and Zulmira reached the road. Arturo held Zulmira with one hand, and opened my car with the other; she couldn't stand. He was using all the old, stored strength in his body to keep her from tipping down to the ground.

He packed her into the backseat of the car. You never lock cars in villages where everyone watches out for everyone else.

Anna said, "You'd better go and help."

I went scrambling down the hill.

Arturo sat in the passenger seat. I clambered into the car, started the engine, and looked back to check the traffic.

Zulmira sat with her head tilted back, her arms loose and slack. I saw that her eyes had rolled up in her head.

I recognized the smell, at last: a spoiled version of sweat and flesh, overlaid with sweet, cheap soap. Zulmira was dead.

=

Nobody expected the police reaction. The kindly, courteous Mello was abrupt; he insisted that Arturo had concealed a death, found suspicious circumstances, had him taken down to the prison in the city for the duration of the investigation even though the man could walk only when he exercised all his will. The police occupied the village, checking everything and everyone; people came in from the fields to find their identification cards. Everyone was a material witness, quarantined in the village.

I love Anna's outrage. She would have thrown herself between the police and the women if she could. But she had no Portuguese, and she could never quite work out the exact wrongs being done around her, so her anger stayed general and ineffectual. She hated that.

She made her apologies to the college. I made my apologies to the deputy director, explaining I was held in Portugal for reasons beyond my control.

"You do have an eventful life," the deputy director said.

I thought the world could not close down on us any more. It was Anna and I, rattling about in the box of our house, and Hart always watching. He sniffed out tears and arguments, and studied them. He tried to measure the distance between us.

I missed talking about the bees with Arturo, or the city or the dust.

Formentina, which seemed such a perfect backdrop for a life, was beginning to spoil, the way a drawing crumbles or glaze crazes over paint, or vandals cut up something as lovely as the Liber Principis. But there wasn't any room for my usual bright, righteous anger at such a change. Arturo had done nothing wrong. Zulmira certainly hadn't. Hart hadn't changed the place; I would never have found it without him.

Anna wanted to go. She said so once or twice. She asked why I wouldn't go talk to my friend Captain Mello, to see when the witnesses could leave.

I found Mello at the GNR barracks.

"I do apologize," Mello said. "We've had to take rather extraordinary measures. You understand."

"I just understand that my wife needs—"

"Your Professor Hart," Mello said. "He's of interest to us. There's another inquiry. But I expect you guessed that."

"Indeed."

"You don't need to tell me why you're interested in Hart. I have a good idea. The Dutch police talked to the Rijksmuseum people, that sort of thing."

His sentences worked like interrogation, so I tried very carefully to show no reaction at all.

"Listen," he said. "This other inquiry is extremely serious. You should know that. I can't say much else. I've said too much already." He talked stage talk out of some Victorian gaslight story, because that was the English he knew: novelist's stuff.

"You mean you're holding Formentina so you can chase Hart? Isn't that a bit excessive?"

"It's only a day or two. This other inquiry is extremely serious."

"But my wife—"

"If we have to go over Mr. Hart's house in any case, you could happen to be there."

I stared at him.

"I'll call you," he said. "We can work this out to everyone's advantage."

≡

Maria Mattoso had never handled a criminal case, didn't usually deal with the Portuguese; but Anna persuaded her, and I supported Anna, and she went down to the prison in the city. It had once been a bishop's palace: a massive oval of wall, and all you could see from outside was a gold-and-white cupola with big glass, set about with guards. The gates could have served a palace still.

Maria Mattoso parked, presented her identity card, and walked inside. She was alarmed by the stillness of the corridor and the sense of pressed life everywhere else.

Arturo was produced, wearing an orange overall and his own, old shirt.

He said, "It is very kind of you to come."

"How are you?"

Arturo didn't try to find an answer.

"I brought you some food." Anna had insisted.

Arturo said, "I'm not hungry."

"But you will be hungry."

"I don't want to have anything they can take."

"Who takes food from you?"

Arturo said, "We're in bunks, you know. Fourteen to a room. I'm in the bottom bunk and the man above isn't clean. I can't go out."

"I know it isn't good in there."

"They have toilets but they don't work."

"Even when you're charged, you have rights. You might get bail."

"I don't know these people," Arturo said. "They're young. They mutter at night. They have marks on them."

"You don't belong here."

"But I do," Arturo said. "I have to be here."

For a moment, she was unsure how to continue. She could be the lawyer, the calculating protector. She could be Maria Mattoso, who saw a man petrified by sadness.

"This is only a technical offense," Maria said. "There's no question Zulmira died of natural causes. An undiagnosed heart condition."

"Then why am I here?"

"I don't know. You didn't hurt her."

"I cleaned her. I did my best."

"Everyone knows that."

"She should have been the one to have the tests and see the doctors. Not me."

"That's not a criminal mistake. That's the doctors' problem."

"Then why—?" But he did not bother to finish his question. He had had a whole lifetime of being handled by authority with willful indifference; he was not surprised. If he allowed himself to be angry, he would have to be angry with his whole life.

"It's going to be worse. I made it worse."

"You don't mean that."

"These men in the room," Arturo said. "I think they might be toxicodependent. They might be sick. I don't like to sleep."

He got up.

"Yesterday," he said, "they forgot to give us food."

Maria stood too. "I'll complain," she said. "I'll do what I can."

Arturo said, "It's God's will, I expect. I wish you could ask Zulmira. She knows about God's will."

Maria watched him walk off, trying to march but on shaky, compromised legs. She watched the door swing behind him and close. She smelled a little disinfectant warring with a slurry of old sweat and shit, with windows closed on a merciless day and air used by a dozen men.

I suppose Arturo lowered himself onto his bunk bed. He sat watching the sundry cracks in the wall for the tiny movements they seemed to make now his glasses were gone. The guards had nothing for the men on remand to do; they would be better off convicted, in larger cells. So Arturo planted a garden on the wall. With his bad eyes, he could see vines again, and beans on poles and the dense green of potato tops.

=

The funeral was not like the funeral of my father. The body came from the police morgue in a cheap pine box. Arturo was brought from prison, humiliated by handcuffs, unable to do anything but stand and keep back tears. The gravedigger made a scene about his fee and the proper tip before he'd lower the box between the dry clay sides of the hole.

The family of Arturo and Zulmira stood about, a little knot of people, until the coffin was covered.

Anna said, "He doesn't know she's dead."

"Of course he does."

She shook her head. "He was sleeping with her for a couple of nights. Maria told me."

I said, "The women almost never die first. You just have to count the women in black."

"So nobody worries about the women? They take the men into hospital and they don't even ask about the women."

I remembered what the nurse had said about country people when she said Zulmira should see a doctor. But even the nurse did not press the point.

The graveyard was a box of hot white walls, bright with the shine of chippings and marble, of pale stone and polished metal. We stifled there.

She shrugged. "I'd like to see your father's grave," she said.

I put a hand on her shoulder, let it slip a little. "I know you have to go soon. I wish you didn't have to go. I wish I could just come back."

"Then come back," she said. She wasn't interested in rhetoric anymore.

"I have to see this through."

"Why?" she said. "Why do you have to see this through?"

I couldn't be quite sure what I meant. My leave was up in a week, but I had police orders not to leave; that was an excuse. I watched Hart's irritating assurance, his bright-eyed chat, and I wanted to catch him out. I needed an answer to all the riddles Mello set about my father's past.

Anna found my father's grave easily, the only marble hut. The doors were already dirtied with a bit of lichen.

She said, "They put the coffin on a shelf? Like that?"

I said nothing.

"I'm sorry, I didn't mean—"

"It's a family home for the dead. I don't know who else he was expecting."

Anna waited.

"I still want to know," I said, "who he was before he went to London and who he was when he left to come back here. And whether London was just an unfortunate gap in his life."

"He loved you very much."

"He wanted me to be English."

"He wanted to protect you."

"Or he wanted to hand me off, to make me someone else's responsibility who wouldn't come back to him. I don't know."

"You can't know."

"I still wonder. I'm wondering what it means to feel at home in a place you don't know. And wondering, and wondering. And wondering why I can't feel as he felt. Don't fathers and sons come from the same place, usually, wherever they go, however they change?"

Anna said, "Come somewhere we can sit. It's very hot." She looked once more inside the tomb. She saw four shelves set back a little from the door, and a single coffin lying to the right with a small marble label. The coffin was still immaculate; you couldn't cheat on the shine and the brass like you can on boxes that will go down in the ground.

"You know as much as I do now," I said.

"I want to see his house," she said. "You could show me his house before someone else buys it."

I said, "I haven't decided to sell it."

We kicked up dust on the path between church and graveyard, live, skirling dust that stuck at the top of the mouth and pricked our eyes. Hot-weather flowers, blue paper discs, stood open at the end of green sticks along the path.

"What do you mean you haven't decided?" I expected her to sound exasperated, but her tone was flat, like a teacher sure of her authority.

"I can't decide," I said.

"So let me see it," Anna said.

We said nothing on the drive.

I parked outside my father's house. Anna stood leaning on the car and looking at the stone lions, the paired putti, the dry fountain with the tall brown rods of grass around it, the great fake chimney of field-stone and the wrought iron everywhere. The house was assorted dreams and aspirations cut up and pasted together in an ambitious muddle. A single, tough red rose, the blooms open and almost black, flourished by the wall.

"I didn't know what to expect," she said.

"He wanted all the things other people have, only bigger. I never knew that. I guess that's what all the *emigrantes* want. You have to show it was worth all the pain of going away." I opened the gate to the small front yard. "He couldn't do that in South London."

"He liked lions."

"Everyone has lions. He has plaster pineapples, too."

"And terraces—"

I fussed with the keys in my pocket. The London keys wouldn't do, nor the Museum keys. The set of light keys, the color and weight of aluminum, was for the house in Formentina.

"I don't have the keys," I said, and, as I turned to Anna, "I really thought I did have the keys. I didn't mean to leave them behind."

Anna was already up the steps, at a window, looking in on the dark, cool space, picking out the heavy chairs, the brass lamps on tables without pictures.

"I don't think he brought anything from London," I said.

"I suppose he wanted to start again."

"But he didn't bring pictures or photographs. Nothing. It's as though his whole life in London never happened."

She looked down on me. She says now she saw a man loyal and
habitual and out of his depth. She felt a great sadness because she
would have liked to hold me, but that couldn't work anymore.

≡

Women cut greens for the goats: grass, dock, lavender. Zulmira's
daughter caught the morning bus because on Thursdays she cleaned a
house in Vila Nova. Some of the village men were working day shifts
cutting eucalyptus to clear a whole hill of red clay that the tile factory
would use. The others were out on construction jobs as usual, basted
with sweat, pushing beams and stone around or taking green wood
and varnishing it so carefully it was like walking on mirrors.

I know that Arturo in his cell regretted his ordinary occupation more
than anything, the cleaning of ground, tying gold willow branches for a
fence, staking trees, sharpening something and using it until it needed
to be sharpened again. He could run through a year of occupation in a
day's imagining, but without the satisfaction of having moved, used
his muscles, been of use; and without usefulness, he lost himself.

I know this because it is my feeling, too. I was obliged, somehow, to
pin down Hart and bring back those pictures. My job, my credibility,
might depend on it, but so did my sense of self, now that so much else
had fallen away: my sense of my father, my marriage, my place. There
were consolations, of course: woods, the mountain, peace, spring
water, maybe even the dignity of labor, the cycle of seasons, everything
that was a wonder if you had a ticket out and a prison if you didn't.

≡

There was another *festa* over the mountain, Maria announced. She
made herself social director of the day.

We assembled, like a convoy, in a triangle of park with a bandstand
at its center, and the heavy shade of lindens. Hart said he wanted
Coca-Cola, and went off to the little local store. I came in behind him,
wanting coffee, and watched as he paid the woman for large garbage
bags, a length of chicken wire, a screwdriver, a pair of small pruning
shears with stout metal blades.

Garbage bags, shears, chicken wire, a screwdriver. Such things had nothing to do with art or theft, and I forgot them.

Maria went home that evening with her mother. They had things to talk about, she said; already she made excuses for not being with Hart. Hart said he understood, that she worked, she had a life. He was just a visitor.

Then he offered her a present. She could collect it anytime in Formentina.

He knew at once he'd done the wrong thing. But she did not refuse. She said, "I'll collect it now."

She followed him up the hill, and sat in a chair like a judge.

He disappeared into the bedroom. He thought he could bring out a book, perhaps, or a bottle. But he wanted to give her one of these famous images that Hart had stolen.

He searched again. He created an odd kind of magic: by promising a page to Maria, he made sure he would have to find them.

There was nothing in the lining of cases, in the obvious smuggler's spots. He looked among the clothes he had brought from Hart's house, just to clear the place.

Jackets. Nobody would elaborately sew a valuable picture into a jacket lining; Professor Hart was not likely to have been nimble with a needle. Trousers, ditto. Socks do not ball up big enough to hide a picture.

There was a pile of shirts, of course: neat, cotton shirts from the laundry. Five were marked in Dutch, one in English, from London. It was a perfectly respectable shirt, too: button-down, white. But it was thick, too thick.

The professor was not so elegant he'd carry about a perfectly washed shirt for months.

Hart tore off the plastic. Where there should have been card in the body of the shirt, there was paper and plastic and some kind of protective tissue. Between the tissues were bright painted images.

He took the first of them and went back to Maria.

He showed her a great cat confined in a cage of watercolor wash, the black in its coat as bright as new ink, the force of its jaw and teeth made obvious. He offered it.

"No," she said. "I don't think so."

At the door, she said, "I don't want anything. You'll be gone soon."

He sat down on the tiled floor. He was stalled—everything to do, no will to do it, like an athlete who breaks with age and finds his muscles will no longer throw him off the ground.

He'd found Hart's damn pictures now it was too late simply to get the Museum man off his trail and move on. He had waited too long, been stuck with other people's questions. He needed my life for his own.

He'd offered the best he had, better than stories, better than promises, and Maria had turned it down.

He was a killer. He deserved the really black headlines, politicians' speeches, a spike in the sales of the very best mortice locks and pepper sprays and 9mm guns. And here he was, confined to a village because of some incident that was more like an image: a dead woman walking in her husband's arms.

It was much worse than he imagined, of course.

≡

Christopher Hart had a dentist in Cambridge, who faxed the records to the local police, who copied them on to Amsterdam and Inspector Van Deursen.

There was no reason a skull found in a river lock in Holland should match the records of a British citizen still officially alive. But it did.

≡

Hart considered the pictures. He set each in a plastic envelope.

It made no sense for him to keep such things. He did not acquire or collect. He moved on; that was the essence of his scheme for a life.

Hart's crimes were not his crimes. These things might be better with me.

He slipped one plastic envelope under my door.

I watched it arrive, shining. I picked it up. I saw that the cat was ruckled a little, that the paper was bruised at the edges. I felt again that clean, inspiring anger at a perfect thing spoiled.

Everything extraneous had to go.

Of all the issues, Anna was easiest. The police said she could leave now they no longer needed the cover of investigating Arturo. She had a ticket home out of Oporto, and although she said she'd take a later flight, and wanted me to come back with her, she also had her teaching duties and her visible exasperation with the place.

The drive to the airport was unbearable. She nursed me with bits of memory on the way: sometimes big issues, how I was the only one who never showed surprise that she gave up music, how much that had helped; sometimes shared trivia, like the time we were lost out walking in Switzerland, or a meal in Siena, the tiny cuttlefish with crisp tentacles and bodies unctuous with ink.

"I read all your thesis," she said. "Every word."

"You didn't have to."

"I wanted to."

All this was in the manner of a deathbed conversation: someone determined not to let things lie unsaid, but afraid there would never be another opportunity to say them. She told me about an afternoon in Siena, a white room, the Bach pieces for unaccompanied viola, the breeze slight and warm on our bodies. The image was lovely, but it wasn't memory anymore, not wired into our lives.

At Oporto airport she said she needed *The Guardian*, and bustled into the newsstand. There were all too many foreign papers; she thumbed through French scandals, *Billboard,* pink Italian sports. She found what she wanted, and came back to me on the concourse.

"Don't wait," she said. "There's no point in your waiting. I'll go through and get a coffee."

"But it's an hour before the flight."

"I might buy some presents," she said.

"I love you," I said.

"Oh, yes. I love you, too." She said, "Doesn't do us much good, does it?"

She passed the police check and the security check and I could just see her still. Then she turned to passport control for flights to London, and she was gone, truly gone.

≡

I called Mello from the airport. I said I had something I'd like to explain, and could I come to the Guarda station.

I showed him the picture: the great cat roughed up by careless handling. I explained that fourteen others were missing from the Museum, that Hart was the suspect, that this picture had been put under my door.

"Prima facie evidence that the man carries stolen goods," I said. "I need police help now." Then I heard the communal voice of the Museum, a great chorus of quiet. I added, "It's a slightly tricky matter."

Mello grinned. "We don't want complications, either. If the pictures are there, you take them back to London. There are bigger issues."

"Thank you."

"We don't even know how to charge the man, not yet. We couldn't make a legal search without you. The Dutch police were very insistent on a legal search."

Two carloads of men went with us, and the convoy hit Formentina deliberately, a statement on wheels. The village froze: men moving gently by the beehives, walking out with the goats up the mountain; the two women picking beans; the barman stacking gas bottles by the roadside. The police stormed up the slate steps between still people who watched and only slowly, whisper by gesture by whisper, started to move.

Mello thundered on Hart's door. There was no answer.

"His car's not here," I said, helpfully.

Mello beckoned three heavy-shouldered men forward and they went through the door as if it were paper.

An old man among the beans in his garden shouted. His wife pulled him inside.

The house was pitch black and smelled of old breath and sweat. There was a mess of laundry in the bedroom that the cops picked over fastidiously. Every drawer was opened, rifled, shut. Hart's jackets hung in a shallow closet; each pocket was checked. Passport. Credit cards. Checkbooks.

The stacks of paper were winnowed for the wrong documents. The computer was treated like some kind of contraband, turned on to check that it was what it seemed to be rather than for any information it might contain. And I, for the first time, was licensed to go rummaging where I wanted to go.

I wanted the pictures. I also wanted to know why. I turned the piles of paper upside down and spread them slightly, checking for anything with a different weight or texture. I went through drawers of socks and shirts. I could be a good thief too; a licensed thief.

I opened a promising cardboard roll that contained only a poster. But the poster was interesting in itself: a van Gogh, a field of poppies under a placid, almost plastered sky, a dark parade of grass, a huddle of houses off to the right, and a great sense of flatness. It lacked ferocity or decorative form, and I looked at it too long because I kept wondering why Hart, an Englishman programmed to dream of seashores, Tuscan hills, dales, and everything that rolls, should put such a value on flatness.

Mello said, "Find anything?"

"Not yet."

"We got one thing. An ID from New York in the name of Thomas Galford."

"Who's he?"

"Maybe it's an ID for somewhere you give false names," Mello said. "It's just a laminated card."

One of the policemen held up the old Vulcanite trunk. Mello felt for a false bottom.

We went looking for some kind of attic, or at least a hidden crawl space in the roof: nine men looking upward, hands and eyes up to the ceiling made of fine wood strips. I found a rectangular cut in the wood in a corner of the main bedroom.

"Ladder," Mello shouted, and his men stamped away to find one. While they were gone, Mello said, "These are pictures you hope to find?"

"Pictures," I said. "Paintings from an album. It makes no sense for him to bring them here, not if he meant to sell them, but you saw what came under my door last night."

The ladder came and Mello, out of kindness more than deference, let me be the one who went up and pushed aside the rectangle of loose wood. I found my face pressed into raw fiberglass insulation. I coughed. I brought up the flashlight and looked around where the beam stabbed over the lawn of fiber to the ridges of the tiles. I felt around, too. My fingers closed on a plastic envelope.

I was so hopeful for a moment. "I've got something," I shouted, voice smothered in the fibers.

"Everybody hides something," Mello said. "It doesn't always matter."

I came down the ladder carefully. "It might not be his," I said.

It was a clear, foolscap envelope, full of receipts, an airline ticket, scraps of the kind of documentation people keep to prove their lives for tax purposes. I handed it automatically to Mello, but he let me open it.

The airline ticket was from Amsterdam to Lisbon on KLM, business class, open, paid for with a Visa credit card.

"But he drove down, didn't he?" Mello said.

There were car rental papers, but they did not fit the car Hart was driving. There was a driver's license, expired, in the name of Gregory Keller, with a photograph very like Hart. There was a used Dutch railway ticket, Amsterdam to Utrecht. There was a pass for the Bobst Library at New York University, soap from the Georges V in Paris, a pack of cards from a Nassau casino, a single Ting Ting ginger candy, several taxi receipts from different cities, and a ticket on the rack-and-pinion railway that climbs Mount Pilatus just outside Lucerne.

"Souvenirs," I said. I tried to keep the disgust out of my voice.

"I'm taking the driver's license," Mello said. "Is there anything you need?"

The men put back the envelope, tidied the papers as they were, closed down the shutters once more, and made the house dark and tight.

Once they stepped outside into the sun, they were plain officialdom again.

A woman watching from her gateway came forward, stolid and strong and nerved up to talk to officialdom. "Arturo?" she said. "What about Arturo?" She spoke very politely, but she said only those words, as though she didn't trust language to carry her any further.

Mello said, "You'll have to talk to headquarters."

The small gray army marched to the cars, slammed doors officiously, and drove off fast, leaving me on my doorstep.

I could see the woman still standing at her gate. Children tugged at her dress, and she gathered them to her and stepped out of sight. She was smiling, or rather giving a smile like a present to the children.

Nothing. Fucking nothing, I thought, except the oddity of a few strangers' names. I was too angry to waste time wondering what Hart's other names might mean. I only knew that Hart was taunting me now, binding me to him with the possibility of bringing back those pictures. I had become his joke.

≡

Maria Mattoso made sure I could hear her arrive: a squeal of tires on tarmac, then a revved engine, then a slammed door. She seemed unsure for a moment whether she should go straight up to Hart's house, or see me first. She chose me.

"Thank you for calling," she said. "It was the Guarda, was it? And they spent how long at the house?"

"Thirty minutes maybe."

"You were with them?"

"Look, I just called you because Hart wasn't here and I thought someone should know—"

"But you didn't think I should know while the search was going on? You waited until the evening."

"I had to take Anna to the airport—" I said. It was not a workable excuse, but I needed something to say.

"Did you find anything? Did they?"

"I don't know what they were looking for." But I could have told her: discrepancies, gaps in the record they could fill with investigation and suspicion.

"You'd better come up with me," Maria said.

She stood there engaged for once, not edging out of the center of things at all. I'd never had occasion to see her so clearly before.

"Come with me," she said.

She strode up the slate steps. I was watching her legs work, the round of a walker's calf, the slim, busy thighs. Her presence was electric to me, like a charge in a vacuum jar, now I was so absolutely on my own.

The door was back on its hinges, but it rocked slightly when Maria opened it. She walked inside.

There was something almost metallic on the air along with the sweat and breath: the smell of uniformed intruders. It wasn't just papers, clothes, that were subtly out of place. A cleaning woman could do that. A thief could do that too. The insult came from men who poked about in private places to discover a story, or make it up. There was simple proof how little they understood: they could never put things back as they were.

They probably found traces of Maria, too, and traces was all they wanted. From traces, they could invent sagas, romances, mysteries.

"Who was it?" she asked.

"Mello," I said.

"He had a warrant?"

"I think so."

"How many men?"

"Seven. Altogether."

"With guns?"

"Yes."

"Did they explain exactly what they wanted?"

"Mello said it was a question of identity."

"And what did you want?"

She pinned me with the words and I stood there with my eyes standing wide open and my hands neatly at my sides. I felt exhilarated. Her attention seemed huge enough to animate all the lacks and spaces forming in my life.

"What did you want?" she said again. "I take it you didn't find it, or you would never have called me."

"You know why I'm here, don't you?" I said. I felt entitled to confide at last. "The Museum believes that Christopher Hart stole something. I'm here to get it back."

"Pictures," she said. "He showed me one of them. I couldn't believe he was just some thief who cuts pictures out of albums."

"So you put it under my door?"

"I didn't. I didn't think of that."

"This—something—these pictures—the Museum shouldn't have," I said. "So they want it brought back without anyone knowing they own it, let alone that it was ever stolen. You see."

She was still angry with me, wound up tight, but it seemed to make her cold and clear. "And you didn't find anything?"

"Mello told me they found nothing."

"So you can go home now."

She had me marked down as a perfect type of a visitor, the kind that always has a very good reason to go away again: job, wife, children, house, mortgage, fear of alternatives and choosing between them.

"I don't have a home," I said. She didn't listen. "This is where I come from."

All the time I was a child, I missed the point of confession. I'd dredge up a few meager sins for a busy priest, offer them as dutiful evidence that I was interested. Then I grew up and away from all that. But I had listened to Anna all morning, and now I really wanted to say everything at least once so it could die on the air and be out of my way; or so Maria would accept and forgive it all.

"Listen," Maria said. "Did they take anything away?"

"I'm not sure. Not much."

"Can I borrow your phone?"

She called the Guarda and asked to speak to Mello, but he wasn't available. She asked what had been seized in Hart's house. She asked about warrants. A sergeant told her nothing belonging to Christopher Hart had been taken from the house. Only when she put down the phone did she realize how oddly he had phrased his denial.

Maria didn't waste time on me.

=

She first thought of storming the GNR barracks, demanding to see Mello. But an angry individual makes mistakes of etiquette, enough to be properly turned away. Instead, she phoned from the cool of her kitchen. She was very proud of her common sense when she told me that.

"Is this about Arturo de Sousa?" a sergeant said.

"No," Maria said. "I wouldn't call at this time about Arturo. This is about Christopher Hart."

"Yes," the sergeant said.

"I'd like to talk to someone."

"You want to talk to someone tonight? You represent Mr. Hart?"

"I'm not calling as a lawyer."

"But you do represent Mr. Hart?"

"I am not calling as a lawyer."

She never knew what convinced him to take her seriously. There was a pause, the phone seemed to fall, she heard some talk on the other side of the room. The sergeant came back.

"Senhor Mello will come to see you. In fifteen minutes."

She imagined Mello being dressed and polished by his quiet wife, packed into a car, and put out to drive to Maria's house. He would drive through the town with great self-importance, insistent the town acknowledge him. And he would be happy to correct whatever Maria thought of Hart.

"This is rather unusual," Mello said when she opened the door.

"I know. Can I get you a drink?"

Mello hesitated at the door. She could tell he wondered if it was entirely proper to be in a woman's house after nine in the evening, that he would be far more comfortable if she were an old, potbellied gouger of a lawyer who could be instructed over a pool table or in some clubby bar.

"A drink," Mello said. "Perhaps a glass of—"

"A glass of port," Maria said.

"Yes." Mello settled in the parlor in the pool of thin light from a floor lamp and looked around him. The old dark wood, the bits of fancy china, and the heavy curtains seemed to reassure him. He was still in a branch of his own world.

"Not white port," he shouted after Maria, patronizingly.

Maria put down a bottle of a twenty-year tawny. She was overdoing it, she knew, but she was playing an unfamiliar game: trading on mutual secrets of professional people, nothing to do with law, or due process, or justice.

Mello sipped. "What exactly can I do for you?"

She said, "I wanted to talk off the record, if that's possible."

Mello shrugged.

"I wonder what you know about Christopher Hart," she said.

"Mr. Hart," Mello said. "You wouldn't have a biscuit, I suppose—"

She was the supplicant; he had the answers. She brought the biscuits.

"I thought you were his lawyer," Mello said.

"I found him the house and organized the lease. When your men want to get a message to him they ask me to pass it on. They often do that, because I speak English."

"And very well, too, I'm sure."

"You searched his house today," Maria said. "That must mean you have some pretty serious suspicions about him. I don't want to get more involved if there's something I should know—"

"Involved," Mello said. "I thought you were already quite involved." He set the word up and hung it with assumptions: what women do, how the world should be, how well the cops know sin.

"You know me," Maria said. "I know all the foreigners."

"Of course," Mello said.

"But I wouldn't say I understand Hart's story."

"You ought to know," Mello said, "it's a very extraordinary story. I don't know how he presented himself to you—a professor, I suppose? With a university and all his degrees. It wasn't a very interesting story, so I don't suppose anyone would have bothered to question it. He came down from Holland, where he was supposed to spend his sabbatical year. Except"—Mello fiddled with a biscuit, mock delicately because he was in a woman's parlor—"that he encountered someone on a tram in Amsterdam who thought she recognized her own son. Not Christopher Hart, but Martin Arkenhout—who was supposed to have died in Florida ten years ago. They found Hart's hotel, photocopied his passport, and this Mrs. Arkenhout said it was just like Martin would have looked."

Maria said, "You'd like some more wine? Just a *copito*?"

But Mello was in serious mode. He laid out the story of how Arkenhout's traveling companion had later vanished too. "You see the pattern," he said. "I would like some more wine."

Maria poured.

"We did search Hart's house. We found an identity card in yet another name—a man who was reported missing in the Bahamas. A man of independent means, that sort of thing."

"You haven't arrested Hart?"

Mello said, "The evidence is in six or seven different countries. There isn't much of it. There's a story that needs explaining, that's all, and there are plenty of those."

Maria paced the small parlor like a courtroom, three paces across, three paces back, edging past the low, sharp-sided table. "I suppose—"

"If the Dutch police are right," Mello said, "then this man will kill and go away. But he'll go away with a new name."

"He couldn't find anyone in Formentina," Maria said.

"You know John Costa, don't you?" Mello said.

Maria poured herself a half-glass of port, although she hardly ever took wine. She raised her eyes to meet Mello's gaze.

She said, "I thought he'd be the last person you put at risk."

"You think I'm a saint?" Mello said.

"But he's the son of José Costa."

"We can't touch Hart at the moment. We need him to try just one more time."

Mello stood up as though manners required it.

"Just to try," he said.

≡

Everything else extraneous had to go.

My father's story itched and nagged at me, spoiled my concentration; it had to be resolved. I didn't realize, at the time, how information hollows a man out, takes away the faithful knowledge of boyhood and offers only thin facts. I was becoming just the shell that everyone recognized: John Costa, a man with no more secrets.

I know libraries. I'm a library rat, a museum person, dust on my whiskers; I turn back to books when I need to know things, like I turned to the big, brown-bound encyclopedia when I was a child, with its postage-stamp pictures of what seemed to be absolutely everything. My father was very proud of the encyclopedia, of having books.

The local library was new and white and empty. It wouldn't do.

The university library, twenty miles away, was barricaded by spinster angels who admitted only the ticketed few. But I charmed them with the authority of my Museum card.

Index boxes, sense and order. I sat at a desk with every book I could order on the history of the Portuguese secret police. The generalities would not do anymore. I wanted names.

There were histories of resistance to the old dictatorship, immensely long studies of how everything worked, studies of the links with German and Spanish and especially British Intelligence; even a 1920 account of a five-day monarchist revolt in Oporto. I found diagrams, theory, cartoons—crude ones from a magazine called *O Verdade*, "The Truth"—that showed what might have happened in any white room in a basement: electrical chairs, men with the faces of angular heroes being beaten by men with the faces of fascist beasts.

I could pass as an expert in a few hours. I didn't want to go for lunch, because I was absorbed, because I feared the spinster battalion might throw me back next time.

I did not find my father's name, not in studies of the Portuguese Legion, which helped out the secret police, nor in the memoirs they kept bringing to my desk: about a Fortress of Resistance, a Communist Intellectual, the memoirs of an Inspector of the PIDE, of prisoners, of "A Life in Revolution" and time spent in "Salazar's Inquisition."

But I did find Mello.

It's not that uncommon a name, but this Mello was in Vila Nova de Formentina, about the right age. But he wasn't a policeman, fretting about change and the state of the youth. He was in the opposition to Salazar and he was betrayed. The informer, of course, was not named. It seemed that one in ten Portuguese had reported at some time to the secret police, or helped denounce people of "bad character," who kept "bad company," who dared to wear red shirts in public or missed Mass. There were far too many names to remember.

My father had asked Mello's permission to come back. My father owed Mello some old duty.

My own father betrayed Mello.

I said out loud, "Am I making this up?"

My father was born in 1920. In 1953, when he left, he was thirty-three: a grown man. But Mello was now around sixty, still in uniform, still working. In 1953, he would have been—what?—seventeen, eighteen, nineteen. A boy. My father gave the PIDE the name of a boy.

Listen. You think you're walking in a garden and suddenly you're on the lip of a cliff. You think you're swimming in the comfort of a great pool and a current starts to take you out between high waves. This was a moment like that.

I wondered which would be worse: to invent this story, to libel my own father, or to find this scenario was fact? I sat at my desk, the examinee looking hard into space.

I knew that if my story was right, then everything my father had told me about Portugal and being Portuguese was tainted, the smell of police behind each heroic frieze of courage and victory. I just lost all the history I thought I had regained.

Suddenly I was very afraid of being my father's son.

=

Mello ordered me to the barracks with all the authority of law and uniforms, and he ordered me out of town. I needed, he said, a few days in Lisbon. He said he had a friend who insisted I have his apartment.

I couldn't resist Mello. He was practical: he said the police would be making certain searches while I was away and he personally would be responsible for seeing that my interests, the Museum's interests, were considered. But I couldn't stay around, because I would complicate matters.

"I wanted to discuss my father," I said,

"We can discuss that later," Mello said. "I don't know how to impress on you the seriousness of all this. The issue is"—and he seemed to be trying to snatch a euphemism out of his limited stock, but he failed—"murder."

I hadn't expected that. Why should I have expected that? Murder is a subject for novels and headlines. I didn't expect my life would take in either.

But I wouldn't be distracted. "Your officer took me to see a room," I said. "A white room in a basement. Why was my father there? When was he there?"

Mello tried to pretend he never heard the question.

"I need to know," I said.

I remembered: trying to reach my father in that high climate that settles around grown-ups, trying to make him listen to my questions about Saturday or why he was cutting back the roses.

"There are things you can't tell a son about his father."

"Tell me."

Mello sighed. I know now what he must have been thinking. He had chanced into a multiple-murder case, complicated by these allegations of theft from a great museum, and he found himself plowing up a past he had long ago survived.

He said, "He was in that room five months ago. Now will you go to Lisbon? Please?"

"Why?" I heard myself at four or five: always that same question, after every statement, "why?" "why?" "why?"; the last time we're all philosophers.

"Listen," Mello said. "We all have a duty to forgive those who trespass against us."

"But why—"

"I just wanted him to understand what he did," Mello said.

"I don't understand how you knew each other. He was miles away from Vila Nova de Formentina."

"I don't have time for this."

It was not a very dignified struggle. I simply sat there.

"Vila Nova's a long way from anywhere," Mello said, after a while. "Things happened here, things that couldn't happen somewhere like Lisbon. The Communist Party had conferences here, late 1940s, early fifties. They met and talked and planned. Of course, the PIDE wanted to know every move."

"You were a member? My father was a member?"

"You don't know what it's like to live under a dictator who wants everyone's lives opened up and visible and the same. You want to fight, but the only ways you know are the ways the dictator keeps denouncing and forbidding. So you use those ways."

"What did my father do?"

"People just forgot what it was to betray someone else. It seemed ordinary."

I had my moral certainties all lined up like toy soldiers, but Mello seemed determined to forgive, to glory in forgiving.

"After the Second Congress, the PIDE chased your father down. He could have confessed. He could have denied everything. He didn't do either. He sort of confessed, said he did know people who knew about the CP in general. They said they'd let him go for one name."

"Your name?"

"I suppose he thought nothing would happen to me because I was too young. He didn't think they would take the story seriously. Or I would get away."

"But he was safe to leave for London."

"I never wanted to leave," Mello said. "I didn't mind him leaving. It made everything easier."

"Was it easy to forgive him?"

"I don't think he understood what happened in those white rooms. I had to explain to him." Mello stood up. "He should have known. Everyone sort of knew."

I stood up too.

"I do not think the sins of the fathers should fall on the sons. If they did, we couldn't have a country."

Sometimes you feel entitled to examine a man: to study him for traces of old rhetoric, choosing the simplest things to say, for bullshit or simply lies. I was part awed by his capacity for forgiveness, part suspicious. I didn't know what part of him to trust. Maria told me later he was the kind of cop who did best when things were impossible, who in ordinary circumstances was an official bully.

"Just go," Mello said. "Go to Lisbon. For Christ's sake, go."

≡

Maria woke up cold in her own bed, she told me. For comfort, she dressed and went down to the kitchen, where her mother and Amandio were drinking coffee.

"You're up early," Amandio said.

"I woke up very suddenly."

"Someone calling you," her mother said.

Maria poured coffee from the pot.

"I said, someone calling you," her mother said.

"Love," Amandio said, beaming, oiled with easy certainty as always. Maria was shivering.

She called Hart twice, tried to suggest she could come out for the afternoon.

She said to me, when she came to the bar for her usual coffee and water, "I hope you get the pictures back."

"Thank you."

"It doesn't seem a good idea to be around here for a while."

"Mello told me to go."

"To go where?"

"Lisbon."

She sighed. "I could go to Lisbon," she said. "Go to the opera, go to the *fado*, go somewhere. I need to go somewhere."

I said, "Please come."

"I've got some business to sort out. I suppose I could come this week."

"Tomorrow?"

I hadn't expected to be so eager; a schoolboy's eagerness.

≡

The apartment was in a new block on Avenida do Brasil. It was a paradox of a zone: where the airplanes come roaring low, but well-off people still like to flaunt their closeness to the airport. The view was jacarandas, the pavements blue with the old flowers, and at the back, a courtyard of washing lines.

I checked the place. The living room was stuffed with bulky green sofas. The bathroom had taps in the form of gold-plated swans, forever vomiting water down the drain. And the main bedroom, a square box of intolerable dry heat, had a triangle for a bedstead like some altarpiece, set about with cherubim and seraphim in rows and ranks up to a fat fairy at the very top. I pulled open the drawer in the bedside cabinet: spare seraphim.

There was no fan, no air conditioner, and the apartment had been empty for weeks. I tried lowering a shade and opening a window, but new heat crept in to disturb the blanket of old heat. I tried showering, distracted by the odd glitter of gold swans around my feet and the water that ran lukewarm from either bird.

I took Luso water from the fridge and drank from the bottle.

I didn't know how to make a place ready for someone else. I knew what Anna would want, but I wasn't expecting Anna. I wondered what I should do: buy wine, buy bread, buy coffee. Buy condoms, nowadays. Make sure the rooms seem fresh and appealing. I was entirely out of practice because it was so long since I had chased, or courted, or even furiously desired.

But that was my occupation now: desire. It was like being drunk, like a headache, like anything obsessive and chemical. Only I was alone, and in a stuffed, airless apartment in a city I didn't know.

I wanted to be outside more than anything. Not that the streets were promising: broad and without character, pale-cream blocks. I could not find a cafe in the shade. There was, however, a seafood bar with tables under a tree, and in its window were piles of crayfish, salt-water and freshwater. I ordered some of both, picking between the piles, trying to judge which one I liked best and therefore which one I should offer Maria when she came.

I didn't even eat for myself anymore.

I could watch myself doing all this, as though from a great height, see the absurdity of it all; and yet I went on. This was infatuation without excuse, without even the object of desire. I couldn't even call Maria until evening. I didn't want to leave messages on the office machine, if I could avoid it. Maybe she'd be home, maybe not.

Clean sheets. Good coffee. Wine, of course; but what kind of wine? Did she even drink? I knew her only in circumstances where perhaps she considered herself on duty, and she drank only water and coffee. I needed good soap in the bathroom, too: what my mother used to call "nice" soap.

I didn't know affairs, you can tell. I could fancy the notion of the plot: the fake phone calls to establish alibi, the calculated meeting, the rush and grapple and then leaving the moment two bodies were tired enough to separate. I could see a certain excitement in all that. But my habits were far too constant and domestic.

A woman passed. She was lovely enough: rounded, ample, eyes

bright as knives. But she was the wrong woman. Just for a moment, I thought I knew how to cure myself, to prove I was riddled with non-specific romance. I'd stand, talk to her, drink a glass of wine, go to bed with her and join together fiercely enough for nothing else to matter, and remember this even when, hours later, it was only memory on the skin, not the scaffolding of some new domestic life. Then I wouldn't need to fuss about which crayfish, seawater or freshwater, or both, the decisions that showed how prissily difficult I found it to do what I knew I would inevitably do: call Maria Mattoso, call her now.

I thought I was just being human.

I didn't call her that night. Instead, I sat in the apartment with a loaf and some cheese, watching an old Portuguese film about students at Coimbra University. The men wore black academic gowns and sang *fados* in the corners of small rooms. The girls frisked on steps, or sat romantically still in windows to be serenaded. The two did not seem to connect very much. It was a love story.

≡

I left my number on Maria's machine, just as a reminder. I asked if she wanted to see the new *King Lear* at the National, or some visiting ballet out at Belém.

She thought this could wait, she says. She had a life in Vila Nova de Formentina that could not be interrupted on a whim—certainly not by a man unconnected and not at home, who might as well be on vacation.

She sat down at table with her mother.

"Where's Amandio?" she said.

Her mother chewed both her meat and her wine.

"Traveling," she said, after a minute. "He has to make a living, you know."

"Gone far? For long?"

"Santarém. Then he's going to the Alentejo. Évora."

"I like Évora," Maria said. "I remember a lemon tree hanging over a white wall."

Her mother glared at her.

"And the fountains. They have lovely Moorish fountains." She watched her mother work a piece of bread into oblivion, first between her fingers, then between her teeth.

Her mother said, "You're not going out this evening? You're thinking of sleeping here?"

"Yes," Maria said. "You don't mind?" She poured wine into her mother's water glass almost by accident, and her mother drank it anyway. "We'll be company for each other," Maria said.

She shouldn't have said that. By way of apology, she said she would wash the dishes.

"You don't know how," her mother said. "Lady lawyers don't do that sort of thing." The two women got up simultaneously and moved plates to the sink.

"He's just making a trip," Maria said quietly. "It's nothing serious."

"Perhaps not for you," her mother said.

Maria touched her mother once, very lightly on the shoulder, and as she expected, her mother brushed the hand away and also smiled.

"He's been very useful," Maria said. "Amandio."

"You didn't like him. But yes, he was."

Maria should have picked up on the tense and worried out its meaning. But she felt too tired, and too kind.

"I mean it," she said. "I'll do the dishes."

When the phone rang again, her mother went to answer it, and Maria heard her talking flatly. When she came back, she said, "It was that Senhor João. Costa. I told him you weren't here. He sounded drunk."

"Thanks," Maria said.

≡

I wasn't drunk, but the words still butted up against one another and bent and scattered when I tried to say where I was, who I was, what I felt.

I climbed into the bath, in the shade of the sharp gold swans, and I lay there for a moment before panicking.

I ran through the apartment, wet and naked, and found toast burning on the stove. So I was right to panic, I thought.

Christopher Hart could be sleeping with Maria. I could not. I hated Hart, wanted him arrested and confined; or dead.

I was the hollow man, no solid past anymore, no father's reliable stories, no place of birth that mattered, no residence, no wife. But I had been a hollow man for years, doing things at one remove, respecting systems and courts and orders and regulations. I was unused to this rush of feeling, like bile or hormones. I thought it could fill me up with purpose and found a new life.

But perhaps she'd come down to Lisbon, after all. One more call tomorrow. I could always make one more call.

≡

I imagine this next part, from everything I know.

There was a road, a sand track, a man with bagpipes, one with a big drum, one with a snare drum. Beside them walked other men, one with a bunch of raw-looking rockets in his hand, just paper pockets of blast. They weren't going to war. They were only announcing a *festa*.

The youngest man lit up a fuse like the wreckage of a cigar, and waited until it glowed. He held a rocket in his left hand. He pushed the lit fuse into the touch paper and waited for the rushing sound, and then, just in time, let go, with a twist and a curl like a javelin thrower.

The mortars almost always went up. Sometimes they'd raise some dust, or some bird nests in a drain; but usually they flew and a few minutes later exploded and left farts of brown smoke high on the air.

This one didn't. It rumbled. It flew. But it flew flat horizontal. It cleared vines and phone wires and bougainvillea, made a pig scream, grazed a neon cross on a tiny white chapel, and shot out of the village into the woods.

The men lit the next mortar.

But the first wasn't history yet. It zipped through pines and eucalyptus until it caught in a ball of loose bark and let off brown-yellow smoke.

The next mortar—and I'm guessing here—shot up into a bare blue sky, and the next: a flash, a bang, then smoke. You could hear and see them in the next valley. In that part of Portugal, you can't have a village *festa* without advertising: loud, explosive advertising. You can't have a party, a sacred procession with banners, without the sounds of trench warfare.

Back in the woods, the trails of bark from the eucalyptus began to smoke. There was a weak little wind, but that was enough. A few leaves, the new ones heavy with oil, burned down to their veins and blew around. Some scorched the grass, which had overgrown itself in a wet spring and was now dried out to brown tinder.

The woods went quiet for a moment, then little flames began to chatter, as insistent as water over rocks and, for a strange moment, just as soothing.

The young eucalypts were still brilliant blue-green and juicy; they went up like fireworks, orange and yellow. Swags of old bark went dusting through the branches, flaming dead twigs and leaves. Bits of fire fidgeted about in the light, sparkling, jittering.

The men in the village most likely thought the rogue mortar had spluttered out without doing damage. They were out raising money for the chapel, so they went back to their rounds, the bagpiper roughing up "Y Viva España" on a red and gold bladder, with jazz riffs, and the bridge passage done without breathing.

The drummers drummed.

There were two fires in the woods now. The grass fire baked pine cones and opened them, licked the scaly seeds inside. It heated up the spindles of heather and lavender. Smoke left a track along the rocks.

As the fire fanned out, the treetops started to spit and crackle. There were fatty white squares on the pine trunks where they had been cupped for resin; the squares burned with a pure gold light, aisles of terrible candles.

The two fires married at a thicket: the ground fires tumbling up the trunks, the tree fires throwing down flame.

Then the wind got up. It blew away from the village, so there was no taste or soot to warn the men with the mortars.

By nightfall, the fire had roots. The grass was cool; the fire rested. The next day, the flames grew up like sudden vines, and the fire bent the trees in its direction. Now it was going uphill, it seemed to move even faster.

≡

Maria went to the GNR station because Mello had something to show her.

It was a portrait, formal as anything in a ruff and a gallery: Christopher Hart, who'd broken surface in a muddy lock when the Vecht was running low in summer. Mello called it the "real" Christopher Hart.

But it was only a head on a clinical white background, details fudged, teeth broken with pliers, one eye out, hair shaved, cut marks of a garotte still clear at the neck. It had been manipulated as though by an artist, planes changed, soul exposed with a few surprising lines, but mostly it had been savaged for the sake of rudimentary disguise.

"They haven't found the body yet," Mello said.

"I see," Maria said. "So you'll want to talk to him?" The name Christopher Hart no longer applied. The man had slipped into a category of appalling things that could exist without names.

"You'll be seeing him?" Mello asked.

Maria made herself look again at the photograph. The head had been hacked. The black must be blood scabs. She didn't feel revulsion; the image was as remote as a car wreck on the nightly news or a painted martyrdom in a church. If she'd had time, she could have taken an interest in the technical, forensic details.

But there was still a man called Christopher Hart, up in his long, white house on the mountain. He seemed like the ghost now: a stunt projected on the sky, flickering, insubstantial, fantastic as his stories and the places he'd been. She'd liked his lies, once.

There was also this specific, bloody thing.

She couldn't stop herself. "What did it smell like?" she asked. And then: "Can I use the phone?"

She dialed my number in Lisbon, still thinking it would be so easy to save my life by keeping me in the city. I didn't answer.

She says she called me seven times that morning. It's a magical number; perhaps she is exaggerating. But I was out in any case, or asleep. She worried I might have left to come home already, that I'd be waiting in Formentina and Hart would be waiting for me.

She called one more time, just in case.

Seven

Maria was used to fire.

I saw it only on the nightly TV news, where it was generalized to orange flames, sooty wreckage, and firefighters struggling with old-fashioned hoses.

Hart, however, was in the thick of it.

The fire rested overnight, but next day the flames hunted one another uphill, faster and faster. Fire had been just a rumor, a stink on the wind, but now it was driving home.

Hart must have heard the bells and sirens down below Formentina. It wasn't the police; he knew the police come silently. It was volunteer firemen, working around a small clump of houses between the village and Vila Nova. He could make out trucks at the roadside, men running pipes to take water down from the little brick reservoirs on the hill, using the few minutes they had pressure to flush away the tinder grasses and wet the earth down. They made a broad line of mud around the houses, and they moved on.

Hart had everywhere to go, so he had nowhere to go. He didn't have anything out in the woods to protect. So he did what everyone else did: he waited the fire out.

There's no way you can go to meet fire and block it at a distance. It's alive. It can flare away from you with the wind, crackle up an old tree's dry dead branches and sparkle prettily into dry grass, fan out in a dozen directions all at once. It does seem to attack sometimes, but even in retreat it is emptying out and blackening the woods. You wait and wait until you can fight it at home.

Some of the older women went to the chapel to pray together, then joined the men who were watching the woods from every angle. The smoke, they could see, was gray now, which meant there was no juice left in the leaves. The woods were burning dry.

≡

Maria had wanted to talk to me. Now she needed to talk to me. She thought I might quit Lisbon and come running back to Formentina. She thought Christopher Hart would be waiting for me.

She says she thought of going to Lisbon. She couldn't. She says she needed to distract Hart. And there was another reason: the police, finally, decided that Arturo had done nothing worth prosecuting, and were putting him out of the jail at nine in the morning. Somebody had to collect him.

The old man was thinner still, his strong forearms gone almost white. He was resigned to being released, as he had been resigned to being imprisoned, and he seemed unsurprised that there were no charges at all. He knew Zulmira had died of natural causes. He simply could not face the fact, not for days, not even now.

He asked about the fire, but Maria did not have the exact local knowledge he needed, about the wind and the tracks around Formentina.

Fire blustered in the grass, crackled in the trees.

Hart told Maria he was on the steps of his house and a moth, like paper under gold leaf, flew out of the bushes. It circled, rose as though it had caught some tiny thermal, and then burst into flames in midair.

Maria was brave, I know that. She wanted to distract him, to save me. But she also wanted to stay at the center of this one story she had lived. She had been ragged with waiting. She was not going to miss a single scene.

A few roads were already blocked off, makeshift trestles in the way where the smell of smoke started. Beyond the trestles, the edges of the road were soft and vague, as if in evening light. There was an occasional rain of soft, black smuts.

She took shortcuts on paved lanes, rocked along over sharp stones, and found a back way onto the mountain road. The sky was varnished brown at the edges. The air smelled used and dusty; in back of it was the taste of great heat. You couldn't mistake it for the night perfume of wood fires in the villages or a bonfire upwind; it was a great breathing body just out of sight.

She crashed gears for the steep switchback road. She tried closing the car windows, but she stifled. With the windows open, she coughed; it wasn't much of a choice.

The bends were sharp angles, the road like a spring that might any minute snap in the heat and fling the cars off the mountain. I know how she thinks. She'd rather worry about the road as a spring, which was absolutely impossible, than think of what she had to alarm her: the heat, the smoke, what she had to say to Hart. How she'd get home. If she'd get home.

Arturo studied the roadside for clues to the fire. At a blackened clearing, gold threads of straw still standing, he sat up very straight.

Maria made up mantras as she went along. So she thought she'd be safe when the water was safe, up above other houses with nothing to spoil it. These high woods weren't so dense, so they wouldn't burn the same way; and there were firebreaks cut up and down the mountain. Anyway, there was always mist and cloud in the mornings, even in high summer, to smother the fire.

But she didn't feel safe.

She imagined herself saying, in a neutral voice, "But you did kill those people, didn't you?"

She imagined Hart saying, "Well, if you put it that way. I suppose so. Yes. Does it matter?"

≡

Arturo insisted on knocking at his own door. His daughter answered, and they stood looking at each other for a moment until Maria turned away. She never knew if they cried or held each other because she knew it could not happen if she stayed.

She locked the car as if she were in the city, climbed the slate steps. She was out of breath all at once. It was only the dust and heat, but it felt like the moment your diaphragm forces all the air from your body. The girl was dizzy. She might as well have been in love.

"Hey," Hart said.

He was on the porch of his house, framed in daisies. But you can't sit anywhere in Formentina without the big, white shine of daisies. He looked like one of those wooden puppets artists use, all gangling articulation.

Maria said, "They're closing roads in the valley."

"Good of you to come."

"I had to talk to you."

He pulled his cell phone out of his jeans.

"Face to face," Maria said. "We don't have much time and I don't want anyone listening in."

Hart shrugged. "Come on up. There's no air, but I can get you some water. Or some wine or some soda or some beer?"

Maria looked around her. This day the whole valley looked sepia, like a photo lying on flames.

"I'll have some water," Maria said.

"I'll get it," Hart said. "Or come in."

She stepped into the shade.

"The police came back," she said.

"Really?"

"The next thing," she said, "they'll want you down at the Guarda Nacional. They'll want you to volunteer for questioning. Of course, you'll need to prove identity."

"I've got a passport."

"To prove it," she said. "Beyond doubt."

"They don't believe papers anymore?"

You can rest your eyes on this landscape. People expect it. Hart saw a train of goats come down the steps, followed by a man in his fifties with a sweet, senseless grin and a quick dog.

"I've got credit cards," he said.

"You don't understand," she said. "They're serious."

The goats seemed to know their own way.

"It must have been tough driving today," Hart said.

She shrugged.

"You'd better come in," Hart said. "Put a fan on. Let's move the heat around a bit."

The house seemed dark, even after an occluded sun. The walls were white, the floors bare, the furniture a clutch of expedients spaced apart: couch, chair, table, a dresser with four embossed paperbacks and an ornamental cockerel from Barcelos. Add company, and it was obvious this was what someone thought would be just enough for someone else's summer.

Hart turned on two fans to blow into each other. A picture— amateur watercolor, bougainvillea on white stucco—rattled against the wall. Where the shutters were slightly open, the dust went scouring through the block of light.

"Cool enough for you?" Hart said.

Maria went to open the shutters wide.

"Hey! Don't let the light in. You'll let the heat in."

Indeed, the air was stifling: new ash as well as all the dead ash.

"I know that you do have papers, Christopher," she said. "Whose papers are they?"

"Christopher Hart's papers. So I'm Christopher Hart."

She said, "It might help if I could give them something they could check. Perhaps you wouldn't have to go down to the GNR then."

"Does it matter?"

"You won't like interrogation."

"I mean, what can they do?"

She said nothing, but her body squared off like an exclamation point.

She'd left her purse on the table, so he fumbled in it, fingering her own plastic parts. "It says here," he said, "you're Maria de Sousa de Conceição Mattoso. I bet the bank card says how long you lived in town. The ID has your medical record. It certainly says you live in your mother's house and you do law."

She snatched the purse back.

Hart could hear men striding down the steps; to be exact, their talk, grim and contained. He could see Maria wanted to be outside because it seemed much safer there, even with the prospect of fire. She didn't like to be with people like him, who slip out of their proper selves at night and go around nameless.

He said, "It's like this. Don't you ever think of being someone else? Of starting again, but radically? You could make up a whole new life."

"I don't know what you're playing."

"You could be anyone or anything. You could be in any of those places you see in magazines, not just Vila Nova. You get to finish off someone else's life and do it better than they do."

"I love fantasy," Maria said. "I don't live it."

"But why not? When you were a girl, didn't you want to be Inès de Castro and die for love, or Madame Curie or Lizzie Borden, or Marilyn Monroe? Didn't you want to choose a new world for yourself?"

"I chose a world," Maria said.

"Are you happy there?"

"Happy?" Maria said. "Listen, I don't have time for this. You are someone the police want to interview. It's serious. I'm your lawyer. This isn't play."

"Isn't it?"

"You think you can reinvent yourself before they get here?"

"I've got time. If the fire is like you say, they won't be here for a while."

"You could give them an account of where you teach," she said. "Your subject. What your last book said, what's in the new book. You do know that, don't you?"

"Why do they want to know all of a sudden? Nobody here ever asked me for a lecture on Dutch imperialism. Hell, that's why I came here."

"That's good. It's good you talk about Dutch imperialism. They'll believe that."

"You really want Christopher Hart?" He couldn't help sounding disappointed. "I thought you wanted someone you could change. Someone you could make up as you went along."

Maria slapped her hands once on the wall.

"Sit down," he said. "There's nowhere to go. I could tell you things."

"I don't need to know."

"You're talking as my lawyer?"

She shook her head.

"So what's the problem? You don't want to know about other lives, other places?" He bent at the waist and put his face against hers. "You'd disappear if you left here, wouldn't you? If it didn't say 'lawyer' after your name. If people didn't know you, your father, your grandfather."

She said, "The police are serious."

He slammed the shutters together and tried to force the bolt into place.

"Are the lights working?" she said.

"Maybe."

"I'd like the light on."

"Sit. We won't do anything. You just listen."

It would have been easier to touch just at that moment. The room crackled with the fact that they were not touching. Breath stuck in the throat.

A sound began overhead: mechanical, distant. The sound became more distinct: one of the small planes that go up from the local airfield to spot fires. It circled and then seemed to veer across its own path. Then it must have passed over the ridge, because the sound was distant again, and then gone.

"Hey," Hart said, and he was laughing. "You want someone to save you?"

=

I went around the bookshops on the Carmo while I was waiting for her: great vaults of books, odd hallways with trestles of books, shelves of paperbacks treasured so long they seemed almost pathetic, old art books from the twenties with their air of embalming culture and sewing it up in good cloth.

I couldn't concentrate, of course.

I called Mello. When finally he took the call, he was brusque and impatient.

"I took your father to the barracks," he said, "so he could understand what he did. He never knew what he did. He was out of the country before the worst happened."

"I apologize," I said. "I apologize for my father."

"We've had a revolution since then," Mello said. "We've tried to change. You forgive and you get on with things."

"You showed me that white room."

"I should never have done that. You're entitled to a father who's a hero. Maybe he was a hero when he got to London."

"I need to talk—"

"John Costa," Mello said, "half this district is on fire. The roads are shut down. Maria Mattoso's left town, and she's probably up with your friend Christopher Hart. Now we're waiting to bring the bastard in for questioning but we can't get to him. I don't want apologies. I want you out of the way."

"Is Maria all right?"

"How should I know?"

"Is she all right?"

Mello said, in English, "Don't you be a fucking hero."

≡

Two men rattled Hart's door, then landed fists on it.

They stood there, shoulders deep as they were broad, skin stained with smoke over shiny red cheeks. Maria opened the door.

"The fire's moving," one man said. "We're cutting a new break."

Hart said, "What do they want?"

"Help," Maria said. "You got scythes or anything? Brooms, then. Anything."

"I suppose there are brooms."

She found a scythe tucked back under the sink. Hart carried a broom. They followed the two men down the slate steps to the road. Nobody talked, not even about what the outsiders were meant to do. They walked until they were out of sight of the village.

Hot air smothered them. The path wound about, no wider than a goat track, then opened to show the whole valley below.

It was like a harvest day: a stir of people in field clothes, bent, cutting, thrashing, breaking down and clearing out the stuff that could burn between the woods and the village. There was a dust of seeds and broken stems that prickled the throat. The ground itself felt hot. A half-dozen women, round and young or old on their bones, cut grass and pulled it away on two-wheeled carts, tugged up bramble with hard, cut hands; and sometimes stopped as if they were listening for the fire.

Dark birds circled where everyone was working, hawks, even an eagle waiting for the woods to give up all the winged things flying from the fire. Dragonflies flared up out of the grass in natural panic. Gold beetles lumbered into the sooty air. And the moths mobbed the working line, soft, velvety creatures, some tiny, some broad as small birds in dark and phosphorescent blues and greens, a plague of them born out of a long, wet spring and a sudden hot summer. They flew into eyes already reddened with smoke and work and wine. They fluttered on women's thighs as they tugged the carts, making skin sing over tired muscles. Hart felt their wings like powder clumped on his wet back.

The birds above kept turning and diving, closer and closer to the eyes and the dry throats of the people working below.

≡

"You won't get home," one of the village women said. "They must have the roads closed."

"I could go down the other side of the mountain," Maria said. "Something has to be clear."

The barman said he'd rung the trout farms that lay just over the ridge, and they said the roads down were pretty much impassable. Nobody had bothered to close them because nobody would try to get through; most corners were dark with soot and smoke, and around any of them you might meet live fire. He pushed another espresso to Maria across a table filmed with fine dust.

"We've got some time," Hart said. She reached for a cigarette.

The little bar by the road was a single white room, branches of bay drying over a coffee machine, a rank of bottles, a counter with jug wine under it, and a shelf of odd groceries: hot sauce, firelighters, tampons, biscuits. It usually smelled of work or of Sunday best. That day, it smelled of the smoke and sweat of everyone's skin. Nobody was rushing to go home to their own houses, not while they were mounting a communal defense; they'd be weaker apart. But it was almost dinnertime.

"I've got food," Hart said. "In the freezer."

"There's no electricity."

"Then we'd better eat what's left."

She couldn't go now. The women were watching them as though they were a couple.

"I'm going," Maria said.

So he stood up, too. There wasn't anything to say because she had no hope of leaving, and the whole village thought she was with him.

They faced each other for a moment.

There's no rule here about how you fight in public. Shouting, the village might have understood.

The barman said, conversationally, "Everything all right?"

"I'm all right. *Tudo bem,*" Maria said.

"You could stay at my place. There's a couch," Hart said. Then, after a pause: "I'll sleep on the couch."

The barman said, "It'll get cold soon. Colder, I mean. The fire doesn't move so fast at night."

"You mean we can all sleep?" Maria said.

She looked around the room, the people packed against one another on benches: old women in print smocks, old men in trousers they might recover someday for church, the few younger people, all used to using their bodies fiercely all day but still, with the prospect of fire waiting just below them, desperately tired.

"Go sleep!" the barman said. He implied: the rest of us are stronger. We'll stay awake for you.

=

And I lay staring up the skirts of seraphim, fretting from one side of the bed to the other, surprised at how I could be in a big city and stay bored and purposeless. After all, I was visiting; I could be a tourist. I could remember my expertise and search out art, fuss about relationships between Flanders and Portugal, Italy and Portugal, about whether the Portuguese imported their Renaissance, and the Italians who built great churches in Lisbon. I could always eat: *bacalhau* or a fine John Dory or shrimps in hot pepper sauce. I could take trams or boats, the funiculars, or the lace-sided elevator up to the sociable bars. I could drink. I could whore, I supposed. Why shouldn't I, now, treat sex as just another appetite to be routinely satisfied? You don't feel unfaithful buying a meal away from home.

All these years, I'd completely lost the habit of being alone, of shopping for a life. I knew the sense of someone else breathing in the house, of surprise, of things happening without my always willing them to happen. Piles of books, the top shelf of the fridge, morning letters all grew for two. I did like touch I hadn't organized, words I did not expect.

No Anna. Nobody.

There was Maria, but she was far away. Maria. Golden black hair on her forearms; I'd never noticed that on a woman before, much less liked it so much, much less got hard when I thought of it. Not a fetish, I promised myself; a detail.

There was never this much time to think inside my marriage. But I realized there were details of Anna's body I could not precisely remember. I could remember the touch and warmth of her, but I was used to looking away as a body grows looser, older, to seeing her with my own weakened eyes and not noticing; she returned the favor. But now I had time.

I wanted Maria in detail.

≡

They rigged a hurricane lamp, all pale gold light out of embossed steel, and cooked half-thawed pork steaks on the gas stove, and opened a bottle of wine.

"Listen to me," Hart said.

But Maria only ate, furiously. On an ordinary day she'd eat very little. She'd worked under the sun, had unfamiliar twists in muscles and bones, but that didn't explain her appetite. She was eating just to be ready.

"Suppose the cops are right," Hart said.

She said, "I don't know what the cops are saying."

She slipped her plate into the sink. She opened a set of inner windows and fanned herself.

The air seemed cooler at last.

The first lip of a huge moon came up over the mountain, and spread into a block of cold, plain light. The valley went quiet, cicadas stopped, frogs abandoned their rasping song.

She turned to him and she held him. She says they made love watching each other's eyes: sex as interrogation. But she only keened, and Hart grunted, and they separated awkwardly like stuck paper. She didn't know any more afterward. Hart didn't tell.

She found her watch by the bed. There were seven hours still to dawn, seven hours of this steel light outside and the quiet. She just had to occupy this man for seven hours.

≡

I drank too much, so I woke up fast, knowing things.

I knew Maria couldn't be safe with Hart, with a man whose record cut across murder and who shifted name and identity so willfully.

I knew because of paperbacks and films, the stories that sink much deeper than fact. We fancy ourselves—scholars, students—held up by a net of references. If you want to talk pictures, churches, dukes, or politics, cire perdue or monetary union or pentimento, or Proust or last night's news, that works very well; the books are everywhere, securely knowledgeable, referenced and footnoted. But when it comes to the melodrama of love, killers, risk, and nighttime terrors, then we have read nothing truly authoritative except the airport chillers. So that's where we learn what must happen next.

Since Hart was a villain, Maria must be the victim. If Maria was the victim, then in two hours' fast drive I could at long redemptive last be what Mello thought I never should be: the designated hero.

Do you understand that I never once thought this was madness talking in my head? The drink helped convince me.

≡

Stillness. The huge moon. Maria stood looking out on a shining suspense, a world stopped and top-lit.

She heard Hart say, "You wanted to know about New York . . ."

Hart stood just behind her. He was wonderfully absorbed in his stories; he still thought he was a whole library to her. He seemed not to know that the stories amounted to a confession, and confession reduced him to one thing: a killer, that's all.

There was the disturbing smell of green things smoldering. The village was still, but not settled, just exhausted. The moon caught the rush of the stream, and even that cool light flickered like a parody of fire.

"I was very young when I was in New York," he said. "Seventeen."

The cool and the moon soothed her eyes. She was happy with the shine of the world. But she made herself turn, smile, appreciate him.

She couldn't go with him this time: to parties, to bluffing through the art world, to Hamptons summers, dealers on the edge, to watching the famous work their way through the pharmacopeia and, sometimes, back again. He sounded like a gossip sheet, or like a brief exposé in some Saturday magazine, as though he had no history of his own, only this shell of other people's stories. He said only one interesting thing: that he'd been in the art world after it was heroic—the Abstract Expressionist heroes wrestling wild paint—and before it became social work to improve the nation. He'd had the fun: the years of the souk.

So she could at least act interested. She wanted him absorbed until he said things she could report.

She closed her eyes. She didn't mean to do it. She saw, also shining, the cut head in the photograph, the mouth gaping on teeth that had been gouged out after death.

She'd had this man inside her only an hour ago. Now she couldn't be sure of his name. If she had wanted to tell him to stop, instead of pulling him to her, what name would she have used?

He was edging around the house, bigger than she seemed to remember, magnified by the vagueness of the light and the big night shadows. He rattled knives in a kitchen drawer, just to find coffee spoons; but she thought of the knives.

He shouted, "Don't you want to know?"

She thought she heard dogs shifting in a yard, throwing themselves against corrugated iron, claws rattling.

"I mean," he said, "I thought you'd want to know everything now."

"I have to make a phone call," she said.

"Use the cell phone."

"I was going to."

She began to dial a number. It wasn't local, he could see, since it started with a zero. She waited for the faint clicks of the old rotary system to fade.

"John Costa?" she said. "This is Maria Mattoso." Pause. "Yes, I'm sorry. I just wanted to tell you the roads are closed. Yes, fire. In Formentina. The roads are very bad indeed. You must stay in Lisbon a few more days." Pause. "I'd love to come to Lisbon," she said.

She put the phone down on the table.

"You didn't have to do that," he said.

≡

She called back only once. And late. She didn't say where she was, except that I was not to come back to Formentina.

She was the victim. She was with the villain, Mello said so. So she could not be saying what she meant. She was saying I ought to come back to Formentina. She must be there. She was in peril, a gun up against her, eyes desperate for the sight of a hero.

If Maria was in Formentina, she must be with Hart. If she was with Hart, she must be in danger.

I finished dressing, threw my dirty clothes in a bag, forgot about the shaving gear in the bathroom, and ran down the wide building stairs. The street was a fluorescent blank: the blues and oranges of artificial light and linden shade and full moon. I ran for my car and found myself wondering what a cop would think if he saw me: a man running for no reason, therefore running away.

I missed a turn between low concrete factories, tried again along avenues of wasted oleanders. I got down almost to the river, to the warehouse blocks with their old graffiti and the rust-red freighters whose masts grew convincing after dark, before I picked up the signs for the highway north.

I'd driven this road before, straight off the plane from London, going to find my father and bury him, to bring back what Hart had stolen. I was as various as anyone then: a mess of memories, mistakes, decisions made and avoided, feelings buried, indulged, and simply forgotten for the time being, a husband, an official of a great institution, a predictable statistic tied to my credit rating, my parking space, my medical record, my morning route to the Museum, my dietetic tendencies. On the road this night I was—I thought the word was *distilled*. All the detail had been subsumed in one great, purposeful fire.

I almost knew (a long train of a truck passed me going fast) in my heart (I noticed bright bar lights in a small town, saying Sousa's Bar, in English) that this was (the road ran in a tunnel of trees) madness. But diagnosis mattered so much less than the chance to act at last.

After an hour I was still rolling, but the certainties had begun to fade. I'd been used to making cases, adjusting to the office, not always telling Anna what I meant exactly, tacking my way through; now I was trying something simple, to be a hero.

It was tough to hold on to a great moral cause while the road slipped under me, a banal carpet. Besides, sleep was tugging me down. I blinked, and the blink seemed to last a minute, like a blackout. I shifted in my seat, made myself concentrate again. I could sleep my way off the road very easily.

I was a ghost now, without all the details that anchor a man in a particular life, no wife, no father I'd acknowledge, going after a man who had thrown away all those details. I was rushing through a landscape proper for such a war of ghosts: visions and spinning suns, guardian knights, hidden treasure, hidden princesses. I didn't know the particulars, only the postcard, guidebook notions, so I could flood this countryside with any story I ever knew, with a thief of lives, an ogre and a knight, killer and cop, all avatars of an old business that grew more literal as the story aged.

I still had a good fifty miles to go.

=

She stood naked by the bed, one hand on her sharp hip, body turned like a fighter, with the absolute purpose of one of her mother's saints.

He stretched himself and threw off the sheets. Desire didn't happen. Instead, he patted the bed and said, "I could tell you about the Bahamas again. About the hurricane."

"Don't you ever run out of stories?" she said. "Don't you ever stay anywhere?"

"Is that an invitation?" He said it without thinking, for once. It was what another Christopher Hart—sexual opportunist, he supposed cynically, not so experienced except with wide-eyed students, given to playing with hearts for the sake of vanity—might have said.

She walked into the living room.

"Dark of night," he said from the bed. "Terrible winds, coconuts and tin roofs flying against the house. The rain. The car we'd parked out back so it would be away from the trees, and something shorted: the lights came on suddenly in the middle of the night, so we could watch the trees bend down through the rain. And these three old ladies wearing hats, playing bridge, discussing the possibilities of the next season. They drank. They chatted. They were starched in place. And then I realized every one of them had pissed herself, and gone on talking . . ."

"What were you doing in the Bahamas?" she said.

"I could tell you. I could tell you about the time I was a New Age minister. Crystals and balls. I was a bodyguard once, in Cannes. I was—"

There was a clatter of dishes, like sliding rocks.

He raised his voice. "I was—"

She shouted from the kitchen: "How did you ever find time to be Christopher Hart, then?"

≡

Trees closed in on the road. At first I thought it was the high moon that somehow made skeletons out of the branches; the moon was the change I noticed. But the trees, too, had changed, become sticks and charcoal, branches broken close to the trunk. Brush had been burned back and trimmed, and the trees stood around like ruins. I saw the ground smoking, or imagined I did.

I passed through Vila Nova without a problem, and took the main mountain road. The suburbs looked as they always looked: proper, gated, bland. The first stretch of woods was intact. But after another kilometer the road was blocked with a line of trestles.

I could have run the line easily. There were no cops out that late to check the traffic. But if the road was closed there, it must be closed by something more alarming farther on: live fire, fallen trees, the volunteer firefighters commandeering the road.

I took the side road that snakes along a contour to the castle at Vila Nova. I was used to seeing only trees at night, trees that came down to the edge of the road and surrounded the small, round, hollow castle that was tucked back in a valley. But tonight, the cover had gone. The castle sat in a bright winter of its own: bare trees, white ashy ground.

I pulled off the road for a moment. The woods used to soak up sound, even in the folds of the high *serra*, but now they might have lost that power. They might hear me in Formentina working the bends and sharp, stony rises on the back roads. But the back roads were all that I had.

I ought to have mapped out a strategy for this, but instead I had only what I could see and smell: the castle in its sea of ash and the cold, brilliant moonlight.

=

Hart brought tea through to Maria. He'd spent too long in the kitchen, fussed in drawers. She couldn't tell why he needed a screwdriver and wire.

She hadn't dressed. The breeze was slight but enough to raise faint prickles on her skin.

She says she didn't move in her chair when my car stopped below. Doors slammed once, then twice. The quiet returned.

I slipped on the slate outside, in a hurry, and went away and came rushing back. I thought if I waited a moment I'd somehow be unnoticed.

I saw that the reading light caught her across the neck, left her face in darkness, tinged her high, neat breasts with yellow light. Hart looked hard, as though he needed to memorize her.

She said, "There's someone at the door."

Hart looked at her and it didn't matter. She waited patiently.

I started shouting outside: "Maria! Maria!"

She didn't move. I mean that; she didn't even tense herself to stay still. She seemed to think that stillness and quiet would make me think she wasn't there and then I'd go away.

I, of course, muscles bunched up and adrenaline coursing, was still sure that she must be the victim.

She was smiling.

Hart never had a witness before. He never had someone else who knew what he did and what he could do, who would record him and keep him; love him, even.

I hammered on the door.

Since she wouldn't speak or move, Hart shouted, "She's here," and he threw the door open. A gust of night breeze scattered brown leaves into the room.

≡

I rushed the house and stood very still, breathing hard. I'd expected obstacles, and found none. I'd expected Maria in danger, but she was only undressed.

Maria said, "Go away. It's just a game. Go away."

I couldn't read the story in the room. There was Hart, with tea: domestic, half-naked, curiously busy for the middle of the night. I wasn't interested in Hart. There was Maria, not moving but quite free, sitting so I could not quite see her face but only her body. I'd had so much time to think about her body.

"You have to go away," Maria said.

I'd burst into some private moment, a cozy moment after making love. Perhaps.

Hart said, "You want some tea?" He said it with real kindness.

I didn't know what a man like me would do or say. I had nothing but TechniScope and De Luxe Color thoughts. I thought of *The Searchers*, and the girl who doesn't want to be saved.

Maria got up and went into the bedroom. Hart went into the kitchen to fetch another cup.

I could have invented all this. I could have made up the story about my father, the informer in that bright white room. Hart might be who he said, might not have done what he denied doing, might not be dangerous at all. Maria and Hart might simply be having a quick summer affair, or perhaps not even that. Perhaps she had stayed the night just because the roads were closed.

Everything in my own past had dissolved, so why should all the fixed points of a collective past, the books, records, papers, reports, mean anything more?

Hart and Maria hardly made noise in the house; they slipped around on agile, quiet feet. From the window I could see the village going down the valley like a fall of tiles and slate. Beyond that, the woods began again. There were no dogs barking, no talk, none of the reassuring city noises that meant life continued even when it was deep night.

Below the road, three men—young men—were throwing a barrel of liquid on a field in the moonlight: shadow figures, furiously active. They stepped back. One of them struck a match, and the gold of the flame was brilliant for a moment before he lit the field. It went up in billows of orange smoke.

"They're making a firebreak," Maria said, as though she could see what was going on. By the time she was beside me watching, the fire was raining sparks upward. The men were dancing.

≡

Maria came out dressed, talking urgently, almost whispering. "You've got to go," she was saying. "You don't know about Hart."

"Mello told me," I was saying.

"Did he tell you the whole story?"

"I know he's wanted for murder."

"Do you know how many murders?"

I stared at her. I shrugged.

"And you still came back here?" she said.

"I thought you were in trouble."

"I'm not in trouble. You are. I told you not to come."

I wouldn't believe it, of course. I have chivalry in the genes, and I know how proper stories go: woman at risk.

Hart walked into the living room.

Maria said, "We have to talk."

So he sat, and he tucked something down at the side of the chair, something springy that resisted being hidden. I was still standing, and Maria pacing like an advocate. Dogs took to barking.

She said to Hart, "Who are you?"

Hart said, "You mean me?"

"Listen to this, John," she said. "If you won't go, then listen."

"What do you want to know?" Hart asked.

She said, "Mello told me. You have a real name. You're Martin Arkenhout. You killed some kid in Florida, took his name, and a year later that kid's name disappeared; so you must have killed again. Now you're Christopher Hart, so knowing how you operate, you must have killed Hart."

"You say so," Hart said. What else was he meant to say? It was obvious this version of his lives was lying in a police file somewhere, an open, active file. They'd got it right, at last.

I said, "That's all you've got to say?"

"Exactly. What do you expect?" Hart tried to sound morally superior. "You want to know how to kill someone? You want the details? You get off on this kind of thing?"

I didn't lunge at him. I wanted to, though. My whole body was a policeman.

"Why don't you call the police?" Hart said. "You have a phone. I have a phone. I'm not stopping you."

"You know the roads are closed," Maria said.

"I expect the cops could risk it. Costa got here, after all."

Maria said, "I'm not leaving without Costa."

I sat down as if to make a point.

We were a stalemate nicely expressed in social terms—two men wedged in chairs, a woman pacing between them—but at a grossly early hour.

There was tea on the table: cups, milk, an old pot with the glaze cracked. It wouldn't do. There was no wasted furniture in the rooms, in the corners where the pale yellow light did not reach, and no big ornamental things. There was nothing I could use to take Hart down.

I thought animals would have done this better. Cats would arch backs, spike their fur, pose to say who was attacking, who was being attacked, then yowl and spit and jump. We had manners. Hart was the child of good middle-class Dutch parents who know how to sit at table and kneel in church. Maria wanted quiet most of all. As for me, I had this quaint residual notion that a man's guilt ought to be proved, and it was enough to hold me back from saving my own life.

Whatever Hart hid down by his chair, it sprang up for a moment: a circle of wire. He'd always been so efficient when it came to killing. Now he hesitated, in a nervous state of being ready for a crime he had not yet committed.

He tried to hide the wire.

≡

Maria smelled gasoline. The smell was faint, and it caught in her mind like a memory, but she knew it was close.

"You're crazy, both of you," she said. "You could run, Christopher. Or Martin. Or whoever you are. Get moving now, and they won't have alerted the frontier police. You could get into Spain without a check, and then you can go where you want. What's stopping you?"

Hart said nothing.

"And you, Mr. Costa. Why don't you go home now? There's nothing for you here. Nothing."

"I come from here," I said.

We were pacing behind a fence of words.

"You don't belong here."

"I know some Portuguese already. I know about Portugal from my father."

"You're from London. You have to go back."

I said, "But I don't have any reason—"

I stumbled up to my feet, not looking at Maria, fixed on Hart: on Hart, who'd fucked Maria, who'd doubted that she told the truth, who'd brought me here and wrecked things, who refused to be properly guilty even of theft, let alone murder. I know only genteel business on the whole—things purloined, the confederacy of dealers, some fakers, not the kind of street attitude that grins and teases and boasts—but I knew then the cold, useful rage that can come down on you when you want to punish as well as persuade with your fists.

Hart didn't back away. He stood in the yellow light and he let me fall toward him, right fist out, as though I were punching through a door. He was making me into a caricature: like a drunk professor. He dodged sideways and out of the light. I was shocked that the punch did not connect, and twisted around.

Maria saw Hart fetch the wire from the side of his chair. The wire was a ring twisted around wood at the side, around a screwdriver. She couldn't shout for fear of distracting me.

Hart dodged in and out of light. I waited, blocking the doorway. The man was only making shadows, huge, gangling shadows, on the wall and the ceiling. He had nowhere to run. He was casting about for an open window, but they were all closed: glass, and then bolted shutters beyond. If he tried to get out that way, he'd be caught before he could get the shutters opened wide.

Then Hart stopped dodging quite suddenly. His arms hung at his sides. I ran at him like a rugby forward, got him around the knees, and threw him down on the floor. Hart's head connected with the red-brown marble of the windowsill and his neck cracked.

Maria tugged her skirt into place and she walked out, down the shining slate steps, through the white of daisies and the sharp agapan-thus leaves that both caught the fading moon.

She sat by the chapel and she waited.

≡

Hart's eyes opened. It was as though he didn't have the force or will to keep them closed.

I thought he might have broken his spine. The only movement was those eyes, and they stared ahead. I felt pity for a moment, but only a moment. Then his arm jerked across his chest as though he were look-ing for something in an imaginary pocket.

He began to inhabit his body again, as a photograph slowly inhabits the paper as it develops, detail by detail: becoming Hart again.

So he wasn't crippled. He was only numb and dazed. I watched his eyes begin to seek out objects, to see me.

I knew that he wanted to kill me. He had chicken wire fixed around a screwdriver in a loop the size of a neck. You couldn't fix anything with it, but you could kill.

So there were no petty rules anymore. This was the unimaginable moment: an actual matter of life or death. We're always nervous of people who have known a choice like this: veterans, grandfathers with medals, cops on a street.

He tried to pull himself to his knees.

"What do you want?" he said.

He wasn't able to stand properly. There was blood on his head. When I went toward him, he scooted back awkwardly on his buttocks. I had never felt such power. He was the one who had always made choices, but now I could choose if he lived or died.

I squatted down beside him. "Tell me what you did," I said.

This is where I meant to play the hero. But mostly I wanted to fill the man's file and put him on proper record: the instinct of an archivist.

"What I did?"

"And where the pages of the Liber Principis are now."

"I'm not Christopher Hart," he said. "You know that, don't you? I was Christopher Hart for a while. I've never been in the Museum."

I hit him once across the face. It was pure cinema. It didn't mean a thing and it couldn't possibly have been useful.

"You want the whole story," he said. "Do you?" He thought he could defend himself with this whole story, and make me step back. He thought the story was some kind of advantage.

"I take lives," he said. "I take people's lives and I use them better than the previous owners ever could. So I've had all kinds of names and passports. I've been many ages. I've had cards and papers that prove I am a dozen men. And you know what? I get to make all the choices I want, one good choice after another. I make a mistake, I start again, in a different skin. Do you ever make a choice, John Costa?"

"Give me the names."

"I don't remember half the names. Why should I? I have to forget the names when I'm someone new. Did you ever slip out of your skin, John Costa?"

I didn't know why he was using so much of my name. Sometimes my father's friends did that, out of confusion about whether to use a name like an ID, as Americans and the British do, or like a history as the Portuguese do, with the family names lined up in a grand row.

I shouldn't have let myself think that, not for a minute. He wanted me distracted.

He had his hand up on the kitchen table, reaching. I couldn't stop him. He tugged down the oil bottle and it broke on the tile floor. He held the broken bottle.

In that moment, I could act. I, the man who was a spectator at the ruins of my own marriage, who only looked on when my father died and did not even know what had happened, who did nothing effective to bring back the pages and pictures I had come here to find. But now I was licensed to act.

The man had killed. The police wanted him, at least out of the way. Nobody would mind what I did. I had never before been so sure that I was morally superior, the better man.

I still couldn't take on all that glory and make myself kill. But I kicked at his hand and the broken glass flew in an arc of oil across the room.

The blood from his hand was very dark. He smeared a little on his face.

"Is this what a killer looks like?" he said.

He painted a bar across his forehead, another at his neck, all in blood.

"You look," he said.

He put his hands on the table and levered himself upright. I could see that his cut hand bent back at an odd angle.

He kept painting the blood across his face, stripe by stripe, as though he were inventing a monster everyone would recognize. Then he stood, and he waited.

He must have thought that every second I delayed was a chance for him. It meant I was indecisive. It meant I was still attached to my sense of order and reason.

And I was. I was mad with reason. I went for his throat.

He let himself die. He was younger, more resilient, had better wind, but he let me force the breath out of him. I broke his head on the tiled floor. I reduced him to a mess of blood and fiber. I obliterated the man.

I never heard a silence quite like that one. The world seemed to be keeping its distance from me, leaving a cold vacuum in which I could hardly breathe. I sat down heavily on a kitchen chair and waited for my heart to stop sounding in my head.

There was paper on the table, and a pen.

I drew a tree. It started simply, two pairs of branches, a solid trunk. I fussed with it, put branches to the branches, and then added twigs that crisscrossed: a bare tree. I began a geometric shape, a kind of rhomboid, and then put on each face another shape, until I had a mosaic of empty, awkward boxes.

I suppose I could have been a hero, there and then. I could have walked out of the house and declared myself the man who brought down a killer. But if I did that, I was shackled back in my old self, John Costa only: the same home and garden, marriage, hopes and prospects.

I broke the shell. I was thinking of Maria when I picked up the pen and I began to write purposefully: to draw a signature, then to practice and practice the signature of Christopher Hart.

≡

The dawn started over the mountain: only a wash of pale white, clouds touched up a little, a rooster shouting early, dogs shouting back, people already regretting their beds.

Nobody had slept very well. Fire was on everybody's mind.

Maria still sat by the chapel. She says she knew she could not budge either one of us from our private war and she preferred to wait, and deal with the consequences.

The dawn made a muddle of shadows up and down the hill. The first thing she saw was not a man moving, because anyone could move at will and stay invisible in the dappled light, but fire: orange flames that licked up suddenly in a straight line, then ran like a fuse around the corners of a building to the side of the village. She'd been looking at Hart's house, but this was lower and closer. The fire sent up dervishes of hot grass.

The building must be the old oil press, she thought: a stone square full of old wood and iron. There might be oil still lying there. The shadows played shapes on the wall, ghosts faded by the rising sun.

Then the building lifted, or else the shock rocked her to her feet. Flame came from inside: no smoke, just clean orange fire. For a moment, she couldn't think what blew with such drama, but every house had propane gas for cooking and heating water, and a single tank might throw out that force. A minute later, a second tank blew, and then a third.

Someone must have put space heaters in the oil press. She liked an explanation, any explanation.

The sound of the explosions ricocheted between the folds of the mountain and only when it died away softly did she hear the crisp, distinct sound of flames.

The village opened at once: courtyards with gates swinging, doors wide, shutters back and windows open in the same grand morning gesture that usually welcomes clean air. But the fire at the oil press was dirty and chemical—the gasoline she remembered smelling, the propane tanks she knew must be there—and the sound and stink of it were unfamiliar, even there where fire visits every summer.

She ran up the slate steps, people joining her from each side, a riot of worry. The houses were so close there was no chance of making a firebreak; they had to fight the fire directly. Some of the men disappeared into the woods to open each farmer's reservoir, and run the water in fat rubber hoses to wet the press down. Women came out with buckets and set them down by the public fountain, ready to start a chain of water up the hill. Some brought brooms, still hoping the fire was a natural one that would keep its distance.

The village didn't have time for words. It was all muscle, bringing down the heavy snakes of hoses, dragging up water from the fountain. The smoke fretted inside lungs, made eyes bleed red tears. The slow rise of the dawn had made the shadows on the mountain faintly pink, like an echo of fire.

Maria felt the weight of the buckets wrench her shoulders. She'd seen so much evidence go up in flames each day: petty evidence, garbage in woods, grass flattened by lovers, skins where snakes passed, bottles and what was in them. Fire took it all. But now the fire was inside the walls. It threatened the contents of houses, the shapes of lives, the crops in the fields, and the woods themselves, which were crops, after all.

The village was impersonal as a machine. Some of the younger women, strong and round, beat the flames down around the oil press so at least the fire could not jump. Three men played water on the roof, to stop the tiles cracking and bouncing out of place, to soak the old eucalyptus beams below. But the heat inside caught at the old oiled wood and melted it down.

It seemed everyone was busy with the fire. Nobody stopped; stopping was not an option. And yet, in the shouting, Maria heard a car start down below.

Later, when the fire was down and a small, sooty crowd stood around outside the bar drinking wine and listening, she saw that Christopher Hart's car had gone.

≡

Fire found out everything natural inside the oil press and ruined it. The walls, of mud, stones, and clay, were blown out and baked; the water that fought the fire had soaked them and they fell down to rubble. Inside, the different levels were still clear on the hillside, and there were huge bent metal cogs, but everything else was a kind of archaeological trace. There was a steel band running round the top of the walls, the kind used to hold houses together; it must have concentrated the explosion.

She got into the building while the stones were still hot and spars of wood or metal sagged overhead. She picked her way over timbers whose resin had boiled away in blisters. She dodged the remains of circular machines and stones. She wanted to be the first one, even pretended to be quasi-official, because she did not want the children to see what she had to see.

Gears had fused; they looked like eels in a bag. The floorboards were burned and ashy. Scorch marks flared up and down the walls.

He could be under timbers, or under the stones themselves, or the fallen metal details of the two presses. Perhaps the explosion had been enough to blow him apart. She stopped in her tracks, appalled at the thought, but only for a moment. She had to know.

She found him in the lower of the oil reservoirs, curled in a circle and crushed. The body was so blackened that, for a moment, she failed to see that it stopped at a garotte, the wire like a stopper on the body. The head was somewhere else.

She wanted to throw up. But without the head, she wouldn't know which one of them had survived; she knew now how little was proved by cards and papers.

She kicked about in the ash. She looked at the base of the great screw for the larger oil press. She looked up, and falling soot cut at her eyes.

She found a skull, broken, with coy veils of flesh and no eyes. It lay by one of the propane tanks. She made herself look carefully. She'd seen something almost as bad in Mello's office: the face of Christopher Hart. But this thing was terrible because it had not yet been put away in the secure category of evidence. It was suggestive, like a guessing game.

She turned away and the wind went out of her belly all at once, and she crumpled and propped herself on a hot, wrecked mass of gears and pulled her hand away burned.

This skull belonged to a man she knew: the man who made love to her and told her stories, or else the man who came chasing to save her, the one she tried to save from dying quite so soon.

She could not tell.

Eight

The first night, John Costa stayed in a small hotel on the road out of Oporto: short, square bed, red silk flowers, and a bathroom stinking of new paint. It took me ten minutes in a cafe to decide what name I'd use to take the room.

I still had this sense of continuity, maybe honesty.

But the next morning I was Christopher Hart on the road across Spain. John Costa killed a man. I couldn't be John Costa anymore.

I let the road carry me north, across a bare red plain, skies cracked with occasional storms, as if some old Victorian panorama were unfolding alongside the car: a wall of paint and make-believe, not hot land dowsed in sudden rain. The road placed me, told me the names of destinations, but also stopped me from ever quite reaching them; I was always on the outskirts, behind screens of fence and wood that were meant to keep my traces, sight and sound, from the living, settled people.

Three and a half days I rolled on like this. I did not stop unnecessarily. The next time I risked a hotel to sleep and shower, I woke up angled like a driver in my bed.

I liked borders best when I had passed them. At least they put some necessary definitions in the continuous roll of the road: signs to prove that I had left Portugal for Spain, Spain for France, France for Belgium.

Then I worried that I hadn't been cleared at the borders, so I might be checked and challenged anywhere on the road.

This fizz of nerves changed to anger. There was nobody, not even paid bureaucrats, to care who I was. The anger became fear. I broke off from my past entirely, a perfect escape, but I escaped into emptiness, carrying nothing. I particularly could not carry, didn't have the shoulders or the back to carry, the fact of killing someone.

The weather soured around me. After Paris, I crossed the flatlands around Lille, the brick skirts of Brussels, tracking rail lines and power lines. The rain was persistent. It curtained off some gray towns, some cold neon ones, a few churches, and once a stretch of plant with high chimneys between a scaffolding of pipes.

I drew money as I went, bank machine after bank machine, a fat pocketful of colors: pesetas, French francs, Belgian francs. The cards might stop working any day and I had to be ready. The name Christopher Hart could wear out.

I risked another hotel.

Nobody ever checked the signature for the credit cards. For a while, only incongruity would give me away: a dead man traveling.

I wiped the steam from the bathroom mirror to look at myself. You fade as you age, gray about the muzzle, eyes softened, face less full of blood and life; and I was fading.

I kept wiping the steam away with my sleeve, but all I added to the picture was a reflection of white walls, the plastic shower curtain, the glimpse of a bed through the door.

≡

Maria Mattoso saw the Oporto train coming from a distance: a great shiver of orange metal in the haze. People crowded the shade on the platforms, bags and cases and kids in piles, old ladies with fans, very young soldiers. Gentleman travelers with shirts still magically starched went picking their way between them all.

She finished her water and waited for the train to come to a perfect stop. She was here out of duty. She had no wish to rush things.

The train opened. The crowd milled at the doors, scrambling up, struggling down. Some families, from aunts to newborns, pushed past.

After them all came Anna Costa.

"I'm very grateful," Anna said. She was dressed seriously, but not in black.

"I'm very sorry," Maria said.

Anna stared. "At least I didn't have to find him," she said.

On the road, Anna seemed to relax a little, even to grin at olive trees overwhelmed by brilliant blue morning glory.

"The police would like you to make a formal identification, I'm afraid," Maria said.

"Is that even possible?"

"It won't be easy. After the fire, and the explosions—"

"Can I do it now?"

Maria said, "You're sure you want to do that after traveling?"

The road crossed a long iron bridge. Below, on the shoals of a wide river, sheets were laid out to dry on the pebbles and children played in the shallows.

Anna said, "I wanted to come back, you know." Then, since Maria said nothing, "It must be terrible for you, too." And then, relentlessly, "You think they'll find him?"

"I'm sure they will."

"And how will you feel—"

Maria concentrated on the road as it climbed through a steep valley, one side pines full of summer dust, the other the black-spike remains of a burned wood.

She said, "Do you have anywhere to stay?"

"I hadn't thought. There's the house in Formentina."

"Stay with me. There's not much furniture, but it'll be easier. You'll need help with the police. Translating." When Anna didn't answer, she thought she should add: "I won't charge you."

She went with Anna to the morgue.

Anna noticed the cracks in the white wall tiles, the cold air stale as a cave, anything except the body. That, she saw from the corner of her eye. The flesh was burned and blistered away, bones broken up so it was hard to get the measure of the man on the slab, if it was one single man; and the skull was wrecked, more like a carved totem than one particular person. She didn't bother to ask questions about teeth or measuring the bones.

The cops showed her a ring from close to the body. She identified it. So she said the body must be John Costa.

The cops' shoulders relaxed. They still felt the blasphemy in cutting up the dead just to give them a name.

At dinner that night, Anna said to Maria, "He belongs here, doesn't he? I want to bury him here." Then she said, "This way it won't be a failure, you see. John Costa and me. We never quite had the time to fail."

Maria Mattoso poured wine.

≡

She unlocked the office door. A postcard had been pushed under it; she almost slipped on a cliché picture of trees around some Metro sign in Paris with a boulevard falling back out of focus.

She picked it up and took it to the light. It was signed with a single letter, *C,* made with a big and almost theatrical movement of the pen; so it was Christopher Hart.

The message was in block capitals. "WISH YOU WERE HERE."

≡

I couldn't believe I had disappeared properly. I thought there must be all kinds of official networks following me: police, banks, border guards. I cut off the grand roads and started toward the sea.

When I was a kid, I used to think that everything began and ended at the edge of the sea, that I could find a safe no-man's-land with my heels in the surf. I thought if I just swam out between the waves and rested on the power of the sea I would be safe from anything that ever happened on the land.

But it isn't that easy to find the sea now the Dutch have built their dams and defenses against it. I drove slowly through a bit of Zeeland, flat except for the defensive dikes that carry the roads, full of bare autumn orchards. The water, when I got there, began slipping away from the shore, leaving a farm of stakes for the mussels and oysters. Far out, the raw waters chopped at themselves.

I found a small town, with a shelter above the harbor, full of old-timers smelling of wet and smoke, all variously crouched and bent as if they were complaining. I couldn't hear anything for the wind.

I didn't want to go to a restaurant and be the conspicuous outsider. I looked through the glove compartments in case there was a biscuit, maybe chocolate. There was a Virgin Mary, of all things, a little blue ceramic with a perfectly satin pink face.

I soaked in self-pity. But you can't pity a self that doesn't properly exist. Q.E.D.

I started laughing.

Cities seemed to make sense, for safety's sake. I secured myself in a stream of other traffic, sure of my direction, no idea of any destination. Perhaps Rotterdam would do. Perhaps Haarlem. Perhaps Amsterdam.

Then I knew I was exhausted.

I knew it when I had to jerk the wheel to keep out of the path of a huge black truck in the fast lane. I thought I heard a siren, but it was the truck's horn fading on the wind. I couldn't afford to be pulled in for some traffic offense, so I slowed as though the car were crippled and went off at the next exit.

I stopped almost at once on an avenue of poplar trees. I wound down the window of the car. The sound of the rain merged with the rustle of wet tires on the highway.

A heron sat at the edge of black water, gray and bearded, completely still.

It occurred to me, the first time because I was not always thinking straight, that the only reason all Christopher Hart's cards still worked must be that they left an easy trail across Europe: statement by statement, buy by buy.

So I thought about selling the car. It was the one major asset left: muddy, but with a shine underneath, and a quite-new model. But selling meant turning over papers, meant opening the chance that someone would get to ask why Christopher Hart, who'd been murdered twice already, was doing business with some garage in a small Dutch town.

I wanted somewhere to stop and get warm and be noticed, even known, by someone else: to find some boundary of myself.

I woke up in full dark.

I turned on the lights and started the engine. The world could have seen the sudden burst of light and sound across the bare flatlands, in between the thin trunks of the poplars. I edged forward.

The trees kept cutting into the beam of the headlights, a flicker of silver bark. My foot slipped on the accelerator. As for my hands, they were a little late on the wheel. The car jerked forward off the road, veered over the wet grass, and hung at the edge of the water.

I heard the rain beating on the roof.

You fret like a child at moments like this. I kept worrying that I had no truly rainproof coat, that I'd get a cold and not be well enough for the rest of my life.

I tried to reverse, but the wheels had no traction on the slick grass, and the front wheels were catching on the muddy sides of the water. I heard the wheels spin, and the car jolted forward again.

I got out fast, collected what I could, pulled a leather jacket around me to keep my papers dry. The papers still seemed to matter. I remembered to pull the wad of banknotes out of my trouser pocket before they turned to papier-mâché.

The car slithered forward, paused, moved again, paused again, settling very slowly past the borders of the water, off the grass and mud and into the river. I didn't know how deep the water might be.

I couldn't save the car. So it had to drown before anyone turned off the road and tried to be helpful, and asked the same kind of questions that had ruined Arkenhout before me: careful questions in a logical line.

I pushed. My feet slithered on the grass. I pushed again. The car levered up in the dark, nose down. It stayed put, lights now below the water, metal belly flashing to the world. The river glowed from the lights, like quick and brown stained glass.

I should report this, I thought. Walking away is a crime. It's curious how much more proper and exact you become when you have a killing to forget: a model citizen.

I washed my boots off in a puddle of still water, being as neat as I could.

The lights under the river went very bright and died. I heard a nightbird call through the new dark.

The car listed to the right with a comfortable creaking sound.

At last, that was a process I could help. I pushed and the car began to shift in the air, from an upright monolith stinking of oil to a ruin at an angle. It stopped again. I felt the mud of the bank slipping under me. I jumped inland just in time as the car swung down and bit into the water, and then settled, threatened for a moment to float, sucked air down deep into the river as it settled under the water.

I saw myself in the car, under the brown water, breath coming in a sigh of bubbles and then stopping dead. But I knew I would struggle and shout against dying. Even this doubtful, hollow self of mine had a quite horrifying will to go on.

The rain started up again.

I picked up a plastic shopping bag of food and water, and the flight bag I'd bought in Paris, a bag on wheels that I couldn't drag through the puddles, and I started walking. I could smell oil on my skin, feel the mud caking wetly on my legs. I came to the railway line three miles on. I changed in the station lavatory, stuffed my wet, muddy clothes into the plastic bag, and walked out almost respectable, but with sodden hair.

The first train was for Amsterdam Central.

The carriage was empty except for a restless boy who kept rolling and rerolling a cigarette as though he wanted to make something perfect.

When I traveled with Anna, a long time ago, two seats on a train became a warm and private room. I remembered this. I kept the boy in sight all the time.

≡

The next postcard was from Amsterdam. Maria called Mello at once.

He seemed glad of the information, such as it was.

She said to Mello, "I'm sorry José Costa's son had to die."

Mello said, "Any death is terrible."

"But of all the men—"

"I forgave the father," Mello said. "How could I want to harm the son?"

Maria waited him out.

"I said, how can you think I would have wanted to harm the son? I tried to keep him in Lisbon. Of course I did. I'm grateful for your information. Please inform us if you receive any other communications."

Mello's men took the card away with ceremony, as though it might contain the whole story encoded somewhere in the picture of gabled houses, the stamps with the Queen's head, the usual message: "Wish you were here."

They left Maria furious with Hart. He must think she could see a body blown apart and take it as just another story like all the others, a sensation to share down a phone line at night. Or else he was teasing her: the clichés on the cards, picture and message, suggested a tease. She wished the police had left the postcard behind, so she could hold it, stare at it, try to sense with her fingertips what he meant and what he was doing: wandering, without a life after taking so many lives of his own, looking for his next name.

The phone rang in her office. She thought of letting the machine answer; she didn't want another boundary dispute, another minor criminal escapade or urgent rewriting of a will until she had closed the matter of Christopher Hart. Anna Costa, at least, had something to bury.

It was a collect call. She could hear the operator's voice through the machine: speaking English, but overprecise, maybe Dutch. She picked up the phone, but the line had already gone dead.

She knew it was Hart. She couldn't say precisely why, whether she was truly sure, or whether she was just eager for the comfort of finishing the story. But she stayed in the office for a while, waiting.

There were no more calls that day.

≡

I put down the phone. It wasn't sensible to call. It wasn't possible to avoid it. Maria was my only connection to my own whole story, the one who knew what nobody else must or could know. I thought I needed her.

I had a headache from all the empty time I now owned. The hotel corridor, pale walls, shining linoleum, the green-white of cheap fluorescent light, didn't help; but I could hardly choose. This hotel did not seem unduly interested in passports or papers. It was cheap. The management, briskly, took a cash deposit for a week.

I counted out the money I'd drawn driving north. I walked over to Dam Square, a wide-open shine of black cobbles in the rain, to find the automatic change machine. I fed it pesetas, French francs, Belgian francs; it handed back guilders. I felt organized for a while.

I slept with the money beside my pillow, shifting throughout the night to check it was still there, like a boy with a treasure or a man in the wilds.

≡

I couldn't talk to anybody. I couldn't talk to nobody. The subject I had to discuss was responsibility for a death, and it had to stay private; but without chat, bluster, jokes, it always threatened to burst out like some madman's curbside sermon.

I needed dinner, anyway. I found a Portuguese restaurant, took the table next to a man who was working construction in Brussels, no family, up for the weekend to riot and drink beer. Then, overcome with *saudade*, which is to nostalgia as a whirlwind is to a breeze, he'd come to this restaurant for something familiar from home: pork and clams, maybe, the authentic cracked egg of *pudim Molotov* and some red wine from Bairrada. He had a list in his mind of how to conjure his home on a table: pig, sugar, rice, potatoes, wine.

"You know Portugal?" he said, the second time.

"I was in Vila Nova de Formentina this summer."

"Everything's good there?"

"Everything's good. You got family there?"

He shook his head. Then he said, "I'm from the Minho. I had a wife, but she died. I haven't been back to see my parents in two years, not since we buried her."

"It's all work," I said. "You want a drink?"

After a quiet moment, I said, "Everything's new around Vila Nova. New buildings. New houses. They're building a new swimming pool."

"Indoors?"

Another beer.

"Work's easy in Brussels?"

"There's work. And you come in legally now. It's good to be in Europe."

"There must be other Portuguese—"

"They have families. I don't. They stick to themselves mostly." He wanted to change the subject, obviously. He wanted to claim a bright, good life for himself. So "What's money?" he said, and ordered a serious bottle of Colares red, which he poured with a flourish. "I once drank the wine at Bussaco," he said. "In the palace. In the gardens. It was a white wine, very old. Tasted of varnish. But good varnish."

He was dark like me. Our builds weren't very different, except he had used his body hard, so its mass was entirely solid, like good rope.

I saw he was paying cash. I wondered if he even had credit cards, bank cards.

"I need a walk," he said. "I need somewhere with girls."

"There are girls in the windows."

"I need someone to talk to. I can fuck anytime."

We strode along the canals, although we had nowhere particular to go, just the hope of a low, warm bar with company.

He said his name was Boaventura.

"Good name," I said, weighing it in my mind.

≡

Maria went back to Formentina, just to check on things. The morning had been cold and wet, but the sun had broken through and the lanes had begun to smell of grapes—musky, sweet grapes—and the quite separate smell of the new wine rising.

The oil press, she could see, was now a low ruin. The scorch marks shone black. Water must be getting into the rubble walls. She was glad it couldn't stand much longer.

She climbed the side track, alongside the ashy edge of the forest, to what had once been Christopher Hart's house.

She needed to organize a new door because policework had left the old one only parked in place. She thought: He paid all the rent in advance, so there's no urgency in letting the place again.

She pushed the door open carefully and propped it against the wall.

The house was dark and stale, which is what she expected; she had closed all the shutters and windows herself. Even the brilliant light from the door made only a tentative square on the floor.

In this darkness, she kept just missing things from the corner of her eye. She thought events must somehow have imprinted themselves on the dust and the dead air. If she wasn't careful, she'd start catching hints and signs in the corners.

She put on the lights, to be reasonable.

The kitchen and the living room both were empty now and unmarked by anything that had happened: it was a house for rent again, just enough chairs and spoons for the summer. She checked some of the drawers in case she had missed something: a book, a brush, something small.

She looked into the bathroom. The rack held a little survey of sunscreens, in white bottles, orange tubes. They seemed useful, so she'd left them.

She stood at the door of the bedroom. It was framed in surprising light.

He was there, she thought, in the next room, always in the next room. She kept opening doors to find him.

She pushed open the bedroom door.

A man stood in the middle of the bright room. Against the sun from the open windows, she thought at first she was seeing Hart: tall, head down, hands laced together. She imagined how he would be when he turned to her.

But when he turned, she knew he was wrong. Hart had never carried a sack of a stomach. The hands, too, were wrong: the fingers did not taper as she remembered.

It took her a moment to accept that she was facing Mello.

"Why are you here?" she said.

Mello was not used to being challenged. Besides, it was as though she had interrupted him in prayer or meditation, and he had to remind himself to answer her.

"I'm sorry if I alarmed you," he said.

"There's no police car down below."

"I walked here from Vila Nova."

"Why would you walk? You never walk." She knew his grand and impressive transits into other people's lives, his official progress through the town.

"I wanted to be here for a moment," he said. "On my own."

"I have to inspect the house," she said. "We'll need to rent it again—"

"I needed to be on my own."

Maria said, "I have things to attend to."

"Please," Mello said. She thought of him as a presence in uniform, with very still eyes; it was startling to see his face properly for the first time, all animated with lines and feeling. "I wanted to think."

Maria went to close the shutters.

"You'll have to leave," she said.

She wondered if he had walked here as some kind of pilgrimage.

"You know I killed them both," Mello said.

Maria, disconcerted, said, "Both of them?"

"John Costa. And his father."

"But how could you kill his father?"

"The PIDE beat me. They used water and sound on me. I've had a ringing in my left ear ever since. It never stops. Then they decided I was too young to know anything, so they talked about crippling my legs so I couldn't get into more trouble, and they could catch me if I did."

Maria said, "I don't want to hear all this."

"José Costa didn't want to hear, either, at first. But I went to talk to him the day he died."

"He died of a heart attack. He wasn't a healthy man."

"He was healthy. He was stronger than I am, and healthier."

The brilliance of the sun, the white of the walls, isolated Mello in an interrogator's light.

"That morning, I thought everything was resolved. After all these years," he said. "I was glad he came back, glad I could settle things. That afternoon, when I heard he had died, it was as though I was suddenly to blame, as though I had to take back the burden of my own damned suffering. And then John Costa comes, and John Costa dies and—"

Maria saw the man's officialdom and authority broken down into tears. She was frightened. She knew he would have to reassert himself, deny everything he was saying, in order to go back to being the police-man who expects compliance. He would assert himself against her later, she was sure.

He said, "I thought I was such a good man that I could forgive José Costa. I suppose I wasn't. I suppose John Costa's death proves that."

Maria watched him make his back rigid again, and his face stern, and his eyes dry.

She said, "If Hart had never come here—"

"Some things would be just the same," Mello said.

At the door to the house, she asked him, "Will you ever find the people who vandalized the grave?"

"No," Mello said.

"You don't want to know."

"Everyone knew the story. It could be anyone."

She realized what he meant: that it was a civic duty to enforce the memory of even little treasons. He had put on authority again, and he would not be questioned.

≡

I thought I should use Hart's bank card while it lasted.

I looked for a bank machine, stepped up, fed the card to the wall, opted for the English language and three hundred guilders—a nice, average transaction, the most the bank wanted to hand out.

The transaction is being processed. There was a sunflower on the screen.

A few people milled behind me, waiting in the rain.

The transaction is being processed. The sunflower stayed.

An English tourist started bobbing from one side of me to the other, as though I was willfully taking my time, and other people's. I couldn't be bothered to explain.

The transaction is being processed.

The transaction cannot be processed. The sunflower did not change.

The card came back.

Christopher Hart was dead.

I slipped the card into my shirt pocket and closed my jacket against the wind. I thought I could try John Costa's card, but the little line of people was radiating impatience. Besides, John Costa must have lost his credit by then; Anna is a practical woman.

I walked briskly. I felt a boy's shame at being noticed or conspicuous. Then I was all mind, working on the possibilities. I didn't feel the cold for a while.

Maybe the machine in Dam Square was just a bad moment in the wired world. But if anyone wanted to know where to find me, I'd just told them: a walk away from Dam Square, with no extra money for a cab.

That night I dreamed I was a schoolboy out running, cold and wet and breathless, pounding along mud tracks and suburban streets in a convoy of misery. I couldn't leave the course; I'd be seen. I couldn't stop running because I was being timed.

I woke up cold.

I had lost all my possible names and lives, except one: Martin Arkenhout. I even thought, just as he had always thought, that I could do it better.

≡

Boaventura said his father had worked one time in London, but not for very long. He should have gone when he was twenty, but that was during the world war, so he had to wait. He came back when he couldn't bear the separation from his real life anymore, and he was famous for buying a little car—a third-hand Renault—which he still drove too fast through the village, too slow on the big roads.

It was very early in the evening to ease down into drink, but it was pleasant enough. Besides, I didn't want to show Boaventura that I was jealous of a father who had come back to him.

He would be my father, anyway, if I was Boaventura.

The idea of killing was still quite abstract. I had no weapon, no plan, no notion of what to do with a body in the middle of the city, except perhaps that it could be weighted down and dumped into a canal. I could see only the need to be someone else, and the possibility of being one thing at last, which is Portuguese, and not a half-dozen mixes of class, nation, attitudes. I would put away the complications and become whole.

But to get there, I had to stab, shoot, bludgeon, drown, or throttle this particular man, had to edge myself out of jealousy and into a clear sense of superiority: Arkenhout's perpetual state of being the northerner in Europe, and sure he was somehow better, more advanced, more rational than anyone else.

"Those women," Boaventura said. "They're smiling." He called over the waitress and had her take a couple of beers to the two blondes, around forty, faces like good bread, who were sitting together at another green baize table across the bar.

The women did smile. One of them beckoned us over.

You can't agonize so much under a blanket of beer, thighs brushing up against you so casually, time passing without it mattering, a plate of mussels with sauces and bread to mop up the drink and the talk about families, homes, intimacies so casually brought to strangers like children bring each other their favorite toys.

Nobody went home with anyone else, either, except that the two women caught the Metro to the south and we saw them off. They kissed us, big kisses full of beery warmth.

Boaventura wandered off, happily. He said we should go drinking the next night, too. See how our luck holds. See what comes up.

≡

I kept walking. I walked half the next day, despite the wet and the cold. I walked the long, blank avenues leading out of the city, with their parade of warm windowscapes: parlors, cats, libraries, kitchens so white and clean they looked like a lesson in morals. Then I doubled back into the old city, dodged into alleys between leaning buildings, past the pimps trying to keep casual on the street corners. I stopped every so often for a beer or a coffee, just to be sure I could still get warm again.

I do not remember thinking about murder, or Boaventura. I felt myself as clean and empty as paper taking impressions.

I came up against all the Gothic spires of the Rijksmuseum, on the other side of a cold, black canal. I saw it as a refuge, and not just because everything inside was subtly ordered, period by period, case by case. All my life, I could always lose myself in paint and forms and signs, even in the jostle of a public gallery. I knew where my history must be: in books and pictures.

I paid and entered. I walked the steps, and I turned into the print room: cases full of engravings, all country scenes and hayricks and tavern drunks, so I imagined. I couldn't see them for the lights shining in the glass; at least I thought the problem was the lights.

I wandered into galleries of furniture: like parodies of settled, domestic rooms, but not yet cluttered enough by living people. There were dollhouses, small lives sliced open.

I walked past paintings that I used to think were glories and lessons, because I used to let myself admire and revere. But now the paintings hung inert on the walls, a line of facts of oil, canvas, board.

I stopped in front of a painting by Frans Post. This at least should have some grand significance: it was painted, I knew, on the same expedition that produced the Liber Principis. The books were the catalog of wonders and this big canvas was a window dresser's version of them all.

I saw a panorama, caught in a great carved frame of strangling vines. I saw: breadfruit clustered on a tree, scarlet birds, a louche monkey lolling, a pangolin snouting at a gourd, a great frog, a pineapple, all making a chorus line of specimens arranged on swags of bush in front of the big, wide stage of the picture; and on the stage, ruins of a cathedral and assorted visitors, whites ahead, blacks in respectful ranks; and beyond that, blue ripples of hills merging up into a sky the same, faintly purplish blue. I could see each item, one by one.

But I wanted to be lost in the picture, to feel a prickle of excitement on my skin. Instead, my mind turned over like some card index. I picked out facts: Post was the first trained, official landscape artist to go to the New World; he painted this panorama in Holland when he came back, a propaganda piece; he'd taken the brilliance of a bird's wing and made it just a flourish in a provincial mind.

Post took to drink soon after. I knew that.

I stood there long enough to start the guard fretting.

If I couldn't read the picture for myself, perhaps I could read the picture as someone else would have done, say a Dutchman in the 1660s: proud the Dutch controlled this rich Brazilian coast with all its wonders, prouder still the Dutch had burned out the Portuguese who used to be there and ruined a Catholic cathedral in the Protestant cause. But I was stuck on the dusty surface, among dates and facts.

I wanted to touch the frame. I suppose that was obvious.

The guard stood up and paced a bit. She used her telephone. She made long passes across the gallery, each one coming closer to me.

I was flattered she thought I was still capable of obsession.

I tried to look at other pictures, a contorted swan, a famous face, a landscape of fields and picturesque woods, but the Post drew me back. I had such a hopeless need to feel, and I felt nothing.

I panicked. I walked away.

The guard followed me into the next room, talking again on her telephone. Two guards appeared on either side of the far door.

I walked steadily, carefully, not wanting to provoke the guards, but my self-consciousness worried them even more. Then I could not see them for the tears.

≡

I had the pictures from the Liber Principis spread out on the bed.

There was a butterfly, and a parrot flying away, the butterfly black and folded with pink flourishes on its wings, the parrot looking over its dark shoulder with sharp eyes; and a long, plated armadillo painted as if in a sunset. There was a strangely mottled horse with the face of a medieval saint. There was a man, gray-haired and yellow-pale with a little belly, sitting naked on a rock with a pipe in his hands; the rock had been chalked or carved with the picture of an ox.

I couldn't sell the elder. For a start, he was too obviously someone out of the Amazon; he needed explanation.

I bought a plastic case to fit the pictures, and I took the armadillo first.

I tried a dealer in a street of stamp shops. He had a store almost without light, dusty frames of prints; and he was faded, short, indistinct in a corner with a rolltop desk full of papers. He frowned a lot, but that may have been his pince-nez. He liked the picture, obviously, saw it in the window alongside the tinted maps of Amsterdam.

"Fair condition," he said. "Looks seventeenth century. Nice subject. But there's a lot of this stuff about, you know. They bake the

paper. They use the right paints. They turn them out in a studio somewhere." He looked at the edges of the paper. "The paper looks right,
though." Then he grabbed back his bargaining position. "I'd need to
know a bit more," he said.

"It's a family thing," I said.

"But it's not framed," he said. "Families frame things."

"I was told," I said, "by my grandfather that it was painted by—"

Then I stopped. It wasn't shame at selling something stolen. Shame
comes and goes, especially when you're frightened. This was habit,
something so fixed it felt more like an instinct: I couldn't separate one
image from the others. I had built a career on the proprieties of keeping
sets together, of knowing origins and provenance in an unbroken chain
back to the day the paint dried; so I could never be the one to take the
significance away from this paper and reduce it to something pretty.

I didn't have principles. I had habits. That was a disconcerting
lesson.

"Well," the man said. "Families tell one another a lot of stories. A
scholar, your grandfather?"

I shrugged.

"It's pretty," he said. He named a price: three weeks in that small
hotel room, some decent meals.

I took back the picture.

"If you don't have a provenance," he said, "I can't go higher. Too
much risk. It looks like someone cut one edge."

"Do I look like a thief?"

"I wish I knew what thieves looked like," he said.

I stood outside the shop for a moment. There was a print dealer
next door, one across the way, a book dealer I remembered just across
the next canal.

It was almost dark. I took the tram back to the hotel and slept in
sweaty starts, as if I had a fever.

≡

The whole next day needed killing.

I wanted no more reminders of what I had lost, but that meant I had
to stay away from everything that would usually have been kind or

exciting or absorbing, just in case I had lost the power to respond. I was on an iced sea, drifting with my eyes closed, in my mind.

Only I was in a city bar: coffee, coffee cream, orange juice, tiny glass of water, wrapped biscuit, cigarillo smoke in my eyes, a middle-aged couple reading a newspaper at the next table, handing each other the world page by page. A very thin, very blond girl left her bicycle against the window.

It didn't seem enough to anchor me to reality. I thought that if I had lost the ability to respond, to fancy the girl, to taste the coffee, to see a picture, then I had nothing to lose by dying.

I wondered how, in an orderly city like Amsterdam, you arrange your own death. I thought there must be a form to fill.

The middle-aged man at the next table slammed down his water and the glass cracked open loudly. The middle-aged woman looked briefly at the spreading water and the chunks of ice and glass, and went back to the news from Algeria.

I couldn't sit and indulge myself this way, like some mooning adolescent, like someone entitled to the privilege of meditating on death instead of fighting it off in the obligatory, commonsensical way. I had killed a man. I didn't have privileges.

I could see the Arkenhouts. I could tell them about Martin. I could close the story for them.

It seemed like such a luminous idea at the time, because I had no other ideas: a mission of mercy, in a way.

I had the name of his parents' town; Arkenhout had given me that. I took the train there, over wet flatlands that lay in the shadow of enormous stormy skies. I checked the phone book in a station booth.

"Mrs. Arkenhout?" I said, although there was no doubt.

"Yes."

"My name is"—and I was unsure for a moment—"Christopher Hart."

Silence. Mrs. Arkenhout was just a silence at the other end of the line.

"I have a photograph of Martin—"

"I know all about photographs."

"It's a photograph from two months ago."

"Oh."

"I would have sent it to you, but I didn't want it to be a shock."

"You don't think it's a shock when someone rings you up like this?"

"I'm sorry."

"Well, well," said Mrs. Arkenhout, but she did not put down the phone.

"I'm at the railway station—"

"You want to look out for pickpockets. There are pickpockets at the railway station."

"I could get a taxi. If you could spare me a half-hour? An hour?"

"I can't stop you coming. I might not open the door, but you can come."

I should have said "Thank you" as though this were an ordinary conversation.

The price of the taxi was three times what I expected, although we hardly left the town. I paid, got out, and felt the cold cut at me.

I walked through a garden of autumn wreckage, neatly tied. I rang the doorbell.

"It's me, Christopher Hart," I shouted.

The taxi driver stayed waiting. There were lights in the house, and somebody to take in this foreigner, but he didn't want to take chances.

Mrs. Arkenhout said, "I'm not sure?"

"I just wanted a private talk."

"My husband isn't home."

"He doesn't have to know," I said, thinking that must be what Mrs. Arkenhout wanted to hear.

After a moment, the door opened.

Mrs. Arkenhout knew only one Christopher Hart. I was someone quite different.

I saw the disappointment, then the fear in her face. She tried for a moment to block the narrow hall, her hips between the sideboard and the pictures on the opposite wall, tried to push the door shut so she could lock it properly against ghosts and strangers. But she lost her nerve.

"I don't know anything about Martin," Mrs. Arkenhout said. "Martin left a long time ago."

"But you let me in."

"Oh, yes. I let you in." Then she recovered herself, a physical recovery like scooping up a trailing skirt or straightening a slouched back.

"Would you like some coffee?" she said.

I almost laughed at her nice manners. I felt obliged to offer something mannerly in return. I took a photograph out of my wallet and showed it to her as some proof of good intentions: a summer picture, Maria and Arkenhout on a wall by a tiled fountain, the light and shadows brilliant.

"This is Martin, isn't it?" I said.

"No." But Mrs. Arkenhout held the picture like a talisman. "It isn't a very good picture," she said. I think she meant it was not the picture she wanted: not crisp and certain enough, not respectable, not tolerable. "I'm entitled to an explanation," she said.

"Of course. I'd really like some coffee."

Mrs. Arkenhout glared. "I'm getting there," she said. "Hold your horses."

She left the room and I heard the coffee grinder running and running until it could only be sifting the powder. I followed her into the kitchen.

"I used to love photographs," Mrs. Arkenhout said, with the machine still running. "Martin on his first tricycle. Martin in his crib. Martin on the beach. He was a perfectly ordinary baby, you know. My husband wouldn't say so, but I would."

I turned off the coffee grinder.

"You think it's ready?" Mrs. Arkenhout said. I nodded, and supported Mrs. Arkenhout through the business of putting coffee into a filter into a machine, adding water, moving a switch, like one dancer shadows another's moves.

"It's been very difficult," she said. "We never saw Martin in America, you see, what they found of him. It was soft ground, very wet, they told me. They cremated him." She hiccuped. "I never get to talk about him."

"Did you ever see him again?" I asked.

"Oh no," she said. "Not really." She put out her hands for the tray, but she was shaking too much to take it; so I carried it into the living room.

Mrs. Arkenhout said, "You really shouldn't stay. My husband won't understand." She said it with her fingers holding a biscuit as though it were lace. "Was Martin eating properly?"

"I think so."

"Nothing ever seems to touch him," Mrs. Arkenhout said.

I told her about meeting Martin, having a house in the same village. "He went swimming a lot. He was very healthy."

But I wanted her to explain him.

"There was a terrible fire," I said. "Martin was very brave—"

"Rubbish!" she said. She used the word like a gunshot.

"The police told us what happened," she said. She still sipped her coffee, seeming calm and rigid as a matron, but her voice raised up from its deferential quiet into the roar of a church alto. "I don't want lies. You can go away if you tell lies."

I heard the house door open and close then, and a coat rustling in the hallway. Someone coughed.

Dr. Arkenhout stood in the doorway.

"Who are you?" he said. And to his wife, he said, "I didn't know you were having a guest."

Mrs. Arkenhout said, "He knows Martin."

Dr. Arkenhout said something in Dutch that I did not understand. Mrs. Arkenhout answered.

I stood, an odd politeness in the circumstances, and he came to stand so close to me I could taste his breath. "I don't know your name," he said, with elaborate, daunting politeness. "I'm sorry."

"He says he's Christopher Hart," Mrs. Arkenhout said.

"I think you should go," he said, giving orders without the possibility of refusal, like any doctor.

"I want to talk about Martin," Mrs. Arkenhout said.

"It is not an appropriate subject," the doctor said.

He stood between his wife and me, as though he could block talk with his body. I could see he was calculating his strength, and mine.

"I thought he was all right. He's always all right," Mrs. Arkenhout said.

"I must insist that you leave," the doctor said.

But Mrs. Arkenhout talked on, without taking a breath, a great spool of talk that she'd recorded many times and never once had a chance to play. "It happened once before, you see. That's what they said. They found him in a pool in the park. He was almost drowned, but he didn't drown. He didn't drown. He grew up perfectly well after that—"

"How old was he?" I asked.

"I shall call the police," Dr. Arkenhout said.

"He was four. He was beautiful."

"He was very beautiful," Dr. Arkenhout repeated. "I'm going to call the police."

I said, "Tell me what happened."

"She doesn't know," Dr. Arkenhout said.

"It's true," Mrs. Arkenhout said. "I don't know. They gave me drugs, so I don't remember exactly what happened or why. But they found me standing by the side of the pond as though I'd been watching him drown and it was cold and wet and there were no other children playing and he was big enough to wade out of the water and so—"

She hiccuped again.

"He always told me," and she pointed to her husband, "—well, he didn't tell me so much as he let me know—that I was very sick, that I tried to kill Martin. But you see, I couldn't have killed him. So I wouldn't have tried, would I?"

She picked up the empty coffeepot like a proper hostess, but she poured it into thin air, watching her husband's eyes.

"My wife is very distressed," Dr. Arkenhout said. "She is not well. I don't know what you hoped to achieve here, but surely you can see—"

When I didn't respond, Dr. Arkenhout rushed at me, scrabbled at my coat, pushed me as I walked into the hall. He couldn't bring himself to break decorum and hit me properly, but he couldn't stop himself shoving and chivvying, as though I were some inert obstacle to be pushed out of his house. He talked calmly, but in Dutch.

Mrs. Arkenhout's whole soft, pretty body, high breasts and neat hips, rose and fell on the ignominy of a hiccup.

"We had to send Martin away," she said, catching her breath, "because how could he ever trust us?" Her voice could have carried an anthem over the flatlands. "He didn't worry about the dark on the stairs like other children. He worried most when he was sitting with his mother in the light of the kitchen. By the stove. With the smell of cookies. Like in the paintings in an old advertisement."

≡

In the rain and the dark, I saw myself in the train windows: alarmed again. The Arkenhouts now knew which one of us had survived the fire, and if the proper Dr. Arkenhout knew, then so would the police, within minutes.

I had a future, but under arrest. I had a reason to run again. I have to think that this is what I had wanted, a fear strong enough to bring me back to life.

I had a week of money left, but no name. I could sign on as a trucker's help, a job with no questions asked, maybe work a Rhine barge up to Switzerland, ship out on some amateur freighter. But sometime I'd need papers, official papers, union papers. I'd be checked.

From where I stood, in the hollow between lives, Martin Arkenhout's career began to seem almost reasonable, even inevitable; people can always talk themselves into believing that killing, thieving, and cheating are entirely reasonable in their own tight terms, the only way out and on.

I needed another entire life.

I had killed one man already, you see. I had lost the protection of the ordinary moral rules, which stop you killing, thieving, cheating.

It should have been easy to find a mark in Amsterdam, a tourist town. The French come north to blow a joint on weekends. Queers roister around the streets they can finally own. Onshore tourists cruise the lighted brothel windows as though sin's no fun when it is licensed and permitted; they're like kids at a sweetshop with money, who would much rather steal.

But they were all weekenders, who'd go back to different skins and different ways on Monday morning: in some French ministry, heads officiously cleared, or some English bank, weekend riots covertly admired by less lively colleagues. I could buy at best a few days, a few weeks, before a whole machine began to miss them.

Then there was Boaventura and me. We had a few beers, some schnapps, and we were warm enough to brazen through the cold city.

The lights were low along the canals, meant to look like the light from torches a few centuries ago and warm the off-center gables and the bare trees. In this near-dark people passed, a few on bicycles even in the wet, a few heads down under the steady rain.

"You know about art?" Boaventura said.

I said, "A bit."

"You know about Vermeer?"

If I were Arkenhout, I thought, Boaventura could slip on the cobbles, go over the side of the canal. Hearts stop in cold water, I remembered; the shock, and then the debilitating cold. But bodies float, and tell their own story; and besides, this body was no use to me unless I had his papers first.

"I saw some Vermeers. I liked them. I want to go to Delft," Boaventura said.

If I were Arkenhout, each recess in the light would matter. There were gangplanks to the long wooden boats moored on the canalside, boats with wide windows and chimneys and potted plants. There were sometimes steps down to the water level, by a hotel, by a landing stage for pedal boats, by a marble monument.

I picked up Boaventura's jacket in a bar, but he noticed what I had done. I said it was a mistake. He had a brochure about Delft in one pocket, with a picture of a church huddling behind this monumental shout of a tower and spire.

≡

In my hotel room, I put all the images from the Liber Principis into the plastic case. There was a slight rust along the edge of the portrait of the elder, damp from the open window, perhaps, or the shower-in-a-box that stood at the foot of my bed. Either way, the paper had begun to soften.

I had one last duty attached to my old name: to return the pictures to London. I couldn't pack them perfectly, but I wrapped each one in plastic and put card between them, and then assembled them in the plastic case and wrapped that. I put in a postcard of a van Gogh—poppies and yellow butterflies—and signed it "Christopher Hart."

≡

I checked out of the hotel the next morning. The management, two short men, didn't mind; they had cash in advance, and they did not even think of returning it.

I wanted to go away. I was too tired to want to go far, but I wanted absolute distance between me and my life. I got only to the end of the street, where the tramlines cut across the stately, shabby file of apartment buildings.

Boaventura was standing there. He said he was looking for my hotel. He said he wanted to go to Delft.

I had tried to escape him. I couldn't. I took that as an omen.

He did know about Vermeer, a bit. He had the idea of me as the *senhor doutor*, the learned man, who'd make sense out of all the culture that always seemed at arm's length from him.

I left my flight bag at Central Station. I was traveling now with nothing to mark me or name me: a mirror man, reflecting only what people bring to him.

Boaventura expected lessons, explanations, news from Portugal that he could pretend was news from home. Sleet stung the windows, and he said, brightly, "It snowed one winter in my village. I remember. It was eleven in the morning, and everyone went outside to see."

The skies at Delft were saturated grays and blacks, like washes of watercolor that are still wet. We had a beer and a piece of apple pie in the first bar before we went walking.

We found the site of the *View of Delft*, of course. We wandered through the Prince's House. We had some lunch: Boaventura, by mistake, had a piece of chicken deep-fried in cornflakes. He looked startled.

Behind each range of pretty houses, each neat cut of canal, there was always the same bleak presence: that spire on a great blocky tower, a rise of cleaned gray stone, then a clock, and then another spiked Gothic steeple stepping up to a final cross. It was a corporate tower before its time, a monstrous boast on the genteel streets, aspiring to be the personal staircase between God and the best gentlemen of Delft. It haunted the corner of my eye whichever way we turned.

The pull of warm places was strong, especially places far away from windows.

Boaventura, though, liked shopping streets. He liked the windows of marzipan stew, chocolate pigs; of taps for a bathroom, cheap Bordeaux, computer monitors; a bookshop; clothes stores with beige mannequins under browns and greens; and televisions.

I saw my face on one of the televisions, held for twenty seconds, gone.

I stopped short, of course. Boaventura mustn't see that. But I needed to know what they'd said, what the flash of my own face meant.

There was a newscaster, with that intense look that comes from speaking words she didn't think or write.

A map of Bosnia.

I didn't know how long the midday news might run, or whether stories were repeated, or whether we'd seen only the headlines and later they'd come back to the subject of the man whose face they had showed: a killer on the run, presumably.

A forest fire. I couldn't tell where. A fireball bursting through trees.

I wouldn't have understood the language, even if I could have heard it through the plate glass.

I felt panic, muddled with a kind of gratitude: after all these anonymous days and weeks, running nowhere in particular, I was known and wanted again.

The acknowledgment came a little too late.

"I'm in your hands," Boaventura said.

≡

The square opened quite suddenly: a parade ground of wet, slick cobbles, a town hall stuck with shutters like an advent calendar, the great dark tower and spire rising much too high on the far side.

Boaventura said, "It's going to snow."

"You want a beer? There are plenty of bars."

"No," he said. He looked disappointed in me.

I was almost afraid to enter the church. Its bulk spoke of a tradition that is not mine: a kind of personal, contractual claim on God like merchants have on one another, and a threat to the town in God's name.

"You've seen all this before," Boaventura said. "I haven't. I want to see things."

"We could go—"

But he had already gone in through the high front porch of the church. He negotiated in a kind of history boutique, all souvenirs and glass cases, for tickets to the tower and the spire. He handed me mine. He brushed through the turnstile that counts the visitors in and out.

I said, "But the weather—"

"It's the wind you have to worry about," the woman behind the counter said brightly. "It isn't really windy today."

I did not want to enter the narrow chimney that held tight wooden stairs, or to start the climb round and dizzyingly round between stone walls. Ahead and behind was never more than the sight of a few wood steps, an occasional slit of light from a dusty window, the walls always turning and turning.

The fact of climbing was real enough in my muscles, but there was no way to test how far we had gone, how high we now stood above the shine of wet cobbles on the square.

Once, I almost collided with Boaventura, who'd stopped to make sure I was all right. "It's a long way," he said.

I could hear only his footsteps. I imagined nobody else would climb the tower on such a threatening day. I began to feel dizzy with the constant repetition of steps, turns, steps.

I heard Boaventura slip and curse. I caught up with him on a tiny landing, by a window that showed almost no light.

"It's nothing," he said.

"We could go down."

He looked contemptuous.

I went ahead this time, working upward, sometimes checking my dizziness by holding the rough rope strung between iron circles on the wall.

I was an item on the news. I had to take the consequences, or I had to be someone else.

The stairs opened suddenly into a vast room full of church air, that odd mix of quiet, dusty light and reflections off metal. The room was full of bells: behemoth bells hanging high.

Boaventura saw doors to ledges around the tower, and he bounded over to see the view at last. He also noticed that we could take the stairs still higher.

I was separate now from the world below, separated by dizziness, by muscular effort, by the sense that I had finally thrown off everything certain: my names, my possessions, my freedom if the police now identified me and arrested me. I looked down on everything.

All I had left, as we climbed on, was the shaft of the stairs as they turned ahead of me, and the fact that I was with Boaventura: a man who could be mistaken for me, who could be me, who could so easily slip again.

We came out at the highest point of the tower, onto narrow terraces fenced in with intricate stone. I saw the stone was softening, its details corroding in the air. I saw dark clouds out across the port at Rotterdam. I couldn't quite make out whether we were above them or not before the sleet started.

Boaventura stood into the wind, braced like a man on a ship's deck.

I tried to look over the stone and down to the shine of the square, the rank of official buildings, the angle of canal to one side. Anyone could slip. Nobody could survive the fall.

The sleet began to close down the world, take away the town below. Whatever happened, whatever I did, the world could only open up from now on—the sleet thinning, then becoming rain, visibility growing back a few hundred meters, then the rain stopping, the lights shining doubled from the wet stones below; and then, if I moved, other cities, other chances.

Boaventura said, "I thought we could see the sea from here."

The world had shrunk to this tiny space inside a storm, a protected and comfortable place to make a choice.

I spent almost too long on thinking this.

Boaventura shivered, and he started again down the stairs.

I followed, keeping a turn behind him so I could not see him. I didn't want to see him. Arkenhout had been such a different matter: a man who was nothing more than a murderer, one single dangerous word, whose names were uncertain and changeable like devils in a book. This man had wonder, panic, too much drink, the pain of separation from a dead wife and a distant family and a place whose very simplicity turned glamorous in memory. He was almost too particular to reduce to a corpse.

I missed my footing, slipped on the shine of worn wood.

Without my fixed place on the stairs, I thought I could fall forever inside this stone chimney, falling and bouncing against the great blocks in the walls.

I cannoned into Boaventura. I heard him let out breath like a fart. I grabbed for the rope rail, and as I stopped my own downward course, I realized that he was now the one falling and falling, arm bruised and torn against stone; and then he was out of my sight, a sequence of shouts and bumps and then silence.

I couldn't imagine how he could stop falling.

I held on to the rope. Below me was such distance that I felt dizzy again; I needed to anchor myself. If I could have, I would have stopped there forever: a man suspended.

But I had to go down, and Boaventura was bound to be between me and the way out of the tower.

I found him lying across the stairwell just before the bell chamber. I heard the chiming of two o'clock in the afternoon, then the harmonics of the chimes persisting in the dusty air, then the sound of sleet cutting on glass.

He wasn't dead.

I had slipped. I do not think I meant to kill him.

But here was a man with papers that connected him to innocence, to irresponsibility in a way, to another possibility of life. I could take those papers in a moment, and leave mine. Two foreigners in a tourist spot are easily confused.

I did not want Boaventura to live.

The presence of bells alarmed me: huge, judgmental engines on their high trestles.

So high above the ground, the windows showed only wild sky and not roofs, streets, and other human lives. I felt for a moment free to make whatever decision I wanted. I was in the spirit of that grim, tall tower: its defiant sense of moral superiority.

I went to the windows to look down. I saw only the weather skirling about me, so loud I was certain I could not be heard when I started to shout: "What do you want me to do? What do you want, then?" I had no idea who I was addressing: God, or my father or Boaventura or even Arkenhout.

The shouts set off a faint, shivering song among the bells.

It was then that I realized if I were truly free in this high place, then I was free to do the right and moral thing, not obliged at all to lift papers and switch them and abandon a man: myself.

I knew I could not give away the crime of killing Arkenhout. It stands as a debt I somehow have to pay.

≡

I was speechless in the glassy, prissy shop down below, just pointing past the turnstiles, up the stairs. The woman had to guess what must have happened.

They brought Boaventura down on a stretcher. He was concussed, which he said felt like the night he lost his wife, and his arm was torn; his leg, too, had snapped across the shin. He wouldn't work for a while, since his muscles and their perfect coordination were what he had to work with, but he would live.

Me, they put into a police car. Nobody said anything. In the local police station there was a flurry of phone calls, but of course they were in Dutch. Then I was put into the back of another police car, and driven out of Delft. I watched the tower of the church go back into the storm.

From the road signs, I knew we were going back to Amsterdam. I did not know what would happen to me next: whether I would be charged with Arkenhout's murder, whether Boaventura's accident would make me a double suspect. I was almost sure it was an accident.

But in the next police station, the same one on Warmoesstraat where Mrs. Arkenhout had begun to unravel her son's history, the cops smiled too much and gave me hot, sweet tea. I suppose my Englishness seemed suddenly obvious.

"We've been looking for you," Inspector Van Deursen said.

"I saw the television. I just saw the pictures. I didn't hear the words. I wouldn't have understood the words—"

Interrogated prisoners gabble this way.

"The Arkenhouts told us about your visit. So we had to assume the body was misidentified in Portugal."

I said nothing, since he was right.

"So you know how Arkenhout died?"

I was being invited to confess murder, with a thick white mug of tea in my hands and an amiable policeman across the table not even scowling or shouting. All the pressure to speak came from a bundle of pressured nerves in my chest.

"You want to tell me about it?"

I tried to drink the tea but it was too hot.

"You can tell me," he said.

He must have known everything already. There was no ambiguity in the record, except for the question of names and identities. The other facts were nicely cataloged for display: assault, fire, the explosions, the severed head and the poured gasoline, which did not fit a simple plea of self-defense; the flight, the theft of money from a dead man's already plundered credit; the visit to the dead man's family.

But I told it all, anyway. I wanted him to propose my penance.

He said, "You know, you're a kind of hero."

"What happened to Boaventura?" I said. "They took him away. Is he all right?"

"The guy in the tower, your friend? He's fine."

"You don't want to know what happened there?"

He smiled. "I told you. You're a hero."

I stood up. "Don't make fun of me," I said.

"Sit down," he said. "Sit down. We couldn't have stopped Arkenhout, not yet. The evidence was all circumstantial, no witnesses, a dozen countries. We couldn't make the case. Now he's gone, and the file closes and we have you to thank—"

"But I stole the money," I said.

He smiled. "You were in shock," he said. "A good man who had to do a terrible thing, so naturally you were in shock. Nobody will condemn you."

"I set fire to him," I said.

He said nothing.

"You don't know the half of it—"

He said, "You just weren't yourself."

≡

The Museum in winter has a shuttered look, the great stone portico closed up against the rain. The guards open the gates ceremoniously, but it is a ceremony without an audience; people come a little late to be sure they can go straight in.

I went back, of course.

I opened the letter from Anna's lawyers, who seemed outraged at my bad manners in coming back from the dead. I found lawyers to answer it.

I walked again into the maze of corridors, grateful for the order underlying the apparent jumble of scarred columns, stones in pieces, bits of bone. The Museum offered me a kind of sanitary leave, embarrassed to have me back, knowing it was impossible to fire the new hero for drawing attention to himself.

"You did go to extraordinary lengths for the Museum," the deputy director said dryly. "Rather too extraordinary for our dull Anglo-Saxon minds."

Just once, Maria called me. She found me at work.

"I'm calling," she said, "as your lawyer. In a way. I want to know what to do about your father's house."

I said, "I hadn't thought."

"There are other houses," she said. "There's one up by Granja, with seven terraces of olives, and a stream. And bougainvillea. It's a stone house, white walls."

"I suppose," I said, "I must leave things as they are."

But I could hear the warmth in her talk. If she'd been there, she would have brushed against my arm, smiled too much.

"You should have told me what happened," she said. "I want to know."

"It's not something I can discuss here," I said, retreating into my official and affectless persona.

"I almost came to Amsterdam, you know. The police said it might help them if I was there. Christopher might talk more."

"You want to talk about Christopher?"

"You knew him. I knew him. I thought that gave us something in common. One thing in common, to start with."

A possibility opened, a kind of prophecy, really: that I would redeem my murder by doing what Martin Arkenhout had planned and so nearly achieved, by going back to my father's Portugal, to the place I knew, to the woman I had wanted so fiercely only a few weeks before, and to my own name with its new meaning. Then I could live my life better than before, and still put away the burden of killing a man.

I suppose she wanted a hero to replace the fugitive she had lost.

"—Arturo is well. He didn't need an operation. It's raining a lot, but that's the season—"

I thought of a life between green mountains, in cropped forests, under skies with eagles, on ground that smelled of mint and anise from the leaves you crush while walking.

"—the grape leaves are still on the vines. They're so red, they look like stained glass with the light behind them—"

≡

Today, I crossed the road to conservation to watch them working on the Liber Principis. They have such ingenious expedients to meld the paper fibers along the cuts. They make sure the pictures again lie in the arbitrary order we knew and cataloged, the order that survived centuries.

"We can't make it perfect again," my assistant, Carter, said. "It's not possible. The pictures were not at all well kept."

"It wasn't ever perfect," I said.

He looked shocked.

"It'll do," I said. "It's what we have, and it'll have to do."

Then I came back to this borrowed apartment and lay down to sleep.

I dream too much nowadays. Sometimes, there are mountains, Maria, even Anna's face, a memory of castles and wine.

Martin is always there, also: the child who was scared in the warm and in the light, in the smell of baking and in his mother's arms. I try to stay awake not to dream those dreams, which do not ever seem to end.

A Note About the Author. Michael Pye, novelist, historian, journalist, and broadcaster, is the author of nine other books, including *The Drowning Room* and *Maximum City: The Biography of New York*. He lives near Coimbra, Portugal.

A Note on the Type. The text of this book was composed in Melior, a typeface designed by Hermann Zapf and issued in 1952. Born in Nuremberg, Germany, in 1918, Zapf has been a strong influence in printing since 1939. Melior, like Times Roman (another popular twentieth-century typeface), was created specifically for use in newspaper composition. With this functional end in mind, Zapf nonetheless chose to base the proportions of his letter forms on those of the golden section. The result is a typeface of unusual strength and surpassing subtlety.

Composed by Creative Graphics, Allentown, Pennsylvania

Printed and bound by Berryville Graphics, Berryville, Virginia

Designed by Iris Weinstein